When The Lights

Turn To Green

Jan More

Love takes us down unseen and unknown paths as we journey through life.

Without love, we might not travel very far.

Prologue

It was a bright day that had dawned late in May 1980.

This was the day she was to set off alone.

It was the first holiday she had really wanted to take.

Before now, even contemplating a holiday had been out of the question for her.

Francis Doyle had spent the past six years in a void, working mechanically, day by day, learning to live with the reality she would never see her parents again or her so-called boyfriend. He had said he couldn't cope with her grieving through the loss of her parents, though he was sympathetic in the first few weeks. He had confided in her friend first. Together, they had decided that Francis had become too much hard work for him to cope with.

It was true she was going through a traumatic time, but why should it have created his cold-heartedness? She didn't understand his inability to show her genuine kindness and friendship when she most needed it. It didn't take long before she would find out exactly what his problem was.

In a very short time, he had switched his affection, finding solace in the shape of none other than her friend and colleague.

The suited pair had married since that episode and moved away, much to her relief.

With all that committed to her unfortunate past, her state of mind had become focused. She fervently threw herself into her work with renewed energy, leading her to forge a position in her career, exceeding her own expectations.

Francis had always favoured springtime as a get-up-and-go time, a time of new life, an awakening from the depths of slumber. Yet this was the first springtime she had felt that way again since her losses. It was time for a new beginning and adventure.

There was nothing planned, nothing pre-booked. Francis had no idea where she would lay her head that night, except that it would hopefully be somewhere in the south of Ireland.

CHAPTER 1

The very idea of not knowing exactly where she would end up gave her a thrill. That morning, butterflies fluttered in her stomach with excitement. The only thing she knew for sure was which roads she would soon be travelling on.

The day had finally arrived. That first day would take her away from all that was familiar to her to that which was most definitely not. Francis lived alone without commitments to anyone or anything apart from her work. She had found her working life had become tiresome and an endless chore of late. Working in a solicitor's office had been all Francis had known. In fact, all that she had wanted. Her first paid employment. Now, ten years later, she was still there, having remained with the same firm since leaving her college days long behind her.

It was not as though her education had ended there; far from it. Having joined the firm of Spector & Spector, lessons of life itself were presented and were received, through the solicitor's office, every hour of every day.

Having worked her way through the different departments, starting as the office junior and general dogsbody, she found herself now secretary to one of the partners. With the tenacity that she had found since her parents' deaths, her career had propelled at speed. Francis had given her all to work and work alone.

Quickly, she had been promoted through all the different departments of the firm, along the way witnessing and learning about the many varied cases the firm could handle and meeting with all manner of people in their various situations. She had learned much about divorce, legacies, criminal charges, estates, conveyancing, court representation, and personal injury.

The list was endless.

Spector & Spector were relentless in their pursuit to cover all aspects of the law. It would be fair to say that she, too, had cloned their ethos.

Their premises lay in the heart of London with the firm headed up by several top solicitors, each in their own field.

In the beginning, Francis was very eager, dependable, earnest and totally committed. As her industry experience grew, she grew, too, earning respect from the firm in general. Praise and promotion had been inevitable. Francis had equalled most challenges with astute comprehension. She was now recognised as a first-class secretary.

Those past ten years since joining the company and losing her parents had flown by with the same relentlessness as night follows day.

Now fully accomplished, she found it all became less challenging, leading her to feel restless. In her twenty-eighth year, she was independent and entirely in control of her life. Now Francis was more than ready to have and enjoy a much-needed break.

For peace of mind, Francis had filled her car with petrol the previous day, it being a Sunday. The car was a few years old. It was comfortable, well maintained, small enough for town driving, yet big enough for four people.

Nothing fancy, but reliable and straightforward, somewhat like her character. She had never driven far distances in the little car. Francis felt confident, having had the car regularly serviced. It was ready for the trip. She needed to feel safe within its confines. How the car looked was immaterial.

Knowing herself well, she would not want to make a stop to fill up for some considerable time, apart from calls of nature.

She just wanted and needed to drive some distance before even thinking of stopping now that she had made her mind up to go away. These past couple of weeks had made her feel almost desperate to put as much space behind her that was familiar, and all the open roads ahead that were not.

Her packed suitcase now stood in the hallway by the front door, containing the minimum clothes and cosmetics, making it the lightest load she wanted to cope with.

She was all set for the off with ample money in her bank account to see her through.

That final resounding crash of the front door as she exited from her own domestic little world couldn't help but bring a smile to her lips. Satisfaction and excitement washed through her.

The small Georgian terrace house in a suburban street, known to most as a two-up-two-down, sat comfortably between its six neighbours in south London. It was set back off the main Wands Road. It was very central for the daily commute to work. Another tedious necessity she had had to endure.

It was the house where she had come so gently into the world, as her mother used to say.

Her parents' first and only home. It was where she was born. It was the one connection left to her by her deceased parents.

All that was theirs was now hers, their only daughter, Francis Doyle.

Now, with the house keys separated from her car keys, she had stowed them into the safest compartment in her shoulder bag and slung it across her shoulder. Taking hold of the suitcase handle, she pulled it along on its sturdy little wheels, down the front garden path and out onto the pavement to her car and freedom.

The drive out of London was uneventful, except to say, at first, the time was passing quickly, yet without much headway.

London was far too busy for her liking. Francis was glad she had decided to make a decent, early start. Even so, there was still unexpectedly a lot of traffic.

Concentration was needed as she safely found her way along. It was tedious, all the stopping and starting created by numerous traffic lights. People scurrying off to wherever their destinations lay. Cyclists weaved in and out of the traffic, pedestrians gambling with their lives as they criss-crossed the roads, though they deftly negotiated the gaps between the cars, lorries and buses. This was Londoners' lot. Mayhem!

Some hours later, Francis had made it to the Severn Bridge.

Now, from a distance, the massive construction of the bridge was looming. It appeared as if it were suspended from the heavens rather than man's efforts, building up from the Severn's muddy banks and cold, uninviting waters, running its course between England and Wales.

Now with the tantalising realisation that there was just the journey up to Fishguard ahead of her, she pressed on with mounting excitement.

3

Just over five hours ago, Francis had left London and all therein behind her. The motorway and tolls had made the journey relatively easy without incident. Only her stomach reminded her it had been quite a few hours ago that it had received any nourishment. Just as she thought she would stop for a while, the signs for Fishguard and the ferries were being shown.

To appease her now rumbling tummy, she reached across to the passenger seat. There, an assortment of chocolate bars lay. Knowing any of the bars were as good as the other and not wanting to take her eyes off the road ahead, she let her hand take the first bar it found.

Francis was still savouring the delicious flavour of the final mouthful when she arrived at Fishguard.

Following the signs, she quickly found her way to the terminal for Rosslare. After parking up she sought the ticket office, only to be told that the afternoon crossing had been cancelled. Not being particularly fazed by the idea, Francis bought a ticket for first thing in the morning. The ticket man had assured her there was a nice little B&B just several minutes down the lane.

Without delay Francis found the bed and breakfast. It was a sizeable house of character. A pleasant little lady showed her a room that was available for the night. We can offer you an early breakfast in time for you catch the ferry, she had assured her.

The next morning, Francis felt refreshed and was now thinking, it had been a blessing the ferry had been cancelled yesterday. She had enjoyed an early breakfast and was eager to start the next part of her journey.

The early morning sun was bright and a soft breeze was blowing in from across the Irish Sea. Deciding to stand outside her car while other cars arrived to join the queue at the termina, she climbed out of the parked car. The breeze teased at her hair, as she faced the sun and sighed. She was ready to depart, quite near the front of the queue. Enjoying the sun on her face, the breeze refreshed her with a pleasure that was new to her. With a goodnight's sleep behind her she was more than ready for the adventure to begin.

Her mind felt free.

Strands of hair were now escaping from the blue ribbon tied at the nape of her neck, the ribbon failing to hold on to her long, curled Titian tresses. Now in their freedom, they were glinting like soft copper-coloured threads in the sunshine, floating across her green eyes as she stretched her gaze past the ferry boat and beyond. She took a deep breath and sighed again as she surveyed the blue-green water. It was sparkling diamond bright. The sun rode the gentle swell and rested on the crests of the sea waves out beyond the harbour.

Behind her and to the west lay Wales' dark green gentle hills, forming a protective back drop to the village of Fishguard.

There were fewer cars than she had imagined, now getting ready to load onto the ferry.

After five more minutes of taking in the area, Francis returned to her car. The cars ahead were moving. Without any delay, she was on board with her car neatly parked on the outer row below decks. It afforded her just enough space to open the car door and retrieve, at a stretch, her shoulder bag. It was lying in the medley of chocolate bars amidst spent wrappers. She picked up the bag and left the chocolate and wrappers where they had landed.

Finding her way to the upper deck she decided a quick visit to the bathroom was her first priority. After that, she would see what the cafe had to offer, though, in truth, she was not feeling in the least bit hungry. Settling on the thought, a cup of tea would be very welcome.

Quickly scanning the area for a place to sit and favouring a seat by the enormous windows, she thought it would do nicely. There was hardly a lack of space, but she hoped it would still be available in the time it took to buy a cup of tea. First was that visit to the bathroom.

As she arrived at the door to the ladies' room, a young woman was coming out. Francis smiled in greeting and waited as the young woman passed by. The young woman had bent her head down as if to avoid looking at Francis' gaze. Then, as if it were an afterthought, she lifted her chin shyly and tried to give her a slight upturn of her lips.

In that brief passing, as she scurried by, Francis was surprised to see her watery eyes. They looked full of what she detected as fear. Hoping she was all right, Francis carried on into the bathroom. The queue had gone down considerably by the time she had returned. Tea was her choice, and the seat she had noticed

5

earlier was still available. The ferry was moving from its moorings, now slowly gliding out of the harbour towards the open Irish sea.

Francis took her seat.

Lulled by the ferry's movement, moving gently through the sea's swell, she relaxed in her space, happy in her thoughts, she allowed her mind to drift without purpose.

Watching the rhythmical motion of the sea, feeling contented now that she had had something to drink, she felt totally at ease.

Now the ferry was negotiating the Irish Sea. It was full steam ahead and over two hours into the crossing. Time was passing quite quickly without any interruptions to the order of the passage. The rolling of the waves was therapeutic to Francis.

After a while, whilst she stretched her neck around, she began to notice the other passengers around her.

An older couple were seated nearby. Occasionally, the soft sounds of their conversation drifted into her hearing.

Her mind rested on the older couple. They looked happy, and she wondered if they had met and married, perhaps thirty years ago. They certainly seemed close, now possible grandparents to a bunch of loving grandchildren. She was wondering, too, whether they lived in Ireland and were returning home from some event or other.

Who else was there? She glanced around, finding people interesting. In her solitude on Sundays, she would often take a walk in the park, sometimes just to sit and people watch.

Further over at the bar, several younger men were chattering. Every so often, she could hear their laughter as they told their stories and enjoyed one another's company. They were having a pint or two of beer to pass the time. Not wanting to look for too long or before catching unintentional reciprocation, Francis looked away towards the far side of the lounge area.

Two men were getting up. They now alerted her curiosity. She watched as they walked to the exit door. They were tough looking men, wearing donkey jackets. Probably Irish labourers, no doubt going home with a pocket full of cash after labouring on a building site or perhaps road works.

The thought provoked a memory of her own father, Robert Doyle. He had told Francis that he, too, had come over to London when he was a young man searching for work. Then laughed and said he had gotten more than he'd bargained for when he had met her mother.

Francis turned her mind back to the two men. Perhaps they would be returning to their wives and children.

She watched as they made their way outside.

Now the men were out of the way. She had a clear view of the girl she had seen earlier, the girl with the watery eyes and fearful gaze.

She was sitting with a man. He leaned towards her as she leaned back. The girl wiped her eyes to stem the flow of tears that seemed desperate to run down her ashen face.

Francis observed the young woman with renewed interest. She was almost trembling as her hand reached into her coat pocket. Francis felt an overwhelming sadness for the girl. She looked so pale and slight, but then decided rationally that she needed to mind her business.

Hadn't she had enough of her own misery? Francis was on holiday, after all.

She took her mind away from the other people and thought it was time to move from that spot and walk on the upper deck. It would be nice to breathe the sea air in the afternoon sunshine and perhaps then another cup of tea.

She checked her watch.

The ferry should be arriving in Rosslare in an hour or so.

Standing up, she looked over, thinking she would take the same route as the two men to go outside. Passing by the couple, perhaps she would overhear something that would tell her it was just a lover's tiff and all was well. As she approached, Francis could now see the young woman was speaking to the man earnestly.

He was listening attentively, with a serious look on his boyish face. Francis thought all would become clear if she got within earshot.

Except that it was a fruitless exercise.

The girl was speaking very quickly in a language she could not understand. Carrying on out the door, Francis was disappointed that she was no further forward in her nosey quest and still wondered why the young woman was so upset.

The freshness of the breeze as she exited the door surprised her with its force, almost taking her breath away. It brushed away all previous thoughts and cleared her mind. The ferry was moving faster through the dark green waters of the Irish Sea. Faster than she had thought while safely inside. She needed to climb the stairs to get to the upper deck, finding it exhilarating as she made her way. When she reached the top, she gripped at her flying hair and kept walking on the near side, away from the rails. As she turned the corner, she bumped straight into another passenger. He was standing with his back to the bulkhead, keeping out of the wind's full force, as the ferry ploughed its way through the sea.

"I am so sorry," she said, looking up now into a smiling, handsome face.

He looked down at her from his six-foot height of masculinity, with all-knowing, all-seeing, beautiful dark blue eyes. Francis immediately thought his eyes seemed to twinkle in a mischievous way.

"No problem. Are yer all right there?" he asked.

Feeling her cheeks blush at what she was thinking, and more importantly, within those few seconds, what he was thinking, from how he looked at her. Smiling back at him, Francis felt like she wanted to run but instead found herself almost mesmerised by his charm.

They stood looking at each other for what seemed an eternity. Then finally, they both spoke in unison.

"I just wanted to get some…"

His was in a deep Irish tone. "I do believe it's one of the most delightful crossings..."

They both trailed off and laughed. Francis waited for him to carry on.

"I have ever made."

He raised his eyebrow at Francis.

"Oh, really?" she replied coyly. "Do you often take the ferry?" Francis felt a little foolish at her reply.

He had no hesitation. He spoke again. "Mostly for my work. I'm kinda used to hopping back and forth." Before she could ask what his work was, he carried on. "And what were yer going to get some of, if I might ask?"

Again, those twinkling blue eyes were as engaging as his musical voice.

8

"Tea," Francis explained, looking down. "No, I mean, some fresh air and then some tea."

They both laughed again. Francis rather nervously, and him somewhat confident.

While looking out at the rolling sea, he spoke again. "Well, we have had plenty of fresh air," he said, turning his gaze back to her. "Let me buy yer that cup of tea." He held his hand to her. "It's a pleasure to meet yer. I'm Michael Connor." With a tilt of his head, covered with dark long scruffy curls blowing in the breeze, he asked, "And ye are?"

Francis brought her hand down from her hair, the blue ribbon failing in the breeze's force, now allowing more of her hair to fly about her face.

She put her hand out to reach his. "I'm Francis Doyle. How do you do?"

His hand felt strong as it wrapped around hers with a firm grip.

"Well Francis Doyle, let us get that tea, shall we?"

He was still holding her hand as if to steady her.

"Oh right, let's."

Francis hardly had a choice, as he was already leading the way, striding assuredly, yet courteously mindful of her. Inside was a stark contrast from the outside. Letting go of her hand as soon as they came through the door, Michael strode without hesitation to the counter. Francis came behind him, attempting to compose herself.

He turned and asked over his shoulder, "How der yer take yer tea?"

"Milk, no sugar, please."

The woman behind the counter was already adeptly placing on a tray two saucers, two cups, a little jug of milk. A whoosh of the water machine filled a small pot of tea for two, which she placed neatly on the tray.

She added two packets of wrapped biscuits as she smiled. "Anything else?" she asked.

"No, that's grand," Michael said.

He held out a £5 note to the lady. Just as speedily as she had made the tea, she went to the till and gave him change. He dropped it into his pocket and carried the tray to a nearby table.

9

"Will this do, Francis?"

Francis nodded and sat down at the table. Michael sat himself down opposite her.

"Well, Francis Doyle. What brings yer to Ireland?"

Michael was pouring the tea for her. In what she thought was an assured way. Feeling a little more confident now in his company, she slowly replied with a smile. "I'm on holiday."

"Ah, 'tis a lovely place to see. Have yer been over before now?"

"No," she replied, but then went on as he handed her the tea. "I thought I would drive down to Kinsale first. I have researched the area and hope to drive around the coast of County Cork. A colleague at work did something similar last year and said she had had the most wonderful time."

"Ah, sure. There are many places to stay along the way."

The chatter was easy between them. Michael spoke about County Cork and the different places she should visit. She listened and enjoyed the tones of his Irish accent that she felt so charmed by, remembering her father's Irish accent briefly as she took in the look of Michael Connor.

He had a wonderful, relaxed way about him. She noticed now the dark thick eyelashes sweeping across his blue eyes. She pulled herself up from her reverie as he went on.

"I am heading that way myself, Francis. In fact, I hope to be staying the night with my brother in Kinsale."

"In Kinsale?" she replied, a little too pleased and eager.

His face changed slightly. She was aware he had become more serious. He cleared his throat before he spoke again.

"I have to tell yer, Francis. I am working right now," he added quickly. "But that said, I have to eat, and I would like it very much if we could have dinner together tonight in Kinsale. Where are you planning on staying?"

Her heart felt as though it had jumped out of her chest. This most attractive Irishman was asking her to have dinner with him. A man she had only just met. Yet in the short time they had been in each other's company, she felt she could trust him. She wanted to trust this man, not only to go to dinner with him, but her whole life.

So, without giving it another thought, she replied, "That would be lovely."

Their eyes met, and she added, "I guess there are guest houses or a small hotel I could book into."

Sitting back in his chair, he gave her a lovely smile. "Indeed, there are all manner of places to stay. If I may offer a bit of advice, if yer heading down to Kinsale, take the main Cork Road then turn off towards Cobh for the Passage West. That's just a hop and a skip across. It's plain sailing after, down to Kinsale."

Francis smiled.

"Thanks for the tip. How long do you think that will take me?"

Michael replied, "I would say two and half, maybe three hours tops. That'll get yer to Passage West, then it's another, say, half hour before you drop down to Kinsale. Sure, yer be fine."

They finished their tea. Michael smiled at her as he stood up to make a move to leave.

"Look, I have to go now. If you are heading down to Kinsale, it's an easy route."

He carried on as she listened intently to what he was saying.

"As you arrive in Kinsale at the bottom of the approach hill, turn left into the town car park. From there, you can see Donovan's. They have comfortable rooms and a very nice breakfast that'll set you up for the day."

Before she could reply, Mr Wonderful reached for her hand and took it to his lips, not taking his eyes from hers. Slowly and meaningfully, he kissed it. She felt her cheeks flush again.

"I will come and find you, Francis Doyle. Be sure of that. Until tonight."

He turned and, in an instant, was gone.

She sat at the table, alone now with her thoughts. Almost trance-like she was holding her hand, the hand he had just so tenderly kissed. With her mind racing, she wondered exactly what she thought she was thinking about.

It was so unlike her. Had the fresh sea air scrambled her brains? Why did she think she would meet up again with a stranger? Agreeing to have dinner with him in a foreign country, no less?

Then she rationalised that Ireland was not really a foreign country. Hadn't her own father hailed from somewhere over there? Perhaps Michael had the gift of the gab. Was this what was known as a bit of Irish blarney?

Perhaps he really didn't mean it.

She looked down at her hand he had kissed, thinking if she would see Michael Connor again.

CHAPTER 2

As the ferry slowly drifted towards the dockside and people were on the move, Francis had running through her mind, *Head for Cork, then Passage West, finally Kinsale.*

Francis needed her wits about her. She would have to stop thinking about Mr Connor. Well, for now, at least.

Standing up, Francis checked in her shoulder bag for her car keys. It had remained draped across her body the whole of the journey. An interesting journey across the Irish Sea.

She rummaged for the keys to the car. Arriving back on the lower deck, people were getting into their vehicles. Francis looked around the other parked cars before squeezing into hers, hoping to see Michael getting into his, but to no avail. She couldn't see him anywhere.

The drive towards Cork city was easy enough. Finding the little ferry at Passage West was exciting. In no time at all it seemed to her she was heading for Kinsale. Michael had been right. It was one of the easiest journeys to negotiate. Francis was used to driving only in England, with its far busier roads.

The first and best thing, as far as she was concerned, was the lack of traffic. The second was that they drove on the same side of the road.

Even though the surroundings were unfamiliar to her, Francis felt relaxed. There was no rush. She could take her time.

Slowly she wended her way down the winding lanes. She noticed how a bright green freshness of new leaves was breaking through from the old branches of the many trees, towering in their ancient twisted forms. Her passion for trees and plants knew no bounds. Those trees she likened to a beautiful lace. They were covered in a bright green haze. It made them stand out in stark relief against the blue skies above.

Francis had many plants in her home, now being looked after by her neighbours next door. She had known the couple all her life, and they were friends of her parents. They had been only too pleased to look after her babies, because that meant Francis was taking a holiday.

Flanking either side of the winding road and between the mighty trees, Francis could see wild fuchsias with pink buds, ready to pop into bloom. It was a beautiful, wild hedgerow. The gorse bushes displayed their bright yellow flowers, while the wild dog rose was still holding onto last year's rose hips. Elders grew; also, wild blackberry mingled in between hawthorn. It was a feast for the birds that frequented the ample store of berries and seeds.

There were views across fields of green that someone had manicured into small sections. Each was divided by the hedges, creating a patchwork of nature. It was all a delight to her senses.

On passing the occasional homestead, she wondered what living in such a remote location would be like. The idea was appealing to her. Living in London was a million miles different from what she had been used to. The parks and commons of London afforded some green places in the capital. Nothing like that could compare to what she was witnessing now. Again, she found she was smiling to herself. Feeling alive and happy, she was finally driving in Ireland.

Francis pulled over at the side of the road, just at the point where a farm gate gave entry off the little lane and onto the fields. It allowed her to get off the road. Though she hadn't passed a single car.

She switched off the engine, pulled on the hand brake, and exited the car.

The only sound to hear was the sweet chirping of the birds. Francis walked to the gate and just gazed out at the sweeping countryside. She took several deep breaths and watched as little birds darted in and out of the hedge. Stretched and refreshed, Francis returned to her car and drove off down the lane. Her heart was light, not knowing what would happen along the way. She was still excited with the knowledge she had nothing to worry about, no work pressures or commitments and weeks of doing just as she pleased, in what she thought now was an idyllic place.

The drive had been a joy, and within what seemed no time at all, Francis found herself driving down quite a steep hill. Then the thought came back to her. *This must be the hill into the town of Kinsale.*

It was just as Michael had said it would be, and now,

14

following the road around to the left, there was the car park.

Francis thought how picturesque the view was as she parked the car and got out for a better view.

Looking around, right there was the harbour. Francis could see many boats as they shimmered in the late afternoon sunshine. Reflections of the boats echoed in the still waters of the harbour.

In the car park, a low wall allowed a clear view across that part of the harbour and towards the hills beyond. She assumed that looking ahead was the way out to sea.

Looking over to where she had driven down the hill into Kinsale, on the left, she could see now properties interspersed with all manner of trees and shrubs.

Donovan's was clearly visible across the road, just as Michael had told her. The name blazoned across the front of the building left her in no doubt.

Knowing she needed change for the parking machine, Francis left the car park for the nearest shop, which happened to be almost next door to the tourist information centre.

That would do; she could buy a map.

All sorted, she put her euro into the parking machine, retrieved her case from the boot and set off for Donovan's.

***

Donovan's had six wide, white-washed steps with railings on either side that led her to the front door of the building from the pavement. Two glass-fronted doors, an added feature she assumed, as the building was old, at least Victorian or more likely Georgian and perhaps someone's family home back in the day was now being used in its grand capacity, as a hotel. All had crossed her mind as she entered.

Once inside, Francis took in the full charm of yesteryear. Ahead of her was a sweeping staircase with a dark red carpet. Several sconces were housing soft lights on the walls, creating a welcoming glow in the foyer.

There was a large, dark wooden counter to one side. It ran almost along the whole length of the wall. The surface was highly polished. The lights reflected in the shine. There was a table with two comfortable chairs tucked in the corner. It created a cosy, homely feeling.

Francis noted a stand with different pamphlets at the far end. An enormous book for the guests to sign lay open in the middle of the counter.

She waited for a little while, checking herself out in the huge gilded mirror on the wall behind the counter.

A lady came through a door next to the ornate mirror. She greeted Francis with a huge smile.

She spoke as she stooped to put the piece of paper she was holding beneath the countertop. "May I help yer?"

She was small in stature, plump, with a jolly, rounded face. "Welcome to Donovan's."

Francis gathered herself and asked politely, "I would like a single room, if that's possible."

"Ah, sure it is." Her words flowed in a sing-song way. "Now, where is it?" she said to herself, stooping again behind the counter, looking for another something, eventually retrieving a smaller book from somewhere below. She produced it to the countertop with another smile on her jolly face.

"Here we are now. How long will yer be staying with us?"

Francis felt silly that she hadn't given it a thought. "Oh, at least a couple of days. I'm not sure."

The jolly-faced woman replied, "Well, now, I can't see that'll be a problem."

As she spoke, the woman looked at the now open book, running along its columns of information with her finger.

"There is a single on the second floor, with its own little bathroom. Would that suit yer now?"

"I'm sure it would."

"Here we go, if I can get yer to sign in our register," she said, pointing to the large open book further along the counter.

Francis entered her name and address as the jolly-faced lady said, "We can leave it open for you until yer know how long yer want to stay." Hardly drawing breath in her chirpy fashion, she continued. "The dining room is through there." She quickly motioned with her hand, showing the general direction. "Breakfast is usually from seventy-thirty until around ten. Would yer like to have an evening meal with us tonight? That starts at seven until about nine."

16

She was smiling again as she waited for Francis to answer. Her small pale blue eyes twinkled with a knowledgeable look at Francis. Francis' mind went straight to Michael Connor, thinking about dinner tonight and whether he would find her.

"Oh no, thank you," she said. "I am meeting someone tonight."

"Your room is up the stairs. I'm afraid there's no lift." Noticing Francis' small case, she added, "I think you can manage."

"See you in the morning, then."

The cheery woman handed Francis the keys.

"We lock the front doors at ten-thirty. You can use the second key to let yourself in if yer any later."

Francis watched her as she disappeared through the same door she had come from. Then she started up the stairs in search of her room.

CHAPTER 3

Michael Connor had been working under cover when he met Francis Doyle on the ferry. He had been sent from Cork over to Wales, where he would follow a certain criminal who was wanted and known to the Gardai. The day before, Michael had been contacted by a colleague in London. He had informed him their man was on the move again and would be on that particular ferry crossing. Michael was asked if he would pick up on the job from Fishguard.

It was hoped that this was the last stage of pinning down one of the largest organised operations of drug smuggling and people trafficking. The Gardai had been involved for a while now. It was their job to complete the surveillance of the organised ring, by getting the very last man involved. They couldn't afford to pounce too soon, not now after so much had already been achieved, with so many months of careful surveillance and information gathered.

The team of officers involved were specially selected for this particular mission. Men were pulled in from various departments.

There in Ireland, Garda officers of the highest calibre were involved.

Michael was one of those officers. He belonged to the National Surveillance Unit and was specially trained after ten years of service in the Garda. Michael had worked his way through the ranks since finishing his education, deciding he would join the Garda like his father before him. Working diligently, he found his way to become a detective inspector.

His proud father, Joseph Connor, thought that, like himself, Michael would be happy and continue in that role as he had done.

That was not to be.

Now in retirement, Joseph Connor watched his son with an experienced eye. Worrying and watching over him, being the concerned and loving father he was, Joseph would speak to his eldest son, Andrew, when the opportunity allowed, about Michael. He knew at least that Michael would call in at his brother's home occasionally. That way, Joseph was in touch with his boys more often than some.

His wife Martha would say, "'Tis all unnecessary, all this pacing up and down, saying how yer wish he would settle. I wish it too, but leave the boy alone, will yer? You're wearing out me carpet."

Michael had always been his own man, but since he was in the NSU, Joseph thought his son could become a little remote from his family. He didn't like to think of him as being alone and single. Hadn't he, himself, had his first son, Andrew, by the time he had made detective? And with another on the way, his darling little Bridget. On occasion, when they met up, Michael patiently listened to his father with the respect he deserved, but he was not yet ready to settle. Sure enough, one day, he would, but not yet, he would say.

Michael had had other ideas. On being invited to join the NSU, he accepted. Michael decided he wanted to join the other one hundred men, specially chosen men. There he would work covertly, enjoying the secrecy of that particular armed unit.

He had taken to it like a duck to water.

With an exemplary service record thus far and fifteen years on, Michael was still enjoying his chosen path. Now aged thirty-four, he was beginning to think he might like a proper home of his own. Michael was getting too used to being independent, perhaps too used to living the way he was.

Michael occasionally thought he didn't want to do this forever. He knew that time would run out on him, eventually. Thoughts of starting a family kept creeping into his mind, but he needed to find that special someone first.

He had become accustomed to always carrying an assortment of clothes and toiletries in the back of his car. The strange hours he had to keep when on an undercover operation meant his car had almost become a second home. Empty cartons and foodstuff containers lay littered along the back seat, newspapers too. Michael's wardrobe was in the boot.

It was safe to say he didn't take too much notice of his appearance, or that of the car. The car would remain just as it was until he had time in between jobs to clear the accumulated rubbish, and that was usually back home with his folks or his brother's

19

His mother would kindly see to his laundry, making many comments as she busied herself with the task. Martha could be heard saying things like, "No son of mine will be seen in this state."

Michael enjoyed his day or two's break at home with his parents. Likewise, he would stay over a night or two with his brother, duties allowing.

All in all, he was a man ready for action at a moment's notice. Deep in his heart, he would like to please his devoted parents and one day present them with the grandchildren they longed for.

He hadn't even met a girl yet.

That part was true, even though plenty of willing girls would have loved to settle with him. He did not commit to any. He might venture on a casual date here and there, but not one so far had come remotely close for him to contemplate marriage with.

He told himself that his parents would just have to wait and be patient. They had Bridget, his sister, to be getting on with. She was married and now expecting her second baby.

Settling for a less active role in the Garda was something Joseph and Martha both looked forward to and prayed for, but as far as Michael was concerned, he was happy just the way he was, for now.

With their love and support and love of family life, he had had a wonderful childhood, brought up on the outskirts of Clonakilty, a charming little town in the west of County Cork and known to the locals as Clona.

Out of the town of Clona, the road wended its way above the coastline and through the gentle hills and pastures. A little further into the west before Rosscarbery, the Connor family had lived for at least three generations. Three, that is, that they knew about.

Joseph Connor never wanted to leave the beautiful old house when he got married and had begged his would-be wife to accept that they would live there after they were married. It was never regretted by Martha, who loved the old house with its many rooms of character.

Ash House was not just a house. It was the well-loved and looked-after home of the Connor family. Joseph's wife couldn't say no, even if she had wanted to.

She loved the old house and the land surrounding the

20

impressive building, with the paddocks, where the old donkeys lived, outhouses with chickens, a yard and a pretty garden, not to mention the beautiful mature ash trees, tall and strong. They had held fast in the rich soil for hundreds of years, their great height towering on three sides of its boundaries.

The front drive from the lane was shaded from the main road, with more trees and great rhododendrons. There was a dense hedge around its perimeter too. All thrived in the mild climate and rich soil of the land.

Within its handsome grey stone walls, Joseph had said he couldn't think of anything better than raising his family beneath its secure roof. Joseph Connor's siblings had not been as keen, after the death of their mother. It seemed fitting that the old family house remained in the family, and Joseph, being the youngest son and very close to his father, would and could be on hand.

Joseph's father would not be alone. Old Mr Connor agreed wholeheartedly, and Joseph' wife, Martha, had moved in, as planned, as soon as she and Joseph were married.

The area of County Cork was usually quite quiet. People knew of one another's backgrounds. Families understood each other. Many were held together by their Catholic religion. They met regularly at church or in the local pub. It was a close-knit community, as the generations followed one another in their particular way.

It was a secure life in a style all of its own. Their own myths and legends abounded, as did their faith.

It was there that Michael still lived, from time to time, with his parents Martha and Joseph. He had been well loved and a well-educated son. He grew up to become a well-balanced, upstanding member of the local community, and respected by most, as his father's son.

Very few knew exactly what Michael did in the Garda, only that he was in their offices up at Bandon, which were his headquarters.

Joseph said his son worked in communications, which seemed to satisfy the general curiosity of the local folks who knew him.

***

Michael was called on to step in at the Garda proceedings. The men he was targeting were on the front line of the operation and were now the priority.

Sure enough, Michael had waited in Fishguard. It was his job at that point not to intervene but to watch, unnoticed, two particular fellas and where they were heading.

Michael had followed up on his first man, who he had kept within his sights unnoticed since Fishguard. He was to witness him meeting up with another unsavoury-looking fella, who Michael had recognised immediately.

This was the first time they had been spotted together. This would be another vital link in the chain for Michael to report.

The two men had joined up at Fishguard, leaving one car behind and travelling together, driving out of the terminal at Rosslare at high speed. Michael followed at a safe distance as they headed west.

The Garda knew who the top men were and had enough evidence to convict the perpetrators, but did not want to pounce too soon, until every last man in the smuggling organisation had been uncovered.

Keeping up with the car and his suspects, Michael followed without detection. They were driving along many of the roads Michael had known all of his life. Finally, they turned off the main road, taking the long, bumpy ride down the lane to Union Hall.

Knowing these roads well, Michael avoided detection and waited until the men were nearer the harbour and over the bridge. He would then easily spot the car if he took the road around the other way near Glandore. They all arrived down at the harbour of Union Hall. Michael was already out of his car and on foot as he watched from a safe distance.

Union Hall was a quiet fishing village with a mixture of little houses at its heart. There was a pub and one or two small shops, plus the fisherman's outlet occupying the corner position of the main street. The catch of the day was always on sale. There, the fishermen sorted the fish and refrigerated them, ready to sell on. Beautiful fresh fish, straight from the Irish Sea.

Further along the harbour lay several large fisherman's boats and trawlers moored alongside the harbour's dock. Their bright colours created an artist's perfect painting. The smaller craft had another section of the moorings. Michael watched from his undetected vantage point.

He could see the two men clearly. They had arrived and were making their way down to the small jetty. There, they got into a small rowing boat.

A couple of fishermen were sitting on crates at the quayside, their bright-green coloured nets stretched out before them on the ground. They checked and repaired them diligently. With their expert hands and practiced eyes, they were chatting while working in the sunshine.

Michael watched as the suspects now rowed slowly and silently across the harbour. They seemed to be heading towards the small bridge that spanned the distance between Glandore and Union Hall. He watched until they were under the bridge and out of sight, knowing they would not be going too far in the small boat. He decided to amble down to where the fishermen were working, to see if he could gain anything from them. If anyone knew anything that might help, it would be these fellas. They noticed much of the activities in these waters.

"Hi," he said in greeting.

They gave a nod of their heads in return. Without causing curiosity, Michael passed a few congenial remarks. The way the Irish do.

As luck would have it, the weather-beaten men did not disappoint. They told Michael they had seen a yacht, a big one.

"Not seen the like of it before. She was moored further out in a cove that lay after the bridge. Been there since last Saturday."

"Aye," the other man offered. "A week, perhaps, at least."

"Rich tourist, no doubt," they mocked laughingly.

Michael thanked them with a wave of his hand, saying he hoped the sun would keep shining for them.

Now at speed, Michael needed to set other wheels in motion. A quick call to HQ would result in other Garda units taking up position.

Where was the nearest phone? No doubt the pub!

Setting off at apace, back along the harbourside, passing the fisherman's store, he was soon at his destination. On entering, he looked around the room. Even though it was a fine spring day, a fire was burning in the old grate. Memorabilia of bygone times covered the dark walls. It was a small room at the front of the building, leading on down to a door and another small area.

Dark old furniture afforded several places to sit. By stark contrast, the bar itself shone as years of continual polishing had made it glow. Behind the bar, Michael assumed, stood the owner of the pub, who gave out a cheerful welcome to greet him.

"How's it going?" Michael asked before the barman could open his mouth. Michael swiftly put in, "I'll take a pint if I may. Is there a phone I could use?"

An old man was reading a newspaper in the corner near the fire. He popped his head over the top of the paper, hearing Michael's voice.

The owner of the pub started off the pint.

"Sure, out the door at the back, mind the step as yer go."

Michael was off towards the back door before he had time to finish hearing what the barman was saying.

"Always in a hurry, the younger folk are…" His voice floated off.

There wasn't anyone to reply.

CHAPTER 4

Francis was very pleased with her room. It was larger than she would have expected, for a single, that is. A large square glass-paned window let in the daylight. She was at the back of the hotel, so the view was over a few rooftops and trees.

There was a small double bed covered in a cheerful flowered cotton bedspread. The curtains matched. A kidney-shaped dressing table was draped with the same material. All looked bright and fresh. It had been carpeted in the same rich red as the stairs and hallways. Under the window, there was another table, suitable, she guessed, to carefully put her case on.

A quick look at the bathroom, and a quick lie on the bed, told her she would be very comfortable there.

It was cheerful and bright.

"Thank you, Michael," she muttered to no one.

Unpacked and refreshed, she wanted to get out again and walk around the town, and perhaps she could walk along the side of the harbour.

Off she set, with a light step and back out into the late afternoon sunshine.

Before going around the town, she thought it might be better to walk along the harbourside first, seeing that it was so close by, and then explore the town.

There were many boats moored out in the harbour. Their masts made a loud sound in unison. It drifted on the stiffening breeze as though they were clapping as she passed. Their flags fluttered gaily. Smaller boats bobbed here and there, pulling at their ropes that were made steadfast to the harbour quayside.

A few cars were passing along the road, and on the other side, lying back from the harbour, were different houses, shops, and a recreational area for people to sit.

She walked along, taking deep breaths of the air, looking at everything with a pleasure she had not felt in years. Wondering why she had never made an effort before now to find this place. It suited her well. Her mind then went to her father. A gentle man, with a quiet, steady manner. Simple in his pleasures and

25

occupation. She sadly remembered that he had been so kind and loving to her. Always seeing her point of view in times of uncertainty, taking her side against her mother's unreasonable instructions or reasoning. This Ireland was his homeland. Why had he never spoken of it?

Francis' thoughts were interrupted as someone caught her eye. She thought it was the girl with the watery eyes from the ferry, recognising the red coat she was wearing on the ferry.

Francis watched with interest as she noticed the watery-eyed girl was accompanied by another young female. Their arms linked, heads bent down, locked in conversation. Two men, who Francis thought looked like could take care of themselves, were behind them. They were tall and broad, manual working looking men, with woollen hats pulled low across their eyebrows. The baby-faced man on the ferry with the girl was not with her now.

Francis felt relief, as the young girl appeared to be much happier, possibly due to being with her female friend for company.

The group of four went down onto the pontoon to climb aboard a motorboat. Within a few minutes, the men let go of the mooring ropes as the engine jumped to life, and they slowly headed off. The girls broke from their conversation and looked up. Both were waving to someone up ahead on the pavement.

Francis followed their gaze, and her eyes fell upon the baby-faced man from the ferry. He was smiling back and lifted his hand from his pocket to wave back at the girls on the boat. The boat went out of view as it meandered through the harbour.

Francis watched him as he turned to get into the driver's side of a parked car. He saw her looking at him. He looked back at her, gave her a smile, jumped in, and drove off.

Francis felt happy in her surroundings, and with a shrug at her nosiness, she continued with her walk. Now she had seen the girl with the watery eyes, looking happy, and off on a boat trip to who knew where, all Francis' concerns about her were forgotten.

She headed back, thinking how lovely it was there. Feeling optimistic, she cheered herself further by thinking there might be something she might like to buy.

The man with the baby face turned his car around further up the road. He had parked up again on the other side to watch

Francis. Her beautiful red hair blowing in the breeze like a beacon made it easy for him to keep her in his sights. He followed her back towards the town.

"Damn," he said to himself. "She is going into the car park."

He stopped and wondered if he should return to his car to continue observing her. Stopping with hesitation, he watched on.

No, he thought excitedly, she's coming out again.

While returning the way she had come, Francis thought she would be walking past the car park.

She thought it might be a good idea to check on her car, and pay for another parking ticket for twenty-four hours. Perhaps even move it. All these thoughts ran through her mind. On entering the car park, she spotted her car, just where she had left it.

Francis noticed that overnight parking was free. She fished in her bag for the keys, still there safely. Then she hesitated and decided the car would be fine right where it was.

Finding herself now in a narrow lane, the kaleidoscope of colours that greeted her completely took over her mind. On either side of this particular lane that curved interestingly, packed shoulder to shoulder with old buildings and shop fronts, each building had been painted a different colour. Each property had done its utmost to outdo its neighbour. Mauves with bright green, orange and red, pinks and purples.

Francis thought it was quaint. It looked so pretty. The goods in the windows equal in their diversity pleased her, with a lovely old bookshop, a florist, and small attractive boutiques. She was having such a lovely time, enjoying everything with fresh eyes. Walking on, she turned the corner where more shops were located.

There was a lady's fashion store. Francis stopped and looked in the window at the attractive items it had to offer.

It was there she saw a lovely dress on the mannequin in the window. It was a gorgeous shade of green, quite simple in its style, which appealed to her. She could imagine herself in that.

"I wonder if it's my size?" she muttered.

The thought now jumped into her mind. She hadn't brought anything suitable to wear for her dinner with Michael.

How could she go out for the evening in her jeans? Francis hadn't packed anything remotely suitable. Why would she? In her wildest dreams, she never thought she would be going out on a date with someone like Michael. She so wanted to create a good impression.

He was certainly worth her making an effort for. She wanted to look as attractive as possible. All these thoughts ran through her mind in a rush. A bell tinkled on the door top as she entered the little boutique.

The baby-faced man leaned against the wall at the corner of the road. He had taken a cigarette packet from his pocket. Took one out and put it to his lips. It occurred to him that she might be in there for a while.

Not taking his eyes off the shop door, he lit the cigarette, took a long drag of it, and inhaled the smoke deeply into his lungs.

Fifteen minutes later, Francis emerged from the shop carrying a large pink carrier bag.

She had bought the green dress after trying it on and seeing herself in the mirror. Even the shop assistant was surprised at how good the dress looked.

"That's made for yer, you look fabulous, so yer do," the assistant said.

Francis didn't need confirmation about the dress. She loved it. The woman in the shop took her time folding and wrapping the dress up for her.

Heading on, she thought she just had enough time for a cup of tea before the sun disappeared below the horizon. Then it would be time to return to the hotel and prepare for the evening.

The Singing Kettle had all types of teas, coffees, and cakes. It looked just the perfect little place. Inside, the walls were painted a dark red. Wooden tables and chairs of different styles were arranged within. A little vase with a few sprigs of flowers had been placed on each table.

There was a pleasant level of general chatter and still a few empty tables.

Francis went straight to the counter.

A cheerful woman greeted her.

28

"What can I get yer there?"

Sounding very British, she asked, "May I have a cup of tea, please, and one of those tea cakes."

"Find yerself a seat, and I'll fetch it over."

The woman gave Francis a pleasant smile. Francis smiled and thanked her before she went over to a little table for two in the corner.

She was enjoying the tea and the toasted tea cake, looking about and taking in the quaintness of the Singing Kettle. The door opened, and a man on his own came in. Francis glanced up, and there at the counter was the baby-faced man. He smiled over at Francis, ordered himself a coffee and waited for it at the counter. After paying the woman who served him, he made his way to Francis' table.

Smiling at her, he said, "We have seen each other before, I think."

Francis felt slightly uneasy but smiled back. He had a foreign accent and said his words slowly and deliberately.

"Have we?"

"Yes, two times. I sit with you I drink my coffee."

Francis relaxed a little, now thinking he had noticed her on the ferry, and that was why he had smiled at her earlier.

"Oh, yes."

Francis pointed to the chair opposite her.

"I thought I saw you on the ferry crossing with your…" She trailed off, not knowing what to say.

He immediately jumped in. "Ah yes, how do you say..." He was waving his hand as if to recall a word. "Hmm." He stuttered and then finally came out with, "My sister."

Francis smiled. "Oh, I see."

He went on to tell her in his broken English that his sister had been distraught by the news of the death of their mother back home, who had passed away.

Francis didn't want to ask anything in return, as she found his broken English hard to listen to.

She felt a bit sorry for him as he seemed a bit lost.

He carried on. "I needed to bring her back here, to her husband." The man knew Francis had already seen them on the ferry. The truth was he had been trying to keep the girl calm. He was bringing her to Ireland on the pretence of helping her.

The truth was far more horrific than he was relaying to Francis. Lies came easily to him as he looked at her open face. He could see her believing every word he uttered in his emphasised broken English.

While Francis was enjoying all the delights Kinsale had to offer, the girl with the watery eyes was most definitely not.

CHAPTER 5

The harbour out of Kinsale was a long affair. It passed through the land like a ribbon. On either side, the rocky outcrops, topped with green fields, would finally reach the open sea.

All was well aboard the motorboat as the men kept watch. The two women chatted, occasionally looking up to see the sights along the way, now passing an old fort that had been a protector of Kinsale in the olden days. The girls expected to be taken to a safe place. The air was now cold as the motorboat picked up speed. The full force of the open sea caused the boat to pitch, riding the deepening waters.

The two women stopped talking and looked at their surroundings. They seemed to be heading straight out.

"Where are we going?" the girl's companion enquired to the girl with watery eyes.

They looked at each other with concern. The girl with the watery eyes answered. "We are supposed to go further along the coast to the house. Somewhere safe for me and my baby."

Clenching hold of her stomach, as if to hold herself together, she managed to stand up. Still the boat was ploughing through the sea towards the horizon. The two burly men stood facing forward. One was seated at the wheel, whilst the other stood at his side. The sea was now rushing by faster than the woman thought was safe. The girl with the watery eyes reached to get the attention of the man standing.

He was surprised as she tugged at his jacket.

She was yelling in her broken English. "Where are you taking us?"

The boat raced on, creating a plume of white spray high on either side. The man on the wheel threw back his head and laughed. The other woman was now bent down as the wind tore at her hair, trying with increased difficulty to maintain any feelings, other than panic.

Ignoring her plea, he said, "Stupid bitch."

She thought the wind had carried her voice off, so she tugged again at his coat.

31

"Where are you—"

The man turned before she could finish her plea, and with all the force he could muster, he drew back his arm. His meaty fist was clenched. When he straightened it, he had landed the punch, full in her pale, frightened face. Already with uncertain footing, the force of the blow and sway of the boat propelled her back to the far edge of the vessel. Seeing her lying there, he lurched forward towards her. She lay unconscious and limp. His overpowering body bent over her as he pummelled more blows into her face until the blood began to run from it. Her face became unrecognisable, squashed and broken in a bloody mess. Now looking down at her with a distasteful smirk, he picked her up and tossed her over the side. Then he casually let the spray wash over his hands to remove her blood.

The other girl was screaming and petrified on the boat's floor as she had witnessed the horrific episode. The boat sped on out towards the horizon. Before the remaining terrified girl knew it, the same dastardly, heinous fate had found her. The motorboat then turned and proceeded along the coast, where it would enter a small cove near Union Hall.

CHAPTER 6

Michael made his call successfully in the little back room of the pub. He returned to the bar, picked up his pint, and put his money on the counter. The place was deserted. Even the old man in the corner had left. With no one there to thank, he drank half of it and decided to get going. Now at a more leisurely pace, he was travelling back to Kinsale, thinking over what was to happen next. He had done his bit these past four days. The vital information he had witnessed had been handed over post haste. He felt he could relax now.

Although Bandon Garda was just under an hour away, his superior had told him to take a few days off. The paperwork could wait a bit longer. His superior had told Michael he would contact him when and if he was needed. The other units would now be given the information, taking over where he had left off. Michael listened and was grateful for the breather. He wanted to return to Kinsale to call in at his brother's. He had really wanted to see Francis Doyle again, too. The daytime would soon be giving way to dusk.

Thinking as he drove along about how happy his super had sounded on the phone conveyed to him the same feeling, a feeling of relief and happiness.

Finally, this drawn-out operation called *Traffic Lights* was almost at its end. There had been months of surveillance. His super had been very grateful. Many men had been and were still involved. He told Michael he was pleased with how all the men had worked together. All had played their part.

It was one of the largest cases of drug smuggling and people trafficking that the Garda had had to handle in County Cork. The gendarmerie in France, the Metropolitan police in London, and even officers in Wales had all pulled together.

Now all eyes would concentrate on the quiet backwaters of County Cork, with its many coves and undetectable places to hide.

It had proven to be an easy area for criminals to carry out their crimes so far.

Back in time, it had been booty from shipwrecks floundering on the rocks. Now it was class A drugs and people. It was a crackdown of mega proportions and one that would go a long way to getting Ireland back to a safe place for its people to live. Now with all the evidence in place, the perpetrators would be rounded up. The Garda had to wait possibly a day or two to pounce. Hopefully all at the same time, everything would be wound up.

***

Michael, all the while, was nearing Kinsale. The thought of meeting up again with Francis Doyle made him accelerate his speed. He allowed his willing mind to think about how attractive he had found her.

He hadn't failed to notice the excellent tight fit of her jeans. The jacket suited her petite frame, with an overall casual yet, he thought, chic look. She appealed to him in so many ways. He thought she was a girl in a million. The kind of girl he could really fall for. He already liked her. He had loved the colour of her hair and those meaningful green eyes and the way her creamy, clear skin had blushed when he kissed her hand.

The look on her face told him, if he were not mistaken, she, too, had liked the look of him.

With a smile, Michael realised he needed to get to his brother as soon as he could to ask him for a bed for the night, and a long soak in a hot bath, which would be just grand.

In just over an hour, his car pulled up outside the parochial house and parked alongside his brother Andrew's car. There was plenty of room in front of the large side gates.

"Ah, it's good he's here," Michael said as he climbed out and took his overnight bag from the boot.

Choosing a few clean items of clothing that were always there in his case in the boot, he strode to the huge front door found in the deep porch that befitted the large church building. Lifting the heavy black knocker, he gave a couple of raps. It was almost dark, yet the sky was a blaze of crimson red. There was a good view from there, as its location was high.

Michael stood with his back to the door, admiring the beauty of the changing sky. The trees about the property were silhouetted, like black cut-outs against redness, making him think it was a glorious end to the intense time the past few weeks had been. All he wanted now was a long hot bath and to enjoy his evening.

The door swung open and there stood Father Andrew Connor, beaming a huge smile at his brother; a shorter man than Michael, curly-haired the same as his brother, though Andrew's was cut short, now mostly turned to a silver white.

"Michael," he exclaimed, holding out his arms in welcome. "Come in, come in," he beckoned fervently.

Michael stepped over the threshold and into the large entrance hall. Putting his bag and clothes on the table, he went straight to his brother, and they embraced in a manly way with back slapping.

The kindly faced priest spoke again. "So good to see you, Michael. It's been a while." His brother took in Michael's appearance with a critical eye. It was duly noted by Michael, and he felt a little self-conscious, though he remained smiling while his brother was speaking.

"Sure, sorry it's been a while, but I have been busy with work. You know how it goes, better than anyone." In an absent-minded way, he was running his hand through his curly hair, with the realisation he must be looking pretty rough around the edges. "It's good to see yer, too, brother. You look well, so you do."

"Come on through," his brother said, leading the way.

Michael followed.

"Will you be stopping for yer dinner?"

It had been the way of it when Michael happened to be in Kinsale. The two brothers would eat together, there at the house or the Italian place in the town.

They made their way through another door and into a sitting room. There a fire burned low in the grate. No lights were on yet. Two leather armchairs were positioned in front of the fire's meagre glow, favourably preferred by Father Andrew. He liked to make people visiting him comfortable.

"Sit yerself down now." Father Andrew pointed to one of the chairs. "Will yer take a drop?"

"Thanks, Andrew. I think I might."

He was already standing by a side table, where a decanter and glasses sat. He poured two large whiskeys from the decanter, handed one to Michael, and added a couple of turfs to the fire. The sweet aroma, as it caught, was pleasing and comforting to both men. A true feeling of home.

They had made themselves comfortable in the fire's increasing glow. The flames started to lick around the new clods of turf, creating a mellow glow around the darkening room.

Looking at each other with a lift of their glasses, the brothers, in unison, hailed, "Slainte!"

Each brother took a healthy gulp of the amber-coloured liquor.

"What's new then, little brother?" Father Andrew asked as he cast an eye over Michael.

Michael downed another gulp.

"To tell the truth, first things first, I was gonna ask if I might stay a night or two?"

Michael raised an eyebrow cheekily and waited for his brother's reaction.

"Sure, Michael. How can I refuse yer?"

Both men chuckled.

Father Andrew was Michael's older brother by twelve years. There was almost a generational gap in the way they lived their lives. Their parents thought of them as different as chalk and cheese. Though their boys were equally loved, both Martha and Joseph were immensely proud of their two sons.

Andrew came across as very proper in his manner, even as a child. Not wanting to partake in the usual boyish pranks, he had, then and still now, behaved in a gentle way.

He had shown a very sensitive, almost unworldly side to his nature, even as a boy. Then later, he became very studious and serious, always finding a quiet corner to have a read. Away from anything rowdy, solitude became his way. As Father Andrew was Michael's senior, he had watched him grow into the man he was now, albeit from afar. Yet he had a deep understanding of his little brother.

The two brothers' lives had panned out so differently, yet their love for each other was as strong as any love between two brothers could be.

Father Andrew was every inch a priest. He had wanted to do things his way and take up his calling, as he referred to it. He had

36

announced to his parents at fifteen that he, Andrew Connor, wanted to become a priest.

Martha had been delighted at the news. She thought it would suit him well, and who were they to interfere with the Almighty's choice? Surely it was the good Lord that had chosen Andrew, her son, to his calling, but Joseph wasn't so sure. Time would tell. His wife told him to let the boy live the life he wanted.

So it was that the young Andrew was sent off to college to take up the priesthood. All through his studies, he was thought to be a remarkable talent and of good conduct. With his studies for the priesthood completed,

he had naturally taken his vows.

After various locations of learning, even abroad in Rome, the young Andrew served as curate to Father Ignatius.

Father Ignatius was the parish priest at that time in the town of Bandon. In fact, that was where Andrew's proud parents witnessed his ordination. The church had been packed, filling all the pews back of St John the Baptist Church. The Bishop of Cloyne oversaw the whole affair. Father Andrew, after serving quite a few years right there in Bandon under the guidance of Father Ignatius, was overwhelmed to be offered the Parish of Kinsale.

The young priest had been favourably accepted. In fact, the confessional had seen a huge increase, since he had been so well received by the church-going community. Andrew had worked hard to make a difference in people's lives, and they felt it. His homilies were witty and interesting. He had time for everyone. He always seemed cheerful. His latest endeavour, in which he had been particularly instrumental, had been the setting up of *the young mother's helping hands*. They met once a week with the help of the Sisters of Mercy. You could say he tried all of his days to make those in the community one happy family.

**

Now, with the knowledge he was welcome, Michael said to his brother that if it were all the same to him, he would be skipping dinner with him as he had a date. At this, Andrew smiled, raising his eyebrows.

"About time, too," he said playfully. "What's taken yer so long?"

Michael was used to his ways and loved it. He got up from their cosy spot.

"D'yer mind me taking a bath?" Michael said with a smile and a laugh.

"Help yourself, Michael. You know where everything is, and take the room you have used before. I'll see you when you come down."

While Michael lay luxuriating in the deep bath, dreaming of Francis, Father Andrew went over to his desk that was positioned prominently in the middle of the vast bay window of the room. He fumbled with the lamp switch. It always amazed him that he never quite located the switch on the first attempt, though it had always been in the same position. Finally, the lamp was illuminating across the desk. He sat down, opened a drawer, and took out a key, the one he would always give to his overnight visitors.

With that now placed on the dresser, he thought he would take another small tot and take it back to sit for a while by the fireside. The merrily flickering flames were too good to miss.

Gazing into the comforting dancing display, his mind remained on Michael.

How he himself favoured his mother in ways and looks. Michael, on the other hand, was very much his father's son.

Though Andrew and their daddy had now gone grey, they all boasted a head full of curls. Albeit, he had kept his short and more akin to their father's.

He knew only too well how his parents longed for their youngest son to find himself a wife and create a home and family.

Ah well, he thought to himself, all in God's good time. He drained the glass and set it down on the table next to him. He put his hands together in his lap as he spoke in a soft whisper.

"Be with my brother Michael, dear Lord, and keep him safe."

He was pleased that Michael was at last going on a date. By all accounts, she had sounded, from Michael's description earlier, a cailin worth pursuing.

CHAPTER 7

As Francis had sat listening to the baby-faced man, she had begun to feel sorry for him. He seemed genuinely upset about the loss of his mother. He had confided in her that it was his sister he was most concerned about.

Francis thought that he just wanted someone to offload his sorrows to. Perhaps he thought he had found that in her. She was the one, after all, who'd witnessed his sister's misery at losing their mother. So she believed.

He told her he lived in London after coming from Romania. He and his sister had been brought up in a small village at the foot of the Carpathian Mountains. He spoke in his broken English of the many castles there, and churches. "Like this place," he added.

"Oh, here, like in Ireland, you mean?"

"Da, Da. My sister like Ireland here. Her husband here too."

It was falling into place now for Francis as she put together what he was trying to tell her. His sister was now with her husband. He must have been one of the men on the motorboat.

Francis listened patiently, being polite and smiling in her manner. She hoped she had brightened his day. Watching him now as he endeared himself to her, while listening on, she thought he must be in his thirties at least. For some men, she really couldn't tell. At a glance, she would have thought him younger.

His complexion was clear and fresh looking, without any signs that he needed to shave, his dark eyes hooded with heavy dark brows. He had a square jawline that framed a tight thin-lipped grimace.

It was the way he spoke that caused Francis to listen to his story. Trying so hard, she thought, to put it into English made him seem vulnerable.

After offering to buy her another tea, Francis declined and thanked him, telling him she really must get back to her hotel.

He smiled, stood up and almost bowing to her replied, "I hope to bump again, to you. Two more days I go to London."

Francis smiled. "Perhaps," she said, smiling again.

He left the Singing Kettle.

Picking up her pink carrier bag, she peeped inside, glimpsing that the green dress was there and safely wrapped in orange tissue paper. Now checking for her purse inside her shoulder bag, Francis went to the counter to pay.

"Are you off now?"

It was the lady who'd served her earlier.

"Yes. I would like to pay, please."

"There yer go."

The lady handed her a slip of paper with the amount written on it. Francis took out a note.

"Please put the change in the tips. It was very nice, thank you."

She went out into the fading light of day. The sky was crimson, and there was a bit of a chill that greeted her. She turned her collar to the freshening breeze.

It was not too far back to her hotel.

Everything there seemed to be an easy walk for her. So different to London. She was totally charmed by all that she had so far seen.

That night she was meeting Michael and now wondered, as she walked along, what time he would show. Perhaps he wouldn't. She quickened her step, feeling the need to be back in her room where she could collect herself, wondering now if she was being foolish and that he had probably forgotten all about her, thinking he had just enjoyed chatting with her to pass the time on the ferry crossing. He was just too good to be true, she thought. Ah well, if he didn't show, she could get something to eat in the hotel.

The glum thought would vanish very shortly.

As she climbed the steps up into the foyer, the warm glow looked welcoming through the glass doors. At the reception desk was the lady she had seen earlier. She was chatting to a man, telling him mostly the same as she had told Francis before about the dining room times. Francis was just passing them by and went to turn to take the stairs.

"Hello there," she called out to Francis. "There's a message for yer."

Francis stopped and stepped back in surprise.

"Is there?"

The woman moved along slightly so she could deliver the message.

"Michael Connor will be here for yer at 7.30."

Francis felt immediate gratitude for the message conveyed.

"Thank you so much," she said as she turned and skipped up the stairs.

Putting the light on in the room, she put her bags on the bed and then drew the curtains. Looking at her watch, she had over an hour to get herself ready.

The green dress now lay on the bed. Francis went into the bathroom and started running the bath.

She was lying there in the comfortable hot water with a dash of the fragrant bathing liquid she had found in the complimentary basket. She began to run through the events of the day. How she had driven all the way to Fishguard, crossed the Irish sea, and met the most handsome man, who just happened to be taking her out to dinner that very evening. Not forgetting how lovely the drive had been down to Kinsale.

It then crossed her mind about the baby-faced man and his sister. It was quite strange that they had headed that way and that she should see them again here in this particular place. Another thought occurred, as she lay soaking in the bath, also strange – his coming into the Singing Kettle. It was just one of those things, she told herself, that their paths had crossed yet again.

She was glad, in a way, that the baby-faced man had come into the Singing Kettle. It had appeased her curiosity. She was sorry for them, being in a strange country. Such bad news she fully had an understanding of. Relieved at the thought, though, that the girl with the watery eyes was in fact his sister.

Bringing her all the way home, back to her husband here in Kinsale, showed a kind and caring nature. She wouldn't dwell on them any longer. The bath was beginning to cool.

Francis was nearly ready to go. She had slipped into the beautifully fitting green dress, looking at herself in the mirror.

She had pinned her hair high on her head. A few twisted curls had escaped, but she decided she rather liked it like that. Not too formal.

The way she had styled her hair flattered her neck, accentuating its gracefulness, and the neckline of the dress revealed her pale soft skin. The shade of green, she thought, seemed to bring out the colour of her eyes. She was not wrong. They looked clear and bright.

Satisfied that she would do, she lightly bit into her lips, bringing the colour to the surface. She picked up her cream jacket, her purse already in the pocket, just in case. Lastly, the keys. She was outside the door and locking it at exactly 7.30.

CHAPTER 8

Michael came down from the bathroom, looking a whole lot better than when his brother Andrew first saw him earlier this evening.

Dressed now in clean clothes, his freshly shaven face looked the picture of health. His too-long hair, so Andrew constantly commented, was still damp from the vigorous shampooing it had received.

He had taken one last look in the mirror at himself before deciding by the time he had walked down the hill and along the road to Donovan's his hair would have been dried by the breeze. He had deftly cleared the stairs down and entered the room where he knew his brother would still be sitting.

Father Andrew eyed him from his chair.

Michael spoke first. "Will I do then?"

"You look fine, Michael. Smell pretty good too."

"Do yer think I've overdone the aftershave, then?"

"You're fine, Michael. Stop your worrying."

Michael dropped down in the chair opposite.

"To tell the truth, I'm a bit nervous. Francis is something else. First impressions and all that."

He cocked his head at his brother. Michael had always conveyed his deepest thoughts to his brother. There wasn't anything he wouldn't tell him. He was his confessor and always listened without judgement, always giving him the best advice. Michael knew that it would go no further, whatever he told him.

Father Andrew replied, "Look here, Michael, didn't she see you already? Hasn't she agreed to be seeing yer tonight? Trust me, Michael, you've nothing to worry about. Take another wee tot before yer set off," he added. "That'll settle your nerves."

Michael looked at his watch. "No thanks. I don't want to be late."

"Sure, it's only ten past seven by my reckoning. Only takes five minutes to get there," he said with a nod of his head. "With those long legs."

As Michael got up from his chair, Father Andrew reminded

him to take the key from the dresser.

Lastly, as Michael reached the door of the room, Father Andrew called, "Enjoy yourself."

With Michael gone, Father Andrew recalled how many of the local girls had confessed in the confessional, how they thought they were in love with Michael. There wasn't a girl in Kinsale or Bandon, and come to think of it, Clonakilty, that hadn't one time or another fallen for Michael.

"Ah," he muttered to himself with a smile. "My little brother. If you only knew."

***

Francis reached the last three steps down into the foyer of Donovan's hotel. There was a general hum of voices to be heard that came from the open dining room doors. A fleeting thought entered her head. There were more people staying in the hotel than she had thought previously.

She stopped where she was on the third step from the bottom. Casting her eyes over to the far corner, she could see Michael Connor sitting, waiting for her. Unknown to her, Michael had been waiting there for fifteen minutes.

To him, it felt longer. Michael had left his brother's home far sooner than he needed. It only took him five minutes to reach the hotel. As he sat there watching the comings and goings, it occurred to him he should have accepted the nerve-settling drop his brother had offered him before he left the house. He couldn't remember ever feeling this nervous before. Andrew was right. It would have calmed his nerves.

Just then, he looked over at the stairwell. He stood up, and at last, there was Francis standing on the stairs, smiling over at him. He thought how radiant she was. She was still smiling at him as he rushed to greet her.

"Hello, Michael," she said.

Michael couldn't take his eyes off her.

Finally, he spoke.

"Francis, you look gorgeous, so you do."

She smiled.

Her polite reply was a sweet, "Thank you."

He offered her his arm.

"Shall we?"

He linked his arm with hers and thought they made a handsome couple. He took her through the open doorway, down the wide stairs, and then turned to walk up the road and into the town.

"Do you like Italian?" Michael asked.

"I love it," she replied with a beaming smile.

The knowledge that Francis loved Italian food put Michael at ease. The evening air was fresh, and they ambled along in conversation about the restaurant they were heading for.

Not more than ten minutes through the town, they arrived outside Toni's Italian restaurant.

It was quiet inside with just two other couples. The restaurant was small and had a friendly vibe. Soft music was playing, and the room was dimly lit, creating a romantic feel. The occupied tables had lit candles adding to the atmosphere.

They were greeted by a small Italian man. On seeing Michael, he threw his hands in the air in welcome.

"Ciao, Michael, good to see you. Your table is ready."

The man gestured to the corner table. Going there himself, he promptly pulled the chair out for Francis, beaming a smile at her. She sat down, taking off her jacket.

"Bellissima!" he exclaimed, taking her jacket from her.

He draped it over his arm and turned his attention to Michael, who had taken his seat.

"A vast improvement to Father Andrew, Michael," he teased as he flicked a lighter to the waiting candle on their table.

Michael just smiled. "How's it going, Toni? This is Francis."

With a flourish of his hand, looking at Francis, the little Italian man said to her, "Buena sera Signorina, Benvenuto a Toni's."

Francis smiled back and thanked him. With another flourish, he handed over the menus.

"What can I bring you to drink?"

Michael raised an eyebrow at Francis and asked her, "Would you like some wine, Francis?"

"Oh, yes please, red will be fine. You choose, Michael."

Michael ordered. They sat in comfort, with eyes only for each other. The evening was theirs. They spent it well, getting to know each other. Michael told her some of his work but not all. He was guarded somewhat, as he was conditioned not to speak of a case that was not fully closed.

He told her about his family. His parents, brother and sister were all mentioned. He felt he wanted her to know everything about himself immediately. The more he looked at her, the way she listened, laughed, and spoke, made it all the more urgent. He just wanted to make her his.

Francis enjoyed every moment, concentrating on every contour of his handsome face and the way he looked at her. She had never felt the way she was feeling tonight. She drank her wine and listened intently, taking in every word he spoke. The food, though delicious, was just a means for them to sit in the pleasant surroundings of the restaurant, learning about each other in the candle's glow. The wine relaxed them. With the conversation easily flowing between them, as they gazed at each other, anyone could see they were falling for each other. Everything was pointing towards this not being a brief affair.

***

On the outskirts of the town of Kinsale and down a dark little lane, another set of events was evolving.

Inside the almost derelict house that stood within its own overgrown area of land, the baby-faced man was sitting at a table in the kitchen. A dim light hung low above a table, illuminating his clenched hand around a can of beer.

He pushed the used plate away from him. Taking a cigarette from a packet on the table, he lit it. He was thinking about the girl he had followed earlier.

In the sink sat dirty dishes and crockery. In general, it was a bit of a hovel. The house itself, with a little bit of love, could have been quite idyllic.

Now it was in the hands of a group of men that used it as a temporary safe house for their illegal and corrupt dealings when they were in this location.

It was there that drugs were sorted into different packages and stored ready for delivery.

Girls had been brought there too. Young girls that had been groomed by the baby-faced man, Dario Dinu, otherwise known as *The Chaperone*. He was wanted by the Garda, the Metropolitan police and the gendarmerie, and was part of this particular operation in Kinsale.

He was an illegal immigrant from Romania, living between the countries of France, Ireland and the UK. He was known to be working with several others. Boats loaded with drugs from Europe and beyond would find their way to the undetected and remote Irish coastline, easily hiding in small coves.

The sea was Dario's friend, his honey pot. It had become solely his means of survival. His life now had become easy. He was dispassionate, even excited by the chase of a new find.

Those females, he thought with disdain, were stupid creatures. To be used by strong, capable men, such as himself. He loved that part of his work the most. Once they were in his grip, he knew how to handle them and give them what, he thought, they really wanted, with a little help from him, to loosen them up.

He found it easy now to travel openly, without hindrance. He had his routes and his helpers when a bit of muscle was needed.

Dario had spent many hours chaperoning the innocent victims, who became his prey. He took delight in weaving his tales of lies to the vulnerable and needy young women. He had become proud of his charms and could easily snare them into becoming his friend.

Once they had a bit of a liking for the drugs, they could be persuaded to do anything. Some would become mules, taking the drugs from one place to another, easily passing them on undetected. Dario would keep track of those mules, travelling occasionally with them. It was his job also to hand them over when they had become a liability to him, rendered unable to carry on. Some were stupid enough to become pregnant. That sometimes could cause disruption for him, but nothing was insurmountable.

As he sat at the table drinking his beer and smoking alone, in his mind, he was hatching a plan.

***

Michael and Francis' evening couldn't have gone better. Toni's had been a good choice. Its warm and friendly atmosphere had been the perfect backdrop for their intimate dining.

Outside the restaurant, Michael and Francis naturally linked arms and huddled close. A few steps further down the road, Michael turned to Francis. He gently lifted her chin and kissed her. It was a gentle brushing of his lips on hers. Then he pulled away.

"Sorry, Francis, I just had to do that. I have been looking at yer all evening, longingly, wanting to kiss yer."

She dropped her head coyly and smiled.

"I'm glad you did."

Francis smiled at him.

He then took her in his arms. This time he didn't pull away. She lifted her face to him, and they kissed fully without restraint. She felt wonderful right there, in his strong embrace. Everything for him was lost in their first embrace. Who they were, where they were, it didn't matter. It was the perfect summing up of all he was feeling for Francis. Michael didn't want to pull away, but he had to stop. He was aroused like never before. Looking at Francis, still in his arms, he spoke.

"Can we meet tomorrow, beautiful?"

"Yes, I would like that very much," she replied, looking into his eyes.

Michael slowly let her go from his arms and took her hand.

"Come on, let's get yer back to yer hotel."

They walked along the now deserted pavement towards the harbour. It was gone eleven, and a chill wind was blowing in from across the sea.

When they reached the hotel steps, Francis fished into her pocket for the hotel key. Sure enough, the large glass doors were shut, but a soft glow shone from the foyer. Again, on the steps, Michael pulled her gently to him and pressed another gentle kiss on Francis' lips.

"Goodnight, Francis. I'll pick yer up, say eleven?"

"That will be lovely."

Francis put the key in the door and let herself in.

Michael ran the whole way back up through the town to his brother's home. At the summit of the hill, he stopped and drew breath. He had needed to run. It had helped to expel the exhilaration he had felt most of the evening.

Francis sprawled in the pretty flowered covered bed. She was tired and felt sleepy. The day's activities were finally taking over. It had been a very full day. Yet she felt the need to stay awake, wanting to relive what had happened to her, on this, her first day away from London in years.

Feeling comfortable, with two plump pillows behind her head, pleasantly fatigued as she lay there recalling the day's events, she looked about the room. It was now bathed in a soft glow from her bedside lamp. It was, or had been, such a different day to any previous days that she had ever lived.

Firstly, she relived the crossing of the Irish Sea, thinking about the different people she had seen. The girl with the watery eyes? She didn't want to linger on that again, so shifting her mind, she recalled the drive to Kinsale. It had filled her love of nature more than she could say.

How lovely the countryside looked to her, so verdant and lush in the spring sunshine.

But most of all, Michael. What was there not to like about him? She wrapped her arms around herself. The look of him made her feel like a teenager who was star-struck about their particular idol. The way he looked at her, with that enquiring look. His blue eyes were framed with dark, thick, long eyelashes. His voice!

How lucky had she been to meet such a man as he? So far away from home and on a ferry of all places.

So, he was a detective, she mused and wondered what her parents would have thought of him.

"It is good he has a career, non?" she could hear her mother saying, with the French accent that she had never managed to lose, even after living in London since she was a young woman of sixteen.

Francis' father, on the other hand, would have liked Michael straight off. "Good fella that you've found yourself there, Francis, and Irish too."

She was smiling to herself, recalling her parents. Sighing, she thought on both accounts, on reflection, Mum and Dad would have most certainly liked him.

Snuggling down, she reached for the lamp switch to turn it off. Softly she said, "Good night, Mum, goodnight, Dad. God bless you both."

It had mattered deeply to Francis what her parents might have thought of him. Having no one else, not one person she had wanted to confide in, even at work, Francis would not tell anyone about Michael. She had been down that road, trusting and open, confiding in who she believed was her best friend until the betrayal.

It had been an added blow that she had had to deal with. The deceit of it had totally undermined her perceptions of people at that crucial time. The time after her parents had had that fatal accident and all that had happened after.

No, these days, Francis looked only to Francis. The only outside help she had received at the time of their departure from the world was from Gerald Bagster. He was her immediate boss, to whom she would become secretary a year or so after the life-changing episodes.

CHAPTER 9

Another fine day was to greet the people of County Cork. Spring was beginning to give way to the promise of the arrival of summer. The showers throughout April had brought about the fresh young shoots of all manner of vegetation, thriving along the lanes, in fields, hedgerows and woods. Even in the crevices of the craggy rocks, ferns had found their homes. Small sedums spread like beaded necklaces along old low-laying walls, intertwining over soft moss. In some places, bright orange lichen had formed, spreading like a slow invading carpet, close to the surfaces of ancient rock faces. All thrived without pollution in fresh, clean air blown from across the vast Atlantic Ocean. The land was warming. A variation of birds were in speedy flight. Some nesting, some feeding their young, all could be heard, warning off intruders from entering their territory, or singing with the sheer joy of freedom that was theirs. The people in this part of Ireland were living out their days in a quiet, easy-going way.

They seemed to hold a secret within their hearts, 'The Irish', that is completely theirs.

People lived in a way that was known to one another. There was a camaraderie of understanding that belonged to the community. Always engaging and never in a hurry.

Historically, that particular part of Ireland had been known by locals as *bandit country,* especially there and into the west.

It was on Bandon Road, in the area of Beal na Blath, where Michael Collins, the revolutionary leader, was shot in an ambush and killed in the 1922 troubles, after the treaty had been signed.

His home was a small farm that lay between Clonakilty and Rosscarbery. The house itself had been burned to the ground by the Black and Tans.

Further along the coast from Kinsale and to the east, in that quiet backwater of gently rolling landscapes, long sandy beaches and numerous rocky outcrops, also small coves and inlets with stretches of beach, lay hidden.

It was around eight o'clock on that Tuesday morning, and Old Tommy Walsh was picking his way down through tufty grasses that afforded a path away from his cottage, a small cottage with its advantageous view out across the mighty Atlantic.

From there, he could see, offshore, an island, home to the Bally Cotton lighthouse. Since the 1840s, it had warned sailors of the dangers, and proved an invaluable help.

He would look out at night and feel the comfort of the lighthouse as it shone its intermittent beam across the sea.

Old Tommy Walsh loved his isolated situation with just his faithful dog for company.

Every morning, come rain or shine, Tom and his dog would go down to the unused hidden beach to see what the tide had washed up that day. He had, over the years, collected many items, taking them back up to his home for careful consideration, seeing what he could make or use. He had different piles of detritus lying in different areas of the land that surrounded the cottage. Some were now covered, long forgotten and hidden from view as the long wild grasses made their home.

That morning, as usual, off went Old Tommy and his best friend.

"'Tis another fine morning, Bess," Tom muttered in the breeze.

Old Tom surveyed the skies as he made his way to the beach. "Let's see what the tide's brought us today."

Bess wagged her tail as she scampered down and sniffed her way along. She had reached down to the sands and was running about, happy in the sunshine, waiting for her master to catch up.

They had gone a little way along, with the sun still low in its transition. Bess had started to bark, as she ran faster along the shoreline. Old Tom had the sun in his eyes and couldn't make out why Bess was barking. Was there someone coming? He put his hands up to make a shade for his old eyes. Peering off into the distance, he could now see Bess dancing around something, still barking as she danced. This was most unusual. Old Tom hastened his step. Getting nearer, it looked to him like a pile of twisted red cloth. Seaweed clinging to a sodden mass.

He got close and could see a leg protruding from the pile. He didn't want to touch it. It looked like a woman's body, twisted and distorted, wrapped and mangled with seaweed and cloth. His heart raced.

"Enough, Bess," he shouted at the dog.

He raised his arm to make her stay away, and the dog's tail went down between her legs. She came around to sit down behind her master.

Old Tommy uttered the words, "Holy Mary, Mother of God." He then turned to Bess. "Come on, Bess. We need to call the Garda."

With much panting and as much speed as he could muster, Old Tom and Bess made their way back along the beach and up the steep path to his cottage.

Within an hour, the little unused and unseen beach was a hive of activity. Garda were everywhere, combing over the beach. At the top of the lane that led down to Old Tommy's cottage, Garda cars were parked, blocking the exit. Not as though there were any neighbours to get in the way. Well, not yet!

CHAPTER 10

Michael's mind was full of Francis, now going over what he knew about her. He had hoped his brother Andrew was there to have breakfast with him. He wanted to talk about Francis. He was so smitten with her.

He would have to make do with his own thoughts as Father Andrew had already left for St. John's and would be taking Mass that morning. Andrew had left earlier before Michael had come down. No doubt, after Mass, there would be other duties he would be called upon to attend to.

Michael was in the kitchen of the parochial house frying himself some eggs. He was in the mood to eat. Bread was on the table, tea was ready, brewing in the pot, and he had cooked himself some bacon.

While Michael tucked into his breakfast, he began recalling what he knew about Francis so far. She was an only child. He found that incomprehensible and sad, knowing how his life and been with a brother and sister. The other thing that saddened him was that by age eighteen, she had lost both her parents in a fatal head-on car crash.

How did a girl so young cope with that? Then, if that was not enough, her best friend, when her parents were killed, had struck up an affair with her boyfriend.

Francis was so sweet-natured.

Michael ran his fingers through his hair, thinking fate had really dealt her a hand.

Now though, she was pretty level-headed, having come through such an ordeal at a young age.

By all accounts, she was very much self-sufficient. Nothing Francis could say to him about her past would change his feelings about her, nor about making her hopefully part of his future.

He had mopped up every last residue on his plate with the last bit of bread. Taking the plate to the sink, he washed and cleared all the surfaces.

Then he downed his tea, and a thought hit like a ton of bricks. The car! Holy mother, he needed to get outside and clean it up.

Broken from his dreaming, he got moving by ten thirty. He and the car were ready to pick Francis up from Donovan's.

First, Michael wanted to make a phone call to his mam and da to tell them he might be in the area that afternoon. The phone was soon picked up.

"Hi, Ma."

"Michael, hello, son. How are yer?"

"There's someone I want to bring along, if you're in, that is."

"Today?" Martha Connor queried her son. "Who is the someone?"

"Yer just have to wait and see, Ma. We won't be stopping that long."

Michael thought he might add that to the conversation, knowing full well it wouldn't be easy to get out once they had met Francis.

"All right, Michael."

"It'll be sometime this afternoon, Ma."

"Fine, son. We'll be here."

Perhaps it was a bit too soon, he thought after he had hung up. Too late now!

***

Francis started her day very slowly, luxuriating still in her bed at eight a.m. It had been a long while since any morning had offered her such a treat. The very thought that there was no rush, no need to catch that train with all the other sad-faced commuters who would be making their way right now, made her smile. She wrapped the covers about her, thinking *Not today.*

Michael would be calling for her at 11 a.m.

Plenty of time yet.

Breakfast was being cooked by someone else and would be ready at her leisure. She could hear a few sounds outside her room. She thought other guests were making their way to greet another day in Kinsale.

"Ah sure, here yer are," the jolly-faced woman said as Francis entered the dining room. She greeted her with a beaming smile. "Did you sleep well?"

Francis was quick to reply. "I did, I really did."

The jolly-faced woman looked about the room. "Well, yer can sit yourself anywhere yer fancy."

Francis looked about. There was only one other couple finishing their breakfast. The room was quite large, with five or six tables and an assortment of chairs. Nothing looked at all like the usual kind of formal hotel dining room. It was far more homely.

Francis chose a small table set near the wall. "I'll sit here if that's all right?"

"'Tis grand. Shall I bring yer tea, or is it coffee? Help yourself, over there is cereal if you fancy it. Would yer be liking something cooked now? The full Irish perhaps?"

It was Francis' turn to speak. "I would very much like some tea, and I think I'll try your full Irish. Sounds interesting."

"Grand choice. I will be back with yer tea."

Francis took in the room. The couple got up from their table. She detected an American accent as the man said to his lady, "That'll keep me going."

He was rubbing his rather large tummy. His wife, smiling back, said, "I should think so too, dear."

On their way, passing Francis, they both looked over to her and wished her good morning.

"Enjoy your day," Francis said as they exited.

She was thinking now perhaps she had left it a little late to arrive for breakfast. There was no one else about.

Just then, the jolly-faced lady brought in her tea, a basket with different breads in it, and a dish containing butter.

"Did yer not have your cereal then? Can I get you some toast? Perhaps some porridge?"

Before Francis could answer, "Well, now it's another beautiful day, so it is. Have yer made some plans? Where yer off to today?"

Francis smiled. She loved the jolly-faced woman's cheerful manner.

As she paused, waiting for Francis to respond, Francis wasn't sure which question she should reply to first.

Her eyes fell on the breadbasket. There was plenty there. "I don't think I'll be needing any toast, thank you."

"If you're sure now, 'tis no trouble, yer know."

Francis caught on quickly. She was getting the measure of how things were.

"I have a friend picking me up this morning."

"Ah, would that be the same fella waiting on yer last night?" Francis smiled. "It would," she replied.

"Well, you have a nice day for it. Was it Michael Connor?" Francis smiled again.

"I'll get that breakfast for you," the woman said.

Satisfied with the little exchange, she returned to the kitchen, returning quickly with a plate full.

Eggs, black pudding, sausage, potato, tomato, and beans.

"Oh my!" Francis exclaimed.

Mary beamed.

"Now there yer go, everything all right fer yer?"

"Just perfect, thank you."

Mary was about to return to her kitchen when Francis asked, "There's just one thing. I was wondering about parking?"

"Should have told yer," she said, smiling, and carried on. "Yer can drive along the side of the building and go round the back. Plenty of space there."

She smiled to herself as she went back to the kitchen.

Francis made a start on the feast that was before her.

***

Michael's car was parked outside Donovan's at ten forty-five, the cleanest it had looked in a long while. Looking around the interior, Michael thought he had done a grand job. He waited a few minutes there, then decided he would wait inside, as he had just the previous evening.

Mary Donovan greeted him as she was busying herself around the foyer.

"Well, I see you're back, Michael."

Mary Donovan was a fount of information. Nothing much passed her by. Most of the locals could rely on her for the comings and goings within the community. She had lived in Kinsale all of her fifty-three years. She had opened up for business at Donovan's after the loss of her husband. Mary fed her need and curiosity within the local community by opening her home to different guests. Not only guests but locals too. She had started the *Twice a Week Club*. There, she would provide a meal for locals and a get-together, Monday evenings and Thursday afternoons. She let out six rooms, but only if she liked the look of the people who happened to enquire.

Mary Donovan didn't go chasing business. She had told her daughter she would rely on the Good Lord, who she had relied on all her life. Hadn't He been her generous guide so far for her? Also, hadn't He gifted her with an aptitude and astute comprehension of people?

Now looking at Michael, she knew he was smitten for sure. Hadn't she seen him waiting for the pretty young woman just last evening?

"Isn't he all of a flutter," she muttered to herself as he kept passing back and forth, sitting down and then standing up again, pacing about the foyer.

Now here he was again, looking very happy with himself.

"Hi there, Mary. How's it going?"

She gave Michael her all-knowing look. "Oh," Mary replied. "It's a grand day for a drive, I'm thinking." His handsome face was not lost on Mary.

"Sure, it is," Michael replied. "That's what I'm planning."

He gave Mary a smile. With a nod of his curly-haired head and a cheeky wink, he continued, "Looking forward to it."

"Would it be with a particular young lady, this drive?"

"It would. Would yer mind telling me this, Mary? Why is everyone so interested in me love life?"

"Ah, love is it, Michael? Nothing wrong with enquiring about love. Sure, 'tis a beautiful thing. 'Tis the lack of it that's the worry, so it is."

As if on cue and just before Michael's retort, Francis came in from the main door, seeing Michael in conversation in the foyer. Mary Donovan nodded over. "There she comes now. Your driving partner."

Michael spun around to see Francis smiling. He rushed to greet her as she came through the main door.

Francis called over to Mary Donovan, telling her she had parked around the back, and thanked her for it.

"That's fine," she called out. "Enjoy your day, the pair of yer."

They were soon gone from Mary's gaze.

Once in the car, Michael looked over to Francis. "Are yer ready then?"

Francis smiled. "Yes, I am. Where are we going?"

"I'm taking you to Drombeg."

"Drombeg?" Francis repeated. "Strange names you have here, but nice."

"It means small ridge," Michael replied.

"Ah, I see." Francis was watching the road ahead as they drove along the side of the harbour. She was sure she had just seen the baby-faced man again. He was with two other men going down onto the pontoon. Michael turned right to exit the town.

Though she had noticed him, she said nothing to Michael. It was just a coincidence and not worth mentioning.

They now headed over a bridge, leaving Kinsale behind them. Michael was telling her they were heading away from Kinsale to a place called Timoleague and then on to Courtmacsherry, which was close by.

"Those are nice names," she said.

"I think it's a very beautiful place," Michael told her. "If I'm not mistaken, you'll love it, as I do," he added. "It's worth taking a look at, for sure, especially today."

Francis was enjoying herself so much. She just wanted to smile all the while. As they drove along, Michael told her stories of when he was a boy and visited these places with his parents and sister.

Francis asked about his sister.

"I think the two of yer would get along. She is possibly a couple of years older than you. She is married to Con, and they have a little boy of, ah…" He thought for a while. "About three, so he is. Now they are expecting their second."

"Oh, that's nice," Francis said, thinking to herself, *Lucky sister*.

There she was at twenty-eight, not married and no babies. She then asked Michael, "What's her name?"

"Bridget," Michael replied.

"Nice name," she said and then laughed, realising how she was repeating herself. Did she think every name was nice over there? Michael got her drift and chuckled. The two of them went on their way to Timoleague.

The road was narrow, and once again, Francis was admiring the trees. They were a little way into their journey when the road turned. There, lying in front of her, she could see how that land gave way to the sea. They were following around a large inlet.

Michael pointed out that they would be going all the way around this inlet. She could see over on the opposite side. Homes were scattered along the inlet.

"That's Courtmacsherry," Michael told her.

"Oh, how lovely. Can we just stop here?" She excitedly looked at Michael. "Just for a moment, please?"

Michael parked where there was a very small place to pull in, just in case a vehicle needed to pass. So far, they had not seen another car in any direction.

Francis got out and stood at the low wall. It separated the road from the mud flats. The tide had turned and had headed out. It left behind rivulets between grass and mud banks, creating weird and wonderful designs in its absence.

"Oh, Michael," she sighed. "This is so beautiful."

The sound of birds and a gentle breeze was all she could hear.

He was standing directly behind her. He wrapped his arms around her from behind and put his head to her neck, whispering in her ear.

"So are you."

Michael turned Francis towards him. She looked at his handsome face as he bent his head to hers. Closing her eyes, she readily accepted his kiss. The kiss was long and meaningful. Eventually, Francis had to pull back.

"Michael, you take my breath away."

Her voice was soft and low.

His reply wasn't spoken as he kissed her again but more in jest as he said, "Now don't go fainting on me, Francis Doyle, will yer. I want to show yer the village."

Getting back in the car, they set off.

"Not far now, Francis. Don't go holding your breath," he teased.

It was not far at all.

Michael crossed the little bridge and told her the Argideen River had made its way to meet Courtmacsherry Bay. The wildlife there was a bird watcher's paradise. She agreed as she looked at the numerous birds on the mud flats. They were pecking for fishy treats and preening, some perched on the higher banks calling out, perhaps with the sheer joy of living.

They parked the car and started their walk. Michael was delighted to show Francis this ancient bit of Ireland. He was getting to know her by showing her the places he loved. In doing so, he watched her every move and her reactions to everything around her. He was falling in love with her more and more.

Right there, in Timoleague, were the ruins of a thirteenth-century Franciscan abbey. The old Friary building rose up from the side of the road, and from its vantage point looked straight out down the bay towards the mighty Atlantic. Ancient ruins, defying nature, still standing, though any roof had long gone, the abbey walls protected old and new gravestones. The bright sun shone through, glassless windows creating shadows within, in part, casting an eerie glow on some of the old tombstones, in shadowy corners and recesses.

Michael took Francis' hand as they walked around, in and out of the stone walls and graves.

Francis had a distinct mystic vibe, telling Michael she could almost hear the prayers raised to heaven from this very place. He raised an eyebrow at her and laughed. She said nothing more but just let her mind imagine perhaps she could hear a whispered, singular voice before the altar, or a distant chant coming to her as the hooded monks recited their prayers in unison.

There were also impressive stone Celtic crosses with elaborate patterns, reaching in silhouette towards the blue, cloudless sky.

Michael, holding her hand, brought her back to the here and now by saying, "Come on, let's take a walk around the village, and then we can drive on a bit."

The village of Timoleague was not that big. Francis never thought the less of it because it was very pretty. She noticed the telephone box standing on the corner. It was the same shape and size as back home in London, but instead of red, it was predominantly green with a yellow trim. She told Michael that she preferred the green. It had fitted so well into its landscape. The village was surrounded by verdant green pastures, separated by hedgerows and trees, to the beautiful bay.

Now back in the car and heading towards the place she first saw from across the bay, Francis was really enjoying herself. Everything she saw felt really special to her. Her mind was taking it all in. Then like a dark cloud descending, a sad thought came to her. But for how long? Time had a habit of flying by, and she wondered how long she would be able to enjoy Michael's company and when he would be called back into work.

"You all right there, Francis?"

He put out his hand to get hold of hers.

"Yes, fine."

She held tight to his hand until he needed to change the car's gear.

They were driving along the other side now. As Francis looked across the bay, she could see where they had gone earlier. She thought immediately she wanted to stay here forever, with Michael by her side. That place was filling her senses. It was as though she belonged there.

What was there back home compared with this? Who was there? It was as if she had stepped into a whole new life, a life that would and had far outweighed the old.

Back home, in London, she was on a treadmill and lonely. Francis realised that now, more than ever. The stark difference had been almost shocking to her. In Ireland, she had come to life. All her senses had been awakened in just a few days. Already she knew she was in love with Michael. Now she was also falling in love with this country, as it was weaving an unseen spell over her.

Michael's voice interrupted her thoughts, bringing her back.

"Shall we get a drink?" he asked.

"Yes, please. Lovely!"

They were now in Courtmacsherry. Francis let go of Michael's secure, strong hand so he could slow down and park up on the roadside. He brought the car into the kerb and stopped.

"We can go in here."

Michael nodded towards the building they had parked in front of. When Francis looked out through the windscreen, she realised he had stopped right outside the pub.

"Do they serve coffee here, Michael?"

"They do." He gave her a wink with a cheeky grin. "Did yer

think I'm going to get you drunk, Francis?"

He was laughing at her.

"Well, I don't know. Do I?"

"Sure, you do. Come on."

They got out and took the two steps straight in through the front door.

Francis took a moment inside the pub, waiting for her eyes to adjust to the darkened room. Coming in from the bright sunshine had made the contrast even greater.

Straight off, Michael was greeted by the man behind the bar.

"Grand day for it. How's it going?"

"Well, it's too good a day to miss, so we thought we might take a drive. Haven't been this way for a while."

Francis found herself a seat, listening and watching as Michael chatted easily at the bar. She had noticed how the Irish never got to the point straight off.

They always seemed to start off with a warm-up, heading along six different paths before arriving where they wanted to be.

She found it endearing. Was there anything about this charming place that didn't delight her? So far, no.

Francis watched Michael as he engaged with the barman, just loving the look of him and the tone of his voice.

After a suitable amount of banter had been shared, she heard him ask for two coffees with a drop.

Sitting away from the bar, on a small table in the corner, Michael came over with the coffee and sat down. He just sat there smiling at her as she took a sip.

She licked her lips and smiled, thinking it tasted different.

"Der you like it?"

"Yes, I think I do," she said, taking another sip. "It's delicious."

Michael just smiled. "Thought yer might."

She had never tasted anything like it before, but it had made a nice warm glow inside her.

"What is it? It's not like coffee I have ever tasted before."

Michael told her it had a drop of whiskey added in the coffee and topped off with cream. It hadn't taken Francis long to drink. When they finished their coffees, they bid goodbye to the barman.

"Mind how you go," he called out.

Francis turned and waved.

They got back in the car, and Michael headed off in the direction towards Clonakilty.

She began to feel as though she were in a dream. Everything she saw and felt made her think, *I have come home.* This was an inexplicable sensation for her. Now her whole entire being was responding to the change.

Francis had always known what to expect and how she thought she should behave. What was expected of her every day at work.

Every weekend she would spend Saturdays doing the washing, cleaning and shopping. She would attend Mass on Sundays, going through the same routine, even there, seeing the same faces of the faithful, lighting candles for her parents in the hope they were together in some sort of paradise.

The one and only outlet for her was to perhaps go for a walk on a Sunday afternoon. Then she tended to her plants with the care one would associate with a motherly, caring love of nature. Her neighbours watched her in wonder and concern. The elderly couple that had lived next door to her home in London had known her all of her life. They mused they could set a clock by her very existence.

The treadmill existence had been brought about by losing her parents mostly, then her boyfriend, and the betrayal of her only girlfriend. It was as though she needed to cope that way to survive the trauma she was going through. She had spoken to her doctor very early on. On his advice, she joined a group that dealt with grief.

It had helped somewhat, but the best medicine for Francis had been working. It had become her saviour.

Now this place, this Ireland, from what she had seen in only a few days, seemed to be changing her, moment by moment. Francis was exhaling not just the fresh air but the monumental grief she had held within for what seemed her whole life. The drive that had steered her throughout her career had held her in bondage. She was, without being fully aware of it, letting go at last.

They drove their way through more of the same quiet lanes.

Now arriving in Clonakilty, they went around a small roundabout and headed down a straight, narrow main road. On either side was a whole medley of shops, pubs, a hotel, eating places, cafes, hairdressers, a chemist; in all, everything you needed for your weekly needs. It had an old-fashioned feel to the place. Michael said they were not going to stop there, as there was something of interest he wanted to show her.

As they passed slowly along, Michael mentioned it was there that his mother came to shop. "It's not far from my parents' home."

"Oh really? Well, I think you're very lucky to have been born here, Michael."

Francis had spoken in all sincerity.

"I mean that in all honesty. What's your mother like then?"

"Hmm," Michael said in a playful manner. "Now, what's my mother like? Tell yer what, Francis, would you like to meet her?"

"What? Today, you mean? Are you being serious?"

"Yes, today. We can go there, but only if yer want, that is. I did tell her we would be coming this way. Only if yer really want to. There's no pressure here. Think my da might be there too."

Francis thought for a moment. "I think that would be very nice, Michael, if you want to."

He squeezed her hand.

"First, let me show yer something else. Then we can go visiting."

They had negotiated through the town, and in a short time were on the other side heading to a place called Rosscarbery.

Michael took a turn off the road, onto a smaller lane. Very soon he had parked up.

"What's here?" she said, looking about mystified.

"Come on, I'll show yer."

Once they were out of the car, he was going through the hedge, which had obviously been used before. Francis was enthralled as a tunnel of twisted growth was formed, with a well-trodden path.

"This is all very mysterious, Michael."

"Come on," he said.

She followed as he led her through the opening, and right there, before her, lay an open vista stretching out to the sea. They were standing in the nearest field. On exiting the deep hedge, there was a stone circle before them.

With a dramatic swing of his arm, Michael looked at Francis. "I give yer *The Druids Altar*," he said.

Francis thought it was magical.

"Oh, I have never seen a stone circle before."

They were like a couple of children with no one else to witness their playfulness. They were quite alone, just the breeze sighing across the height of the landscape. An occasional bird tweeted as it flew past nearby.

They walked over to look at the stone circle and stood close by while Francis counted seventeen. Michael watched her as she entered the stones, gently sweeping her hand over each one. He was watching her every move, her hair glistening like copper in the bright sunshine. She seemed to sweep and bend her whole body in the most delightful, delicate manner.

"You've done it now," he said.

She was laughing. She loved the way he played and teased her.

"Oh, yes? What have I done?" she called, swinging her body around like a spinning top.

"Whatever you do, don't stand in the middle," Michael called.

"What, like this?"

Francis ran to the middle and threw her arms in the air, laughing. Michael was by her side in a moment. Grabbing hold of her, he softly said, "You're mine forever now."

Then he kissed her.

They fell to their knees, holding each other tightly, locked in an embrace, deeply lost in their kiss. Francis didn't want this magic to end. She let him gently guide her to the ground. He was on top of her now.

"I want you more than I can say," he whispered.

Their eyes locked as they kissed again as they lay, body to body, lips to lips, locked in a passion welling within them. Finally, Francis pushed him away.

"Not here, Michael, not yet."

Michael broke from his reverie.

"Yer can't blame a fella for trying," he said as he held her there for just a moment longer.

66

He kissed her cheek, understanding that that was as far as it was going. He leapt to his feet, grabbed her hand, and pulled her until she stood.

She knew without a doubt it would have been very easy for her to get lost in his embrace. She knew she wanted him with all her heart.

Michael put a reassuring arm around her shoulder, and they both sighed as they looked at the magnificent view.

Francis slid her arm around Michael's waist.

CHAPTER 11

In Kinsale, the motorboat Francis had witnessed the three men boarding earlier that morning had returned. They were moored up alongside the harbour wall for the rest of the day.

It was now four in the afternoon. The calm weather made the trip easy for the three men as they returned from Union Hall. They were calm in their underhanded dealings. They were used to doing what they did and did their business nonchalantly in broad daylight. They were totally unaware that they were being watched.

Now the three men were making their way by road to their house with a hoard of cocaine and cannabis. They were in the habit of stopping at various locations around the area, bringing the illegal drugs, namely cocaine, from the continent to this quiet location that seemed to them so perfect. Sometimes they would receive a woman or two who they could pass on. The yacht would rendezvous with another sea-going vessel offshore further out at sea. The Chaperone drove the car along with Costie and Leon Balan. All three were illegals, all three were now known, and all three were being watched by the Garda National Drugs Unit (GNDU). Time was running out for them.

The GNDU were now watching their activities closely. Nothing was proven about the body washed up in Ballycotton yet. Forensics were working on the female's identity and were in a hurry to find it out. It was suspected she could possibly be the same girl spotted with The Chaperone, Dario Dinu.

The yacht anchored nearby Union Hall had been the supplier. It had sailed in a few days earlier. They were allowed to remain, so the criminals on board would think the coast guard hadn't detected them.

On his crossing from Fishguard, Michael had picked out the brothers. Following through with his orders, he watched as they joined forces in Fishguard. The two brothers had been told what was needed of them and were now on the move to carry out and perform their heinous duties.

Michael was on it. Another colleague of Michael's on the

ferry crossing had kept an eye on Dario Dinu and the unfortunate young women he was chaperoning.

Dario Dinu had brought the young women from London to Fishguard.

Crina Sava was now no longer required. She had remained unaware of her final destination.

He had told her he would take her to Ireland, where she and another girl had a safe house. He had it sorted. No need for her to worry. Crina would be helped and looked after, especially now she was pregnant.

"Who would be looking after me?" she had asked in her naivety.

"Another woman," he lied.

Still, she had moaned and cried virtually throughout the ferry crossing. Dario had needed to keep her calm and placate her.

He had met her in London a year or so ago. Being Romanian too, she was quickly groomed by Dario Dinu. All alone, she was an easy target for him.

He had led her to think he would look out for her, help her find work, and ensure she was safe.

Firstly, he had confiscated her passport, pretending to her it was for safekeeping. Then he had told her she needed to relax. He would show her how with a little help of the white powder. Once she was compliant and hooked, he finally set her to work. She was trapped, totally at his mercy, though Dario Dinu had no mercy. Now Crina Sava was used to pass the illegal substance undetected. As time passed, she had become totally reliant on him and drugs, just like the many other girls he had had before her.

Crina's final degradation was to become pregnant. Dario Dinu would except money from anyone who would pay cash for a few hours with one of his girls.

This was how he made his living. He was the very dregs of humanity, preying on young women. Occasionally he would ensnare a prettier girl that stood out from the crowd, someone who had more potential to earn him a larger reward. He would sell her abroad on the market, with which he was very familiar. There the cream of the girls would be sold off to the Far East and beyond. Clients he had had in the past were very generous, paying high prices for naturally blonde and fair-skinned girls, and redheads were very sought after too.

He found the chase excited him. The challenge of the chase gave him a reward in itself. He felt empowered over his victims, who were always so easily lied to. These girls were stupid, he told himself. They were nothing to him, just business.

**

Now at their safe house, the three men were together in the dim kitchen, undetectable at the back of the house. No one ever passed that way. The place looked neglected and overgrown in an acre or so of wasteland. Beer cans and cigarette packets were strewn across the old wooden table where the three sat.

Dario Dinu was banging his fist on the table in temper as the other two sat back in their chairs, smoking and listening.

"We need to get the redhead," he was saying. "It shouldn't be difficult. The yacht will be leaving tomorrow, and I need her to be on it. We have the morning to find her. She is alone. It shouldn't be too difficult. She is so small; you can put her under your arm."

They all laughed. A little calmer now, Dario added, "If we can get this shit shorted by tonight." He nodded over to another table with two large bags of cocaine and a pile of small plastic bags. There was also another larger bag containing cannabis waiting to be divided.

The two brothers listened as The Chaperone went on.

"We can all go down the town in the morning, get the motorboat ready and look for her. If I can, I will get her on the boat. The rest, you know, is just a matter of getting her to the yacht before it leaves. The reward will be good, my friends."

They all lifted their cans in salute.

CHAPTER 12

Martha was all of a flutter.

"I wonder who it is?" she asked Joseph.

He looked up from his paper. "Well, how do yer think I would be knowing that?"

"It must be important to him. Michael has never brought anyone home before now, has he?"

Joseph went back behind his newspaper.

"Do you think I'm looking all right in this dress? Perhaps it's someone from work."

Martha smoothed down her dress, as Joseph remained behind his newspaper.

"Ah, yer look fine. Stop your worrying. They will be here soon now, whoever it is."

Martha gave her husband half a smile and left the sitting room, thinking he'd been sitting there this past hour, reading his paper. It was her, getting everything prepared, ready for an intriguing visitor.

It had been a while since she'd seen Michael and she was looking forward to it.

He always had a happy way with him, making her laugh, sometimes until her sides ached. She would hold her tummy, saying, "Ah, no more, Michael. I'll be crying soon with the pain."

The house always came to life with him in it. Martha smiled to herself.

***

Francis was looking forward to meeting Michael's parents. It was so unexpected. She didn't have time to worry about what to wear, which was just as well. Her jeans and jacket would be acceptable, no doubt. Francis looked down at the pretty flowery pink top she was wearing. They were country folk, after all. No need for high fashion here. She looked at Michael. He was casual enough in his jeans and shirt. Her thoughts were interrupted as Michael slowed the car down.

"Here we are."

All Francis could see was a driveway flanked by two tall

pillars and huge open iron gates. He deftly swung the car through. On either side of the drive were tall overhanging trees. The drive gave way as the house came into view, opening up with ample space in front of its impressive structure to park four or five cars. Michael parked up in the middle.

"Oh, my, Michael. This is some house. It's fabulous! Positively fabulous."

Michael smiled. "It's a bit special, I suppose," he remarked as he looked up through the windscreen at the house he had seen and lived in all his life.

"A bit special? It's gorgeous."

Michael looked at her and squeezed her hand.

"Like yourself then."

His eyes were on her, and she felt a tightness in her tummy.

Just then, the large wooden door of the grand grey Georgian house opened. Three dogs came out ahead of Michael's parents. Martha and Joseph waited on the step.

Two of the dogs were barking enthusiastically, one small white terrier with brown patches and one medium mixed breed of a light brown colour. Its coat was scruffy. Then one who didn't seem to bark came loping slowly behind, far more dignified. He was large and noble looking, an Irish wolfhound.

Francis sighed. "What's his name?"

"That's Murphy. We've had them all since they were pups."

Michael got out of the car and greeted them as they came straight to him. Three tails wagging with accentuated vigour.

Francis just waited a moment to take in this happy sight. She loved dogs.

Michael told them to go back, and they obeyed him and returned to the step. Francis thought that was impressive. He opened the car door for Francis.

"Come and meet Ma and Da."

Francis stepped out. Then walking towards them, she held out her hand in greeting.

As she reached his mother, in her polite English tone, she softly said, "How do you do."

Martha took one look at the pretty young woman and knew this was a bit more than a date for Michael. He had never brought a girl home. Martha was not going to give a polite handshake.

72

She ignored the hand that Francis had offered her and placed her hands on Francis' shoulders with a big smile. Martha looked her straight in the eyes, then kissed her on each side of her pretty face.

"Welcome to Ash House. This is Michael's father."

Martha turned to face her husband, giving him a nod of the head as if to give him permission to do the same. With a smiling face, likewise, knowing only too well what Martha said without the need for words, Joseph stepped forward and kissed Francis' cheek.

"It's lovely to meet you both," Francis said, smiling.

Michael gave his mother a hug as she hugged him back. Bending his head, he kissed her cheek.

"Yer look lovely, Ma." Then he winked at his father.

Joseph put a hand on Michael's back, ushering him in.

"Nice to see yer, son."

The four, plus three dogs, went inside.

The hall was quite large, and at once, Francis felt the homeliness of the house. It gave her the same welcome feeling Michael's parents had. Francis had never been in a house quite like this one. It seemed so grand to her. They all went into the sitting room whilst the dogs were sent off to the back of the house somewhere.

"Make yourself comfy," Martha said. "I'll get the tea."

She was out of the room and back in her kitchen, where everything was prepared, so far as it could be, in advance. All that was needed was to pop the kettle onto the range to brew a fresh pot of tea. It would accompany the cake, bread and butter, with homemade jams of two flavours, one of which was Michael's favourite, gooseberry, and her own home-made fruit cake.

In fact, far more than the four were ever going to manage.

Martha's kitchen was warm and homely, far from the modern, pristine kind.

It was a perfect square, with a couple of large dressers, both with pretty plates on display.

The large sink that was snowy white, with big brass taps, was situated beneath a large square window, affording a view straight out onto a garden with yard.

Martha loved to cook and bake. Her kitchen was, on most days, filled with the aroma of her culinary delights. She had accumulated pots and pans of every description, with old inherited ones from her mother-in-law's time. There was a huge range to cook on that kept the warmth going all year round. A large square table dominated in the middle, and several assorted chairs were around, some with comfy old cushions. The kitchen was more than just a kitchen. It had been a well-used hub of homeliness for generations of the Connor family over the years.

Joseph was under the watchful eyes of Michael in the sitting room as he asked Francis where she was living.

This sitting room was seldom used these days, only for visitors, who of late seemed few and far between. With its large soft sofas, it still retained its cosy feel.

Francis had removed her jacket, placing it over a chair near the French window. She glimpsed what appeared to be a very large garden out of the door.

Sitting comfortably next to Michael, Francis readily told Joseph about her home back in London and her work. She told him, too, about her parents. Joseph didn't interrupt but let her talk as much as she wanted.

All the while, Joseph was looking at Francis, not unkindly, but with a deep concentration on his face. Michael looked at his da in silence as he wondered, *What is he thinking about?* There was something on his mind for sure.

Just then, Martha came in carrying a tray. A large pot of tea, cups, saucers, milk and sugar, serviettes, spoons, forks and knives. All were carefully stacked with skill.

"Michael, could you bring in the other tray fer us?"

Michael was on his feet, out the door and back again before Martha had set her load on the table, right next to her chair. Michael put his tray next to his da.

"There's a good fella, thanks," she said.

They were all back seated.

"Now," Martha said. "How der like yer tea, Francis?"

She held the pot, waiting to pour.

"Milk, no sugar, thanks."

Francis stood to take the cup and saucer Martha offered her.

"Take a plate and help yourself. There's plenty. Yer might

need a fork too."

Martha had thought of everything, not knowing who Michael was bringing home. She had not wanted to let him down. She was looking at Francis thinking how lovely she looked, while Joseph continued with a serious look on his face.

An hour had passed. Michael and Francis were full of cake, bread and jam, and the teapot had been filled twice. The conversation flowed much as it should. Francis thanked Martha for the lovely spread and told her she thought her jams were the nicest she had ever tasted.

Delighted at that praise, Martha asked, "Which one did yer prefer, Francis?"

"It's very hard to choose, but if you push me, I'd say the gooseberry."

"Wouldn't you know it?" Martha's hand came up. "'Tis Michael's favourite too. I shall give yer me recipe."

Finally, Joseph was to get a word in. The women seemed to have hit it off. Joseph wanted to ask Francis a couple of questions. Now was the time.

"Now, Francis, where did yer say your daddy came from?"

"Oh, I didn't. The truth is I don't know. All I know, all I ever knew in fact, was he was brought up somewhere here, in Cork."

"I see," Joseph said. "Would yer mind me asking what his full name was?"

"Of course, it was Robert Joseph Doyle."

"Do yer know when he was born?"

"Yes, I know."

Francis was looking bemused. Michael was feeling a bit uneasy as he looked between his da and Francis.

"It was 1912."

Michael had had enough. "Why does it matter, Da?" Michael asked, leaning forward in his seat.

"'Tis nothing, son. I just had a feeling about someone I knew with the same name, is all."

"Really?" Francis said. "That's interesting."

"I'll think on it a bit more." He smiled, adding, "Probably nothing at all."

Joseph took a bit of Martha's fruit cake. He had asked what he needed to.

"Can I help with the tray, Mrs Connor?" Francis was on her feet. Michael stood too.

"It's all right, Francis," Michael told her. "I'll do it."

"Call me Ma, Francis. Everyone else does."

Francis smiled as mother and son went off to the kitchen with the trays.

"Michael, she's a lovely-looking girl," Martha said out of earshot of Francis.

"She is that too," he said. "Look, Ma. I'm still working. And the truth is—"

Just then, the telephone in the hall rang.

"Shall I get that?" he asked.

"Yes, please, you get it, son."

Martha had her hands full of plates. Setting them down now in the sink, she had wiped her hands and was heading back to the sitting room.

Confident her son would deal with the caller; Martha made her way back to Francis and Joseph.

Michael was absent for a while, so Francis took the opportunity to ask about the dogs. Joseph was quick to say Murphy the wolfhound was five. Molly was the mixed breed, she was three or so, and Finn was the Jack Russell. He was just two and full of attitude. Francis smiled and told them she had always loved dogs, but it seemed it was never the right time to have one.

"It's a shame," Martha ventured. "We have always had some animals for the children growing up."

Michael came back.

"It's work."

Francis' face fell. Just what she had not wanted to hear, she was hearing.

Joseph looked at his son. Michael looked at them all in turn.

"Looks like I'm needed tomorrow."

He looked as crestfallen at Francis. He looked at her now. "I think we had better be on our way now."

Joseph knew better than to ask what was happening or where. So, he said nothing, not wanting to add to the disappointment.

Martha sprang to her feet, saying, "Well now, there will be other days, and soon, I hope. It's just been grand to meet yer, Francis. You're welcome anytime."

Joseph added, "Yes, yer must come back, and soon."

The goodbyes and thanks were said. Joseph and Martha waved them off from the step.

Michael didn't quite know what to say to Francis back in the car. He had been so caught up in the moment, he hadn't given it much thought, as he felt now, he should have. Michael was silent, searching his brain for the right words as he drove back the way they had come, so happy, such a short while ago.

Michael was desperate for her to stay close by, even if he was working. He thought anything could happen if she decided to go off on her own. She could meet someone else, even forget all about him, and he might never see her again. He couldn't let that happen. Not now, not ever.

The silence in the car, while they were both lost in their thoughts, suddenly became palpable. He needed to say something right now. He brought the car to a halt on the side of the road and switched off the engine.

"Look, Francis, can I be honest with yer?"

He had turned to face her and took hold of both her hands. "While I can't, at this time, confide in yer and tell you what I am doing, I want to be honest with yer."

Francis wondered what he was going to say as he held her hands in his. "Okay." She smiled. "I want you always to be honest with me."

"I have to go to work tomorrow. Truth is, I'd really like to be with you. You see, Francis, I am falling in love with yer. No, I am in love with yer," he corrected. "I know we have only just met, and it might sound ridiculous to yer, but it's the simple truth. I know I have no right to ask, and I will understand if yer don't feel the same way."

Francis put her hand on his cheek. She knew he was being really sincere. He took her hand, putting it to his lips and kissed it. Then went on.

"I don't want yer to go off on your own tomorrow or any other day come to that. I know you're on your holiday, and God knows ye have earned the right to enjoy yourself."

Her green eyes flashed, and she spoke. "Just stop talking and kiss me, Michael."

He didn't need to be told twice. The air was cleared between them. They both felt relieved and revived. Their feelings for each other were clear. They knew for sure where they both wanted to be, and that was with each other.

"Where shall we go now?" he asked, more or less to himself. "No need to get back yet, is there?" He gave her a wink as they pulled back onto the road. "Shall we have a walk? I know the very place."

Francis agreed, just as she had agreed to stay in Kinsale and wait for him.

They came into Rosscarbery, and Michael turned the car to take a little road heading out along an inlet towards the sea. The town was behind them on the hill. Just a small old-fashioned village with a main square above the causeway. Once on the other side, he parked the car.

"Let's walk along here," he said.

They left the car and headed off in a direction that would eventually lead to the open ocean. There was an hour at least before the sun set. Hand in hand, they made their way, the light slowly fading, as the sun made it way towards the horizon.

***

Back at Ash House, Martha and Joseph were in their kitchen having cleared away the crockery and leftovers.

Martha said that if she were not mistaken, Michael had at last met the one.

"Did you see the way Michael was watching the girl? If that's not love, then I don't know what is. What do yer think, Joe?"

"I think yer might be right, Ma. She's a lovely girl, make no mistake. I have a feeling."

He paused and pulled out a chair to sit at the table, making himself more comfortable for the telling.

"Go on, Joe," Martha said eagerly. "Tell us what yer think?"

She sat down at the other end of the table, all ears. If she wasn't mistaken, her Joe was just about to tell her something she didn't know or hadn't thought of. It usually happened that way when he started off with *I have a feeling*.

"Right, this is what I'm thinking. That pretty young girl is the daughter of Robert Joseph Doyle, a boy I knew quite well at school."

Martha's jaw dropped. "Never! Holy Mary, Mother of God.

78

How sure can you be, Joe?"

"I'm thinking, 'tis the right name and right age. I know he left for London before the war. Now this is the thing, Ma. He had a sister."

"Had, Joe?"

"Well, him, Robert, that is, being dead and all. His sister is, yer know who she is?"

"No, I don't, Joe. Will you stop beating about the bush and tell me who."

"What I'm saying is that yer know her too."

"Go away with yer!" Martha had had enough of this shilly-shallying. "Who is she, Joseph Connor?"

"It's Nuala, Nuala O'Leary."

Martha's jaw dropped for a second time.

"But she never married. So why isn't her name Doyle?"

"She did, see, a brief marriage it was before we were wed. That's why you didn't know, I guess. We've never spoken of it. Why would we? Yer know how she keeps herself to herself. Well, it was always the way of it. Just the same as when she was a girl. I've always known about them. Not much income. Their daddy died years back, and then their mammy died just before we left school. If my memory serves me well, Robert never went back to school when his ma died. Kept himself to himself after that. He got some work in printing. Young Nuala was courting David O'Leary. They married, and then he was killed shortly after. Think he got in the way of a rebel's bullet." Joseph shook his head, paused, and then carried on.

"Don't think she ever got over it." Martha was all ears; this was news to her.

"Then what happened, Joe?" she asked.

"Young Robert, I guess, had had enough. You see, the work situation was pretty bad back then. Times were hard on most folks, so he took himself off to London. That was the last I heard of him. Perhaps he kept in contact with his sister. Then again, perhaps not."

"Well, I never. And there's me, all this time not knowing a bit of it. You've surprised me, Joseph Connor, so you have."

"I'm thinking," Joseph said, "that I might just pop along to see her. See if I can find out anything from her that might throw some light."

Martha's first instinct was to add a caution. "She a strange one, Joseph. Do you think it's wise to interfere? She might be upset that yer go raking up the past."

"It just might be, Martha, that I'm right, and that sweet girl, who has not got a soul in the world, perhaps has an auntie who could tell her all sorts about her family. What can be wrong with that?"

CHAPTER 13

Father Andrew had been busy all day, one way or another. His day started very early. He hoped he might have had a chance to meet Michael at breakfast. That was not the case this morning. Michael was still in his bed when he had to leave the house.

After celebrating Mass, there were the old folks at St Joseph's he had to call in on. There were a few confessions he had promised to hear in the home of the sick. The poor souls could no longer make it to St John's.

He had bumped into Mary Donovan en route that morning. That woman, he thought on reflection, didn't miss a trick. She started by telling Father Andrew that his brother Michael and the pretty young woman were off for a drive today.

"She was over from England, Father, and all for an undisclosed time."

At this point, she gave a nod of her head for added emphasis.

"While Michael, himself, just that morning, was saying all about love and looking very pleased with himself when he came to take her off again."

Without drawing breath, she further ventured, "That the young lady in question had come down to breakfast this morning, all misty-eyed and late. That was after an evening out with yer brother, Father, and who knows to what time."

She nodded her head again.

"I couldn't be certain as I had to lock the door to Donovan's. It's the rule of the house. So, I think it had to be after 10.30."

Father Andrew was listening and looking as though it was the most important information he had ever heard, while the fully committed Mary Donovan flowed on with the telling, seemingly not needing to draw a single breath.

"Though young Rosemary kept a lookout for them, from time to time."

Father Andrew now had the mental picture of Rosemary Donovan keeping vigil in the upstairs room facing front, onto the main road.

Mary Donovan broke the image as she went on. "But by

eleven, at the latest mind, we are both in bed. We don't like to keep late hours, Father."

She smiled. He was just about to give an answer, but Mary barely sailed straight on.

"Well, they had a lovely day for it, Father, so they did, don't yer agree?"

The barrage that had assailed Father Andrew's ears made him want to laugh. Instead, he smiled at Mary Donovan.

"Well, yer can be sure he will be breaking a few, if not many, of the local girls' dreams, including your Rosemary if I'm not mistaken," he said gently. "If the young lady in question stays in Ireland, that is. Not many English folks do now. So, I'm thinking, leave it in the good Lord's hands. I'm on my way to St Joseph's," he said before she could start up again, and left her watching his back.

Father Andrew chuckled to himself, reflecting on his brother as he rushed down the hill. Did a fella ever cause as much interest to the female population as his beloved brother, Michael?

****

CHAPTER 14

Robert Doyle and his sister Nuala had lost their father while they were both quite young, a casualty of the First World War. Their mother had struggled to bring them up alone. As the years slowly passed, their mother had become more and more weary. She felt the burden of making do. There was never quite enough. Sometimes their mother would go without food, giving all she had, to the two always-hungry little ones. She would sit at her table in their meagre home, and the tears would fall for the loss her husband, shot in a skirmish, through no fault of his making. Her babies clung around her skirts, still young enough to remain innocent of their predicament. She had struggled on somehow. Her heart ached, leaving a void only her beloved could fill.

Their mother had prayed morning and night that there might be an end to her suffering. Time went by, and now the children could see her in a distressed state. Her heart had become cold yet would melt at the words of her little Robert. He would come to his mammy and rub her back, saying, "We'll be all right, Ma. I can get a job soon. Yer see, I'm nearly grown."

The pain in her back was getting worse as she bent her head forward for some respite. This had been her only way to help alleviate the pain.

On this particular day, Robert and Nuala were almost grown and in the last stages of their schooling. Their mother hoped things might improve. Robert would find work. He was a good boy. Nuala would find herself a nice young man. Nuala had turned into the prettiest young thing. A smile came to their mother while she busied herself with cleaning and tidying. The pain came again that day while she was alone in the little croft, and she stopped what she was doing. She sat at the table thinking it would go. Some hair had escaped from the bun at the top of her head. Ringlets of hair fell about her once beautiful face. Laying her head on the table, she quietly left the world, beginning her journey to the other side without fuss. Nothing had changed within the croft, except, in the silence, her hands had slipped from her lap to her sides as she exhaled her last breath.

Robert had suffered growing up in this environment. He would always compare what they had, or lack of what they had, to the other boys he knew and their families. It was true that not many Irish folk at that particular time in history had lived an easy existence. Many were struggling in their rural environment.

The young Robert hadn't had much of a boyhood, trying to be the man of the house and looking after his mammy and little sister. He became serious and moody. The day he had come home from school to find his mammy slumped with her head down on the tabletop would be a day he would never forget.

His first thought was that of Nuala. He ran as fast as he could to their nearest neighbour, Mrs O'Sullivan.

"Oh, my dear boy," she had exclaimed as she made the sign of the cross. "Saints preserve us. Go fetch your sister and bring her here first. I'll send for the priest."

The young Robert had managed to meet his sister along the road. She was dawdling along, the way she always had, singing and talking to the birds, lost in her own world of make-believe. Robert had stopped. He watched her from a way off. Robert wondered how he would tell her. She looked so happy. The picture of his mammy slumped across the table flooded into his mind. He had to say to her they'd be all right. They had to be.

In no time at all, Father Kelly came, riding his bike to the little croft. Three of the nearest women knew Robert and Nuala's mammy well and were with her now. They had laid her on her bed. Candles were lit about the little room that was hers alone. Her rosary was entwined about her hands placed upon her still and silent chest.

Robert and Nuala stood in the open doorway to their mammy's room. Silently they stood and watched in the flickering candlelight.

Mrs O'Sullivan was standing behind them. She thought it was important that they should see their mammy at her rest, so they could come to terms with it. Now with a little persuasion, she had guided them away and outside the house.

"Now, yer both should come home with me until it's time for your mammy's funeral. Everyone will want to come by. We won't be leaving her alone now, as everyone will take turns to keep vigil. There's nothing for you two to think about, 'tis all taken care of."

Robert and Nuala had gratefully excepted. Mrs O'Sullivan had been close to their mammy, and Mammy in return always said she was a good friend.

Robert never went back to school after that. Nuala had stayed a while longer. After the funeral had come and gone, the brother and sister went back to the croft. Robert sought work as an apprentice. It was Father Kelly who had set the wheels in motion for him. It didn't pay much, but he had managed to get a position in the works of a local printing firm.

With the help of the locals keeping an eye, the brother and sister made the most of what they had. Robert had diligently kept to his work whilst Nuala stayed at school. The pair became independent and strong-minded, growing into exactly what their mammy had hoped on that very last day she had thought about them.

Robert watched as his sweet little sister left her school days behind. She had now turned into a capable young woman. Even to him, she seemed a dreamy and lonely sort of girl. He hoped she would find herself a nice fella, and then he thought he could get on with his own life. He didn't want to stay there for much longer. Robert was desperate to go to London. He had heard he could get a better job with more pay.

Robert didn't have to wait much longer.

Nuala had turned sixteen and David O'Leary had been coming by their cottage. Nuala had been very keen to accept David O'Leary's proposal. He had told her of his love for her. David just couldn't and wouldn't live without her. They had been courting, without Robert's knowledge, for some months. Since that beautiful spring had blossomed, in fact. Their love for each other had too. David O'Leary would come by on his bicycle and they would secretly go off together through the woods. Nuala, in return, had felt the very same towards him. They had so much in common, particularly their love of nature. He would point out the different birds and flowers. He would read her endless poems and talk about the Celtic otherworld, fairies and ghosts and the mystical land beyond the veil.

Nuala had felt and known with the same understanding as David, for these kinds of matters were in her very nature. She had experienced, from a very young age, the gift of seeing people who had died, though some might have called it a curse. For Nuala, it was just a fact of her life; they were just people who had passed to the other realms, just out of reach to most. The birds that called to her had shown her how humans occasionally could stray during their lives on earth, enabling a glimpse into the next world. It was a world for supernatural figures. She had also been gifted with courage and understanding for as long as she could remember.

Nuala witnessed this, while alone, sitting by the lagoon in Rosscarbery. She was in a reflective mood, just sitting and watching the water as the fish were leaping, enjoying watching the ripples as they broke the surface of the cool, clear water, creating circles that would slowly expand and disappear in a mesmerising way. All was quiet. Just the occasional plop as the fish went back into the lock, breaking the silence.

Her mammy had passed just a few weeks before. Right there in the here and now, in the bright sunshine, her mammy had come into focus, out on the water, smiling and waving, telling her without words she would always watch over her. Nuala had waved back and smiled as her mammy returned to visit her and was gone again.

Nuala knew that life was meant to be lived to its fullest, with the knowledge that death really didn't hold a sting. It was simply a passageway to the other world. There, one would pass their days and nights too, immersed in love, peace, and beauty, waiting until the call came again to return to the school of life, perhaps in another time and place altogether.

How she loved David O'Leary. He was gentle yet manly. He was kind to her beyond belief. But best of all, he understood her ways, as they were his ways too. They were made for each other. A match made in the other world, the other world of love, beauty and peace. The land of eternal youth.

With Robert's blessing, they were married, and he did his very best to get her the dress she had wanted. It was a simple wedding, but, for Robert and his sister Nuala, it had been the best day they had had in their lives.

The troubles since the 1922 burnings throughout the country had left a deep divide. Two now opposing sides would gather momentum. Catholic and Protestant against one another. The Irish Republic Army took Ireland into a civil war that endured, leaving a lasting shadow over Ireland.

David's father was a now-retired doctor. He had hoped his son would follow in his footsteps. That was not to be. David had become a teacher. It suited his temperament far better than being a doctor ever could have. He would teach the children with a kind, loving empathy, mostly about the natural world. That would take their young impressionable minds away from some of the hostilities of man. Ireland was a difficult place to live. Many had left, yet many more of the young were leaving. They wanted to live in peace and find prosperity.

David's mother had been another casualty of a different kind, catching her death by an outbreak of flu. She had never been that robust and had succumbed to the virus within a fortnight and died. David had been their only child. Now his father had insisted that the young, newly married couple, after their honeymoon in Galway, should live in his house. He said there seemed little point in creating an unnecessary expense. His house would be David's soon enough, and he had never wanted to live alone.

It was done as he had asked. David and Nuala didn't mind at all. The house was large enough for them to have as much privacy as they wanted. All was settled. Everyone was more than happy. Robert could move on now with his life, so he had planned to leave Ireland and start a new life in London.

Though Nuala was disappointed her brother had chosen to make a fresh start in London, she wanted him to find happiness too. She knew he had to make his way for himself. The way she had found her own path, she really hoped that he, too, would find that special someone to share his life with.

It was 1930s London, the era of the Great Depression. These times showed a gulf between the haves and the have-nots, shining a light on the stark contrast between the two. The have-nots were living in abject poverty. For those families, life was hard and bleak, dealing with mass unemployment, slum housing, outbreaks of TB, rickets, polio, diphtheria, and more. London sogs were notorious, and the pollution was dense, especially in the bleak winter months.

Robert had saved and scrimped for another whole year after

his sister's marriage. He had wished her well; he could see she was happy and content. She was safe now with a husband to rely on and a very pleasant home to call her own. Robert left for Liverpool by ferry, with all the expectations that possess the young. It was 1933, a time for a fresh start. He had done his best for his sister, and nothing else troubled him. Robert was full of hope, and he was strong and free. He would find work and not be in a hurry to return. Robert's home life had created too many sad pictures in his mind. He needed a fresh start, a new beginning and a whole new way of life.

Perhaps he had had the luck of the Irish in his favour, as it was certainly on his side. While he watched others from his homeland struggling with manual labour finding it hard even to get some sort of lodgings, Robert had found his employment in Fleet Street. He was put to work on the printing presses. Not only was his luck in for work, but a fellow workman told him he could lodge with him, as he knew how most people were against the Irish in London. Droves of Irishmen had sought out the cities of London and Liverpool to earn a living. Guest houses would place signs in the widows, *No dogs. No Irish.* Their reputation for *the drink* had gone before them.

Robert had no wish to be known as such a man. He kept himself straight. He was only too grateful for his new circumstances, spending no more than he had, paving his way and becoming a reliable part of the team. To begin with, he was an assistant. He had learned fast what was needed of him, and he could now load and feed in the inks. He knew how to install and adjust the printing plates and control the ink flow. It suited him, and he worked diligently. He was making his way at last.

Now settled and earning, he began thinking about the next step in his life. Nancy Laurent came into his life one Sunday afternoon. Robert had taken to walking in the park. Nancy, too, had taken to the same walk. The couple came to notice one another. It was after a few polite exchanges over the weeks they finally got chatting, sitting on a park bench. Nancy was a French maid, the same age as him. Her employer was a high society Lady. In an otherwise dull week, Robert and Nancy had laughed and joked and found one another's company a pleasant respite.

With her nose in the air, she had told Robert, "It is considered an asset to have a French maid. One who you could take to Europe and one adept in fashion, hair and makeup."

It was indeed a feather in her hat. Nancy possessed these attributes that were not lost on Robert.

Nancy confided in Robert. Her mistress and her were mostly bound to London, as her employer was getting old and frail. He learned the high society Lady had taken to Nancy when she learned Nancy was an orphan.

The orphanage was run by the Benedictine nuns in a Paris suburb. On reaching fifteen, Nancy was told she had been placed on the books of a reputable maid's agency. She was to be fully trained to become a perfect lady's maid. Nancy didn't mind. She trusted the nuns to help her. Nancy knew they wanted her to make a good life when she was old enough. Nancy had happily attended the day classes a couple of times a week, where she had learned the niceties of her trade to become a fine lady's maid. It was a school for young women to complete their education.

Now a couple years had passed, and Nancy had travelled and learned much from her mistress. She had told Robert that she had been in London for the past year, adding and in a very nice house. Nancy loved city life. It was true to say she loved fashion and hair. She found her work easy. Nancy was treated very fairly and hardly lacked for anything. She had begun to think of how it would be for her to become her own mistress. Robert found it all very understandable. It was not long before he proposed.

He could see and made no delay in pointing out to Nancy that together they could be stronger. He could and would look after her because he loved her. She told him she didn't have anything of her own. No matter, he had said, she just needed to agree, and they could go and see the priest the following Sunday, to tell him they wanted to marry. Nancy said she could see herself as his loving wife.

It had not gone down too well with her employer to start with, though she did concede after getting used to the idea. A few days later, her mistress had decided that she wanted to meet the young man in question who had turned Nancy's head. Pondering that she was not going to live much longer, she had concluded that Nancy should have a life of her own. How could she, a now ailing elderly woman, be responsible for stopping this young woman's wish to marry?

"Bring your young man to meet me," she had asked Nancy. "I should like to meet him before I agree to terminate our agreement."

There were the other girls within her household who could do as much as she needed, especially now with her travelling days over. Furthermore, Nancy had looked after her very well. She had become quite fond of her. Nancy had always shown her the greatest respect.

A week later, after Mass, Nancy agreed to meet Robert as usual in the park. Nancy told Robert what her mistress had said while they strolled along, then suddenly said to Robert, "Let's go immediately."

Half an hour later, Robert and Nancy stood waiting in the elaborate drawing room of her employer's home.

Robert's straightforward and honest manner won the day. There was no doubt these two young people were a good match. Not only did she give them her blessing, but she had insisted on a nest egg. Her wedding gift to them would be a small house. It was the least she could and should do for them, she thought. It wasn't worth much, but it would give them the start, as both had suffered.

After thinking it through, she told the couple, "It's my way of saying thank you, Nancy, for looking after me so well." They were both delighted.

Robert and Nancy could not believe how lucky they were. They were both so overwhelmed. At the appropriate time, they were married and finally moved into their own little home. A small Georgian terrace house on Wands Road.

It was now spring 1939. So happy and now so content, the newly married couple did all they could to make their own home their world.

"I never want to live anywhere else," Nancy told Robert.

Robert was still working in the same place, the printing rooms in Fleet Street, very well respected and secure in his position. Robert Doyle was a happy man.

Nancy was now free to do as she wished. He had told her she didn't need to work. They could manage very well now. Not having to pay rent made a huge difference. They could even afford to save a little each week.

They had four months of married bliss, and then on 1st September, World War II was declared.

CHAPTER 15

The old doctor's house, as it had been known for many years, was a house of character. It was a little way out of the village of Rosscarbery. It stood alone, and these days, it was hardly visible from the lane. No longer did the local doctor live there. Yet the house had kept its identity as such. It was situated in a beautiful location with far-reaching views from its position up a gently sloping hill. A person would need to know these little back lanes, as the house lay hidden mainly by mature trees and shrubs.

Nuala O'Leary had lived in the house since her marriage. As a very young girl of sixteen, she had married the doctor's son. Poor David O'Leary was taken suddenly whilst riding his bicycle back home from school. It was said that he had suffered a heart attack. That story had not been true. A single bullet in the head had robbed him of his life. One of his pupils found him lying alone by the side of the track. His legs were still entangled around his bicycle. The same track he had followed for over ten years, between the school where he taught and his home, had become his final journey.

He was just a young man of thirty-one years. Most of the local folk and children came to his funeral held in St. Fachtna's church in Rosscarbery. Now his body lay in the churchyard. Nearby were his own dear parents and Nuala's parents too.

From that very day, Nuala had remained alone. With plenty of time now on her hands, she called to her strengths to help her, reasoning with herself about those earlier days, it was meant to be, and while on this earth, she would live the rest her days alone. She listened, and she watched as the seasons came and went, and how each dawn followed the darkness of night, content for having known a love that would last this lifetime.

Now she was in her late sixties, still living in the old doctor's house, as she had done since the day she had married.

Some folks who knew her had respected her for her herbal remedies. She was, in fact, very accomplished in her creations and a true herbalist. Word and rumours spread about the woman who lived alone, making her lotions and potions. Some were favourable. Especially those brave enough to have tried a particular remedy and, consequently, had felt a lot better; they had praised her knowledge. She had never claimed to heal people. She was far too sensitive for that. However, she could help with chesty coughs, headaches, rheumatism, and minor ailments.

She could also tell when things were more serious. In that situation, Nuala would offer advice, recommending perhaps a doctor would be better to help remedy their problem. She had never sought to claim any praise or adulation of any kind.

Nuala knew but never minded what people thought; she was at peace with herself and her surroundings. She was very aware that everyone around her was not the same as her. She was perhaps seen as unusual in her isolation.

She, after all, never felt alone. Indeed, she was not alone at all.

Sometimes people would ask her what she thought might happen in a kind of half-interested way, thinking perhaps that she had some sort of powers, like a gipsy fortune teller. She did, of course, but was very cautious to whom she said what.

In those earlier days, the Holy Father had always been kind and understanding to Nuala. So understanding in fact, she felt she could tell him the sad news that he was very unwell. He was amazed at her knowledge and had then confided in her. He knew he didn't have much longer to live. She had proved to him, beyond a doubt, that she was a true daughter of God. She helped him more than anyone else living.

High praise indeed to have received from a priest. Even the priest who was now in the parish, Fr Graham, had sought her advice when he was new to the community. He liked Nuala as he got to know her. She regularly attended his Mass, enjoying his homily, and would receive holy communion regularly. It was then she would witness little sparks of light about him.

She liked the atmosphere and often felt and saw spirits around the little church.

Nuala always lit her candles for those lost spirits, hoping it would help them find their way home. This could happen when the two realms became at their thinnest.

Today she had woken with a start, just as though someone had whispered in her ear to *wake up!*

Nuala stretched and looked out the window. The sun was rising.

"Hmm," she said out loud. "What's going to happen this day?"

There was no one there to answer. Slowly Nuala got herself washed and dressed, ready for what might lie ahead.

CHAPTER 16

At Ash House, Joseph Connor was pacing in the kitchen while Martha was making porridge for breakfast at the range.

"Will you stop your pacing and sit yourself down? It's ready now."

Martha's voice broke through Joseph's thinking.

"Fine, fine," he said and sat at the table.

Martha put a bowl of steaming porridge in front of him and another for herself, at the far end of the table.

"Have yer made up your mind?"

"I have," he replied, blowing on his steaming porridge. "I'm going up to see Nuala O'Leary. It seems to me the right thing to do. If I'm mistaken, no harm done. I think it will be a revelation to young Francis if I'm right. If, of course, Nuala is interested in meeting her brother's only girl."

"Sure, it will be a revelation," Martha replied softly before taking a mouthful of her creamy steaming porridge.

***

Gulping down a cup of tea and a last mouthful of toast, Michael was on his way down to the harbour to meet up with his colleague, Patrick Logan. He had been in on operation *Traffic Lights* for the same time as Michael. They were on the ferry crossing at the same time, but Patrick had taken over following Dario Dinu in London. Michael had been on the trail of the two brothers Costie and Leon Balan, the two ruthless brothers in Wales.

Before that, Michael had also been in London watching Dario Dinu but had handed over to Patrick as the three men had split up. Dario Dinu had a girl with him; she had been pointed out earlier in the operation. It was known that she was pregnant. The woman had been with the gang for some time. The two brothers, also from Romania, had joined up with Dario Dinu, aka The Chaperone, as two of his musclemen. In other words, he used them to eliminate anyone who became a nuisance or surplus to requirements. The three criminals, murdering gangsters, were also illegal immigrants, wanted in their own country for murder and drug crimes.

***

Now Michael was back on the case. That morning the Garda and all units had been given the green light. He was going down to the harbour, where other Garda would be in position. Further along the coast in Union Hall, Garda were also ready and lay in wait. The Garda water division, out of Dublin, had already been alerted and were ready to board the yacht, hopefully before it was due to sail that morning. Also, they were further out, alongside, at the top of Kinsale harbour.

It was now known the brothers and The Chaperone would be down at the harbour. Other officers, undercover at the gang's base house, had witnessed the drugs being unloaded from the yacht and taken by car direct to their house on the outskirts of Kinsale.

Officers were in strategic places all along the route to Kinsale Harbour. This was an operation that had to succeed.

The Chaperone had been following a young woman tourist recently and was expected to make his move, if any, before the yacht would sail. This was speculative, but apart from the previous day, he seemed to have been following the same young woman. The Garda knew she had been on the same ferry, so was unsure if she was part of the operation or just a tourist and possibly his next victim.

A lot of the final information had been gathered and fed through to the Garda by a remarkable, young, undercover woman.

She was Ana Mayer, another Romanian girl, highly trained in her profession and employed by the National Crime Agency.

It was now thought that this brave young woman may have lost her life, along with the woman under her surveillance. There was no body as yet, but she had been seen boarding the motorboat with Crina Sava. Crina Sava's body had now been identified. It was the body found on the beach by Old Tommy Walsh. He had discovered it, washed up along the coastline in Ballycotton. If it hadn't been for him, on his regular beach combing excursion, it would have, in all probability, been washed back out to sea again.

96

Patrick Logan was already down at the harbour, sitting in his parked-up car, with a paper cup in hand full of coffee. Michael rapped on the window and opened the door on the passenger side.

"Hi, Pad. How's it going?"

"So here yer are at last."

"What's new then?"

Michael's eyes were focused out front along the length of the harbour.

"Get in then, and I'll tell yer."

Michael dropped into the passenger seat.

"They're here," Patrick said and nodded, taking a final swig of his coffee.

He threw the empty cup over his shoulder, where it landed with all the others. The back seat was strewn with newspapers, coffee cups, and food wrappers.

"There seems to be a girl in the picture. We're not sure if she is with them or just a tourist."

"Perhaps his next victim," Michael replied.

Patrick dropped down the glove compartment and took out a handgun. Checked it over and put it in the holster beneath the jacket.

"The body of Crina Sava was washed up at Ballycotton."

Patrick's voice was devoid of emotion.

"Jesus," Michael replied. "Murdering bastards."

"That's the truth of it. They are on the motorboat alongside. Can you see them?"

Michael nodded. "Sure."

The two officers fixed their eyes on the motorboat, clearly visible on the high tide.

"Why are they still here?"

"That's what I'm thinking. I thought they would be heading back to the ferry by now."

Michael felt for his holster.

"Our friend, The Chaperone, is going to make one last search for the little redhead."

Patrick spoke without emotion. Michael was listening to this new bit of information without taking his eyes off Dario Dinu as Patrick continued.

"If he can find her this morning, he's going to make a grab for her. We think he will take one last look around the town, coerce her towards the harbour and take her to the yacht before it sails. Not long now. Time's running out."

Within a short while, The Chaperone was on the move. He stood on the pavement. A smile came over his face as he looked ahead. He couldn't have planned it better. There she was, walking towards him. A few people were passing, taking a stroll. Michael and Patrick never took their eyes off their target. They watched as he now took a couple of steps in their direction.

Suddenly a woman was walking towards him. He waved, smiling at her. The two stood in conversation momentarily before Michael realised it was Francis.

"Jesus Holy Mary, Mother of God."

"What?" Patrick exclaimed.

"It's Francis. That's bloody what."

With that, he was out of the car. Patrick too jumped out.

"Who is Francis?" he called, but his voice was lost.

Michael, now with a gun in hand, was off running towards Francis.

At that moment, the motorboat engine started up. One of the brothers jumped ashore and lunged towards her in an attempt to grab her from behind.

Michael had his gun down by his side as he turned to Francis, shouting, *run*. She saw Michael and heard him, and though looking bewildered, Francis responded and took flight. Michael's arm rose as soon as she ran clear, and with his arm outstretched, he fired a shot. The thug who was about to grab her fell straight back to the ground. He lay on his back staring, without seeing the clear blue sky, as a trickle of blood ran from his brow. The shot entered the middle of his forehead, straight between the eyes.

Dario Dinu's reaction was fast as he slid, within a second, a stiletto knife down his sleeve. Without notice or commotion, the thin silver blade penetrated past Michael's jacket, cleanly through his shirt, and into his side, silently making its victim draw in a deep breath, as the pain made him crumple like a rag doll to the ground.

Patrick's instinct seeing Michael go down was to shoot Dario Dinu.

Dario dropped next to Michael on his back. The precision of

the gunshot left Dario Dinu also gazing wide-eyed at the sky. Instantly, the motorboat took off.

Garda came running from all directions.

Francis fled to Michael.

He had managed to get to his knees, bent over, holding onto his side as the blood started to seep through his shirt, two dead bodies on either side of him.

Francis was trembling like she had never trembled before.

CHAPTER 17

Joseph Connor had told his wife he thought he should go alone to Nuala's home. Since he was calling uninvited, perhaps it would be for the best. Martha reluctantly agreed in the end; she could tell Joe had made up his mind and she didn't want to argue the point. Though she was very interested, her curiosity was now getting best of her. She'd had no dealings with Nuala O'Leary and therefore didn't know the woman to make any real judgement. Only at Mass would she greet her. Martha had known other women speak of Nuala O'Leary. Some would think her strange, whilst others thought she was a clever woman. They marvelled at some of her herbal remedies. Martha was now feeling sympathetic towards her, considering the sadness at losing her parents while still a schoolgirl, and how difficult that must have been for the brother and sister. Also, losing her husband and never knowing the joy of holding her own baby in her arms. For Martha, that went so against all that she had held dear in her lifetime. How lucky was she, with her family all around her, a loving husband, though stubborn, she thought, with a small smile. Martha carried on tidying her kitchen, realising, in fact, that she was a very lucky woman indeed.

As Joseph drove up the lane, he was mulling over in his mind how he might approach the subject he was calling about. He thought about various openings but couldn't quite feel comfortable. Now he questioned why he should bother at all. Francis' pretty face came into his mind. Yes, he thought, 'tis the right thing to do.

Nuala was out in her garden. She had seen the wren and the robin. She watched as the little wren flitted before her, whilst the robin just sat and watched. This was a sure sign to her that someone would knock on her door today.

Something to do with Robert, she felt.

The day before, her brother had appeared to her in the garden. She had been tidying in her herb garden, trimming back the unruly, left-over fennel stems from last year's growth, noticing all the new shoots for this year were growing up fast. Nuala deftly

100

cut low with her pruners, aware now she was being watched. A little way down the garden path stood her brother Robert. She paused and stood up from her stoop, pushing her hair from her face back over her shoulder.

"Hello Robert, why are yer here?"

Smiling as he had before, he held out his arm to her without concern. Nuala waited, rooted to the spot, watching Robert as he placed his hands over his heart and smiled.

"Love, is it?" Nuala spoke out gently, almost in a whisper.

Robert nodded to her and faded away from sight.

This was the second time he had come to see her.

The first was some years back. Nuala had known then that that had been the time of his passing from this world. He was on his journey to the next.

At that time, she had seen him through the window. It was one morning as she was in her conservatory, tending to her plants. Glancing up at a sudden movement that disturbed her train of thought about the plant she was watering, she placed the small watering can down next to the plant. Turning, there was Robert. He was standing just outside the window. As they saw each other, brother and sister smiled.

"Ah, Robert!" She gasped. "What are yer doing out there?"

He waved, still smiling for a few more moments and then was gone.

Now there he was again. Why, she wondered, why now?

There was something else for her to know, was the conclusion she had come to. She went back into the house through the conservatory, put her secateurs on the side, and followed into the kitchen, put the kettle on the hob and went to the sink to wash her hands. Throwing the cold water from the running tap over her face, she went to the mirror and looked at herself.

Her hair was tumbling around her shoulders. Looking at her reflection, she thought she should tie up her hair. She wanted to be ready for whoever was coming.

Nuala took the stairs to her bedroom and brushed her hair at her dressing table, then tied it back with a ribbon. Looking left and then right at her reflection, she said, "That looks better."

Nuala took off her apron to reveal a pale blue dress. It was long and almost reached her ankles, with long sleeves and a small white collar.

"I'll do," she said.

She returned down the stairs to her favourite room, her kitchen. The kettle had just begun to whistle. Nuala went through the motions of making a pot of tea, and as if on cue, the doorbell jingled.

"Here we go," she said.

Joseph Connor ran his fingers through his hair as he waited on the doorstep of the fine house where Nuala lived. He hoped he would receive a welcome, but it didn't pay to be too optimistic. Bringing news, such news as he had, was a little daunting. Just as he exhaled rocked back and forth, the door swung open wide, and he was greeted with a smile. A feeling of relief flooded through him as he let go of the tension he hadn't realised had built inside his chest.

"Morning, Nuala." Joseph smiled in greeting and went on. "I hope it's not a trouble to yer, my coming by. It's a grand day."

Nuala looked at the uneasy man standing before her.

"Morning to yer, Joseph Connor. What brings yer here?" She was watching the little sparks of light dancing about him. "Come in now." Nuala stood aside and waved him by her.

Joseph wiped his shoes on the doormat and entered.

"Will yer come through to the kitchen. Tea is brewing."

He followed Nuala through the dark hallway and into the bright kitchen at the back of the house.

"Sit yerself-down now, Joseph."

Nuala went to the cupboard and took out the bread tin, placed it on the table, took the butter dish from the fridge and placed it alongside. All the while, Joseph was looking about her kitchen. He liked the feel of the place, and he particularly liked how the conservatory led off. It was full of potted plants. Beyond, he could see the garden bathed in sunshine.

"It's a very nice place yer have here, Nuala."

"I'm comfortable enough," she replied.

Nuala cut some of her fruit bread and placed it on a plate, and she put it in front of Joseph.

"Help yerself there to the butter."

She poured him out some tea. "There we are now. There's the milk and sugar."

"Ah, thanks, Nuala. That's grand."

He sat back in his chair. "Now I expect yer wondering why I'm here?"

Nuala raised an eyebrow. "It had crossed my mind."

"I have come about yer brother Robert."

Nuala sat silently, nodding.

Joseph picked up the knife and buttered a slice of the fruit bread.

Nuala lifted her cup and watched him over the rim as she sipped at her tea. Still, she said nothing.

Joseph wriggled a bit in his chair. He was feeling a little uneasy again. He wanted to get the right words out of his head and out of his mouth in the right order.

"Well, now…"

Nuala put her cup down. "What is it about Robert? Spit it out, Joseph."

"Michael," he said finally.

"Yes, Michael, your boy," she said encouragingly.

"Yes, that's it. Yer see, Michael brought home this lovely girl. Her name is Francis Doyle."

Nuala sat up straight. "Doyle, yer say?"

"Aye, Francis Doyle. Well, it might be a long shot, but I think, looking at her that is, yer see she looks…"

He hesitated again. Now he could see he was absolutely right.

Nuala's eyes widened. The same green sparkle from them was looking straight at him, just the very same as Francis' had on the day they had first met. The likeness was even more apparent between Francis and Nuala. Nuala was just an older version. She had the same hair, only hers was streaked now with silver. The once rich, copper colour was fading. She still had the same curls as a child and the same as Francis.

"Go on, Joseph," she said, encouraging him to say his piece.

"Well, there is a strong resemblance to yerself, Nuala."

Finally, there it was, out, and now Joseph had said it.

"Her father's name was Robert."

Nuala looked as though the wind had been sucked right out of her. The air that filled her lungs was held in limbo as she inhaled to the limit and waited, wide-eyed and speechless. It hung there between them at the table as they looked at each other.

Joseph was transfixed as he looked at Nuala's expression. A look between shock and disbelief. He almost wanted to leap to his feet and pat her back. It seemed quite a while to him before Nuala let go and exhaled deeply.

"So that's it?" she said, almost to herself.

Gathering herself before her visitor, she smiled.

"Well, Joseph, I knew something was coming my way, but I never dreamed it would be that. Francis, yer say?"

She looked questioningly at Joseph.

"She's a lovely girl, Nuala."

"How old?" That was Nuala's first question.

"I think she is about twenty-eight."

"Twenty-eight," she whispered.

"The thing is, her parents are passed on."

At that point, Joseph winced, supposing Nuala did not know about her brother.

"It's all right, Joseph Connor. I knew he had, let's say, moved on."

She smiled at him, realising his sensitivity.

"Didn't know his wife, though. Yer see, he never came home. He hated the place. Not for him at all. He waited until I was settled before he could spread his wings. I was pleased he did. I met my David and was as happy as a girl could be. I wanted the same for him. Of course I did, bless him. Now yer wondering how I knew?" Nuala paused for a moment. "Well, it's like this." She smiled again at Joseph, and her green eyes twinkled. "I knew he had passed on as he visited me." Joseph was listening in all earnest. "It was about nine or ten years ago, maybe more. Expect that was about the time he left for the other realm." Joseph's eyes widened. "Ah, don't look so shocked. 'Tis nothing to me. I've seen it all me life. I just thought he had come to say goodbye. It might shock yer further to know he came to see me again, so he did."

Joseph was at a loss as to what his response should be. He picked up his cup of tea and drained it as Nuala watched him. "Will yer be wanting to meet your niece?" he finally asked.

She looked at him. "And what der yer think? Of course I want to meet her. Will yer be bringing her up here?" Nuala looked hopeful that he might.

"I will," he said as he stood up. "Thanks for the tea."

"Good," she replied. "Now I think your wife might be needing you at home if I'm not mistaken. Will yer wait just a minute, Joseph? I'll just jot down me telephone number for yer." Nuala went to a drawer in the dresser and found paper and a pencil. She wrote it out for him. "Now, when she's ready, I'll be here." Nuala handed him the paper. "Many thanks, Joseph Connor."

"Think nothing of it. It's been real interesting meeting with yer."

He felt awkward as he put the paper into his pocket and returned to the hall. "Mind how yer go," he said over his shoulder as he reached the front door. He turned, looking at Nuala before opening the door, smiling at this little lady as she stood smiling back at him. "You're an extraordinary lady, make no mistake."

Still smiling, she opened the door for him. "Get away with yer now."

She waited on the doorstep as he got into his car and drove off. "Hmm," Nuala muttered. "There goes a decent man with a bit of sadness waiting on his doorstep."

CHAPTER 18

Joseph drove out of the drive and back onto the quiet lane. He was in no rush, moving slowly, his thoughts still in Nuala's kitchen. What a strange woman she was, attractive too, in her way, still wearing her hair long, tied back in a ribbon, just like Francis.

He prided himself that he had noticed how the two women were so alike. They were the same in stature and had the same colouring and sparkling green eyes. Suppose she took more after her father than her mother. He had that colouring, curly as yer like, a right copper nob.

The picture of Robert Doyle at school came into Joseph's mind. Wasn't he a feisty little fella? Joseph smiled to himself. Sad that he was gone now, his thoughts turned to Francis.

Well, now, wasn't she going to be shocked when he told her that she had an auntie. Joseph smiled again to himself, then chuckled. How strange could life be? After all these years and then she came straight into the arms of Michael. Made for each other. Joseph turned into his drive and pulled up in front of his home.

Martha came rushing out the front door, swinging her handbag and pulling at the collar of her jacket.

"Oh, thank God yer home, Joseph," she yelled as he shut the car door. "Get back in the car."

"What in the name… is wrong?" he muttered.

Obeying Martha, he got back in the car as she rushed to the passenger side and almost threw herself into the seat.

"Hospital." Martha gasped. "Hurry now."

Joseph knew to get a move on. There was something serious going on, that was for sure. "Will yer tell me what's happening?"

"It's Michael. Gone and got himself stabbed, of all things. Holy Mary, Jesus and Joseph, our boy's been stabbed. Faster, Joseph."

"I'm going as fast as I can, now calm yerself. Who did you speak to?"

Though Joseph was beside himself, he needed to stay calm for

106

Martha's sake. He let his lifetime in the Garda help him to stay rational and tried with all his might to detach himself. He would save his emotions till later.

Martha was highly strung, fishing about in her handbag, looking for a hanky, as the tears started to roll down her cheeks.

"It was the fella he sometimes works with. You know him, he was there, they were..."

She was choking, trying to get the words out.

Joseph risked letting go of the steering wheel to pat her arm. "Never mind now. Come on, Ma, he'll be all right."

Joseph stayed quiet for a little while, then asked again, "Now, who did you talk to?"

Martha had composed herself somewhat. She was sitting with her hands gripped on her handbag, as though it would fly off if she dared to let go. Her eyes stared straight ahead as if willing the car to get there as fast as possible. All her anxiety was directed through her hands as she held onto her bag.

Feeling calmer now, as the miles ahead were now less than those behind, she finally found her voice. "It was Patrick, you know, Patrick Logan."

Joseph spoke softly, trying to keep his wife calm. "What did he say exactly?"

"Just that he had been stabbed in his side, he was still alive, and they had taken him to the hospital. He said he was going to call for Andrew. Oh, Mother of God, please look after my boy, don't let him die."

Martha was now rolling her lips together to stop herself from crying.

Joseph patted her arm again. "There, there, now, he'll be all right, Martha. Yer see. He's made of strong stuff."

"I couldn't bear it, Joe. I just couldn't."

The tears had started again.

***

Patrick Logan had managed to get hold of Father Andrew. He was now at the hospital. Michael was in emergency surgery and being seen to. Francis was wrapped in a blanket. They had put her into a little room that was on a side ward. She was sitting in an armchair that was next to the bed. The doctor had seen her. He was happy that she remained there for a few hours at least. The doctor had advised that she should stay longer just in case. Overnight would be safer. He said shock was a strange symptom and could lead to something else occurring.

Francis had been in complete shock on arrival. The nurses had given her a heavy dose of sedatives to calm her. Half an hour had passed, and the shaking had now subsided. The nurse kept popping her head around the door to ensure she was all right. She had brought her in a cup of tea this time. Francis looked up at her.

"Is Michael going to be all right?"

Her voice was almost a whisper.

"Of course he will," came the cheerful reply. The nurse put a hand on Francis' shoulder. "He'll be stitched up in no time. Now, Father Andrew is outside. Will I tell him to come in?"

Francis couldn't think straight. "Father Andrew, you say?"

"Yes, that's right, he's Michael's brother."

Michael's brother, the words seem to echo in her head. "Well, yes, if he wants to," she replied vaguely.

"Try to drink some tea now. That'll make you feel better."

The nurse was then out the door.

Francis stared at the cup of tea on the table next to her. She recalled she had felt like this once before, when they told her about her parents. The drugs they had given her made her feel as though time had slowed down. A few minutes later, there was a gentle knock on the door. It opened, and a grey curly-headed priest popped his head in.

"Hello, Francis. I am Father Andrew, Michael's brother."

Francis' hand came out from beneath the blanket to take hold of the hand offered by the kindly looking priest. He was standing next to her to gently shake her hand. Francis then slowly withdrew, hugging the blanket around herself.

"May I sit down?"

"Yes," she said. "I'm sorry," she added.

"Sorry?" Father Andrew replied. "Why are yer sorry? None of this is your fault."

Francis tried to smile.

"Poor Michael, he will be all right, won't he?"

She looked at Father Andrew with pleading eyes.

"I think he will be as good as new when they finish with him."

Just then, there was another knock at the door. This time, it was Martha. She rushed to Francis and put her arms about her.

"Oh Francis, you poor wee girl."

Joseph looked at his son Andrew and then grabbed hold of him. Father and son clung together in a silence they both understood. For a moment, the room was silent, each in their own thoughts, all thinking about Michael. The enormity of the situation. It was Father Andrew who broke the silence.

"While we are now here all together, perhaps we can say a prayer for Michael?"

They gathered around Francis as she sat huddled in her banket and wide-eyed, silently watching. It was like a dream to her, a bad dream. Her eyes fell on Father Andrew as he made a sign of the cross.

"In the name of the Father, the Son and the Holy Spirit."

All but Francis crossed themselves with their heads bowed.

***

A team of doctors and nurses had repaired the damage caused by the stabbing. It was some hours later that he was transferred to a ward. His parents and brother were still in the same room as Francis, waiting to hear news of Michael. They waited in silence now as Francis lay fast asleep on the bed. The nurse had come in earlier and could see that Francis could no longer keep awake with the amount of sedation she had received. Getting her into the bed, the nurse had said sleep was the best medicine now.

The threesome had taken turns to go outside to walk and get refreshment, giving themselves space to take in all that Francis had tried hard to convey to them.

The Garda had all the information they needed. Half of the force was there to witness what had taken place.

It was that evening Michael came around, and so did Francis. Martha and Joseph could finally see their son. He was awake. They wheeled Francis in a wheelchair through the corridors to the ward. Father Andrew was due to come back after Mass that evening.

Michael lay almost flat on his bed, smiling as they came to his bedside.

Francis watched as Martha bent to kiss her son's forehead.

"I'm all right, Ma, don't go fussing."

"Oh, son!" she exclaimed as a tear trickled down her cheek.

"Let the boy breathe, Martha." Joseph's manly voice brought a bit of reality to his son's embarrassment.

"Yer did a grand job, Michael," Joseph said with a wink and a nod of his head. "We're proud of yer, son. You saved this wee girl, so yer did."

All eyes fell on Francis. She was still a bit wide-eyed, and the drugs had slowed her body down. Her limbs felt like they were floating. Joseph pushed her wheelchair as close to Michael's bed as possible. Her hand reached for his cheek, and very gently and slowly she caressed it. The couple were locked into one another's gaze.

Joseph took hold of Martha's hand and gave it a squeeze, whilst Francis leaned forward from her chair and kissed Michael's lips.

"I love you," she whispered before she slipped back into her chair.

Joseph's voice took hold of the situation as they all looked at Michael lying in his bed.

"Looks like yer might be in here for a while, son." He now turned to face Francis. "With that in mind, Francis, we thought that perhaps yer would like to come and stay at Ash House with us, or am I being a bit premature?"

He was smiling at her and nodded to Michael for his assurance that perhaps it was a good idea.

Martha chimed in. "Oh, yes, that's a good idea. What yer thinking, Francis?"

Francis wasn't thinking at all. She just wanted to lie next to Michael. They waited for her response.

She said quietly, "I'll stay here tonight. They said I should."

Michael now had a broad grin on his face. "That's me girl," he said.

"Well, Francis, if yer think it's best, dear girl."

Martha had seen her son's face light up at the thought. Joseph nodded to Martha, seeing her disappointment.

"Perhaps tomorrow then, when yer feeling stronger," he said.

Martha agreed. "They are strong sedatives you've had."

Joseph nodded back to his wife. "Shall we come back tomorrow afternoon?"

Francis smiled at Michael's lovely parents. Just then, Father

Andrew came gliding down the ward in his black cassock. Standing at the foot of Michael's bed, he looked down at his brother, lying flat on his back.

"Ah, here's the man. How's it going, little brother?"

Michael managed a wave.

"I'm grand. Would yer look at me?" he jested.

"I can see yer are with all this attention. The whole town's a buzzing. And how is our Francis now?" he asked. "Looking a whole lot better, I'm thinking."

Francis smiled at Andrew.

She liked Andrew and had taken to his jolly character. He had the kindest of hearts, if she was any judge. "Much better, thank you."

"Well, the pair of yer had us all worried there. But all's well that ends well. Here we all are."

He turned to Francis. "I was thinking, Francis, perhaps yer would like to stay up at the house with me. There are plenty of rooms."

Father Andrew wondered why they were all laughing.

"That's really kind of you, but I am staying here for the night."

Martha thought she had better put Andrew in the picture. "Yer daddy has already suggested that Francis come and stay with us when and if she wants to."

Michael watched in amusement. He could tell his family already liked Francis. Why wouldn't they? She was the loveliest girl, his girl, and one day, he thought, his wife. With that thought now firmly in his mind, he spoke out.

"Well, tonight," he said, "Francis is staying here." His voice was triumphant.

Martha smiled down at her son. He was going to be all right, she thought.

"Good night, Michael," she said. "Rest well. We'll see you tomorrow in the afternoon."

Martha leaned over and gave him a kiss.

"Night, Ma, thanks for coming."

She went to Francis and kissed her cheek. "Rest up now," she urged.

Joseph had put a fatherly hand on his shoulder. "Night, son."

"Thanks, Da. Likewise."

111

Joseph went in turn to Francis. "Yer both going to be fine now."

Bending over the wheelchair, he pecked her cheek. Francis just smiled and thanked him. Father Andrew waited until his parents were walking out of the ward. He looked at Francis and his brother.

"God bless you both, but I think he already has. Get some rest, the pair of you."

Michael gave him a cheeky look and a wave and thanked him for coming. "Night, Andrew."

Once Francis said a quiet thank you, Father Andrew was off down the ward and through the swing doors, his cassock floating about him.

Michael and Francis just gazed at each other.

"Are you in pain?" she asked.

"No, surprisingly not, if I lie still."

Michael reached for her hand. It was then the nurse came by and said it was time for Francis to leave Michael. He needed to rest, and so did she. He pulled Francis' hand to his lips and kissed it. It reminded Francis of when he took her hand on the ferry and did the same. Except this time, he said, "I'll see you in the morning, dear girl."

Francis smiled. "In the morning. If I'm allowed."

Francis looked at the nurse.

"And why not?" came the reply.

Francis nodded.

"Isn't it special circumstances? Come on now. Let's get you settled."

With that, she wheeled Francis away. Michael's eyes followed, and he held his hand up just as Francis turned and waved back, before she went out through the swing doors.

Father Andrew was out in the car park with Joseph and Martha. They were discussing Michael. Joseph was telling him what the doctors had told him earlier.

"He was such a lucky fella."

"The knife only went in a short way."

Martha crossed herself for the umpteenth time that day.

"Thanks be to God," Father Andrew added.

"Missing all the vital organs," Joseph went on. "It was Patrick

112

Logan's quick thinking shooting the bastard before he had time to jam it home."

"Joseph," Martha exclaimed.

"Well, it's true. It could have been a whole different story, make no mistake," Father Andrew said.

"They had been watching them for days. If not weeks," Joseph added.

"Patrick said they had no idea Michael was seeing Francis, and that she was being watched by the same thug that stabbed Michael," Father Andrew added. "They were about to kidnap Francis, so Patrick informed me."

"Oh my," Martha said. "Would you believe it? Sounds like something in a film, right here on our own doorstep."

Joseph put a comforting arm around his wife's shoulders. "Now don't go getting yerself in a state again, Martha. It's over now. I think we should be getting off. We can come back again tomorrow. Andrew here has had enough for one day, too, no doubt."

He looked with love at his son.

"Yer right there, Da," Father Andrew replied.

"I'll say good night. Perhaps we can have a get-together when Michael's back on his feet. I'm sure Bridget will want to meet this new lady in Michael's life."

"Yes," Martha agreed. "What do yer think of her?"

"From what I can see, it matters not what any of us thinks. Michael is smitten, that's for sure. I think she is a lovely wee thing."

Martha gave her eldest son an embrace and kissed his cheek. "Me too. Night, son."

Joseph looked at him. "It's a day to remember in more ways than one, I'm thinking. Night, son. Drive safely."

Joseph and Martha both sighed with relief as they got themselves into their car. Looking at each, Joseph reached for Martha's hand again. "Well, what a day. Let's get home and relax."

"Good idea."

Martha smiled lovingly at her dear husband. He was a man and a half. She considered herself a lucky woman.

They pulled out of the hospital car park and onto the road

leading out of Kinsale and home. They needed to go by where the dreadful incident had occurred. Martha could see where the Gardai had taped off the area, allowing the traffic to pass by. Two tents had been put up, covering the spot where the shot men had fallen.

All Martha could see was her son, her lovely Michael, running to save Francis. Then the moment when he was stabbed. She closed her eyes and thanked God silently. As if he had known what Martha was thinking, Joseph reached across, took Martha's hand, and squeezed it.

"It's done with now, Ma. Put it out yer mind. Do yer want to hear what Nuala O'Leary said to me this morning?"

He knew that would give her mind something else to think about.

Martha's head spun to look at him.

"I do, Joseph Connor. I had quite forgotten about Nuala O'Leary. What did she say?"

CHAPTER 19

After Joseph Connor's visit, Nuala felt that a wind of change had washed over her. Robert's daughter, she kept thinking. Trying to make it sink into her being. "What a thing!" she said out loud. "What a thing, indeed. Robert's daughter, Francis Doyle."

That was what her brother had come to tell her. Then Nuala thought about Joseph Connor. It was his son Michael that was... was what? Her boyfriend? She would soon find out.

After she had finished her tea, she decided to do a bit of cleaning and polishing. Then after a bit of lunch Nuala spent an hour or so in her conservatory. She found it was the most relaxing thing to do. Tending her plants was an endless pleasure. They thrived under her watchful eye. After that, she would look for some pictures of her wedding day. They were the only pictures she had had of her brother.

With that thought in mind, Nuala remembered they were somewhere in David's study. She hadn't been in there for a while now. She expected it needed a dusting.

Over the years, Robert and Nuala had lost touch. A tinge of sadness stabbed at her heart. She supposed that he had made a life for himself. Nuala had never felt sad about Robert then. Her life with David was all she needed after they were wed.

Later, with a bowl of soup and some homemade soda bread to nourish her, Nuala felt ready for David's study.

She took out some polish and a duster, put on her apron and set off down the hall to the study.

On opening the door, she could smell a mustiness in the room, so she went over to the bay window and pulled the curtains fully back. A shaft of sunshine beamed across the room, highlighting the dusty particles floating about.

Lifting the latch to the window, she threw it up and was greeted with bird song. Outside, there in the old tree, were several chattering birds. She smiled as she could see the new leaves straining to push forth, making a canopy that would eventually shade over this side of the window.

"Could do with a bit of pruning," she muttered. "Ah, what the matter, more shelter for the birds."

Turning her back to the window, Nuala looked about the room. David's room, remembering now, how her husband would bring the pupils' books home in his saddle bags, placing them onto his desk for marking after tea.

She walked to his desk and, moving aside those important things that had belonged to him, she started to dust and remember. With that done, she went over to the bookcase.

She could see him now in her mind's eye, standing there with his back to her as she entered the room. He would be mulling over a page from an open book held in his hands.

"Thought you might like a cup of tea," she had said, placing it down on the desk. He turned, smiled. "That's grand."

Then he and the thought were gone. Her mind returned. Nuala was looking inside the glass-fronted bookcase. So many books. *Now where did he put our pictures?* She looked over the shelves of books, then closed the glass door. Over in the corner of the room, there was a tallboy.

"I wonder..."

It was a bit of a struggle. Sliding the top drawer open, she peeped over the rim, only just tall enough to see inside.

"This piece of furniture lives up to its name," she said to no one.

As she fished around inside, there were some albums. Nuala lifted out the first she could get hold of.

Carrying it over to the desk, she opened up the first page. Staring back at her was a photograph of her father-in-law. Doctor O'Leary.

"My, he is looking serious, such a stern-looking man."

She turned the page over, and David's mother was looking delicate and quite angelic in a lace blouse. She had a sad look in the portrait.

There were more of the same of her in-laws. Nothing of much interest to her.

Nuala went back over to the tallboy.

She needed something to stand on. Nuala carried the chair from the desk and placed it in front of the tallboy. Climbing up, she could now see the contents lying within the deep drawer.

There were some letters tied in a bundle with an old piece of faded ribbon.

"Hmm… I shall look at those later."

She had hardly touched David's room, just the dusting and the opening and closing of the window. It had just not been necessary for her to go rummaging.

This was David's father's office, where he would sometimes see his patients.

Nuala sighed. All these years since David's passing; how many years was it now? Must be thirty years or so. She sighed again. *My lovely David*. He was only thirty-six.

Picking up the bundle of letters from the drawer, she climbed back down from the chair and decided she needed a cup of tea. The dust in the room had been disturbed and had made her throat dry.

Collecting up the polish and dusters with the letters, Nuala walked from the room back down to the kitchen. After filling the kettle, she placed it on the range. Looking at the bundle of letters now, she had a burning desire to open them and read the contents.

"Make some tea first," she said.

Comfortable now with a mug of tea, Nuala sat at her table as she pulled at the ribbon wrapped around the bundle of letters. *Mrs O'Leary* was written on the envelope; she must be David's mother. She looked now at the postmark: London.

"I wonder who she knew in London."

The letter had not been opened. Nuala turned it this way and that, feeling like an intruder into someone else's life. *Don't be silly*, said the voice in her head. *Open it, you silly goose.*

Silly goose. That was what her mother used to call her when she was a child. She hadn't thought that in many a year.

Nuala pushed her finger at the corner of the envelope, a single piece of paper and a photograph. Who's that? She was thinking when the penny dropped.

Robert.

It's a letter from Robert. There in the picture was her brother and his bride.

"Oh, Robert."

Nuala's eyes filled with tears as she gazed at her big brother, looking so proud and smart in his wedding suit and the prettiest of brides standing at his side.

Nuala wiped away the tears so she could see the picture. His words came flooding back as she gazed upon the picture she held in her hand.

Robert had said she mustn't worry about him. He didn't want to return to Ireland and had done the best he could for her. That she would be safe now, now that she had a husband.

Putting down the picture, she turned her attention to the letter.

657, Wands Road. London.

June 1939

My Dearest Sister Nuala,

I hope this letter finds you well and your husband too.

I have enclosed this photograph of us on our wedding day.

My wife's name is Nancy, and I know you would like each other well. We have been very fortunate to now own our own little home. It's small but just right for us. There is a small yard out the back but a larger front garden. I work in Fleet Street and have a good job with the newspaper's printing works. You are often in my thoughts and prayers.

Your loving brother Robert

Nuala couldn't think straight. Why had she not seen this letter before? She had now spread the rest of the bundle over the table, searching.

"Perhaps there's another one from Robert."

Her hands quickly moved from one to the other. There was no other, just this one. The others had been opened and were all addressed to Doctor O'Leary.

Why, oh why, hadn't David given her this letter?

He must have seen it, to have put it in the drawer. Unless his father had put it there.

"No," she thought. "He had passed away by then."

It must have been David. He died in 1939, in early July.

He must have meant her to have it; but then again, she reasoned, why was it put up there in that tall boy, of all places, tied up with these others that were his father's? There was no explanation. She would never know now. Feeling upset that her husband, her beloved David, could do that to her willingly was an ugly thought. Nuala had never felt real anger in her life, but she felt it now, welling up inside her chest, making her so sad at the same time.

Dear Robert had sent her a letter. He wanted her to know he had a wife, a good job and a home to call their own after all this time. Now they were gone, she would never meet his Nancy. Looking at the picture again, she vowed, "But I will meet your daughter, Robert." She had spoken out loud, and suddenly she felt the anger subside.

And she called out again, "I will meet your daughter, Robert, so I will."

Gathering up her father-in-law's letters, she roughly bundled them together, re-wrapped the old bit of ribbon around them, and marched down the hallway and back into David's room. The top drawer was still open; she threw them up, and they landed with a thud in the drawer. She gave it a mighty shove till it slid shut. Nuala left the room and closed the door behind her.

Feeling a lot better for that defiant act, she decided she would get on with some baking. There would be visitors soon, and she would want to lay a table for her newly found niece. Picking Robert's letter up from the table, she re-read it, folding it carefully as it had been, slid it back into the envelope with the picture and placed it on the dresser.

Nuala set about her chores with a renewed vigour. There was a lot to think about. Francis Doyle, her very own niece, would be all she would think about today. As she filled the bowl with flour and began to rub in the butter with an experienced hand, thoughts of the letter returned.

It had not been opened.

Why? There must be an answer. Thinking on it, Nuala came to the conclusion that it had not been opened as David had thought it was his mother's, just had she had done. It must have been that way. That's why it was with her father-in-law's other letters.

Now her curiosity was roused again. What was in those other letters? Without further thought, Nuala went to the sink to wash her hands and hurried back down the hall to David's study. Taking the chair again, she climbed up and pulled the drawer open. There they were. She took them and climbed back down again. Moved the chair back to the desk and sat down to look. All were postmarked London. Nuala took out one of the letters from its envelope.

All Saint's Sanatorium
London
September 28th 1912
Dear Doctor O'Leary,

Concerning your wife's condition and situation. We now have the unanimous decision of all three doctors.

With that in mind, a place has now been located for her here, at the Sanatorium of All Saints.

All three doctors have agreed that Mrs O'Leary will be well looked after at the institution. To assure you, this particular institution has a wonderful record for cases such as your wife's. It is hoped that with the right care and understanding, this will be the best remedy for her and yourself. They agree that the situation has now become inappropriate and untenable for her to remain at home. In due course, we will send you further correspondence regarding the arrangements and the doctor's full report.

We hope that this meets with your approval.

Yours sincerely,

Sr. Delaney

Secretary for All Saints and communication.

Nuala let the letter fall to the table as she sat back in the chair.

"Holy Mary, this is a day of revelations."

She couldn't help but speak out loud.

"Well, I never. What a thing!"

She took out another letter. They were more of the same.

The poor woman had been committed. David had always thought his mother had died young of the flu.

"Well, you wouldn't go telling a child something like that now, would yer? There's nothing to be done about it now," she reasoned. "She is lying with her son and husband in the graveyard."

Still, Nuala's mind was not quite satisfied with the thought.

"I wonder, did David know about his poor mother?"

With that last thought on it, Nuala bundled up the letters for a second time that day, lobbed them back up to the drawer, and took herself back to baking.

"Now I have to think about the living."

Once again, Nuala's hands were back in the mixing bowl, rubbing in the butter.

"I will look tomorrow for my wedding photographs," she told herself.

CHAPTER 20

The next morning, all was quiet. There were no sounds to hear in the little room the hospital had provided for her. Francis lay gazing at the ceiling. She was dressed in the nightgown the hospital had given her. She stretched and looked down at the gown, then over to the chair, where her clothes had been neatly placed, her mind struggling to make sense of all that had happened to her.

She tried to play it back in her mind to see if she had missed something.

The events during the mayhem of yesterday had all happened in such quick succession, like a bad dream. It felt almost unreal, yet lying there right then in the hospital room, Francis knew that it had been very real indeed.

Suddenly, there was Michael, running towards her with a gun held out before him, his arm sure and steady. Shouting at her to run, *run, Francis, run.* She had blindly obeyed, running away. He had stopped just a few feet from her. Then there was a shot, and a man fell to the ground. Michael fell. She thought he had been shot. Francis had fled to him as he lay on the ground. Another shot sounded, and the baby-faced man fell beside Michael, staring at the sky, a bullet hole in his forehead with blood trickling down his temple. Francis closed her eyes, hoping the image of it would not be there when she opened them. Why was Michael there? Then came the thought. Michael.

Michael's family were there. They had come to see him. Suddenly the tears started, and she couldn't hold them back. Michael had been stabbed. What was she doing lying there? She had to get up to go and see him.

Just as she swung her legs over the edge of the bed, a nurse came in.

"Ah, good morning, Francis. I thought you might manage a bit to eat."

The nurse had brought her a tray. She could see a cup of tea, a bowl of porridge, some bread and butter, and a tiny pot of jam.

"How are you feeling today?"

Francis smiled at the kind nurse.

"Not so bad. I was just going to get myself dressed. I was hoping I could go and see Michael. Michael Connor, that is."

The nurse nodded.

"All in good time. You should eat that up first. There's a bathroom through that door."

She cocked her head in the direction of the door in the corner of the room. The nurse arranged the tray on the little table and put Francis' clothes on the bed next to her.

"Thank you," Francis said. "I think I need the toilet."

She got off the bed, a little uncertain that her legs would hold her up. She had slept so deeply.

"Yer bound to be a bit delicate after the drugs they gave you yesterday. That's why you need to eat."

The nurse stood by while she went to the bathroom and had a wash, then left her to eat and dress herself.

She winked at Francis before she left the room. "I'll be back shortly to take you to see yer fella."

Michael had eaten his breakfast an hour or so ago.

The doctor came by, just after, taking a look at him.

"Nothing for you to worry about. You'll just feel a bit sore while it heals. There are a few internal stitches, but they will disperse in a week or two. You're a lucky man, Mr. Connor. It could have been a lot worse."

The doctor shook his head, and he added, "Luckily, the knife didn't penetrate too far. An inch further..."

The doctor stopped talking, thinking better of it than to mention the outcome. Michael knew he could have been lying in the morgue.

The doctor carried on. "Being a thin blade, the wound should heal quickly. Just take it easy. Rest now is the best medicine. I'd like you to stay in for around a week, just to be certain. I'll see you again in a day or two."

Michael thanked him, then said, "All in a day's work, Doc."

The doctor smiled at him, saying, "You're a brave man, Mr. Connor."

With that, he left the ward.

Michael sent up a silent prayer as he lay there thinking about Francis. He was concerned that this incident would have upset her, perhaps even beyond repair.

There she was, the poor girl, supposed to be on her holiday. Now she had been caught up in his work side of his life. It was just the worst thing that could have happened when things were going his way.

Her face floated into his mind.

Ah, Francis, please don't give up on me.

Michael pulled himself up to release the pressure he felt on his side.

He would try to stop thinking the worst, but his mind returned. It was all he could think about until he could see her again. He needed to speak to her.

Why had she come along at that moment? It was almost as though she had planned to meet him. She stood chatting to him, very friendly, the way he waved at her. Him of all people. Michael felt the blood rushing to his face. He closed his eyes, thinking he hoped the man rotted in hell.

"Mr Connor, you have a visitor."

As he opened his eyes, Francis stood with the nurse at the foot of his bed. Francis went to his bedside, and the nurse left them alone. Michael held out his hand to Francis, and she quickly took hold of it. They looked at each other. Michael spoke first.

"I'm so sorry, Francis."

Francis could have cried, but instead, she held on to Michael's hand so tightly.

"Sorry? Don't be daft. Why?"

"I feel as though I have gotten you into this. Truth is, I'm frightened that this..." He hesitated. "Well... that you'll want nothing more to do with me."

"Now you have gone daft," she said. "If anything, Michael, it has made me realise just how much I want you."

She leaned forward, her face just a few inches from his. Letting go of his hand, she slowly and carefully wrapped her arms around him and kissed him fully on his mouth, with as much ardour as the space allowed and without hurting him. Just when she knew he was really enjoying it, she pulled back.

"Now, Mr Connor, did that convince you?"

"I'll show you how much when I leave this bed. You wanton woman," he jested.

Francis threw back her head and laughed. "You better believe it."

She pulled up a chair so she could sit down next to him. "Can I ask you something serious, Michael?" Sitting down, she leaned in towards him.

"Of course. You can ask me anything, but I think it might cost you another one of those kisses."

"That's your lot for now. You're in recovery. What I wanted to ask is, why were you after that man with a gun in your hand?"

He looked at her, waiting a moment before he could reply. "Well, yer see, it's my job, Francis. Those men, those evil men, were drug smugglers." He took hold of her hand. "The man you were talking to was going to snatch you."

"Snatch me?" She gasped. "Why? What for?"

"Oh, Francis, do we have to have this conversation now?" Michael looked at her with pleading eyes and a frown.

"Yes, Michael. We do." She glared at him. "I'm sorry," she added. "I need to get it clear in my head."

"Yes, of course you do," he conceded. "I'll tell you from the beginning."

He cleared his throat and shifted on the bed.

"I work in the undercover unit of the Garda. That's why I was on the ferry. I'd been watching him for weeks."

Francis sat wide-eyed, listening carefully to every word.

"I had earned a few days' rest. That part, yer know. What I didn't know was that you were on speaking terms with him."

Francis' face flushed. "Hey, you don't think... I was, well... you know... interested in him?"

"No. I know now," Michael said. "But you had me going there."

Francis went on. "I just bumped into him by the harbour, and he recognised me from the ferry. He happened to come into the tea shop while I was having a cup of tea."

"Yes, of course he did, the sly little bastard." The words were out of Michael's mouth before he realised it. "You see, Francis, he was stalking yer."

125

Francis wrapped her arms around herself at that very thought. "Stalking me?"

"Yes. Believe me, he has done much worse. He would have got a good price for you."

She was feeling frightened at the thought. "Oh, Michael, don't."

Michael reached for her hand. "Yer safe now, don't look so worried." He winked at her. "I saved yer, didn't I?" he said to make her laugh.

She stood up and leaned over to give him another kiss. Sitting back down, they gazed at each other lovingly. "Yes, you did. Michael, just one more thing."

He tilted his head towards her with a quizzical raised eyebrow. "Yes? Haven't you had enough of that conversation?"

"No. I was just going to ask what about the girl on the ferry. She was with him. He told me she was his sister."

"No, Francis. She was not his sister. She was working with him."

Francis was confused. "But he told me she was his sister, and I saw her again getting into a boat with her husband and her friend. There was another man there, steering the boat. I saw him wave her off."

Michael sighed. He knew he would have to tell her it all. He wanted to, but also he wanted to protect her. Francis just looked at him, waiting.

"Okay, Francis. You really want to know?"

"Yes," she replied almost defiantly.

"If I tell yer everything he told yer was a pack of lies? Does that help?"

Michael was very serious now. Francis couldn't move or speak as he rattled off what he didn't want to tell her. "That poor girl had been groomed by him. First, he confiscated her passport. Offered her somewhere to live. Gave her drugs until she became reliant on him. Then when she was ready, he set her to work, making her carry drugs for him. He also used her for sex, renting her out. She fell pregnant, and finally, Francis, she was murdered. Dumped overboard out at sea. Her body was washed up down at Ballycotton."

Michael watched in his own misery as he saw the shock in Francis' eyes. The words he was saying he had not wanted to say. Yet still, he had told her; after all it was what he did, and who he was. He didn't want any secrets between them. If they had any future together, he wanted her to understand him fully; now the need was to pour it all out.

Carrying on, he told her, "The woman who you thought was her friend was working undercover for us. She also went overboard."

Francis was speechless as the tears ran down her cheeks. She could hardly believe what she had just heard. How close had she come to being taken.

"Oh my God, Michael."

He reached for her. She clung to him and nestled her head on his shoulder, her face buried in his neck, so he couldn't see her tears. Michael soothed her hair.

"I love yer. You're safe. I'll never let any harm come to yer."

As the nurse came onto the ward, Francis pulled herself together just in time. She didn't stop at Michael's bed but went to the end bed, where an elderly man was lying. He and Michael were the only patients on the ward, with just four beds on either side.

"I love you too," Francis said softly, wiping her hands over her teary face.

Michael was back to teasing her. "Yer got a red nose now, yer know."

The nurse came back. "Ten more minutes, and then you'll have to leave," she told Francis. "Before lunch comes around. It'll be visiting time after that."

Francis nodded in acceptance.

Michael rested back on his pillows.

"I'll have to go, Michael, but I'll come back."

"How yer going to get back to the hotel? I don't think it's a good idea to get there on your own. Why don't yer get something to eat in the cafe, there's one in the lobby. My da will be here this afternoon. He can give you a lift. Better still, yer could take them up on the offer of staying at Ash House."

Francis felt unsure. "Oh, I don't know about that. I hardly know them."

127

"Well, I don't think you should be on your own. You've had a bit of a shock, yer know. I feel responsible for letting all this happen to you."

They looked at each other. Michael was waiting for her to think.

Francis wanted to stay close by, but she wanted to get a change of clothes. There were blood stains on her top and cardigan. Michael's blood.

"Look at the state of me," she said to him.

"Ah, Francis. You're beautiful, so you are."

How could she resist him? She was considering what he was saying. "Well, all right then. I will go to the cafe and think about it. I'll see you later."

She was about to turn to go when he said, "Hey, where's me kiss? Also, yer bag is here on the floor. Won't you be needing it?"

She picked up her bag and put it on the chair. Michael reached and grabbed her arm.

"Not so fast," he said and pulled her towards him.

They kissed like their lives depended on it.

CHAPTER 21

Martha was busy in her kitchen, putting various items in her basket that she knew her son Michael would like to eat. Joseph was resting after lunch in his chair in the sitting room.

He called out to Martha, "Are you nearly ready? We should get going."

"Yes," came the reply. "Nearly."

Joseph folded his paper up and set it aside. He was eager to see how the young couple were doing. They had been through a lot in their short time together. He went and joined Martha in the kitchen.

"What's all that you've got there?"

Joseph was looking at the basket that Martha had filled.

"You never know what the lad might fancy," Martha replied. "It's just a few things, really."

"Looks like you're set to feed the five thousand."

"You know how he loves my baking. I'll just get me bag."

Joseph peered into the basket as Martha left the kitchen. He couldn't see much as Martha had packed it away in air-tight containers.

"Here we go then. Bring the basket, Joe," she asked, opening the back door.

Joseph drove steadily, while Martha sat as usual with her handbag on her lap, watching every twist and turn in the road. Now she felt more content and confident that her son Michael would be well.

"Did yer think, Joe, that you might be telling them about Nuala today?"

"I'm not sure that this is the time."

Truth was, Joseph couldn't make his mind up.

"As I see it, it's like this. On the one hand, it could be a good time, might distract them from the terrible ordeal they have both been through. On the other, they are just getting used to each other. Bringing Nuala into the picture might upset the apple cart."

"In what way?"

"Haven't they had enough shocks to cope with? I'm just not sure, that's all."

"Perhaps you'll feel different when you see them both. She's such a lovely girl."

Martha smiled to herself.

"Wouldn't it be just grand, Joe, if she's the one?"

"Yes, I think it would."

Joseph reached over and rubbed Martha's knee. "Just grand."

They drove on in silence through the countryside. Each loving parent was locked in their own thoughts about their son. Joseph's mind had the image of his son running towards danger. He thought Michael's heart would have been racing, seeing his girl there before his eyes, about to be snatched.

Martha's voice brought him back from his thoughts. "Well, what was that sigh all about?"

"Ah, just thinking about our boy, that's all."

He patted her knee as was his way when they were in the car. Martha smiled.

"He'll be all right now, Joe. I can feel it."

The silence fell again. How he wished Michael would leave the unit he was working in. He was not getting any younger. Perhaps Francis would make the difference, he hoped.

Martha's mind was on other matters regarding her blue-eyed boy as the car brought them nearer to the hospital. How she hoped for a wedding; how lovely would that be? She knew from the start Michael was smitten with Francis. She thought about the way he looked at her, and she couldn't help but smile. Then there was Nuala O'Leary. She wondered how they would react.

***

Francis had stayed in the cafe in the hospital. As she ate her bowl of soup and bread, she mulled over what Michael had told her. Her initial shock was over. Now she was trying to rationalise her situation. Should she ask to stay with Michael's parents? They were so easy to get on with.

She was sure that the first meeting with them went well. They were kind and seemed to like her. She liked them too.

Francis would need to get back to the hotel and pick up her things if she did. Then the thought came. She also needed to pick up her car. Michael had said she shouldn't be alone. She had to agree with him there. She didn't want to be on her own, not now.

That was a new feeling to her as she had gotten used to being self-sufficient over the years. Somewhere in the back of her mind, she felt it would be the right thing to do. It was Michael's wish.

The thought entered her head. She had learned to be independent; she had had to, to survive. Now she had met him, she felt she wanted to let go and be looked after. With Michael, she had felt so safe. Francis had sat there long enough. Suddenly her mind was made up. She would see how the land lay when she met up with Martha and Joseph.

Francis left the cafe and went out the main doors of the hospital. She looked up at the sky. The day was not as sunny, as she could see the clouds gathering and only a little blue beyond. Still, it was good to be in the fresh air. She started to walk. As she was on her second lap around the car park, she noticed a couple getting out of their car on the far side. Immediately she recognised them as Michael's parents.

Joseph was getting something from the back seat as Martha arranged herself, flicking her fingers through her hair.

As soon as she was in earshot, Francis called out a cheery "Hello". Martha's head turned towards the voice.

"Oh, Francis. Hello. You're looking a whole lot better than yesterday."

Martha held out her arms, and Francis went willingly towards her.

As Martha held the girl in her arms, she was aware of the extent of Francis' relief at being held. Francis was clinging to her.

When Martha pulled away to look at her face, tears ran down her cheeks.

"There, there, what's all this?"

By then Joseph stood next to them, holding onto the basket. He put the basket on the ground and put his arms around Francis. She buried her face against his chest.

"You're going to be all right, Francis. It's just the shock coming out. I have seen it before."

He was stroking her hair.

"Everything will be all right. You're safe with us. We're going to look after you until Michael gets better. Aren't we, Ma?"

"Of course we are."

Martha's voice was soft. "Come on then, let's get inside and get a cup of tea before we see Michael."

"I phoned in earlier, yer know, asking how the pair of yer were. They said you were doing fine, nothing for yer to worry about at all. Come on, Francis, let's go in and get that tea."

Francis stood back, wiping her eyes.

"I'm sorry," she said, looking at them. "I seem to be so emotional. I'm not usually like this."

"It's not usual goings on either," Joseph said. "What yer went through just yesterday too."

He put his arm around her shoulder. "Come on, let's go in."

Francis, Martha, and Joseph made their way in through the hospital's main doors and made for the cafe in the far corner. Martha left Joseph and Francis sitting at a table and went over to the counter.

Francis looked at Joseph, looking into the kind, friendly eyes that were looking steadily back at her.

"It all seems to be unreal to me. I still can't believe what has happened. I was with Michael this morning, and he told me everything."

She was brushing another tear that had escaped from her pretty green eyes.

Joseph was a bit surprised that his son had decided to tell her everything. "Did he? It's not exactly a pretty story."

Joseph had been in the Garda for many years and had seen some nasty things in his day, but to have gone through what Francis had was another story. She was most definitely still in shock.

"Well, in my experience, sweet girl, it will take a little while to come to terms with it. Now I don't want to persuade you, one way or another, that said, I really think yer will be better off coming home with us. Just until Michael's better."

Francis smiled at Joseph. "That's exactly what Michael said to me this morning."

"Well then, there yer are. Great minds think alike."

132

Francis felt relief. "All right, I think you're right, if you're sure. It's so kind of you both."

Just then, Martha returned with a tray. "Three cups of tea," she said with a smile, and sat herself down. "Now, are you feeling better, Francis?" she asked, making herself comfy and placing the teas down in front of them.

Francis picked up her cup. "Yes, thank you, much better." She took a sip of the hot tea. "Lovely," she added, cradling the cup.

Joseph looked at her and winked. "We'll have this, then go and see yer man," he said.

Francis felt a lot better now that she had spoken to them. Relief filtered down through her back, releasing her shoulders as her muscles relaxed. The tea warmed her inside, and the colour returned to her cheeks. She laughed as Joseph teased Martha about all the baking she had brought in for Michael.

"She's enough in there to keep an army going," he said as Martha retaliated.

"Yer just jealous, Joseph Connor, cause it's not fer you."

"How well yer know me, woman. Come on now, let's go and see Michael, before I get myself in trouble."

They found Michael awake and half sitting up in his bed. There had been another addition to the ward. A man in the bed opposite Michael, with his leg and arm held up by some sort of apparatus and covered in plaster of paris.

Joseph looked over at the sight, then looked back at Michael.

"Consider yerself lucky, son."

Michael laughed at the humour of his da.

"Shh, Joseph," Martha grimaced. "Poor man," she said.

Francis put her hand to her mouth to hide her smile. She saw the funny side.

They each got a chair and sat as close to Michael as possible. Francis sat quietly, just looking at Michael. Being happy to be back in his company was enough for her. Best let his parents do the talking, she thought to herself.

Michael was looking remarkably calm and content, considering that he had been stabbed. Martha had pointed out the colour was back in his cheeks.

"Now I've brought yer a few of your favourites," she said as she started to unload the contents of her basket onto the locker beside his bed.

"Ma, you shouldn't have gone to all that trouble. There's enough there to feed the five thousand."

Joseph chuckled. "I told her much the same this very morning."

"Oh, quiet the pair of yer. You're as bad as each other. Yer can always share it around."

Francis was really enjoying these exchanges. It was a tonic to her.

"Yer very quiet over there." Michael smiled at her. "Yer all right there, Francis?"

All eyes were on her.

"Yes, I'm fine, Michael, thank you."

Her answer was curt, yet happy.

"Did yer think on any more about what we were saying this morning?" he asked.

"Yes, as a matter of fact, I did. I was speaking with your dad."

"Were yer?" Martha shot in. "When was that?"

Francis looked at Martha. "When you were getting the tea."

Martha looked to her husband enquiringly. "What I was saying to Francis is I think she might be a little more comfortable if she came with us and stayed at Ash House for a while."

"And?" Michael asked.

He looked at her with his adorable blue eyes.

"I said yes, I think I would like to. It's very kind of your parents to offer."

"That's my girl. Thanks Da, you too, Ma."

"Makes sense," Martha said as if it were a foregone conclusion.

"Oh, why don't yer tell them now, about Nuala, Joe?" Martha blurted out.

Francis' head spun. "Nuala? That's my middle name."

"Is it really? Well, isn't that interesting."

Martha's eyebrows raised as she took a side look at her husband. Was he annoyed with her for mentioning it? Or did he think the time was right? There was silence. Joseph looked at his wife, then in turn, Martha fixed her gaze on him, still with an enquiring raised eyebrow.

Michael, easing himself up on his pillows, winced. The pain made him draw in his breath before he spoke. The uneasy silence was broken.

Martha was quick to caution her son. "Careful there, Michael. You don't want to go tearing at the stitches."

He ignored his mother and looked towards his da.

"What's all this then? Nuala, did yer say? Nuala who?"

Joseph wriggled a bit in his seat. He had been taken unawares by Martha's decision to blurt it out.

His son's serious look told him that perhaps there was no better time than the present. They were together, be it not in the happiest of surroundings.

All three were waiting for his reply. Joseph decided to come straight out with it. He was praying that it was the right time. Joseph knew Francis had to know. He just wished they were all at home together for the telling.

"Well," he said, not wanting to bear the looks they were giving him a moment longer.

"Nuala O'Leary" – he turned and faced Francis, her sparkling green eyes wide and encouraging – "is your aunt, Francis."

"My aunt? But…" She trailed off. "My aunt!" she said again to reaffirm the unbelievable news she was hearing.

It was Michael who took over.

"Her aunt? Are you sure, Da?"

"As sure as sure, son." He smiled.

Joseph looked back at Francis.

"I hope you don't mind, Francis, my finding out, but when you came to visit us, I just knew I could see the family likeness and all."

Finding her voice, Francis' tone was soft and low. "Well, I am astounded. My aunt! My father's sister."

She spoke the words as they settled in her mind and sunk in.

"It's incredible, here of all places."

Michael reached out for her hand. She looked at him and said, "Just incredible."

Michael was astounded too.

"Sure is," he said as he squeezed her hand.

135

Joseph looked at the pair of them. He knew he should continue.

"I went to see her."

"You did? Where is she?" Francis couldn't wait to hear.

"Not far. I'll take yer when you're ready. She is a bit further on from us. We all went to the same school, yer know."

"Really?"

Everything Joseph was telling her now was a revelation. Her heart began to beat a little faster as she thought about why her father hadn't told her he had a sister.

Joseph's words filtered through her thoughts.

"She said she would really like to meet yer."

"Did she! I was just wondering why my dad never mentioned her."

"Nuala told me she never knew about you. That she never heard from your father again after he left Ireland. She just knew he was going to London to find work."

Martha and Michael watched on in silence, allowing Francis to take in the incredible news. Mother and son, in quiet understanding, knew how important this news was to Francis.

The tea trolley came rattling through the swing doors and onto the ward. A middle-aged, robust woman in a white apron arrived at the foot of Michael's bed. The cups and saucers were finally quietly rested on the heavy-looking trolley.

"Here we are," she said, looking straight at Michael. "Can I get yer a nice cup of tea?"

"Yer sure can," Michael said. "Unless yer got something a little stronger, perhaps?"

He gave her his cheeky wink.

"Tea is all I have now."

She smiled back at him.

The woman set about pouring from a huge silver-coloured tank. The dark brew flooded the cup, leaving just enough room for a drop of milk.

"Milk then, is it?" she enquired as they all watched.

"How's about the rest of youse? I've plenty here."

Joseph, Martha and Francis made no delay in replying.

"Yes, please," they chimed in unison.

136

Martha got up and looked inside the bedside locker. Finding one of her containers, she set about opening it up. It was filled with fruit cake. They all took a chunk out as she offered it around. Sitting quietly, they ate and washed it down with tea. The four were all in their own thoughts, yet all were thinking about the same events of the past couple of days. Now the new revelation about Nuala O'Leary.

When they had finished, Francis was quick on her feet. She relieved Joseph and Martha of their cups and saucers and placed them on Michael's table.

"I think I need to get back to the hotel and check out."

She took Michael's hand. Looking into his eyes, she added, "I really need to get cleaned up."

"You need to pick yer car up, too," he reminded her.

Joseph offered to drive her without hesitation. The relief on Francis' face was obvious to all.

"That would be lovely," she said.

Joseph stood up. "Well, we can go now, so Michael can have a chat with his ma. When you've checked out, I'll drive ahead back here, and you can follow. It won't take us long. Then, when we're all ready, you can follow me back to Ash House." Joseph smiled at her. "It won't take us long at all."

Joseph and Francis set off. It was about a twenty-minute drive back into Kinsale from the hospital. Francis sat quietly, enjoying looking at the countryside passing by. Joseph's steady, strong hands were on the wheel. She tried not to think of the events of the previous day. She just wanted to think about her father's sister. How odd it was that he had never mentioned her. Perhaps they had had a falling out. Suddenly Francis felt there was an urgency about the need to meet her. She would be able to fill in some of the gaps. Here she was, in Ireland, and how sad it was now that her parents were no longer alive.

She looked at Joseph. The strong set of him, his eyes steady on the road, here with her now, and she thought about her own father.

As if he read her mind, he said, "It's such a pity your parents aren't alive."

"You just read my thoughts."

Joseph smiled, keeping his eyes on the road as he spoke again.

"I remember him well, yer know, from our school days. He was a strong character. He was always ready to stand his corner. Looked out for his sister when their Mammy died."

"Oh. I never knew that. I was thinking about Nuala. She would be able to tell me things, perhaps. I really can't understand why he never mentioned anything about her, or here. I think it's so beautiful."

They were coming back into the town.

"It was difficult back in those days, just a lad without his parents. Sure, Nuala will help you understand. Here we are." Joseph had pulled up right in front of Donovan's and switched off the engine.

"Would you like me to come in, or wait here?"

Francis thought for a moment.

"As you wish." She smiled. "I have decided not to bother to change. An hour or so longer won't make any difference now. I'll just grab my stuff and pay up."

"I'll wait here then. Off yer go."

Francis was true to her word. She rushed in and took the stairs straight up to her room. A few minutes later, she was back in the foyer with her jacket hiding the dried blood on her top. A man came out of the door behind the desk.

"Hello," he said.

"Hello." She smiled. "I would like to check out."

She handed him the key. Francis had been relieved that it wasn't Mrs Donovan on the desk. The last thing she wanted was to explain the goings on of the last couple of days. The man in question didn't seem interested in her, and she was very grateful. Francis was out the door with a cheerful goodbye.

Standing out on the pavement, Joseph was stretching his leg as Francis descended the steps.

"All done," she told him. "My car is around the back."

"Right yer are. I'll wait until you come through. Just follow me back."

Francis looked at Joseph. "I'd just like to say thank you." She leaned forward and kissed Joseph on his cheek. "You have been so kind to me. It means a great deal."

"You're more than welcome, dear girl. Come on then," he said. "Let's get back. It would be good to get home before it gets dark. We need to pick up Ma first."

He looked at her and knew that, from that moment on, they would always have a great friendship.

It was another twenty minutes, and they both parked back in the hospital car park.

***

Martha had enjoyed the time sitting with her son, watching him with his eyes closed. She was just so grateful that her Michael had survived. How close had he come to being taken? The violence of it all made her heart ache. She had thanked God profusely almost every hour since. Now here he was, talking to her about Francis as though nothing had happened.

"Do yer like her, Ma?" he asked.

"I do, Michael." She smiled. "More importantly, do you?"

"More than I can say." His reply was swift and sure. "I just know that we are right for each other."

Martha looked thoughtfully at him.

"It's a funny thing. I always knew yer da was the one straight off." She carried on. "People who have not experienced it don't understand. They say, how do yer know? I think you might not know where the two of youse will end up. Yet you know yer want to have a good go at it, to find out. If you see what I mean. I think, Michael, that you need to follow your heart."

Michael smiled at her, her kind, lovely soft face. Reaching for her hand, he said, "I know one thing for sure. I love her, Ma." Suddenly he looked crestfallen. "Why did this have to happen, right now of all times?"

Martha looked down at his hand in hers.

"It's not ideal, but we can't undo what's done. Francis seems to have handled it pretty well so far. I guess she wouldn't agree to stopping with us at Ash House if she was not as keen for you."

He laughed, and Michael held on to his side. Just then, Joseph and Francis returned.

Francis went straight to Michael and gave him a quick kiss.

"All done," she said.

139

The tension Michael had felt while she was not with him had evaporated as he took in her loveliness. His ma was right. She needn't be here, let alone agree to stay at Ash House.

CHAPTER 22

Bandon Garda had been a hive of activity. Most knew about the swoop down in Kinsale. The TV had reported on the case, not in such detail but enough to set tongues wagging. The poor woman's body that had been washed up in Ballycotton had caused much speculation. Now a stabbing and shooting, in Kinsale of all places. The locals would be speaking of it for months, if not years.

Michael's superintendent was making plans to visit him in the hospital. It was now the weekend. Michael had been a model patient, doing as he was told. The enforced rest had been beneficial. It allowed Michael to get to grips with his feelings for Francis. He had been mulling over exactly what he had hoped would happen and how that would fit in with his future in the Garda. The stabbing had brought everything into focus. What kind of life had he to offer the sweet girl, he thought to himself.

Lying awake at night, he ran through many scenarios. There was now no question left unanswered in his mind. Now he felt back in control and more certain than ever. He wanted to ask Francis to marry him. He also needed to speak to his superintendent. Their answers would hold the outcome of his future.

***

Francis came to terms with all that had happened.

It was now early Saturday morning. She awoke from the deepest sleep. The house was silent. Michael's sister Bridget was to visit in the afternoon that day, but this morning, she would visit her auntie.

She stretched beneath the soft, comforting bedding. Martha had been so kind to her, Joseph too; so understanding. Gazing at the ceiling, her thoughts turned to Michael.

Michael was on the mend. The very thought of him and her knees felt weak. Could all this be real? Francis felt giddy and most definitely in love.

Was it just last Monday that she sailed into Rosslare Harbour? Meeting Michael had turned her life upside down. This was just meant to be a holiday, after all. Suddenly the thought of work, her work, flooded her mind. It seemed so alien. This was the first time since being there, almost a week, and now an alien and unhappy thought had entered her mind. For ten long years, she had been stuck in that company. Granted, she had learned much, yet she could see now she had been dead inside.

She got up and opened the curtains. The room was filled with sunshine after the previous day's rain. She scanned the view. Her eyes glanced over the garden to beyond, where the fields, trees and hedgerows were bursting with new life.

Lifting the latch that held the window closed, and reaching down, she held onto the brass handles, there for that very purpose, and she slid the window up, surprised by how smoothly the sash cord ran.

Now with the soft breeze brushing her cheeks, she breathed deeply and filled her lungs with the sweet fresh air. Francis was beginning to blossom, just as sure as the new spring growth.

***

The Garda in County Cork were in the throes of wrapping up the loose ends of the case. There were reports to be written up, and every man involved had to account for their proceedings in what was known as 'Case 717 Traffic Lights'.

There were the dead bodies to deal with, also the people on the yacht who had been arrested. Four men had been captured and taken to Dublin. The one brother who had tried to escape in the motorboat the moment a gunshot was fired was Leon Balan, brother of Costie, whom Michael had shot point blank as he lunged towards Francis.

Leon Balan had been caught by the Gardai water unit as he tried to head out of Kinsale harbour. He was under arrest and being held at Dublin prison, awaiting trial with the others. It was unknown if the criminals would be transferred back to England.

Every piece of evidence had to be numbered and filed. It had been a huge operation for the county. All the Garda involved had played their part well.

Patrick Logan, Michael's colleague, had offered to take on a lot of the paperwork on Michael's behalf. Their superintendent gave him the thumbs up for the time being. When Michael had fully recovered, there would be enough time to tweak and finalise the details.

The London Metropolitan branch that had been working on the case had been pleased with how the Garda had managed to close down this part of the operation. They were trying to wrap up another part of the case they now thought involved the same family of dealers, operating in true mafia style.

It had come to their notice a certain woman had been connected to Dario Dinu. She could be the head of the group.

News had travelled fast in the underworld. Certain people had been captured or killed in Ireland. Drug deliveries had stopped. Word was out now that this woman within the family was out for revenge. The Met had it on good authority Dario Dinu's death had not gone down well.

Michael's superintendent, Jim O'Rourke, needed to speak to Michael and Patrick. Unfortunately, it would seem this case for them was not quite over.

Within a few days, the Met had informed the Garda that this woman was Dario Dinu's older sister. They now knew she would be looking for those who were responsible for the death of her beloved baby brother. There was one big problem; they could not identify who she was.

***

CHAPTER 23

Based in the Bayswater area of London, her home was palatial by all accounts, occupying a corner position on an exclusive square. The residence looked out onto a central communal garden. Though rarely used by the occupants of the houses, the view was pleasant. Tall plain trees and shrubs had created areas of privacy where seating had been installed. All in all, the area was thought of as upmarket in the local community.

Laura Popa was running a high-end, well established brothel, employing young boys and girls. Her clientele was wealthy and therefore demanded the best money could buy. All her girls and boys were attractive, clean and reliable. She also dealt with all manner of drugs and alcohol. There was gambling on the premises and almost anything else their money could buy.

Laura Popa aimed to please.

Each room was decorated inside the house with lavish and ornamental furnishings. Tasteless in its extreme, it was akin to a stage setting, flashy and gaudy, with a plushness that was excessive.

She wore expensive clothes and flashy jewellery, her long black hair was sleek, and she kept it tied tight to the nape. From there, it flowed down to her waist. Her eyes were catlike and dark, and her body slim and agile. She moved like a cat, almost prowling around her premises, surveying all that was hers down her aquiline nose.

She favoured tight black clothes, and her long painted nails completed the picture of this money-driven predator.

She was devoid of feeling, except now her baby brother's murder had filled her with such an overpowering rage, it filled her every fibre. There would be no rest for her until she found someone to pay. There was nothing that would bring him back. Not now, not ever.

It was not long before she had thought of a plan. It would be easy to send someone to this place, this backwater, wherever it was, to find out who would pay the price with their life. A life for a life, she thought.

That was the least she could do, so her little baby brother could rest in peace amidst the angels.

Laura Popa was beginning to feel better. The more she thought about it, the happier she became.

That afternoon, under her instructions, a couple in her employ took a flight and landed at Dublin Airport. They hired a car and drove down to Kinsale, arriving late Friday afternoon.

It was not difficult for the couple, posing as tourists, to overhear the gossip in the cafe and bars they had gone into. Opinions were rife. The locals, it seemed, had nothing else to talk about.

The young couple moved about, totally ignored by most, except the hotel's landlady.

They chose to stay at Donovan's.

"We would like to stay for a couple of days," they had asked so sweetly and politely.

They told the receptionist that they were on a romantic weekend and just wanted to escape London.

"It's so busy there," the girl had said. "Here is so beautiful."

Mary Donovan could imagine and puffed out her chest, ready to inhale and then set off on a verbal tour, taking delight in chatting away in her entertaining fashion.

She told them how she knew the two young people, so in love, much like themselves.

"He was in the Garda for the thrill of it all."

Then the terrible sadness of how he had been stabbed and how the dear girl had witnessed it all. Then there was the washed-up body of a woman in Ballycotton. All told with as much drama as Mary Donovan could muster.

They couldn't believe their luck. This woman knew every last detail. They would show her nothing but respect and listen dutifully and carefully to her every word, prompting her when she drew breath.

"Oh, do carry on. It's so interesting." The girl smiled all the while, putting in just enough exclamations to make them plausible and sympathetic listeners to such a story. In response, the man asked, "You're saying she was actually staying here? Do you know her name?"

"Oh yes," Mary Donovan replied. "Sure, I do." She was so

caught up in the telling, she said without hesitation. "It's Francis Doyle. Beautiful girl. She's very recognisable with that head of hair, the loveliest, reddest long curly hair. One in a million, I'd say."

The couple exchanged looks. "And he was?" The girl thought she would try her luck.

"Oh," Mary said. "Didn't I say? He is Michael Connor. They make a lovely couple, so they do."

"Great story."

They thanked Mary Donovan. She set about arrangements for their room.

"I have a nice double-facing front," she said. "Will that do yer?"

"Sounds great," the man said.

"It's got a nice view of the harbour," she proclaimed.

The man signed the register.

Mr & Mrs Darling.

The woman smiled. "Just perfect," she said.

As soon as they were in their room, the couple threw themselves on the double bed, laughing. He rolled over on top of her and said, "Hello, Mrs Darling. Looks like we're in for a cosy weekend."

She smiled up at him. "Can you believe that woman? She sure can talk, luckily for us."

He kissed her full on the mouth. "Oh, I love this job." He sighed.

She pushed at him, rolling him away.

"Easy there," she purred. "There's enough time for that. We should phone in and tell Laura."

"Not now," he snapped. "There's time enough for that, too. She's not expecting to hear from us that soon," he moaned.

"Fair enough."

Her mind tuned in. She had expected that rebuff. She could never change him, even if she wanted to. Her reply had been soft and gentle, not wanting to upset him. *Keep him sweet*, she though as she got off the bed.

"I think I'll take a shower."

She glanced back over her shoulder as he lay there watching her. She seductively pouted and blew him a kiss.

146

"Good idea." He smiled, leapt off the bed, and followed her into the bathroom.

***

The so-called Mr and Mrs Darling were, in fact, a couple who had been teamed up in the employment of Laura Popa. They both owed her so much. They felt she had saved them, giving them everything they desired. They could not see the depravity that was there all around them, blinded to their way of life by the riches that seemed to matter to them, beyond rationality. They lacked for nothing materially, yet now they were just as unstable and corrupt as the woman who had created them.

Laura Popa had, in her mind, rescued them. She had made them feel secure.

Their lives had been worthless, having been on the streets of London from a very young age. Any morals they might have possessed had been eradicated. Their minds had become extensions of hers.

The evil Laura Popa had liked the look of them. It came to her that they would make a wonderful double act. She had groomed them well, in every way, to perform for her or anyone else who would pay for the novelty. Laura Popa was a woman who liked a project. Wanting to own and possess their young minds was a challenge she had savoured. She had found them willing and easy to coax.

It had amused her. She called them her little darlings. It had surprised her, too, just how willing they were to perform for her. No need to mistreat them. Just treat them with what they want. The fact that they took to each other made the project that much easier in her eyes. A match made in heaven.

Now there they were, a lot older and wiser to their trade. They would do anything for Laura. She had become their mother figure. For them, their treat was a short break and an easy mission. All they had had to do, so far, was to gather information about the killing of Laura's beloved brother. They would phone her tomorrow and tell her what they had discovered in the short time since arriving in Kinsale. It was the weekend, after all.

CHAPTER 24

Francis came down the stairs to the smell of bacon cooking. She followed her nose into the kitchen where Martha was at the range.

"Good morning."

"Ah, there yer are. Now there's tea in the pot. Help yourself."

Francis sat at the table.

"That smells delicious."

"Would yer like an egg with it?" Martha asked with a smile.

"Oh, yes, please."

"Coming right up. Now tell me. How did yer sleep?"

"The best ever," she replied.

She watched Martha standing at her range in the lovely sunny kitchen.

Francis thought how homely it felt and that Michael was lucky to belong there. This was the house he had been brought up in. It had made her feel like nothing in the world mattered beyond its walls. Everything was just so comfortable, easy and secure.

Martha set down the plate of eggs and bacon in front of her.

"There's bread there, in the basket. I'm just making some toast."

Francis looked at the plateful.

"This looks wonderful."

"You need a good breakfast in yer tummy, set you up for the day."

Francis smiled, remembering Michael saying much the same to her about Donovan's breakfasts. She knew now that Martha had taught her son well.

"Morning, Francis," Joseph said, coming into the kitchen.

He put his hand on her shoulder. Francis looked up at him and smiled.

"Good morning to you."

They could hear the dogs barking outside.

"Take their food out, Joe?" Martha asked.

"I'm on it."

Francis remembered the dogs from the first time she had visited. They seemed to spend a lot of their time outside. Joe retrieved some dishes from the pantry and was back off again to tend to the dogs. They stopped barking as soon as he got to them.

"Thank God for that," Martha said, sitting opposite Francis and sipping her tea. "You must be excited to meet your auntie this morning."

Francis put down her knife and fork. Wiped her mouth on the napkin.

"Yes, I am." She beamed at Martha. "It's just so unimaginable. Who could believe it? Not in my wildest dreams. How I wish my dad had spoken to me about his home here."

"I'm so happy for yer." Martha's twinkling blue eyes told Francis that she truly was. "I expect your auntie will be able to tell yer all sorts."

As soon as Joseph came back in the kitchen, he asked, "Are we ready for the off then?"

Martha and Francis were just tidying away the plates from breakfast.

"All done." Martha hung up the tea towel. "Now let me get you something to take to yer auntie, Francis."

She went inside her pantry door. When she came back out, she had a basket in her hand.

"There we are." She handed it over to Francis. "Thought she might like some of the gooseberry jam. You seemed to favour it, as I recall."

Francis took the offered basket.

"That's really thoughtful." Looking inside, she saw two jars and a tin.

Martha was looking pleased with herself. Francis planted an unexpected kiss on her soft cheek.

"Thank you, Martha. Not sure how long I'll be, but I'll tell you all about it when I get back."

"Looking forward to it, love. Have a lovely time."

Francis told Joseph she just needed to get her jacket.

"I'll wait in the car. You follow me up. I'll indicate when we get to her place. Think you'll make it back all right?"

"Yes, I'm sure I will."

Francis left Martha and Joe looking at each other.

He bent down to kiss his wife. "Won't be long, love," he said.

***

Superintendent Jim O'Rourke had found his way to Michael's ward. He strode through the swing doors and saw Michael lying back on his pillow with his eyes shut. Surveying the room, he took in the unfortunate person in the contraption on the opposite side of the ward. There was another bed occupied at the far end. He approached Michael's bed.

"Mick," he whispered.

Michael's eyes slowly opened. Only the fellas at work called him Mick.

"Hi, have a seat."

"How's it going then?" he asked.

After removing his cap, he sat himself down.

"Just grand," Michael replied, trying to heave himself up. "I'll be better when I can get out of this place. There are only so many bedrests a man can take. I'm bored silly lying here all bloody day."

"All the men wish you well. Yer know how it is."

"Sure, thanks. How's the rest of it?"

Michael thought to ask this first. There were things he wanted to tell his boss. Michael wanted to gauge his mood before opening up.

"That's what I want to talk to you about, Mick."

His grave face told him this was not going to be good news.

"Sounds ominous. Yer better tell me then."

"The Met were on. They say there's more trouble. Dario Dinu's sister."

Michael gave a half-cocked smile. "Sister?"

"It's serious, Mick. She's not one to mess about by all accounts. You know what these types are like. It's all about family. Only theirs is akin to the mafia. Think they stem from the Romanian equivalent."

"That figures," Michael said.

Michael didn't want to know, but he needed to ask. "Where is this sister, then?"

"Word is, she wants to avenge her brother's killing."

Michael lay back on his pillows.

"Jesus. I thought this was the end of it."

150

Michael swore under his breath.

His superintendent carried on. "You're in danger, Mick, if it gets out you're lying here in a hospital bed. I've put Paddy on leave for the time being." He went on in earnest. "You're one of the best there is, Mick. The best I know, for sure. Short of putting a man outside the ward doors, I'm not sure what else I can do."

Michael swore again, this time not so softly.

"Do yer know how long you'll be in for here?"

"No," came the short answer.

Both men were silent until Michael growled through gritted teeth. "I might get up later to sit in the bloody chair. So, I guess it can't be much longer now."

Jim O'Rourke looked at Michael. He chanced a small smile. "Could have been a lot worse."

"Yeah, suppose you're right."

Michael had calmed himself down. He was thinking he might as well get it off his chest, tell him now what's what.

"Well, here's the thing..." Michael looked him in the eye. Without hesitation, he blurted out, "I've had enough."

His super looked at him. "Enough?" he repeated. "What?"

"Enough of the job."

Michael's face was straight and as serious as Jim O'Rourke had ever seen him.

"Now, don't be hasty. We can handle this."

"No!" Michael retorted. "I'm not being hasty. I have been thinking it through. I've had plenty of time to think. It's nothing to do with what you've just told me."

"It's not?" Jim O'Rourke was looking flummoxed. "What then?"

Michael's voice took on a gentle tone. "I've met someone."

"I see," Jim said, smiling.

Michael read his face. The super looked at him like he wasn't serious. This was not up for debate. Michael didn't like the feeling he was sensing. Did Jim O'Rourke think he could talk him out of it? He could think again! Staring straight back at him, Michael retorted.

"I mean it. Put me on a desk job, or I'm leaving altogether."

It surprised Michael, hearing the words out loud, just as much as it surprised his superior.

The super could tell Mick was on a short fuse, putting it down to being confined in the hospital.

Michael kept his gaze steady. He was not going to explain his innermost thoughts about Francis, how this kind of life was not going to be what he wanted for her, or for them as a couple. It was okay for a man on his own. Now that he had met her, he was not going to lose her. She had already been drawn into his work in just a few days. Michael's mind was made up. He kept his gaze steady, waiting for the reply.

"Mick, are you sure?"

Michael cocked his head.

"Sure," he said without emotion.

Jim O'Rourke stood up, and put his hand out to Michael, and the two men shook hands.

"I'm sorry to lose you, Mick, she must be someone really special."

"Yeah," Michael said. "Really special. I'll be back at Ash House soon, I hope. Let me know what you come up with."

"Will do," a shaken Jim O'Rourke replied. "Leave it with me and get yourself well and home soon."

Michael watched him leave the ward. Then lay back. One down, one to go, he thought.

"Oh no, now what?" he muttered when two nurses were heading for him.

"Come on, handsome," the older one said as she threw back the bedding. "It's time for you to sit out in the chair."

152

CHAPTER 25

True to his word, Joseph was driving ahead of Francis at his usual steady speed. He had indicated for Francis to take the right turn. She had butterflies in her stomach as she approached the house. The house of her very own auntie.

It was quite a sizeable place, she noted, looking at the grey Victorian villa. It was similar to Ash House, surrounded by old trees and huge rhododendrons. As soon as she had brought her car to a halt, the front door of the house opened. There, standing on the step, was her aunt.

Francis hurried towards her with her arms outstretched in greeting. Likewise, Nuala held hers open to greet her. Both women were locked in an embrace and had tears in their green eyes. A shaft of sunlight filtered through the branches of the huge tree and highlighted them in glorious sunshine.

Francis pulled back. "I'm so pleased to meet you. I never knew you existed." Her voice was soft and emotional.

Nuala stepped back, saying, "Let me take a look at yer." Then she smiled. "Aye, I can see you're Robert's daughter, no mistake. Won't you come in? The kettle's on."

Francis smiled. "I'd love to. I'll just get something from the car."

Nuala stood waiting and watching while Francis returned to the car and retrieved a basket from the back seat. Nuala had noticed that Francis had her hair tied back the same way as her. A loose ribbon held her long curls at the nape. The only difference being that Nuala's once red hair was now sandy and streaked with silver. Her dress was long and plain pale blue. She had put a darker blue baggy cardigan over the top. Francis was dressed in her jeans and a pretty pink fine-knit jumper. Both women were similar in size and stature. The resemblance was there for all to see.

Francis followed Nuala into the house.

"Come through into the kitchen."

"Lovely house," Francis said as they entered the hallway and the kitchen.

Immediately Francis' eyes were drawn to the view of the conservatory, filled with plants and sunshine.

"Oh!" She sighed. "What a lovely conservatory. May I take a look?"

Placing the basket on the scrubbed wooden table, she couldn't take her eyes away from the many plants.

"Of course yer can."

Francis made her way, as excited as a child in a sweet shop.

"Do you like plants?" Nuala asked like she couldn't tell.

"Yes, I do. You have such the perfect place for them."

The two women walked about, looking at the various species. Nuala, so knowledgeable, and Francis, with so obviously the same instinct and liking. There was a small table with a couple of chairs in the far corner, with beautiful, ornate fretwork, making it a perfect place to sit.

"I think I would spend all my time here. You have made it a lovely place. Your plants look so healthy."

One of the windows had been opened, and Francis could hear the birds chirping happily outside in the garden. Her senses were filled.

"Spring," she said and sighed.

Nuala smiled as she watched her every movement and reaction.

Francis was enthralled. "The atmosphere here is delightful."

Nuala was happy to see her niece was so in tune with nature.

"Well now, would yer like yer tea here, or is it coffee yer prefer?"

"Tea, please."

"Come and help me then, and we'll bring a tray."

Nuala turned and went back to the kitchen.

"It's such a beautiful day."

Francis took the contents from the basket and placed Martha's two jars of gooseberry jam on the table, next to the cake tin. "These are a gift from Martha Connor."

Nuala was looking at the jam. "That's kind of her. Yer had better take her something of mine in return."

Francis smiled. She had never known anything like it before. The women here, so far those she had met, were just so lovely. Francis placed the mugs on the tray with the plates.

"Bring the tray then, will yer," Nuala said, walking back to the conservatory.

They had seated themselves at the table in the corner. Sunshine, bird song, and plants surrounded them. The two women would discover that they were indeed very much alike. It was just the years that had separated them and the distance, robbing them of a genuine understanding and an instant liking of each other.

Now, with time and place no obstacle, the two women would find love, friendship, happiness, and the bond of blood that would always tie them together. By the time Francis thought she had better leave, they had covered all manner of subjects. Each had filled themselves with questions and answers. Yet there was still much to say. Nuala, not being used to visitors, was beginning to feel overwhelmed.

"We shall have to meet up again soon," she said to Francis. "You know where I am now, and I can tell yer, dear girl, you are welcome here any time at all."

Francis hugged her aunt.

"I can't tell you how much this all means to me. Thank you so much, Auntie."

Nuala smiled. "Isn't that a thing? I'm an auntie."

They laughed.

"Before I forget." Nuala went over to her pantry and came out with a fancy tin. "Give this to Martha. Thank her for me, for the jam. Gooseberry! I shall enjoy that, and the rest of the cake."

"Yes," Francis said. "It's quite delicious."

"You've got my number. Bring yer man back with yer the next time. I should like to meet him."

"Yes, I will. See you again soon."

They embraced, and Nuala saw Francis off. She was reluctant yet tired, and it had all been quite extraordinary. Nuala watched as Francis got back into her car. A tear slid down her cheek as she watched her niece waving goodbye as she drove away.

Francis was driving slowly along the lane. She could hardly believe what was happening to her. She needed to think. After a little way, she saw a pull-in to a gate onto the fields. She brought the car off the lane and stopped. Switching off the engine, she opened the window. There was silence, apart from the soft sigh

155

of the breeze.

Sitting still and quiet, Francis mulled over her thoughts. There was time enough before the afternoon's events would overtake her again. Bridget was going to visit her brother Michael. The young woman also wanted to meet Francis, longing to see this new woman he had met.

Putting that thought away for now, Francis wanted to think about Nuala. How alike they were. How sad that she had never received her dad's letter and the photograph.

That was a strange thing. Still, there was nothing to be done about that now. That was all a long time ago. This was now the present, and she needed to concentrate on that. It seemed to her that meeting Michael was meant to be. Almost like it had been engineered in some strange way. Such a coincidence was uncommon to her. Even when she caught the ferry to Ireland. Everything had been for her, or so she thought, unplanned, yet here was everything falling into place, and now, an auntie of all things.

She looked over the fields and above at the blue sky. This place was where her father had been born. He had gone to school there. The same school as Michael's father. Another coincidence. Francis sighed. How strange it all was, how lovely it all was. Michael, the man dreams were made of. She loved even the thought of him. He appealed to her in every way. She loved how he made her laugh, how he teased her, and how thoughtful he had been to her. The look of him made her heart beat faster then. There was the way he had kissed her, so loving yet masterful. There was no doubt the man had swept her off her feet. His parents were the loveliest couple. They had shown her nothing but kindness. For all that, Francis thought on, she had only known him for a week. Still, it was undeniable they had fallen for each other. Hadn't they already told each other so? There was no doubt in her mind. Just imagining being in Michael's arms was enough to make her blush. It had sent ripples of pleasure throughout her entire body.

"Michael," she whispered.

Trying to pull herself out of her reverie, Francis told herself time would tell. She had plenty of that at the moment.

Feeling that she had put things in order for now, she started the car. It occurred to her not a single car had passed her by since she had stopped. Nevertheless, she had still looked over her shoulder to pull out before carrying on down the lane back to Martha, Joseph and Bridget.

***

After Nuala cleared away the cups and plates, she went into the conservatory and sat down at the table. Her mind picked over what Francis had told her.

How her brother Robert had been killed outright in a road accident alongside his wife. She tried to visualise the lorry, hitting them head-on. One minute all was well. The next thing they had been swept away. At least they didn't suffer. Nuala comforted herself with the thought. But poor Francis; the real trauma had been hers. On her own since she was eighteen, both parents were gone, and no other living relatives. Well, except her, of course. If only she had known.

No use thinking along those lines. Her mind turned to Francis. Nuala liked her. She had a gentle feminine way about her, pretty as a picture. Nuala smiled to herself. She must be quite clever, too, holding down a responsible job in London. That was no mean feat in her eyes.

It was no wonder Robert had made contact with her. He knew she would be coming. Nuala sat still and closed her eyes, thinking about Robert. The sun had moved to the side of the garden, casting shadows along the pathway. The birds were still collecting bits and pieces for their nests in the garden. There were odd, soft scratching sounds as they foraged beneath the shrubs in the undergrowth, flicking bits out onto the pathway. They were the bits not needed.

Nuala was so quiet that the slightest sound came to her through the open window. Everything slowed in her mind. Even her heart slowed as she breathed in and out. She could visualise the growth of the plants pushing up through the warming soil. In her mind, she was outside. She felt the soft grass beneath her bare toes and enjoyed the fragrance as she brushed against the herbs. The overhanging branches, with their thickening buds, swelled with every passing day, until they would be covered in clouds of pink and white blossoms.

157

It was then she saw her brother, standing again on the garden path, smiling, and she approached him. The two embraced. *Thank you,* she heard him say. *Keep a lookout, Nuala. She will need you.* Nuala slowly opened her eyes. There he was, still standing on the pathway waving, and then he was gone.

"Ah, Robert, I will do my best," Nuala said.

CHAPTER 26

At Ash House, all three dogs were roaming about the kitchen. They were enjoying being fussed by Bridget.

"You shouldn't encourage them," Martha said as Francis came in through the back door.

As soon as the dogs saw her, their affection was transferred to her.

Laughing, Bridget said, "Hi, you must be Francis."

She had gotten up from the table and put her arms out in welcome. The two women embraced.

Looking at her enlarged tummy, Francis said, "So lovely to meet you."

"We're pleased to meet you too."

Francis beamed. "How far on are you?"

"Almost eight months and counting."

The dogs were swirling around them as they picked up on the happy tones of the young women's voices, giving the occasional soft bark.

Martha chirped up. "Will yer put the dogs in the yard? I can see one of you going flying in a minute."

Bridget gave Francis a conspiratorial look. Both of them laughed.

"I can see you're gonna become partners in crime."

They didn't see Martha smiling to herself as she turned back to the washing up in the sink.

"How was the visit then, Francis?" Martha asked.

"Extraordinary. I can't quite believe it."

Bridget looked over at Francis. "Ma told me all about yerself and Michael."

"Oh, did she?"

Bridget hurried on. "Thank God the pair of yer are all right. Could have been much worse by all accounts. Like something out of the wild west. Yer must have been terrified."

"I was rather shaken up," Francis said.

"Shaken up?" Bridget exclaimed. "Bloody nightmare."

Martha's head spun. "Less of that, my girl."

159

Bridget and Francis gave one another a quick smile of understanding for the second time.

"Michael was so lucky. It doesn't bear thinking about."

"Indeed," Martha said.

"What time are we setting off for the hospital, Ma?" Bridget asked as she stretched, then stood up.

"As soon as yer daddy gets back. I thought we might have a bite to eat first. Then we can get going."

Having the habit of turning up whenever his name was mentioned, Joseph came in through the back door with the dogs close at his heels.

"Will yer feed the hounds?" Martha asked Joseph before he could take off his jacket. "They've been having a merry dance in here this morning with Bridget."

Joseph turned back to the door. "I'm on it," he mumbled, entering the pantry to get the dishes.

Shaking the box of feed, he held it in his hand. The three dogs dutifully followed him back outside to the yard.

The two young women between them were laying the table, ready for the lunch Martha had been preparing for them all most of the morning. The smell of the soup was making Francis' mouth water, along with the aroma of freshly baked bread. Martha began cutting the bread into chunks.

With Bridget and Francis sitting at the table, Martha started dishing up the tasty soup.

"Get stuck in, girls."

Martha smiled as the two eager young women didn't need to be told twice.

"Where's that man now?"

Martha's tutting made Bridget raise her eyebrow at Francis with a smile as she blew on her soup.

Francis thought Bridget was very much like Michael. She had that same cheeky, laid-back way about her. Their sense of humour was also the same as Joseph's. Francis was feeling very at home with them. It was an instant liking she was feeling for Bridget.

Liking, too, everything about their way of living all seemed appealing to her very nature. She felt she had been transported out of one life and into another. The world about her now was so utterly different.

As she listened to the banter between daughter and parents, she looked closely at Bridget.

Michael and his sister had both favoured their father's looks. Both had the same blue eyes and the same dark curly hair. Martha and Andrew, on the other hand, were more alike in stature, and fairer. Altogether, she summed up that they made a very loving family. The kind of family she was happy to know. Her thoughts now led her into uncertain territory. How long would it last?

Not dwelling on a negative thought, Francis let her mind return to the people around her. Joseph had sat down at the table and asked, "How did the meeting with Nuala go?"

They all waited for her to answer.

"It went very well."

Francis was happy to share her experience. She was saddened that Nuala had a letter from her brother but had only found it the day before Francis came to visit.

Joseph was shaking his head. "Poor woman, what a pity."

Francis continued. "There was a photograph, too, of Mum and Dad's wedding day. I briefly told her about the stabbing but didn't want to elaborate. I didn't want her worrying about me before we got to know each other."

The conversation continued as Joseph drove them to the hospital. He felt happy to listen to his wife as she spoke to their daughter and Francis. Their intermittent laughter made him smile. It was a tonic after the last few days. Michael was on the mend. The women were happy, and above all, Michael now had this lovely girl in his life, but he couldn't help but wonder for how long. Francis had another life, after all, in London.

When they arrived, Bridget stretched and was relieved to get out of the back seat. Her heavy load made travelling a bit awkward. She was looking forward to the baby's birth in about four or five weeks. Her mother told her on the phone that she shouldn't be travelling so much, but Bridget wouldn't hear a word. She begged her husband to drive her to her parents so she could visit her brother in the hospital. She knew she could stay over with her parents; her daddy could bring her home on Sunday. She was now far too big to sit behind the steering wheel.

Michael had always gotten on well with Bridget. She was just a couple years older than him. Though the pair joked and teased one another, they had a very close bond, loving one another dearly. Bridget had been beside herself when she heard the terrible news that her little brother had been stabbed. They approached the ward Michael was on. The girls went ahead through the swing doors. Michael's bed was empty.

Joseph went straight over to a nurse, who was talking to the man in the contraption. He was still lying there in exactly the same position. His face was the only part that wasn't in bandages.

"Excuse me," he asked apologetically. "Michael Connor?"

"Ah," the nurse said. "He's been moved."

She gave Joseph directions as the women watched and waited till Joseph returned.

"He's been moved," he said. "Come on."

They went back out the swing doors and took a small flight of stairs to the next floor, down a long corridor, a right turn, and then left. Finally, Joseph knew exactly which one of the doors led to Michael's room. There was a Garda seated outside the door. As they approached, he stood up.

"Can I enquire who you are?" he asked.

Joseph spoke up, telling him who they were, then whispered a few words in the young man's ear.

"Thank you, sir."

He smiled and held himself up a little straighter, reached for the door handle and opened it for them. The three women went in first.

"Good work," Joseph said to the Garda as he passed him on the way in.

Michael was sitting in a chair by the window. Bridget waddled towards her brother.

"Well, there's a sight," Michael said, joking, looking at his sister.

When Bridget got near enough, she reached out and ruffled his hair. "Who's the eejit who got himself stabbed then?" Bridget taunted.

Michael was trying to duck out of the way. "Get off, will yer?"

Bridget bent over awkwardly due to her pregnancy and kissed the top of his head.

"Should have taken the knife to yer hair," she quipped.

The women laughed.

Joseph didn't laugh but asked seriously, "Why have they moved you, son, and put a Garda at the door?"

The women fell silent. Suddenly, the mood in the room had changed.

Michael was looking at Francis' frightened face. The realisation that there could still be more trouble had made her shiver. Michael didn't want anything else to upset the relationship that had hardly got going between them. He knew instantly he was not going to tell them the whole truth.

Making light of it, he replied, "Ah, it's just a precaution."

He quickly changed the subject. Michael didn't want any more fussing. "I can come home after seeing the doc." He looked at Francis with that twinkle in his eye. "That, they tell me, will be Monday morning. One of you can pick me up Monday."

"That's grand," Martha said.

Michael watched Francis' face as the relief showed itself, and she beamed at him, unable to contain her engaging smile.

CHAPTER 27

Vinnie and Coral, alias the Darlings, were ambling around Kinsale in no particular hurry. Having had lunch out, they enjoyed themselves in the afternoon sunshine.

It was a busy Saturday afternoon with a market on one of its colourful streets. People had come into the town from the outskirts for their weekly shopping spree, swelling the local community. The church bells had been ringing, following a wedding, creating an almost carnival feeling. All sorts of people were taking their time to browse around the stalls. The cafes were doing a brisk trade, and the restaurants and pubs. Previously the pair had walked alongside the harbour, where many boats were moored.

A playground on the opposite side of the road boasted swings and a roundabout, a place where families were meeting up. Their children ran about happily, laughing and playing. The two walked arm in arm. Having had her fill of sightseeing and walking, Coral turned to her partner.

"Shall we take that drive out to the hospital now and see what we can find out?"

"Suppose," Vinnie replied rather sulkily.

He had become lethargic after his lunch and was thinking about a relaxing afternoon back at the hotel. Coral had other ideas.

"I thought we should phone in and see what Laura thinks about what we have found out so far." She went on enthusiastically. "If we go there first, we might have more to add. See what I'm saying?"

"Suppose you've got something there," he replied after thinking it through.

"It's not far. The hotel said about twenty minutes."

"All right, let's go."

Vinnie plunged his hands deep into his pockets.

The couple walked back to the hotel and got into their car. Twenty-five minutes later, they were parked in the hospital car park. They looked at each other.

"Here we are. What do you reckon now?"

Vinnie had no forethought about what they were meant to be doing. His mind was all about enjoying himself.

"Shall we go in and see what we can see?" Coral offered, as sweet as possible, knowing only too well of his mood swings. He could fly into a temper at the drop of a hat. Coral knew he was a strange mix.

Now he snapped, "We don't know what the copper looks like."

He was glaring at Coral. His brown eyes had a flat, unreadable darkness. The curl of his mouth was like a snarling animal about to pounce. It was his way of venting his temper at what he now thought was an impossible task.

Quietly and seductively was the way to handle him. However, she was beginning to get tired of putting up with his unreasonable ways. She simply smiled at him now.

"Leave it to me. Come on, Vinnie, we have nothing to lose."

Knowing he would watch her, Coral got out of the car, flicking her straight long blond hair over her shoulders, down her back. She looked over her shoulder at him. Vinnie, still sitting in the car, watched her as she began to walk towards the hospital's main entrance. Her jeans were as tight as they could possibly be. She walked like a temptress, flicking her hair from left to right. She knew how to handle him. He couldn't take his eyes off her.

Finally, he got out of the car, locked it and looked about. Not that many cars there, he thought.

Coral waited as he ambled over to her. Soon as he got to her, she hooked hold of his arm and kissed his cheek.

"Exciting, isn't it?"

She smiled and squeezed his arm with her hands. He was calming down again.

"I can think of better things to do."

Laughing, she said, "Later, we will."

They walked into the lobby of the hospital. There were wards to the left and to the right of them. There was also a cafe in the far corner. Coral looked to the reception area and approached.

"Hello," she said. "Men's surgical?" she enquired with a beaming smile.

"On the left," the woman said without looking up.

They started in that direction. There were swing doors leading off at the right and left of the corridor. Coral popped her head in one set of doors. She quickly took in that there were four elderly men on the ward. Each had an equally elderly visitor sitting beside them.

Coral didn't think he was any of those men. A jolly-faced woman approached, wheeling a noisy trolley. The tea trolley was loaded and rattled its way towards them.

"Hello," Coral said.

The jolly-faced woman gave her a smile.

"Don't suppose you know where Michael Connor is? The hero," she added for good measure.

"Sure I do. He's the fella that got himself stabbed. Everyone talks about him, yer know. They moved him. He's upstairs now. I've just taken them tea. His family are with him, and his girl. Are you related?"

"No, not related, but just really good friends."

Coral smiled. The lies trickled like honey from her mouth and as sweetly, too.

"Just take the flight of stairs. You can't miss it. There's a Garda on the door."

She pushed off her trolley again as it rattled its way towards the other set of swing doors. Coral's quick thinking caused her to call after her. The woman stopped her trolley and waited.

"I just had a thought," she said sweetly. "Did you say his girlfriend? You see, I don't want to step on anyone's toes."

Coral wanted to imply she could be romantically connected.

The woman nodded, thinking, *And why wouldn't he have the women after him?* answering "Yes, I did say that. There are his parents and another pregnant one. Think she's the sister."

"Thank you very much. You're very kind."

Coral walked back, smiling at Vinnie, looking triumphant when she reached him.

"Come on," she said. "Let's get a cuppa in that café."

When they got to a table of Coral's choosing, she sat down facing out towards the route that an older couple, a redhead, and a pregnant woman together would have to take to exit the hospital.

Vinnie came back with two cups of tea. "What now?"

166

"We sit here and watch till they appear, and then we follow."

Coral couldn't help but feel euphoric at her success. She picked up the cup of tea and blew gently across the surface before taking a sip, not taking her eyes off the lobby. They sat there for another twenty minutes before their prey appeared. The two young women were laughing together, with the older man and woman walking behind.

"We're on," Coral said, standing up. "Get the keys out, Vinnie. Let's go."

They were hot behind the unsuspecting family. The cunning pair fell in step silently behind, listening to as much of their conversation as possible.

"Yer man's coming home," Bridget said to Francis.

"The girls are getting on fine, don't yer think, Joe?"

"Aye, that they are."

Joseph's mind was wandering. Though he didn't say anything to Martha, he was thinking about Michael and feeling a little uneasy.

"So, what are yer plans?" Bridget asked Francis.

Coral's eyes were on Francis. She watched as Francis turned her head towards the pregnant girl, listening and waiting to hear her reply.

"I'm not certain. I do love it here but I know for sure I will have to go back to London sometime. Finding Aunt Nuala has helped me to think about staying, and then there is your lovely brother."

They were all at the main entrance. Politely, Joseph held the door open and stood aside for the women to pass through. Coral skipped past, too, looking up at Joseph and thanked him. She was really enjoying this task that Laura had set them. It appealed to her conniving nature. She liked being the one in the know. Made her feel authoritative. Vinnie, on the other hand, found it a bit tiresome. He was more for a bit of action. Sneaking around in some backwater in Ireland, of all places, didn't appeal to his nature. He was a sexual predator, and he took delight in performing.

At first, he liked the idea of being away from London, and Laura for a while, having Coral all to himself, but he could tell Coral was really getting a buzz out of this sleuthing lark.

167

He hoped that when they made the phone call, Laura would tell them to return home.

When they reached their car, Coral told him to follow the family.

She hadn't taken her eyes off Francis, watching as she helped the pregnant woman into the back seat. With Joseph at the wheel, they took their time, which allowed Vinnie to fall in at a safe distance and follow. Coral took out a packet of cigarettes from her bag. Taking two out, she lit them both at the same time and offered one over to Vinnie.

Winding down the window a little, she inhaled the smoke deeply. Blowing it out again, she sighed.

"That's better."

As they followed, out onto the country lanes, Vinnie dropped back, not wanting to be noticed. There were few other cars around. Coral's eyes were firmly fixed on Joseph's car. Vinnie decided to let her have her way. She was clearly a lot better at this lark than he was.

Finally, she spoke to Vinnie. "Did you hear?" she asked.

"Hear what?"

"The redhead is English," she said. "Lives in London."

"So?" Vinnie said. "We have been asked to find out about them over here."

"Yeah, well," Coral said. "Laura will be interested that she is from London and that she will be going back sometime."

"Do you think?"

Coral shook her head in disbelief.

"Perhaps the copper is based in London too. Don't you see, Vinnie? They are a couple."

He laughed. "A couple? A couple of what?"

He thought that was highly funny. Coral played along again.

"Well, yeah, I get you."

Coral laughed too. The mood in the car lifted as they followed.

Vinnie's mood was happier now, which had made Coral less tense. Another car had overtaken them and was now driving in front of them. But the roads were so easy to drive along that they were happy to keep their distance.

"Don't they have funny names over here?"

Vinnie had noticed the signpost for Clonakilty.

"Yeah, they do," Coral admitted.

The next signpost was Rosscarbery.

They followed Joseph's car right up until they realised he was turning into a driveway. Coral took a mental note of where exactly they were. As they slowed further down the lane, she asked Vinnie to pull in when he could. Coral took out the visitor's map that she had taken from the hotel. She began looking at it until Vinnie pulled in.

"So where are we then?" Vinnie asked.

The two were looking intently at the map. Coral pointed with her painted red fingernail.

"Here," she said, tapping at the exact spot on the map.

"Could do with a pee," Vinnie said as he jumped out of the car and piddled against the back wheel.

Coral laughed to herself as she watched him in the car wing mirror.

"Dirty little bugger," she muttered.

Vinnie got back in the car and started up the engine.

"Where now, me lady?"

"Let's get back to the hotel, make that call and see what Laura has to say. Then the evening will be ours."

Coral smiled at Vinnie.

"Sounds good to me."

He spun the car around and headed back the way they had come. As they approached the driveway, Coral made mental notes as to the distance they would have to drive, leading them back to the village of Rosscarbery, so she could easily find it again if needed.

Content in their findings, the couple drove the simple route back to Kinsale.

The sky was darkening as clouds had started to gather. The sun was about to dip below the horizon. Though neither of them took any notice of the glorious changing colours created by the sun's salute to the end of daylight.

***

At Ash House, the lights were being turned on. Martha drew the curtains in the lounge. She returned to her kitchen to make the girls a cup of tea. Francis and Bridget had settled themselves in comfy armchairs next to each other. Bridget was chatting away to Francis about her life in Bantry.

"It's quite a large town," she said. "It has everything I need, that's for sure. It's not such a bad place to live."

Francis listened intently.

"Con, my husband, is a school teacher. We moved there because the offer of teaching in the school there suited him fine."

"Does he enjoy it? Teaching."

"Yes, he does. He is a natural with the kiddies. They all love him."

"What age is he teaching?"

"Ten to eleven years olds. A lot of prep work before they move on up to the next level."

Bridget spoke proudly about her husband. Their relationship was going along just fine. They had a lovely home. Bridget was now expecting their second child. She had created a loving, happy home to bring her children up in. The same kind of upbringing she had experienced. Bridget carried on telling of her life in Bantry.

"I was so grateful to Con for driving me up yesterday. Plus, for looking after Liam. He can be a bit of a handful when he gets going."

Before Francis could reply, she carried on. "It was great to see Michael, though, wasn't it? He looked really well."

Francis pitched in before she could carry on further.

"It sounds like you have your hands full in Bantry and now the new baby."

Bridget put her hand to her tummy and stroked it. "I'll be glad when this one arrives."

Francis looked at her. "Your life obviously suits you. You look wonderful."

"Easy living," she replied. "And plenty of fresh air. Straight off the Atlantic."

"Yes, now you mention it, I've noticed the air here is so much sweeter than in London."

"Don't know how you manage that," Bridget replied. "Living in London, that is."

"I guess it is because I was born to it." Francis sighed. "I am not looking forward to going back, I must say."

"Don't then," Bridget said. "Take hold of yer life, and live it how you want."

"You make a lot of sense, Bridget, but I do have a job. My home is there."

"Two things that can be simply remedied," Bridget replied. "Sell up and quit."

Francis laughed. "You make it sound so easy."

Martha came in with tea on a tray. "Make what sound easy?" she enquired, putting down the tray on the nearby table.

"Quitting London, and my job," Francis said.

"You are?" Martha asked.

Her head nearly spun off her shoulders. Bridget laughed at her mother's reaction.

"She would if she's got any sense."

Bridget hoped she would. She had taken to Francis just as quickly as her brother had. Bridget had sown a seed. The three women looked at each other without saying another word about it. Though Francis never answered, she found the idea of selling up and moving over here most appealing.

"Where's Da?" Bridget asked.

"Seeing to the donkey. He's taken it up the lane to Tom's place." Martha cocked her head. "Would you believe he said she needs a bit of company besides the dogs?"

"That's good, Ma. They do like a bit of company."

Bridget was smiling at Francis.

"Tom said his one gets more than enough company. He's got three donkeys up there and a couple of ponies too."

"Now yer Da reckons he will get another donkey for old Blossom."

"I told him, all on your own head be it. I want nothing to do with it. Haven't I enough to do with this big old place, him and three dogs too?"

Ma paused to drink her tea.

Bridget and Francis found it highly amusing.

By the time Joseph returned, the evening meal had been made, with the table set. They all tucked into Martha's good home cooking.

It had been a pleasant evening for Francis. The realisation of feeling so relaxed, to the point where she found she was almost nodding off, was not lost on her. The old clock in the hallway chimed nine o'clock.

"I think I should go to bed now. I feel really tired."

Her small voice sounded sleepy.

"Of course," Martha said. "It's been a busy day for us all. Get yourself off. You too, Bridget. You should make the most of the little bit of peace yer have left to yourself."

Francis was relieved. She was not used to so much chit-chat in the evenings. Bridget eased herself up.

"Think you're right, Ma." She waddled to the door. "Night," she called as she closed the door behind her.

She was looking forward to reading a few pages of her mystery murder book as she lay in the big soft bed that used to be hers.

Francis said goodnight and thanked Joseph and Martha for the lovely evening.

She was beginning to realise that although she lived and worked in one of the busiest places in the world, she had become very reclusive. Nearly all her evenings since her parents died had been spent alone. Being here now within this family, her mind was changing. Although tired as she was, she was still more alive than she had been in years.

Francis climbed the stairs to the guest room with many questions.

Now lying in her bed, she turned off the lamp, and with the curtains open, she waited until her eyes had adjusted to the darkness. Out of the window, she could see the sky. There were clouds passing high above as the wind sent them scudding across her view. Patches of the inky darkness beyond were studded with twinkling stars. She had never recalled such a beautiful sight. There in the silence, Francis thought about Michael. There hadn't been much said between them. Bridget had commanded most of the visiting time. She had been so pleased to see her brother. Apparently, it had been months since their last catch-up.

Francis was just happy to see him more like himself, watching him as he reacted to his sister's playfulness.

As she had been the last to say goodbye to him, Francis now recalled their kiss. His lips had been so firm, commanding and urgent. It had sent feelings throughout her body. Feelings that she wanted more of. She was now longing to be his. Her self-control was longing to give way to his masculine force.

As she lay there now, looking at the stars, she started to think and imagine what it would be like to lay naked next to him. His strong arms around her, his hand exploring her nakedness, and she his. She sighed with the realisation that there was an undeniable electricity between them. She knew it would not be very long before she would give in, giving herself to him totally.

He had whispered in her ear as the others had left the room.

"'There's something important I want to ask yer, and I'm praying you will say yes."

"Is there?" she had answered coyly.

"Tomorrow, we will talk," Michael said.

Wishing now with all her heart, she had replied, "Ask me now."

But the moment had gone. Francis had seen it in his eyes. He had stopped himself from saying anything else. Since then, she had been wondering what. What was he going to ask her? Francis would find out tomorrow when she visited. She felt sure he would ask her to stay in Ireland.

With that in mind, she thought about tomorrow. While Joseph and Martha were taking Bridget home, she would phone Nuala and ask if she might visit later in the morning. Then she would drive herself back to the hospital to visit Michael.

Watching the night sky, her eyes had become weary, her mind settled, and she drifted off to sleep.

After about four hours, Francis' eyes opened, and she was suddenly wide awake. Looking out at the night, there were no clouds now, just a sky filled with stars. Getting out of bed, she went to the window. Was it a dream? Yes, just a dream. Looking at that magnificent night sky, she thought she heard something. No, it was not in the house. All was silent. It might have been a screech from a wild animal, a fox perhaps, or maybe an owl. There was nothing. It must have been a dream, but somehow it felt like a warning. As she returned to her bed, she felt chilled.

It was her father. He was there, right by her bed as she lay sleeping. There was something he was trying to tell her. Something she couldn't quite understand. As he faded away in the dream, he was saying, *follow your heart, follow your heart.*

She heard the clock in the hallway striking three.

"How strange. It had to be a dream."

She snuggled back and wrapped the covers around herself until sleep found her again.

A few hours later, sunshine filled the room as Francis slowly opened her eyes. She felt as though she had slept deeply. A long stretch and yawn helped her wake up. The thought about the dream flooded into her mind.

She sat up, looking about the room, and decided she would have a shower.

The smell of bacon cooking wafted to her as she descended the stairs. Her long hair was still damp, though towel dried as best she could.

There was Martha back at the range.

"Morning," Martha said.

Francis greeted her in return. "Morning, can I help myself to a cuppa?"

"Help yerself. There's a fresh pot. What can I get you to eat?"

Francis did not feel that hungry. She felt she had been eating far too much since being there, though she had enjoyed every mouthful. Martha's forte was to keep those around her well-fed.

"Perhaps just some toast and marmalade?" she answered politely, pouring a mug of tea.

Martha left the range and went to a cupboard. She took out a ceramic pot.

"There's some of my homemade marmalade. Tell me what yer think. Milk's there in the jug."

"Thank you." Francis smiled as the toast presented itself from the pop-up toaster.

"You seem to make everything look so easy," she said to Martha. "Your cooking is just wonderful."

Martha beamed. "Years of practice, love." She chuckled.

Francis spooned some of the marmalade onto the side of her plate, as Martha placed hot toast in front of her.

"Now yer sure that's going to be enough for yer?"

"More than enough." Francis took a bite of the toast with Martha's homemade marmalade on it. "That is so delicious."

"Another recipe I'll have to show yer then."

Joseph came in through the back door. "That's the animals

seen to. Morning Francis, how's it going?"

He dropped into his chair at the far end of the table.

"Morning. Just enjoying your wife's wonderful marmalade."

"Aye, she's a fine cook. I've filled yer car up for you."

"I am beginning to feel really spoilt, thank you. I'm hoping to go and visit Nuala this morning. How much do I owe you?"

Joseph didn't respond.

"Did yer not fancy the drive down to Bantry then?" Martha asked before Joseph could answer.

"I would have, but I told Michael I would go to see him." She hurried on, not wanting to sound ungrateful. "I thought you might like my help to make up his bed."

Francis flushed at the thought of mentioning Michael and his bed in the same breath.

"No, dear girl, that's all sorted," Martha said as she placed a huge cooked breakfast in front of Joseph.

"If you're sure. I feel as though I ought to be doing something."

Joseph stayed silent, tucking into his breakfast.

"Do you mind if I use the phone to call my aunt?"

"Of course yer can," Joseph and Martha said in unison.

Bridget appeared. "Tea, please, Ma."

She sat herself down. Her pregnancy was taking its toll.

"And good morning to you," Martha said. "Help yerself. It's in the pot."

"Bet it's gone cold now," Bridget said grumpily. "The baby's been giving me a right good kicking."

They all chuckled.

Francis jumped to her feet. "I'll put the kettle on and make some fresh, shall I?"

"Thanks, love," Martha said.

She liked Francis more each day.

CHAPTER 28

In Kinsale, the Darlings were having a lie-in.

Vinnie rolled himself on top of Coral. "Sod breakfast," he said.

They had spent their evening in the local pub. It had been an education, listening to the live Irish music from the band. They certainly had got the people singing, clapping and tapping their feet. The pints were being drunk as fast as they were pulled. The atmosphere was great. By ten thirty, all was being wound up.

"Just as I was enjoying myself," Vinnie moaned. "Come on then, let's get back to the hotel. You can dance to my tune now."

He stroked his finger along Coral's bottom lip while the other hand grabbed her around the waist.

She threw back her head and pushed her breasts towards him, sucking his finger until he pulled it away. "Can't wait," she said seductively.

Before they had gone to the pub, they had phoned Laura Popa on the way. They had both squeezed into the public phone box in the town. Coral talked while Laura Popa listened closely to every word. Coral gave her the names Francis Doyle and Michael Connor. Laura had asked her to spell out the names. It was now obvious to Coral that Laura would be writing everything down. She told her adorable Laura about the visit to the hospital.

"The stabbed copper was being guarded, so we couldn't get a look in."

"I see," Laura hissed.

Coral went on. "Francis Doyle and Michael Connor are an item. Apparently, it was Francis he was trying to save. That's when your brother was shot. Your brother stabbed the copper. It looks like your brother was out to take the girl."

"I see," Laura hissed down the phone again. "You have done vell, my darlings," she purred at Coral.

"We know where the family lives," Coral said triumphantly.

"You do? Excellent. Are you having fun, my little darlings?"

"Yes," Coral said. "We are."

With the mentality of a schoolgirl, Coral giggled.

"Vell, give me time to think," she purred. "How far are you from their family home?"

Coral was used to Laura's accent, but now Laura had a distinctly menacing tone in her voice.

"About twenty minutes or so," Coral replied.

"Is there anywhere nearer you can get to stay?"

"Yes, I think so," Coral said.

"Go there tomorrow and phone me again."

"One last thing," Coral said. "The girl, Francis Doyle, lives in London."

"London?" she spat. "Did you say London, here?"

"Yes."

Laura was taken aback. "Now isn't that interesting? Now listen carefully, Coral, I vant you to find out vhere. Do you think you can do that for me?"

"Yes, I'm sure I can. It might take a bit longer," she said softly.

"That's all right," Laura purred. "Just don't arouse suspicion. Stay avay from the hospital now. Ven, you find out vhere she lives, phone me. I hope to hear from you in a couple of days or as soon as you find out."

Laura didn't wait to say goodbye. She just hung up. Coral looked at the receiver of the phone. "She just hung up," she said almost to herself.

Vinnie was standing right next to her. Eager to get out, he asked, "All good?"

"Yeah," Coral said. "I'll tell you outside."

They left the little phone box and headed up the street into the chill of the night air to the pub.

***

Laura Popa had sat at her desk after the call from Coral. She had remained seated in her ornate chair. The single desk light illuminated her hand as she replaced the receiver back on the phone's cradle.

Now she gently strummed her long red fingernails on the desk's surface.

Her mind relived her baby brother's last moments. Dario was dead, and someone had to pay. It was she, and she alone, who needed to avenge his death. There was no one else she wanted to

177

give that task to. There was always someone for the right price. This was personal. She craved that satisfaction for herself. Why deny herself that pleasure? It would be the least she could do for her little brother. An eye for an eye came into her mind.

"I have to take my time and think everything through. Leave nothing to chance."

It had to be right. Even if it took her leaving London for this place, a place she had never even heard of.

Laura Popa was unsure of the exact plan, yet was confident that she would create the perfect gift for her little brother. Then she could rest easy and move on with her own life. She loved a project, after all. Her red lips curled in a twisted kind of half smile. She felt pleasure when she was planning to hurt someone. She needed to inflict pain on someone else, and then she could set her own pain free.

The room's dimness hid most of her face, yet her cat-like eyes seemed to glow as she thought her little darlings had done well.

***

Coral and Vinnie had stayed in their room until midday. They had not been interested enough to seek pleasure out in the sunshine of the glorious spring day. They had stayed in bed. Now with his energy spent with Coral, the church bells had begun to annoy Vinnie, and he was moaning again to Coral.

"Why do they ring so loud here? Bloody racket!"

He threw back the covers and got out of bed, his naked body disappearing into the bathroom.

"Let's get out of here," Coral shouted. "Hurry up, I want a shower too."

His head came out, and he looked at her lying there. "Come on then, there's room for two."

She sprang out of the bed, giggling.

An hour or so later, they were down at reception, paying up to make a hasty exit away from the town, just as the church bells started up again.

"What's the name of the next place, then?" Vinnie asked as he started the car.

Coral had her map out, spread across the dashboard.

"Let's try this place called Rosscarbery. We drove straight past last time. This time we can investigate. Might be some place to stay a night or two."

They drove out through the side entrance of the hotel, along the harbour road and out of the town, leaving Kinsale behind them.

***

Nuala was so pleased Francis had called her earlier. It had given her time to go to Mass, get back home and get the kettle on. It was such a grand day outside. She filled the kettle. There was much she wanted to tell Francis, but she decided to err on the side of caution. See how the land lay.

She had hardly stopped thinking about her since their first meeting. It would be good to see her again. She cheerfully went about her preparations.

Rummaging in the draw of the dresser, she found her secateurs and went out through the conservatory to pick some daffs. It was warm, and opening the window by the little table, Nuala considered setting up there. Francis seemed to favour being amidst the plants. She opened the doors, and the perfume of the garden delighted her.

"Good morning, plants," she said.

Now, with a good bunch of the various daffodils she had picked in her hand, Nuala came back into the kitchen just as the kettle started to whistle on the range.

"Just a minute," she said to the kettle. "My hands are full."

Placing the daffodils on the table, she grabbed the kettle and set it aside.

"There, that's better, peace again."

Taking a vase off the dresser, Nuala arranged the pretty flowers in the vase and placed them in the middle of the table.

"That brings in the sunshine."

Nuala was ready to receive Francis.

***

After Francis had waved goodbye to Joseph, Martha, and Bridget, she was in a thoughtful mood again.

Bridget was a breath of fresh air with her strong character.

Take hold of your life now and live it.

Again, she had said it. They were her parting words after the two women hugged.

"Bring that eejit brother of mine down for a visit, will yer?"

179

she said.

Smiling and waving, she eased herself into the back seat of her Da's car. Martha was next.

"If yer peckish, help yourself. Keep the dogs in the yard. Take the other back door key when you visit yer auntie. Take her something from the pantry. There's plenty there."

"Come on, Ma," Joseph said. "I'm sure Francis will be fine."

He looked at Francis and winked, and got himself in the driver's seat.

"I will," a smiling Francis called out. "Safe journey."

"Give Michael a kiss from me."

Martha's voice was just audible through her wound-down window as Joseph made the turn and drove off down the drive.

"I will." Francis answered.

Though Martha never heard her reply.

Francis felt rather strange being in the house alone. She went out into the yard. The dogs, Molly, Finn and Murphy, got up and came to her, wagging their tails.

"Hello," she said, giving each of them a tickle around their ears. "Well, it's a lovely day," she told them as she started to walk down the garden.

The three dogs dutifully followed her. Murphy, the Irish wolfhound, slowly came to her side and nuzzled her hand as they strolled along.

"Are you all right?" Francis asked.

His beautiful eyes looked sorrowfully up at her.

"They won't be long," she said soothingly.

Francis couldn't help but sit on the grass and cuddle him. The other two, who had been sniffing around, now bounded in, trying to nuzzle up for some of the action. Francis laughingly tried to tickle all three and lost herself in the happy throng. Finally, she got up, walked as far as the large garden allowed, and then decided she had better get going.

Ensuring all was secure, she washed her hands and brushed her hair. Nuala should be home from Mass.

At the last minute, she remembered to go into the pantry. Looking in, she found Martha had already placed some freshly made scones in the basket for her to take.

"Martha Connor," Francis muttered. "You're a lovely lady."

Out into the sunshine once more, Francis placed the basket on the back seat of her car.

She was still thinking about Martha, how considerate she was, and Joseph too. They couldn't be any more helpful than they were, letting her stay in their home, a stranger.

Her car jumped to life as soon as she turned the key. Francis patted the dashboard in thanks. Amazingly, her Auntie Nuala was not more than ten minutes down the same lane where Ash House was situated.

She was still amazed at the coincidence of it all, and it had all felt so right, her being there. She had much to consider, and seeing her auntie might help her decide.

Nuala greeted her as she took the basket from the back seat.

"Morning Francis, 'tis another grand day," she called.

As Francis approached, she reached out to her auntie and kissed her on the cheek.

"Yes, it's lovely, such a beautiful blue sky. I have been so lucky with the weather since I have been here. Someone told me it always rains in Ireland."

Nuala laughed. "Now you know different. Come on, let's go in."

They went through into the kitchen. Francis could see she was all prepared for her visit.

"Is it tea or coffee this morning?"

"Tea, please."

Francis sat down at the table.

"Are you comfy there?" Nuala asked.

"Yes, fine, thanks. I think there are some scones in the basket."

Francis emptied the basket contents on the table: two containers, one with scones, while the other had a sponge sandwich. "Looks like cream and jam this time," Francis said.

Nuala brought a pot of tea to the table.

"That looks like a thing of beauty," she exclaimed. "Martha Connor sure knows how to bake. Let's have a chunk of that with our tea."

The two women looked rather alike at either end of the table. With only the years between them, they were so comfortable in each other's company. No one would guess from the sight that this was just their second meeting.

"It's lovely to see you again, Auntie Nuala."

Francis cut a wedge of Martha's sponge. "Oh," Francis laughed. "That's a big piece."

"You'll manage, I have no doubt," Nuala said cheerfully.

Francis wanted to tell Nuala about her strange dream. After a mouthful of cake and a sip of her tea, she said, "I had a dream of my dad last night."

Nuala looked up and put her cake back on the plate before eating.

"You did? That was nice, wasn't it?"

Nuala looked at Francis with an enquiring gaze.

"Yes, it was, but I thought it was a bit strange."

"In what way?"

Nuala was interested in where this was going.

"I was awake almost instantly, feeling like he was in my room. I feel bits are missing. It was three in the morning. I know that because the clock struck in the hallway."

Nuala was all ears.

"I went over to the window to look out. I thought I heard a wild animal screeching. Perhaps a fox or an owl. It's a bit muddled, but I thought my dad was in the room. I could see him and hear him speaking to me."

"Go on," Nuala said. "Then what happened?"

"Well, this was a strange thing to say, but he told me to follow my heart. Then he faded away, and so did his voice."

"That sounds like good advice to me."

Nuala was looking hard at Francis.

"Have you seen your mother or father before?"

"No, I have never dreamed of either of them."

"Well, Francis, what do you think?"

Nuala wanted to judge how these kinds of matters, which were second nature to herself, affected Francis. Could she believe that her father had really come to her to give her advice to follow her heart?

Francis looked quizzically at her aunt.

"I'd like to think it was really him."

"What if I was to tell you I think it was?"

Nuala spoke in a serious, matter-of-fact way.

182

"Really?" Francis said, half surprised at her for entertaining such a thought, yet really hoping with all her heart it was.

Nuala drank her tea. "I'll start at the beginning," she said. "See what you think then."

Francis sat back in her chair, excited, curious and enjoying very much being with her auntie. She could feel the bond between them growing as she listened to Nuala's lilting Irish tones. Apart from taking in every word, she thought she had come home.

Nuala carried on.

"When I was a child, we lived not far from here. It was always my mother, your father and me. My father was killed; shot, I believe. Leaving my poor ma without support. It was hard living here back then, especially for a woman alone with two small children. She managed somehow. Robert was a great comfort to her; I see that now. I was always in a world of my own. Your da always looked out for me, though."

Francis was enthralled hearing all this for the first time.

"My childhood was a wonder to me. I thought everyone was the same as me. It took quite a bit of time for me to realise I was different."

Francis was all ears. She was gripped. "Different in what way?"

"Well, yer see, Francis, I could see the dead. All those people would appear to me. I don't know how or why. It's just the way of it. I used to see my da, so I never thought there was anything to worry about. We had many conversations when I was growing up."

"Did your mother know?"

Francis had heard of people like Nuala, people with a gift or a curse, whichever way you wanted to look at it.

Nuala smiled. "We never really spoke about it as I didn't think there was anything wrong. I can remember telling my ma that da said, *All will be well, not to worry.* She would just smile and cuddle me to her. When she passed, I used to see her as well."

Nuala paused for Francis to respond.

"Goodness me, Auntie, that truly is amazing."

Nuala decided to refresh the pot, and she stood up. She wanted her words to settle in her niece's mind, giving her time to come to terms with what she was telling her.

It was quite possible that Robert had made himself seen to Francis, knowing perhaps now was a good time. Now she was here in Ireland, where there was nothing to clutter the brain, close to nature, she would perhaps find her way. It was obvious to Nuala now that Robert was concerned for his daughter. Francis was half right, she thought, as the dream was a warning. The screeching she had heard before her father appeared, the time too, all these were warning signs to Nuala. Also, the fact that Robert had come to her twice. Now he was telling her to keep an eye on Francis.

With the fresh tea now in the pot, Francis returned from the toilet, eager to hear anything else her auntie might have to say.

"Here yer are. Shall we have another cuppa and take it in the garden?"

"That would be lovely."

Francis' love of plants made her eager. Her aunt's garden looked rather special, judging by the glimpses she had seen from the conservatory.

"I have quite a few plants of my own but only a small yard. I would love to have a proper garden. I have collected quite a few indoor plants. Lucky for me my neighbours are looking after those whilst I'm here."

Nuala smiled. "I don't think I could survive without a garden. Yer see, I'm a bit of a herbalist too."

The two women went out into the garden. The birds were singing their hearts out, busy flying in and out, swooping closely by, almost in greeting. Francis felt she was in a very special place like no other she had ever known.

"This is quite magical. It seems you have a lot to look after here."

Francis was looking down the garden path. It was long and lay on the right-hand side. It had a broad border on the outside, backed by a tall brick wall. A perfect place for all the herbs. They were now coming back into life. With the protection of the wall came the extra benefit of the sun's warmth, as its rays warmed the old bricks. It seemed to stretch into the distance far beyond Francis' sight. The rest of the garden was a creation that needed to be walked through to see it. It was an old mature garden, full of interest, a garden to delight all the senses of sight, smell and sounds.

Francis thought about how the approaching summer months would take it into another dimension of beauty.

Nuala's voice brought her back to the here and now.

"Do yer like it then?" she asked.

"Do I?" Francis exclaimed. "I think it is just wonderful. I was just thinking to myself how glorious it must be in the summer months. It's a real credit to you. Can we take a stroll?"

Nuala took hold of Francis' arm, and they started their meander, not along the path but through the shrubbery and onto one of the many gravel paths. As they strolled, they chatted about the different plants, trees and shrubs along the way. Francis became lost in what was for her an ideal and magical garden. It was as though it had been created for her. Her newfound auntie had magic, too. Her voice was soothing and calm as she told Francis the various names. There were many Francis did not know.

Nuala had not had this kind of interaction herself for many years. She was just as delighted and eager as Francis. Before them now was an arbour where roses would bloom. There were many buds already swelling. Nuala had placed a welcomed bench to rest there, the perfect place. Come June, the roses would fill the area with their intoxicating perfume.

The two women sat down. Francis was surprised when she glanced back that the house had completely disappeared from view.

"This is such a lovely spot to sit."

"I often do. I sit here to meditate."

"Meditate," Francis repeated.

"Wouldn't yerself, if you were here?"

"I wouldn't know how."

"Would yer like to know? I can teach yer that. I'm sure yer would be very proficient with just a bit of advice."

Francis found the idea appealing.

"Do you think? What would you say the benefits of it were?"

"Well, that can be different for different people. I can tell yer what it does for me."

"Oh, go on then. Please show me how, if you think I can."

Nuala told Francis to sit back and keep both feet firmly on the ground. "Yer should have comfy loose clothes on, and bare feet help."

Francis kicked off her shoes and took her socks off.

"Close your eyes."

Francis obeyed every word.

"Now concentrate on yer breathing, slowly in and out. Listen to the sounds of the garden around yer, and without opening your eyes, visualise what the garden looks like."

Nuala remained silent for a while. Her voice softly came into Francis' hearing.

"From there, let yer mind drift. Once you're comfortable with yer surroundings, not thinking of any one thing in particular, just breathe in and out, in and out."

Nuala's voice was getting softer as she spoke. Her voice faded as she visually saw Francis drifting to where her mind wanted to be. Her shoulders had dropped.

Francis felt distant, only hearing the birds. She felt very peaceful. There was nothing but the warmth of the sun. Her body was as light as a feather. The feather she watched as it drifted silently down before her. All became silent. Not even the birds could be heard. Warmed by the sun, she had been lulled into this comfortable, peaceful place.

Now someone was walking towards her. A woman.

Francis strained to see who it was; the sun had moved and cast a shadow, but as she watched in happy anticipation and curiosity, the shadow moved slowly. Francis was mesmerised, watching as it drifted away revealing the woman's identity. It was her mother.

Oh, Mum! she exclaimed, though no words were spoken. Her mother waved, smiling, and then slowly turned and started walking away. Francis kept looking but realised that her vision had ended. She naturally thought about the birds singing, and their sound returned to her. She slowly opened her eyes.

Nuala was sitting silently beside her.

"I saw my mother. I actually saw my mother."

"Well now, isn't that nice?"

"Nice?" Francis said. "It was fantastic."

"Not bad for a first try. I'm impressed," Nuala said light-

186

heartedly.

Francis took hold of Nuala's hand. "How did I do that?" she questioned.

"I'm not sure," Nuala said. "I guess yer more like me than just looks."

Nuala could feel Francis' energy through her hand.

Suddenly tears started to roll down Francis' face. She was engulfed by emotion. It was as though the floodgates that had held back years of pent-up grief had suddenly opened, releasing from her very core that which had been drowning her.

"Let it out," Nuala said. "Let it out, Francis, you're safe."

Nuala took hold of her other hand as Francis did just that.

It seemed her auntie had given her permission to let go. With every racking sob, she was being cleansed, washing out the old Francis and bringing in the new.

Finally, the tears subsided.

"Oh my!" Francis said. "I'm so sorry. I just don't know or understand."

Nuala handed her a handkerchief. As Francis blew her nose, Nuala assured her that all was well.

"It's all right, perfectly natural for yer to let go. Obviously, yer needed to do that. When was the last time yer cried like that?"

Francis searched her auntie's face and saw nothing but kindness and concern for her.

"Never," Francis admitted.

"I thought not. Well, my dear girl, it's no wonder. Yer have been wound up tight, like a screw, for so long. You'll be feeling a whole lot better now, I promise. Come on, let's get the kettle on. You've been sitting there for over an hour."

Francis gasped. "An hour?"

"Did yer know," Nuala said laughingly, "yer have a habit of repeating things I say?"

They both laughed and took themselves back to the house.

Back at the table with the kettle on again, Nuala asked Francis, "Would yer like to tell me about yer man?"

"How did you know I was going to talk about Michael?"

Nuala just raised an eyebrow at her. "Do you really have to ask me that?" she said.

"I guess not. I think you know me better than I know myself."

"I'm sure when you get to my age, you'll be all-knowing too."
Nuala knew she was catching on fast.

With another cup of tea in front of them, Francis launched in.
"I think I'm in love."

"When is he getting out of the hospital?"

Francis was beginning to look at her auntie in a whole new light. She was something else.

"Tomorrow, and I will see him this afternoon, well, when I leave here. Yesterday, he said he would ask me something and hoped the answer would be yes."

"Did he now? Sounds interesting. What d'yer think that something is, then?"

"I think he is going to ask me to move here."

"What do yer think of that idea?"

"I would have to give up my job," Francis slowly answered.

"How would that make yer feel?"

Francis thought again, then replied, "I'm used to my independence and have been for the past ten years."

Francis realised the way Nuala asked her questions was purely to get her thinking it through for herself.

"And?" Nuala asked enquiringly, prompting her.

"Well, I have worked hard there."

"Is that so important to yer now? You have worked hard, I'm sure, yet yer didn't say you would miss it."

Francis looked at her canny auntie. "You're right. I wouldn't. I've had enough of it, to be honest."

"What else then? There is yer home. What about that?"

"I'm not sure. It was Mum and Dad's home, you see."

"Didn't Robert, I mean, your daddy, tell yer to follow your heart? Where is your heart, Francis?"

"Here," Francis said immediately.

They sat quietly, looking at each other, then drank their tea in unison.

Nuala waited for Francis to speak. She did not intend to tell the young woman what to do. She thought Michael Connor would ask Francis to marry him, if she was any judge. Nuala was also weighing up in her mind the significant meaning of her brother's concern. It would not be because of Michael. Otherwise, he would not have told Francis to follow her heart.

He had asked Nuala to keep an eye on her. What was the danger? Nuala was thinking hard. Her mother came there to this place, smiling and happy.

All in all, Nuala had decided that for Francis, the danger lay elsewhere, but where?

"Are you all right, Auntie?"

Francis wondered what she was thinking. She was looking at her vacantly. She could tell her mind was somewhere else.

"Sorry, I was miles away, just thinking and wondering what yer gonna decide."

Francis had decided.

Speaking to her auntie had cleared her mind. She was feeling energised.

"I love it here," she stated. "I have had enough of London. It has taken me to get myself here to realise what a terrible rut I was in, and the boring person I have become."

Nuala interrupted there. "No, Francis, yer are far from ever being boring. Yer just beginning."

Francis smiled. "I hope so," she said and then carried on. "To think I was working in London all this time, when there was all this just across the water. Finding you has been the best thing that has ever happened to me."

"And yer man," Nuala said.

"Yes, and Michael. He is rather gorgeous. I feel as though I have known him a lifetime."

"That's just how it should be. I felt like that about my David. We knew one another almost from the off. He only had to touch my hand and my knees would weaken. I thought I was in paradise when he kissed me. We couldn't wait. We used to go to the woods, where no one would find us, and, well, yer know what I mean."

Francis blushed pink. "Auntie!"

"It's the truth. Yer can't deny those kinds of feelings yer have. Not when you're young and the hormones start leaping."

"You're a caution and a tonic." Francis laughed. "I shall phone the office Monday morning and tell them to take the rest of my holiday time as my formal notice period. They have a girl in to cover for me whilst I'm on holiday and I'm sure she will jump at the chance to take my place. So no worries there."

"What about your home? You own it, don't you?"

"Yes, outright. Mum and Dad left it to me." Francis thought momentarily and said, "I shall put it on the market and buy something here. Something with a garden."

She couldn't hide the joy she felt. Saying it all out loud made her excited.

"To start with, yer could come and live here for a while."

"Could I?"

"Of course yer could. Why on earth not? I would love to have some company, your company."

Francis leapt to her feet and threw her arms around her aunt. "I am so happy."

"I'm happy too, Francis. Will yer do one thing for me?" Nuala's mind was now rushing on. "Will yer bring Michael so I can meet him? I remember his da and Martha but haven't seen Michael in years, not since he was at school. If he is anything like his father, he's a keeper."

There was that cheeky look again, Francis thought. Nuala was not the elderly aunt she might have expected. She was still very much with it, attractive and flirty, and very knowledgeable.

"Of course I will. I'm sure he would love to meet you too. Perhaps we can come this week if Michael is well enough."

After more tea and other tales, Francis couldn't wait to tell Michael.

"I guess I had better be on my way. Thank you so much for everything. You're right, you know, I do feel so much better, and that, dear Auntie Nuala, is all because of you. Did I tell you?" Francis hurried on. "My middle name is Nuala."

"I'm not surprised," Nuala replied. "It was your grandmother's name too."

"Really? That's lovely."

Nuala reached into the pocket of her dress. "Before yer go, I'd like to give you this."

She had a gold chain in her hand. She hung it out so Francis could see it. It was one single piece that had been carefully twisted, combining a cross. It was simple in its design. It glistened as each finely crafted twist reflected the light.

Francis was overwhelmed. "It is so beautiful. Look how it sparkles. I have never seen anything like it."

"It was yer grandmother's."

Nuala was pleased at Francis' reaction. "Take it and wear it always."

Francis looked at her aunt. "Are you sure?" she asked, tears welling in her eyes.

"Of course I'm sure. Put it on."

Francis put the chain over her head. It slid down onto her chest and nestled there.

Smiling, Nuala said, "Right where it was meant to go."

Francis wiped away the tears and kissed her aunt. "It's a treasure. I shall always wear it. Thank you."

Nuala saw Francis out and watched as she drove down the drive, waving. She uttered the words, "Stay safe, dear girl."

***

Francis was so happy, she couldn't wait to see Michael, wondering what he was going to ask of her. Smiling to herself now her mind was made up, she had something to tell him too. She picked up speed and reached the hospital in under twenty minutes.

The Garda was still at the door to Michael's room. He nodded at Francis as he recognised her from yesterday.

"Hi," she said cheekily.

He nodded back.

Francis gave the door a little rap with her knuckles. On opening the door, she found Michael looking out of the window. He turned as she approached him.

"Ah, my lovely woman."

Francis went to him, and they embraced. Michael found her lips with his. His kiss was as urgent as always, and he held Francis so tight, she could feel every inch of him against her. She gently pulled away.

"You must be careful of that scar tissue, Michael," she teased him.

He saw it in her eyes.

"Oh yeah! I had completely forgotten."

Pulling her to him, he carried on kissing her neck, her ears and finally back to her waiting lips. He felt her respond as his tongue explored her mouth, and she melted more into his arms. She could feel him getting hard as he pushed his body on her, moving gently from side to side. She had to stop him. They were in the hospital, and anyone could come in at any minute.

"Michael," she breathlessly gasped, easing herself back.

He looked at her, his eyes now soft and dreamy.

"Yer the most desirable woman, and I want yer."

Francis smiled at him and whispered, "I want you too, Michael, all of you, but not here."

He relaxed and let her go.

"Sorry, Francis, but I have had enough of just thinking about yer, every minute of the day. All I've thought about since being in here is yerself. Yer have taken me mind and me heart. Let's sit down," he said reluctantly.

There were two chairs by the window, and they sat facing each other. Before he could speak, Francis had a question of her own. Now they were face to face and sitting down, she asked, "Tell me, Michael, was I just part of your surveillance work?"

Her question to him hung between them in the silence of the room. Michael didn't answer straight off. She felt uneasy, not being able to read his look. Not liking the silence or the feeling she had created, she carried on.

"You're coming home tomorrow."

He smiled at her attempt to make him feel better. It was almost childlike, he thought lovingly. Michael set his feelings aside and took her hands in his. Leaning forward, he took in her beauty, searching her face as though he was trying to fathom her, read her mind.

"What is it?" Francis asked eventually.

"Marry me," he said without taking his unflinching eyes from hers.

"Marry you?" she exclaimed.

Michael never wavered but waited, not taking his eyes off her. Waiting for his words, his proposal, to settle on her.

She blushed. Heat rose in her body; she was completely taken off-guard, lost in her random thoughts momentarily.

"Marry you?" she said softly. "Are you serious, Michael?"

"I have never been more serious in me life."

She smiled at him. "And I thought I had news," she said.

"Answer me, Francis. Will yer marry me?"

Francis looked into his beautiful eyes. It was her turn to

fathom his face. She wanted to kiss him, wanting him more than anything, but was this all too soon?

Just then she heard her father's voice.

Follow your heart.

Francis knew beyond doubt this was what she wanted. This was what was in her heart, more than anything she had ever wanted in her life before, she thought.

"Yes, Michael, I will."

The words were out.

He reached over and pulled her from the chair. Once again, they were locked in an embrace. He kissed her smiling lips.

"God, you had me going there," he said as his lips moved from hers and nestled in her neck. "I thought you were gonna to turn me down."

Francis smiled. She felt overcome. She had just agreed to marry Michael. They stayed silent for some time, locked together. They finally released each other.

Sitting back down, Michael asked, "What were yer gonna tell me? And no! You were not any part of me work, let's be clear on that." His eyebrows arched. Francis smiled at him. It was her turn as he waited, smiling back at her.

"I had already decided to move here. I thought you were going to ask me to stay."

"Yer did? Yer are? Aren't yer the dark horse? When did yer decide that?"

"When I realised I was in love with you for sure. I am going to give in my resignation tomorrow. I thought I would phone and tell them to take this holiday as my notice period."

"Wow! Yer don't hang about. I did the same, as a matter of fact."

He looked at her, and her surprise made him laugh.

"No!" Francis' eyes popped wide. "When?"

"Yesterday, when Jim O'Rourke visited from the station in Bandon."

"Are you going to leave the Garda?" she asked incredulously.

"Well," Michael said casually. "I've asked for a return to an inspector. Think that might suit my needs better if I'm to be a married man. Perhaps I'm getting a bit long in the tooth for this kind of lark." He winked at her. "Save my strength for other important matters." His deep blue eyes looked at her, waiting to see her reaction.

She felt her stomach tighten, sending waves of pleasure, and her soul sang.

"Looks as though we are of one mind," he added, looking at her in that way again.

She knew exactly what he meant. Francis wanted to throw herself into his arms. Instead, she tried to remain in control.

"Oh," she said. "I nearly forgot. My aunt wants to meet you."

"Does she now? And why would that be?"

Francis just had to retaliate. "I guess it's because I told her I was in love with you and that you were gorgeous."

Francis could have kicked herself. Why did she say that? Why was she behaving like a schoolgirl? This was not the time and most definitely not the place.

"Did yer now, you wanton woman."

"You'd better believe it," Francis quipped back.

Really, she loved his banter, and, if she were really truthful, his suggestive way of talking to her. Apart from making her giggle, the warm, excited feeling that fluttered deep inside was overpowering, making her think things. He made her think and imagine. Her mind went into overdrive, surprising her otherwise reserved nature.

The two sat looking at one another. Michael knew Francis wanted him.

"Now, don't go starting what we can't finish, Francis. Well, here, that is."

His eyebrow raised in that particular way, and she blushed.

Francis changed the subject. "I guess I will need to put my house on the market. I was thinking I could buy one here. My aunt said I could, in the meantime, stay with her."

Michael was thinking. "Are you sure, Francis? That you really want to move here?"

He had that serious look on his face.

"Yes, Michael, I am. It's not just because you asked me to marry you." Her face and voice assured him she knew her own mind. "I love it here. Even if we were not to be married, I still would want to be here. You see, meeting you and my aunt has made those feelings another reason I feel it is right for me. I have made the right decision."

He didn't interrupt, keeping his eyes steady and attentive. He listened to what she was saying.

Francis carried on. "I don't want you to think it's only about you. I feel I am a different person here. I feel alive."

He stood up and came to her chair. Taking her hand, he pulled her to him. Putting his arms around her, he said, "I love you, Francis Doyle."

"I love you, Michael Connor."

The kiss that followed sealed the love between them. Michael pulled back, looking adoringly at her. With his gentle Irish lilt, his voice spoke close to her ear. "Make no mistake, Francis. It's almost definitely all about you for me."

She melted into his arms as his lips found hers, wanting more.

CHAPTER 29

The Darlings were looking for a place to stay in Rosscarbery.

The location looked like it might be where Coral thought she could find out about Francis Doyle. They had driven across a causeway on arrival, turned up a steep sloping hill and arrived in the village centre. This would be the nearest stop to the house further up the lane where the Connor family lived.

"There's nothing here," Vinnie had moaned to Coral.

"Look, there's a pub over there. Perhaps they do rooms. We'll go in and ask. Fancy a drink?" she asked Vinnie, trying to cheer him up.

"I'll park over there." He nodded to the other side of the small square.

There were a few other cars parked up. The few shops were closed except for a convenience store at the far end of the square. Coral made a mental note as she got out of the car. Vinnie was right. There wasn't much here at all.

They walked the short distance to the pub and entered. It seemed dim as they came in from the sunshine. There were three men lined up against the bar, and all turned to see who had come in. They looked at Vinnie, then past him to the blonde woman who came in a few steps behind him. They all returned to face the bar.

The landlord smiled in greeting. "Not a bad day, wouldn't yer say. What can I get you there?"

Vinnie went up to the bar. "I'll take a pint."

"Of Guinness, is it?" the landlord asked cheerfully.

"Yeah, Guinness, that'll do."

Vinnie was still down in the mouth. The landlord had lost his smile. Starting off the pint, he looked back at Vinnie. "Anything else?" His expression hardly changed.

"Yeah. She'll have a vodka and tonic."

The landlord fetched the drinks, and Vinnie paid. Coral reminded Vinnie about a room.

"Oh yeah."

Coral raised her eyes to heaven. When the barman brought the

196

change over, Vinnie asked, "Any rooms, mate?"

"No, we don't do rooms. Try down the road. There's a B&B along the way, on the right."

"Right," Vinnie said and thanked him.

The barman continued his conversation down at the far end of the bar, where there was a group of men.

They went into a corner and drank their drinks in silence. There was a general buzz of activity in what appeared to Coral an eating area further down past the bar. She downed her drink in two gulps and Vinnie in three. They left, and no one bothered to watch them go.

Once more out in the sunshine, Vinnie was moaning again. "That was a barrel of laughs." Vinnie was even more glum than before the pint.

"Yeah." Coral was now as glum as him. Perhaps this was not such a good idea.

"This place…" She was speaking softly, almost to herself. "I mean, how will we casually meet up with that redhead? Come on, let's look at that map again."

"We could park a bit further down the lane nearer the house and wait," Vinnie offered.

"We could do that for hours, Vinnie. I don't think that's a very good idea."

The disgruntled pair went and sat in their car. Coral took out the map.

"Look, Vinnie," Coral pointed out. "The town of Clonakilty. How about if we head back that way?" She tapped the map showing him where, and continued. "Hang around there a few days, we might learn something. This place, well, nobody even wants to speak to us, let alone give us any information. You never know." She continued gaining momentum as the thought materialised in her mind. "Perhaps the girl would go to that town for shopping. Can't imagine anyone coming here for anything?"

"You might have something there." Vinnie eyed her. "Come on then. It's Clonakilty. Here we come."

Vinnie was only too happy to leave this particular backwater. He started up the car and went back down the little hill leading to the main road and across the causeway. The beautiful bay of Rosscarbery was lost to them. They could not see the beauty of the place at all. They arrived in Clonakilty.

"Not far, was it?" he said.

Vinnie was feeling his mood lifting.

"This looks more like it," Coral said.

The road had led them into the heart of the town. There were numerous shops, cafes, and pubs and a big hotel. They found a car park. As it was a Sunday, few shops were open, but they found a small hotel off the main road, tucked away down a side street.

"This looks all right, Vinnie."

Coral smiled as she rang the front doorbell. They were ushered in by a friendly-faced older woman. While the room she showed them was old-fashioned by their standards, Coral said it was fine.

"It'll be payment in advance if you don't mind," she said sweetly.

"That's fine," Coral agreed. "Shall we say three nights, for now? We're not sure how long we will be staying."

"Sure. There we go, then. There are your keys."

Coral held out the cash to the woman, and she quickly put it into her pocket.

"You might like to put your names in the book on the table there."

There was an open book on the small hall table.

"Breakfast from 8 till 9:30, will that suit you?" she enquired, looking as though she meant, take it or leave it.

"Fine," Coral said. "We'll just pop and get our bags from the car."

"Yes, yes, off you go then."

The woman seemed in a hurry to get back to whatever lay beyond the closed door at the end of the hallway.

Vinnie had been looking at the other room as the door was open. The room faced the front, where there were four small dining tables.

"See you in the morning," Coral said.

"Fine! Mind how yer go."

With that said, she ushered them to the main front door.

Outside on the pavement, Coral laughed.

"What?" Vinnie said.

Coral looked at him, saying, "Don't you think these Irish people are weird?"

"Yeah," Vinnie said. "Weird."

They linked arms and retraced their way back to the car for their bags.

***

The beautiful sunshine of the day had given way to dusk. The sky had turned crimson as the sun dipped below the horizon. Nuala found herself watching from her garden as the last birds sang out their goodnights and the trees became like black lace. It was that most beautiful moment. The birds going to roost for the night. The sky ever changing before turning into that inky blackness. Tonight promised a myriad of twinkling stars. There had not been a cloud in the sky when finally Nuala came in from the garden, still thinking about Francis. She felt troubled since Francis had left to visit Michael at the hospital, feeling that there was perhaps something Francis had not told her.

It was all odd to her. Nuala's senses were working overtime. She had needed to have been in Francis' company for longer, she was thinking, to get a good reading. She wanted a glimpse of what was on the horizon for her newfound niece.

"Ah, well." She sighed. "Perhaps she will come back soon and bring Michael with her. Seeing them together might help."

The visitation of Robert to his daughter, then her mother, right here, and the very next day too, Nuala reflected. She was sure something very serious was going to unfold, and was left now with an uneasy feeling. There was something, but what? What could possibly go wrong?

It had been Francis' first meditation. Still mulling it over, she climbed the stairs to her bedroom.

Quite extraordinary for the girl to be visited by both parents, she thought. Nuala was still puzzled. Her mind wouldn't be still. The girl wasn't aware of her own powers. It had taken for her to come here, to clear her mind. Here, thought Nuala, was where her destiny lay. If nothing else, at the moment, Nuala felt sure of that.

Now ready for her bed, she untied the ribbon from her hair, letting it fall around her shoulders, and sat at her dressing table, brushing as she pondered.

"I need to stay focused," she told her reflection. "I need to be aware there is danger."

She was sure, but where was it? Nuala kept brushing and thinking.

Finally, a deep tiredness overcame her, and she had to go to bed. One thing for sure she knew, she would need all her strength and powers to give her niece the help she felt, very soon, the girl would need.

***

Francis lay in bed that night, far from any feelings of trouble. As she lay looking at the starlit sky, she was the most content she had ever known. Casting her mind back to the events of the day, starting with the goodbyes of Michael's family, Bridget's words rang in her ears. *Take hold of your life.* Francis thought she now had made a start to do just that. Tomorrow would be the next step, starting with giving in her notice. They were all going to be surprised at that bombshell. That was an exciting thought, making a mental note to call the office as soon as she knew her boss would be there in the morning.

Her visit with Nuala had been the most extraordinary time. Francis ran through those events.

What a strange thing had happened there. Enjoying the delights of her garden one minute, then finding herself on a journey of meditation. She had slipped away into oblivion, from reality, really quickly. Where she went to, she had no idea, yet it was comforting. Her body felt weightless, and her mind was as free as the birds she had listened to, their song whispering in her ears. Then silence.

Her mother, smiling and waving. How did that happen? Francis tried to tune into why. Why was this happening to her here? She had never thought, throughout those years of grief, she would ever see her parents again.

It was just last night that she had seen her father. What she thought at first was a dream, then he was here, telling her to follow her heart. Right here in this room.

She sat up. "I am following my dream, Dad. I'm going to marry Michael."

Francis surprised herself that she had actually spoken out loud to no one.

Or, perhaps, came a second thought, her dad could hear her.

She was sure she felt something touch her hair.

Lying back down, Francis pushed at her pillow and pulled it into her neck.

Michael would be there the next day. She sighed, thinking how would he adjust to a new position within the Garda. She knew it was because he had met her that he now wanted a safer position. They hadn't even discussed it. There had been no time. It had never entered her mind. His job was so dangerous. Francis shuddered at the thought, remembering Michael running towards her with a gun in his hand.

Run, Francis, run.

The shots fired, two men's bodies on the ground, oozing blood. Michael crumpled as the knife penetrated his side. Francis didn't realise that her hands were screwed into tight balls until she felt her nails digging into her palms. She released them and sat up again. Tears were on her cheeks.

"Oh, this is no good," she muttered.

Getting out of bed, Francis entered the little bathroom in her room. Turning on the tap, she splashed cold water on her face. Giving a tug to the little string that lit the vanity unit over the sink, Francis looked at her reflection in the mirror. *Pull yourself together*, she told herself. Wiping her face and hands, she tugged at the string again to switch it off and went back to bed.

Michael would be home, and all would be well.

"Goodnight, Mum and Dad," she whispered as she snuggled down.

"Goodnight, Francis," they called from beyond the veil.

Though she didn't hear that, she felt comforted as she drifted off. Sleep had found her and took her to that blissful place.

CHAPTER 30

Michael was up, dressed and waiting for the doctor to come and give him the all-clear to leave the hospital. God, he wanted to get out of there. He had never been so inactive in his entire life.

He was beginning to pace the room when a nurse had come in with a cup of tea. She was full of smiles, in a chirpy fashion, and placed it on the table.

"So, yer off today, I see yer all ready and packed."

Michael's bag was loaded up, ready for the off, sitting at the foot of the bed.

"Yes," he said, turning from the window. "Any idea when the doc's due?"

"Any time now," she said. "Can't wait to see the back of us, is it?"

"Yeah, something like that," Michael said with a smile. "Thanks for everything."

"You're welcome. No offence, but we'll be happy not to see yer again, if yer get my drift. Keep yourself away from those hooligans."

"I'll do my best." Michael smiled. "Thanks for the tea."

The nurse was out of the room, and the door closed behind her. Michael picked up the tea and drank it. Joseph was coming to pick him up at midday. He looked at his watch. Another hour to go. He sat down and closed his eyes. Francis came into his mind.

I need to buy her a ring. I wonder what she would like?

There was going to be a lot to sort out. What a girl, he thought as he recalled her saying she would move here anyway. She knew her own mind. Once her mind was made up, that was it. Time for action.

He knew from the moment he had met her that he wanted her. He knew that she wanted him. They were right together.

The door opened, and in came the doctor.

"Good morning, Mr Connor. I'd like to take one last look at the wound."

"Sure thing," Michael said.

His shirt was off in a flash.

"No discomfort?" he asked.

"No, nothing," Michael replied. "I think you did a grand job in stitching me up."

"Yes, I think we did."

The doctor's smile was brief. "Continue to take it steady. No more heroics." The doctor raised his eyebrows at Michael. "You should be fine."

Michael put his hand out to shake the doctor's hand and the doctor gripped hold of Michael's.

"Take care," he said.

Michael thanked him, put his shirt back on and reached for his jacket. He sat back down and put his mind back to Francis. His da wouldn't be long now.

***

After breakfast, Francis told Joseph and Martha that she thought she would take the drive to Clonakilty.

"I'd like to look at the shops before Michael gets home."

"That's a great idea," Martha said. "Are yer happy to go on your own?"

"The drive is pretty straightforward. I should be okay."

Francis smiled at Martha, hoping that she hadn't been put out. Martha's response left her in no doubt that she had not been put out at all.

"That's good, Francis, for I have a few things to be getting on with me self this morning. Ye take yourself off to Clona. It's another lovely morning. Make the most of it.". Joe's picking up Michael. Aren't yer Joe?

Joseph raised his head from the newspaper. "See yer later. Mind how you go."

His voice emanated from behind his paper. The top of his head was all they could see. He was engrossed in some story or other. Martha and Francis laughed.

"I need to do one last thing before I go."

Martha looked up from the sink. "What's that, love?"

"I was wondering if I might use the phone to call my workplace before shopping?"

Martha didn't ask why, though it was on the tip of her tongue.

"As it's long-distance, I shall pay, of course."

"Not at all," Martha replied. "As if I'd charge. Would yer listen to the girl, Joseph?"

Francis kissed her cheek in thanks and went out into the hall.

Joseph looked over his paper at Martha.

"Did yer say something, Ma?"

"No, Joe," Martha replied, shaking her head. "I said nothing at all, yer fine as you were."

Francis dialled the number of Spector & Spector, the solicitors where she worked. It rang several times before it was answered.

"Good morning, Spector & Spector. How may I help you?"

Hearing the precise English voice of Susie, Francis thought she was putting on her best telephone voice and smiled to herself.

"Hello, Susie. It's Francis, Francis Doyle."

"Hello, Francis. Aren't you on holiday?"

"Yes," Francis said. "Is Gerald, I mean, Mr Bagster, available?"

"I think so," she replied. "If you wouldn't mind holding, I'll ring through."

Francis looked at her watch while she waited. He should be there, she was thinking.

"Hello, Francis. How's it going?"

"Very well. I am phoning because, in fact, I want to give in my notice."

Her voice sounded clear and bright. The line went quiet. Momentarily, Francis thought she had sounded a bit abrupt.

"Hello, are you still there?" Francis enquired.

"Your notice? Francis, is everything all right?"

"Yes, everything is more than all right. I have found an aunt, my father's sister."

Gerald Bagster had been more of a friend to her, more than anyone else she had known, especially at the time of her parents' passing. He had helped with their will and the funeral. He had been a confidant and the best adviser possible. But Francis reminded herself that she had given the firm ten years of her life.

"Your aunt! That's wonderful news. I am very pleased for you."

Francis waited. She didn't want to say any more than just that.

"If I might ask," he said, "why is that going to affect your work?"

"I am planning on moving here to Ireland."

"If it's what you want." His voice fell, sounding a little crestfallen.

Francis spoke up.

"It is, Gerald. My mind is made up. I will be putting my house on the market."

"All right, Francis. When do you want to leave?"

Francis didn't hesitate. "Right away. While you have a replacement there for me. You know she is more than willing to take my place. I'm sure she will be a good replacement."

"I see," Gerald said. "It would seem you have thought it all through. I am really sorry to lose you. You have been a real asset to the firm. When you're ready, let us know your address and I will send you a reference."

"Thank you. Perhaps the firm might like to deal with my house sale?"

"Yes, of course. Happy to help, Francis, in any way."

"Bye then, for now."

"Goodbye, Francis. I hope all goes well for you. Take care."

Francis was pleased to end the call. She put the receiver down, letting out a slow breath.

"I've done it," she whispered.

Excitement arose in her, making her feel like she wanted to dance. Returning to the kitchen, she saw that Joseph was still behind his paper, and Martha was sorting her great store of goods in her pantry.

"I have news," she announced.

Martha came straight out of the pantry, and Joseph put down his paper. They both waited, gawping at her.

Smiling, she said, "I have just handed in my notice. I was going to tell you both this afternoon when Michael's here, but I just couldn't wait."

"Does this mean yer will be staying here, in Ireland?" Martha asked.

"Yes," Francis said.

The realisation of her words filled her with pleasure.

"I'm staying in Ireland."

Martha hugging her, said, "We are really pleased for you,

Francis. I suppose finding your aunt helped you to make up your mind."

"And Michael," Francis said confidently.

"Won't he be pleased?" Joseph replied.

"Yes, he knows I want to stay."

Martha, reading into that remark, beamed at her.

"We couldn't be happier, Francis. I'll have to phone Bridget and tell her the good news."

"Right," Francis said. "I'll be off to the shops. Is there anything I can get for you? Anything you need?"

"Just enjoy yourself," Martha said.

"I was hoping to buy a few bits of clothing, could do with one or two extra things. I really didn't bring much with me."

"That's lovely. See you later, love," Joseph called out. "Mind how yer go."

Francis took the back door, and the dogs came running up to her for a bit of a fuss.

"I can't stop now," she told them. "I'll be back soon, and so will Michael."

The dogs stood staring at her, wagging their tails as if they understood every word, watching her go. Murphy let out his deep soft bark. Francis looked back at him. "Bye, Murphy, see you in a while."

It was yet another fine day. It could not have dampened Francis' enthusiasm even if it had been raining. She enjoyed the drive to Clonakilty, looking forward to seeing what the town had to offer. Francis would be looking at the place with even more interest, knowing she would be living somewhere nearby.

"I'm going to be married," she whispered.

This new Francis was very excited. Her mind was so full of lovely thoughts. She went from one thought to another as she drove along the main road in the town. She was thinking about her parents. They would be really happy for her. Francis felt quite sure of it.

Follow your heart. Her father's words. He would be happy with her choice. An Irishman! And what a man he was. Francis was smiling to herself. *My soon-to-be-husband.* She liked the sound of that. She spied a parking space on the left of the main road. Cars were parked intermittently along both sides. It was a long road. Along its pavements were numerous shops and just a few people here and there, mostly locals and mostly women.

The women there seemed friendly. They were chattier and generally in conversation with each other, even out on the pavements. It seemed to Francis that everyone knew everyone else. It was so different to London. Different and a whole lot better, in fact.

She decided to walk the entire length of the road, down one side, then back up the other. She had seen the shops, as Michael had driven her through. Now here she was, meandering along. It wasn't long before she spied a very nice shop with women's clothes and couldn't resist popping in. Twenty minutes later, she had come out again carrying a couple of carriers.

Her face was alive. She couldn't remember ever feeling this relaxed. Seeing a florist tucked down a side road, she decided to buy Martha some flowers. With a large, pre-arranged, mixed bunch of flowers loaded in her arms, Francis thought putting the shopping in the car would be a good idea. It was impossible now for her to hold anything else. The car was just a little bit further along.

Heading towards her, Coral stopped in her tracks. "Look, Vinnie," she said, tugging at his arm.

"What? What's up now?"

"It's her, straight ahead. With the flowers, see?"

Vinnie could see her now as she stepped out from behind two women who had momentarily blocked his view. He noticed how her long curling hair seemed to dance in the sunshine. She was a looker. Coral was urgently tugging at his arm.

"Vinnie, give me those bags quickly. Go off," she said, taking the shopping bags from him.

"Off where?"

"Go and get yourself a drink or something. I have a plan. I'll see you later back at the digs."

Vinnie shrugged his shoulders and handed over her shopping bags.

"See you later, then."

He wandered off back the way they had come. His hands were deep in his pockets.

As Coral came right up to Francis, she turned her head to look into a window on purpose and pushed into her. Francis was taken off-guard and almost fell to the pavement. Her shopping went flying, and for added impact, Coral let her shopping drop too.

Quickly, Coral grabbed hold of Francis, took her arm, and apologised in her kindest manner.

Francis smiled. "No harm done. Are you all right?"

Coral gave Francis a beaming smile. "Yes, it was entirely my fault. I am so dreadfully sorry. Let me."

She let go of Francis' arm and started gathering up the shopping from the pavement. They laughed as Coral handed Francis her own carrier.

"Oh no, that's mine," she said playfully. "I have just bought this amazing blouse."

She took the carrier from Francis. Opening the bag, she gave Francis a glance.

"That looks lovely," Francis said. "I love that colour."

"You're English, aren't you?" Coral asked.

"Yes, I am. I'm from London."

"Me too," Coral said. "Let me buy you a coffee, my way of apologising. They do a lovely bit of cake too."

"It was my fault as much as yours," Francis said. "Coffee sounds great though. I think I might take you up on a piece of cake, too."

With their shopping sorted, Francis told her, "I was just going to drop this off at my car. Three cars further along."

"Here, let me hold those for you."

Coral took the flowers from Francis whilst she rummaged in her shoulder bag for her car keys.

Coral was looking at Francis, thinking and thinking to herself that she was good at this and should have been an actress. Like taking sweets from a baby. Coral had taken sheer delight in actually speaking to Francis. She felt a power that she had not felt before, enjoying the deceit of it all. She had no idea what Laura Popa had in mind, but she would relish being in on it, whatever it was.

"There," Francis said. She had taken the flowers and put them on the back seat. "I'm ready. Where's that cafe?"

Coral guided her a little further along on the other side. "Over there."

Francis looked across the road. "Lovely!"

It had a pretty-looking frontage of pale yellow, and a soft green outline made the bow-fronted window frames stand out. Inside the cafe were gingham check tablecloths, the same yellow and green as the exterior of the building. The whole look was clean, fresh, with its pale-yellow walls and light ash wooden chairs.

"This looks so pretty," Francis said to Coral.

"There's a table free just there. You sit down. Coffee?"

"Yes, please," Francis said. "With just a drop of milk."

"And?" Coral pointed to the assortment of cakes lined up inside the huge glass cabinet.

"Sponge and cream," Francis said, thinking this had been a good idea.

She looked at Coral waiting up at the counter behind another lady, waiting to be served.

Francis couldn't help but look at her expensive-looking shoes and her beautiful fitted jeans. They weren't cheap, she reflected; such a good fit. Her jacket was well tailored and cut in at the waist with a single vent. She looked chic. Her long blonde hair was undoubtedly coloured, Francis thought. Still, it looked in perfect condition, which was definitely the result of regular hairdresser visits.

Carrying a tray back to the table, Coral sat down opposite Francis. There were two coffees, two large pieces of cake, and a jug of cream. Francis noticed she had chosen the same.

"There we are."

Coral offered her hand across the table. "I'm Coral."

"I'm Francis. Pleased to meet you."

The two girls held each other's hand briefly.

"Nice to bump into you," Coral said, and they both laughed.

Francis had had a very nice chat, with a gorgeous chunk of cake and a welcome cup of coffee. It was almost an hour later when Coral got to her feet.

"It's been really nice meeting you," Coral said with a swish of her hair. "I hope your plans to move here all go well."

"Yes, thank you," Francis said. "It's been really nice meeting you too."

Coral had managed to get everything she needed to know

about Francis Doyle.

She was just so easy to lead. Coral had asked quite openly what part of London she came from, and there it was. Wandsworth, south London, Wands Road.

It was a funny thing about Londoners. They all had the same instinct to ask or tell what side of the river they came from.

Coral's immediate response had been a gasp. "No!" she had emphasised. "I have a friend living in Wands Road. What number are you?"

Francis smiled openly. "Really? That is a coincidence. I'm at 657."

"Ah," Coral said. "She must be further away than I thought. Mind you, she is in a flat 23, I think. It is quite a long road, as I recall. I'm in Bayswater."

Coral confidently looked at Francis. Deftly she had changed the course of the conversation. "Big old house." She smiled. "It's the family home, really."

"More upmarket than Wandsworth," Francis said. "I think the way things are going for me, I shall be putting it on the market soon. Hopefully, next week. I am moving here as soon as possible." Francis could not help but sound enthusiastic and excited.

Coral had left the cafe first while Francis ordered another coffee.

She was enjoying sitting in the cafe, watching the people, mostly women, she had noted, coming and going. The atmosphere was pleasant. The women chatting made Francis feel relaxed. The way of life here, Francis realised with every passing day, suited her.

Ireland was in her blood, and she had felt it so strongly, now more than ever.

As she sat looking around at the other ladies chatting away, Nuala came into her mind. She actually had an aunt living here that she felt she could get along with.

That morning had reinforced, yet again, that this was where she belonged. Drinking down the last of her coffee, she looked at her watch. It was nearly eleven, just enough time to walk a little further, and then back to Michael's parents' house. It wouldn't take long before Joseph would be returning with Michael. There was that feeling again, like an excited little girl. Her tummy tightened and fluttered.

Passing along the pavement, looking into the small independent shops, she was taken by a very nice dress in the window of another little boutique, and without hesitation, she went in.

***

With another purchase in her hands, Francis decided to return to Ash House. She wanted to get cleaned up and changed before Michael came home. The dogs greeted her as she came into the kitchen. Joseph had opened the door to her as he saw her through the glass of the back door.

"Here yer are, yer man's home."

Francis was all a flutter, dropping the parcels on the kitchen table along with the most beautiful bunch of flowers.

"Already," she exclaimed.

Michael and Martha came into the kitchen.

She rushed to him. "Welcome home."

He kissed her right there, fully on the lips, in front of his parents. She hadn't minded but was fully aware that she had to pull away.

"I was shopping," she said, feeling a little embarrassed.

Michael let her go from his strong arms reluctantly.

"I can see that," he quipped, casting his eyes on the array of carriers.

"Martha," she said, as she gathered up the flowers, her cheeks flushed. "These are for you."

"They're just lovely, Francis. I'll put them in water."

The awkwardness, Francis felt, dissolved.

"I'm so pleased you're home, Michael."

Francis couldn't take her eyes off him. He never answered but just looked at her. Joseph left the kitchen, giving them space.

"I'm outside," he called out to Martha. "Call me when lunch is ready."

"Will do," came the reply from the little utility room, where Martha was arranging the flowers into two vases, thinking the same as Joseph.

Michael took Francis by the hand and walked her out of the kitchen and into the lounge.

There he wrapped his arms around her. "Not half as glad as me," he said.

His voice was soft and low before his eager mouth sought hers. They kissed until the need for air broke them apart. They sat on the sofa together, his arm around her shoulders.

Francis spoke first. "I feel a bit awkward now in front of your parents. Now you're here too."

"Thought yer might," he said, kissing her neck.

"I'm serious," Francis said.

"Of course yer are."

His face was nestled in her neck, and the warmth of his breath on her was beginning to have an effect. The softness of his lips and now his free hand was caressing her hair while the other held her tight. Francis couldn't stop him. She didn't want to stop him. She was enjoying it too much.

Martha came into the room. "Look at these," she said, holding a vase of flowers before her.

***

That evening Joseph was going to drive them down to the square in Rosscarbery. He had said he thought they all deserved a treat. So, he organised a meal in the local pub. The food there had a reputation for being very good. Joseph and Martha had first-hand knowledge, as it was their local. It was a family-run affair. Joe and Ma Connor were well known. It was not as though they were there every day, but this was their first port of call for a get-together, if the need arose. It was an easy place for them to drive to. Or, in good weather, it could be a lovely walk down the lane. Knowing most of the people who frequented the place, they were their neighbours. It always felt comfortable and could be very entertaining if they held a music night.

Francis was really looking forward to seeing the place. Earlier, Michael took her on a walk with the dogs. They had gone out of the garden to the back of the house. The dogs were excited and headed off up and over the hill.

Francis asked if they were safe.

"Safe?" Michael said. "Yer kidding me? Of course they're safe. Come on."

He grabbed her hand. She couldn't see beyond the brow of the hill until he led her, and they reached the top.

There the land lay before them. It was unfenced, open, and looked to her as natural as when time had begun. The grasses were soft underfoot, with huge trees that looked as though they had been there since the dawn of time.

"It's gorgeous, Michael."

"I know, just as ye are." He winked at her. "Come on."

Michael grabbed hold of her hand. They walked on further down the other side. Murphy came back to them and nudged Francis' free hand.

"Hello." She stroked his ears. "Where's the other two?"

Murphy looked at her with those soulful eyes and trotted off again. She felt that Murphy could understand every word she said to him.

"Reckon he just came back to check on you," Michael said.

"He is a beautiful boy. I should like to have a dog or two."

"I don't see why yer couldn't. Meanwhile, you've got Murphy, and yer definitely got me."

He swung her around playfully. They were looking into each other's eyes.

"And a whole bunch of kids," he followed up with.

He was looking at her in a way that made her feel weak.

Cheekily, she replied, "A bunch! How many is that? You'll have to catch me first."

He held her tight.

"No trouble," he said. "No trouble at all."

Francis' face burned, and she knew it was bright red.

Michael could have devoured her right there and then; laying her down on the soft grass and taking her would have been so easy. He thought better of it. She was his, and he knew it. That understanding was there. *No*, he thought, *I need her to tell me she is ready. I must wait a little bit longer. Please God, don't let it be much longer.*

All his senses about Francis were right. Deep down inside, he had felt a connection from the moment they met. He had known a few girls in his time. None of them had for him what Francis had. She was special, and he loved her with all of his heart.

He kissed her gently, then took her hand again. "Where've those dogs gotten to?"

He whistled, and as if out of nowhere, the three dogs came

bounding along.

"Let's get back for a cuppa."

Michael put his arm around Francis' shoulders. "I love yer, Francis. We have a lot of things to sort out."

"Yes, we do," she said softly.

They carried on back up to the peak of the hill that they had come over earlier. The sun was going down, and small clouds had appeared.

"The weather's gonna change," Michael said as his eyes took in the darkening clouds.

"Well, I was beginning to think the sun would always shine here. It's been so lovely, all the while you were in the hospital."

"We get our fair share of the rough stuff. Make no mistake about that, particularly when the wind and rain sweep in off the Atlantic."

They carried on walking down the other side of the hill.

Francis could now see Ash House in all its glorious setting. Her thoughts turned to where she was going to live. It didn't seem right to her to stay any longer at Ash House. As lovely as it was, it was not the right thing to do. She didn't want to outstay her welcome. This, she thought, was the perfect time to tell Michael.

"While I'm looking for somewhere of my own, I thought I would take up the offer from my aunt to stay with her, just for awhile.

Francis waited for Michael's reaction.

"Yer could if that's what you want. I'll not persuade yer otherwise."

"I think it's the best option for now," Francis said swiftly.

She had the feeling Michael was not too pleased. She was trying to gauge what he really was thinking.

"Will you come and visit with me to see her? Perhaps tomorrow?"

"Yer know I will, Francis."

He had stopped walking, and she turned back towards him.

He looked angry.

"What is it?" she said. "You're making me feel nervous."

Michael's mind was working overtime. He wanted her so badly. It had brought him to a standstill. The past week he had spent lying still in a hospital bed, with only his dreams for company, with no way of expelling the needs of his restless body. The situation had left him in a frustrated state, in body and mind. He gave way to what was really the matter. Hearing she was now going to move in with her aunt, he needed to tell her and tell her now.

"I'll tell you what it is," he blurted out. "When am I gonna get yer in my bed?"

Francis was taken unawares. She put her hands over her mouth and laughed with relief, glad it was not something more serious.

"Laughing, are yer?"

He swooped over to her, looking her in the eye and holding her tight.

"I'm serious. I can't wait any longer for us to be together. It feels like a bloody lifetime." Michael never gave her a chance to answer. She felt his arms tighten about her.

"Michael, I feel the same. You know I do."

He kissed her waiting lips so tenderly at first, then as she kissed him back, he became more urgent.

She pulled back. "Tonight, Michael," she said softly. "Tonight."

Three dogs waited and watched as they kissed again.

CHAPTER 31

It had been the best night out Francis' had had in a very long time.

The Ross was an old building right in the square of Rosscarbery. The bar area greeted its customers as soon as they entered. It ran along the length of the room. Two men had recognised the Connors as soon as they came in. Francis and Michael were behind them.

"How's it going, Joe?"

"Fine, fine. Yer all right there, Finn?"

"Aye, that I am. Evening, Ma, yer looking as lovely as ever."

His cheeky smile and words encouraged Martha to chuckle.

"Get away with yer, Finn," she said coyly.

Martha looked at Francis with raised eyebrows and said, "Let's go sit through the back."

Francis followed as she led the way. Joseph and Michael spent a bit of time talking at the bar. The other men were more than interested in chatting with the Connors.

The room opened out at the back, where Francis and Martha found a table to sit. Martha sat in one of the partitioned areas. It afforded privacy and felt intimate. There were a few other tables occupied in the eating area. But this evening, it was quiet. She nodded to a couple looking at Francis with interest. Martha didn't want to get into a conversation with them, knowing too well that they would want to know every last detail about who Francis was.

It was one good reason Martha had chosen the seated cubical for them to have their meal.

The lighting in this area was soft. Francis liked how a single light hung directly low over each table. The shades illuminated the tables, not the people, giving it it's intimate feel. It was comfortable and cosy.

Michael appeared at her side with a tray of drinks.

"Thought you might like the wine," he said, placing a large glass of red in front of her.

He gave the same to Martha.

"Lovely," Francis said.

"Slainte," Michael said, holding up his pint of Guinness.

He sat opposite her, thinking how lovely she looked in her new dress.

"Is yer da still yapping?" Martha asked.

"He won't be long, Ma."

Joseph joined them. Michael downed most of his pint before he spoke, his attention on Francis.

"Shall I tell them the news, then?"

Francis smiled. "Yes, I think you should."

Michael had his parents' attention. They were both looking at him.

"Francis has accepted my proposal. We're gonna get married."

Joseph took his son's hand and nearly shook it off.

"Well done, me boy, well done."

Michael laughed at his father's enthusiasm.

"Careful there, Da. Yer nearly taken me hand off."

Joseph then leaned across the table and kissed Francis on the cheek.

"I couldn't be happier," he told her.

Martha's hand went to her mouth as if to stop the scream from escaping. She then grabbed hold of Francis, kissing both her cheeks.

"I am so pleased, yer made for each other."

The rest of the evening was happy and light, with lots of laughter, plenty of food, washed down with plenty of drink.

Francis' face was glowing.

Michael, throughout the evening, hardly took his eyes off her. His mind was on later when they would be alone.

CHAPTER 32

At Bandon Garda Station, Superintendent Jim O'Rourke was seated at his desk. He had just put down the phone. The Met had been in touch again. He scratched at his head as he ran through what he had been told. This case had already lost him one of his best men, Michael Connor, who had been stabbed. Thank God Mick had lived. He was going to be hard to replace. Jim wasn't sure yet where he would best be suited. Mick had surprised him when he asked for a desk job. Standing up now, pushing his chair away, he was thinking he could do without this disruption from London, yet again. Standing at the window, he was now rubbing his chin, thinking on what the Met had told him. It was their opinion that the case was not over.

They had moved the already captured criminals from Dublin prison to London, where they would now stand trial.

Something else had come to light in further investigations. That something else was Laura Popa. She had been unknown to the police until now. They had reopened the case after learning that she was the older sister of Dario Dinu.

They wanted from Bandon every last detail relating to that day in Kinsale. Dublin Garda at Phoenix Park had been happy for Jim O'Rourke's team to continue, as they had been in the front line during this last stage, the final stage, thought O'Rourke, his mind still mulling over the facts as he recalled the events.

He would need to get Patrick Logan in and Mick Connor too. They could go over it together. Two heads were better than one; if necessary, they'd type the whole bloody thing again.

Laura Popa, it would seem, was now the Met's priority. They were making some headway in her direction. They hadn't yet a location for her but were working on it.

In London, a small operations office had been set aside within the police station. Another group of officers were working on finding her and fast. It was believed now that she was holding a lot of the unanswered questions.

Laura Popa had become their number one most wanted for drug crimes, murder and people trafficking. How soon they would bring her to book was anyone's guess. So far, she had eluded all police attempts to identify who or where she was. There was no paper trail of any sort.

Inspector Bennett hoped someone in their custody might know who Laura Popa was. It was unknown as yet by the police in London or the Garda in Ireland.

O'Rourke was now thinking he needed to make a couple of calls. Mick and Patrick's report was needed as soon as possible.

He walked away from the window, where beads of rain were running down in little rivulets. Back at his desk, he picked up the phone. He would phone Mick first to see how he was doing.

"Hello, Martha Connor.." It was Mick's mother, he thought.
"Mrs Connor, trust yer well, Superintendent O'Rourke here."
"You'll be wanting to speak to Michael," she inquired. "He's not here at the moment."
She heard the inspector suck in his breath.
"Can I give him a message for yer then?"
"Yer can," came the short reply. "Will yer tell him to give me a call?"
"That I will," Martha replied. "Though it might not be for a while. He is out visiting."
"I see," O'Rourke said. "As soon as he gets back then."
"No trouble at all. Goodbye," Martha said.
Martha returned to the kitchen.
"Who was that?" Joseph asked, putting down his newspaper.
"O'Rourke at the station."
Martha's eyebrows were raised as she looked at her husband. "I hope they don't push Michael to go back to work too soon. I don't think he has had enough time off yet."
Michael hadn't told his parents yet that he would be giving up working in the undercover unit.

***

Nuala was in her kitchen, watching the burner with the door open, making sure the log would catch. When she was satisfied, she closed the door. The flames had started to lick around the log. The burner created a cosy feeling in her kitchen. She loved to watch the dancing flames. With the sudden chill and change in the weather, she felt the need to feel cosy and make her home

219

welcoming.

Not many more days left in the season when she would light the burner. The month would soon be June. Happy that all was ready for Francis and Michael's visit, Nuala climbed the stairs to her bedroom to remove a clean dress from the large old-fashioned wardrobe. It was one of her favourites in two shades of green. She grabbed a cream cardigan to go over the top. Nuala flung the items on the bed and set about making the change. Once dressed, Nuala caught sight of her reflection in the mirror.

"Not bad," she muttered. "Respectable enough, except that hair, that could do with a tidy."

Taking her hairbrush, she vigorously brushed at her long tresses, and she then tied it up with a green ribbon.

She could hear a car coming up the drive. She thought it must be them. Instead of going straight downstairs, her curiosity led her towards the landing window, where she could take a quick peep.

Nuala watched her niece as she got out of her car. Michael was getting out of the passenger side.

"My, he looks a lot like his daddy. Two peas in a pod, so they are. The only difference was the years between them."

She felt sadness about how time had robbed of her colouring, thinking we all become a pale shadow of our youthful selves. It was easy for her to make the comparisons here and now, whilst looking down at Michael's thick dark curls.

Joseph was still as handsome as his son. The years had been kind to him. Francis, too, was how she had once looked herself. Nuala remembered her youthfulness as she watched the two of them together. She remained unnoticed as the two kissed before coming to her door. Smiling to herself, Nuala was at the door before they had time to knock.

"Come in, come in. It's starting to rain."

Sure enough, the threatening clouds gathering were finally giving way, and a soft, gentle rain was now falling.

Francis greeted her aunt with a kiss.

"This is Michael," she said.

Michael held out his hand for her to shake. Nuala took hold of it. Immediately she felt his power. This was a man who meant business. His handshake was warm and sincere. His gaze was steady and strong.

"How's it going, Michael? It's grand to meet you." Nuala smiled up at him. "So pleased you could make it. Come in now."

Nuala walked through the hallway, and Francis smiled at Michael as he ran his hand through his hair. An attempt, thought Francis, to make a good impression.

Francis loved Michael's hair and the unruliness of it. The curls went where they chose, giving him a casualness that appealed to her very nature.

Nuala's cosy kitchen greeted them.

She put the kettle on the range.

"Tea for yer both?"

"That would be lovely, Auntie."

Francis nodded at Michael. "Fine for me," he said.

"Sit yer selves down then."

Francis and Michael pulled out a chair next to each other at the table.

"We have news, Auntie."

Francis was beaming, and Nuala thought she looked positively glowing.

"What would that be?" Nuala asked, taking in the look of them both.

"We're to be married."

Francis' cheeks blushed just that little bit more.

"Married, is it? That is happy news. Congratulations to yer both."

Michael chipped in. "After we leave here, we're going into Clona to buy a ring."

Nuala got up from the table and came to her niece for a hug.

"I thought yer had an extra sparkle about yer this morning."

Francis squeezed her aunt in an embrace.

"I am so happy, Auntie."

"Yes, I can see. It's how it should be."

Nuala then went to Michael. He stood up and hugged her to him.

"Yer a lucky man, Michael Connor," she said in earnest.

Michael replied, "Don't I know it?" He kissed her cheek. "I'll take good care of her. You'll see."

"I know yer will, Michael."

Nuala smiled at him. The kettle whistled on the range, and Nuala set about brewing tea, leaving the couple to gaze at each other.

Nuala was getting nothing but good feelings about them. She was sure their love was strong, even though they had only known each other briefly. It's either there or it isn't, she told herself. Nuala looked at them while she carried on stirring the tea in the pot. These two were entwined by destiny.

They are both old souls that have known each other before. Before this life, they had walked, loved, lived and parted. Possibly, all too soon, death had called one of them. They knew and recognised each other's souls as soon as they met. They were going to get another chance at happiness together.

Nuala brought the teapot to the table. They could hear the rain now as it was falling harder onto the conservatory's glass roof.

"The garden will be pleased," Nuala said to them with a smile. "Help yerself to the fruit bread." Nuala handed him a cup of tea. "There's milk and sugar. You know best how yer like it."

Francis took her cup.

"I was thinking, Auntie, I would like to take you up on the offer of staying with you for a while. If you're still happy to have me about the place."

"Happy to have yer, sure I am. Yer man, too, if needs be. What's yer plan then?"

Francis looked at Michael, and then she paused. "I have given in my notice at work."

Nuala laughed. "Yer not hanging about."

"Well, there's no point. I've made my mind up. Best to get things moving."

Michael gave Francis a nod and a smile. She knew exactly what that meant. His looks were always loaded whenever their eyes met. Nuala looked back at Michael. She smiled at him, and he knew Auntie Nuala understood plenty.

Francis carried on. "I need to put my house on the market. I thought I would do that next."

"When?" Michael asked.

This was news to him.

"Like I said," Francis replied. "There's no need to hang about. This time of year, is a good time to sell a house. People tend to be on the move, in my experience, earlier in the year. In my experience, through work, that is."

Her aunt and Michael listened, both taking in every word she said.

"I thought I would go back in a few days, sort out a few things and bring some clothes over. You know what I mean?" She was looking from one to the other for reassurance. Michael was not enthusiastic, she could tell, and Nuala suddenly looked a bit odd.

"There is a lot for me to do." She trailed off. "Why are you both staring at me? I am not saying I'm off to the moon."

As soon as Francis mentioned going back to London, the atmosphere had changed in the room. A dark shadow had wrapped itself around Francis, though Michael and Francis hadn't noticed.

Nuala wanted to let Michael speak first. Nuala now knew for sure where the danger lay for Francis.

Something had made Michael feel uncertain about her leaving so soon.

"I don't think you need to go just yet, Francis," Michael said.

He looked at her with a crestfallen look.

"It would only take me a couple of days to sort out what I wanted to keep, plus there are my clothes. My office will sort out the selling of the house, but I need to see the agent and things like that to get the ball rolling. I don't see a problem, Michael."

Her voice had changed, and Michael was getting the message. Nuala listened and thought she wanted to defuse the situation.

Michael spoke again before Nuala had a chance. His voice was far more assertive as he glared at her. "The problem is, Francis, I don't think it's a good idea for you to go on yer own just now."

Francis turned towards him to make her point. They were eye to eye. "Michael, I have been on my own for over ten years."

Michael had an overwhelming feeling that he didn't want her to go. Perhaps it was because of the Kinsale episode. He searched her face, then dropped his eyes. "I know I have no right to tell yer anything. It's just a feeling, that's all."

Nuala looked at him. *Yes*, she thought. *So do I.*

"May I say something?"

They both turned their attention back to Nuala, who they

almost forgot was sitting there, listening to them, getting overheated.

"Sorry, Auntie. Of course you may."

"Why don't I go with yer?" Nuala offered with a smile.

"That's exactly what I was going to offer. To go with her," Michael said.

Francis looked at them both, thinking about what they had said. For a moment, all three sat looking from one to the other.

"I think you are still supposed to be in recovery. What would your work think if you were just to go off to London at the drop of a hat?" Francis said.

"I shouldn't think it would matter to them at all," he said defensively.

Francis thought he would be too much of a distraction. She'd never get to do the things as quickly as she would have liked with him around.

"Are you frightened I might not come back?" she said with a saucy smile.

"There's that, too," Michael said.

"Of course I will," she reassured him. "I think seeing the house would be lovely for my auntie. Especially now it's being sold. It was, after all, her brother's home that she never got to see, not knowing where he was and now, I would be able to show her before I sell it."

Francis looked back at Nuala.

"Are you sure, Auntie, that you would like to come with me?"

Though Nuala wasn't so sure it was what she wanted to do, she knew that she had to go with Francis.

Her brother had come to her and asked for her to look out for Francis. This was his warning, and now Nuala was feeling the full force of the situation, a force she could not ignore. How could she let her go to London alone? It was clear to her Francis didn't want Michael along on this occasion. She watched as the black cloud slowly left the kitchen as she voiced her opinion.

"I want to see the house. I'd love to come with yer, just yer try stopping me."

They smiled at each other.

"Lovely," Francis cooed. "Shall we fly?"

"I've never been on a plane in my life. Come to think about

it, I have never left Ireland. Do I need a passport?"

"No," Francis said. "Just proof of who you are will do."

"I'll have to think about that."

Nuala couldn't think off-hand what she might have.

"We will think of something," Francis told her. "Not to worry now."

Michael felt as though he had been side lined, listening to the women making their plans to fly, Francis clearly excited about taking her aunt. There again, he thought, Nuala had every right, more so than him, to go with Francis. It would be a nice memory for them. They had missed out on so much time not knowing one another all the years. After all, it was only for a couple of days when all was said and done. He didn't want Francis to feel like she couldn't move without him. He recognised in himself; already, he could be a bit possessive when it came to her. He had never had these feelings before.

It was as though he had an overactive desire to protect her at all costs, telling himself it was all because of the shooting in Kinsale.

"Michael, what do you think? Will you drive us to Dublin to catch a flight?"

Francis' voice finally penetrated his thoughts. Both women were waiting for him to reply.

"Sorry, Francis, I was thinking. Sure I will. Have you decided when?"

Francis smiled. "When we find proof of who Auntie is."

She laughed. She looked at him now questioningly.

"Perhaps next Monday? The start of a fresh week will give us time to arrange things."

They all nodded their agreement. Monday it would be.

All three thought it best if Francis came to stay on Sunday before the drive to the airport on Monday morning.

In the meantime, Francis would sort out the flights and times. She thought it would be straightforward. Half an hour later, Francis and Michael left Nuala's and were on the way to Clonakilty. Michael felt as though he had had the wind taken out of him. Francis, on the other hand, was so happy.

***

"Cheer up, Michael," she said as she drove along. "You're looking as gloomy as the weather."

He couldn't seem to shake the feeling that had come over him in Nuala's kitchen. It was a foreboding feeling.

"I'm sorry," he said. "I'm all right, really. Have yer thought about what kind of ring yer might like?"

"Do I get to choose?" she jested.

"Of course, yer can choose anything you like."

He smiled at her.

Francis' world was a very happy place.

"Anything at all," he said again.

When they arrived in Clonakilty, the rain stopped. They parked along the same road as Francis had parked before. They got out of the car. Straight off, two men came up to Michael.

"Hey!" one of them said. "Long time no see."

He grabbed Michael by the hand and patted him on the back.

"How's it going? Got yer out to the shops, has she?"

He nodded to Francis with a beaming smile.

"Something like that. This is Francis."

He took hold of Francis' hand and gave it a squeeze.

"Nice to meet yer, Francis," he said rather roguishly.

"Take no notice of him, Francis. He's nothing but trouble." Michael turned back to him. "What's new then, Tom?" Michael asked.

"Just helping out yer man here." He put his thumb up to the man standing next to him. "His car's in at Joe's. We've an hour to kill until he picks it up."

Michael nodded to the other man.

"Good luck to yer then. Catch yer next time, Tom. We've got one or two things to do."

Michael wanted to get away, Francis thought.

"Yeah, sure thing, mind how yer go. Nice meeting yer, Francis."

Michael had hold of Francis' arm as he was gently moving her away.

"Watch him now," Tom added cheekily, nodding at Michael.

Francis gave half a smile, just to be polite. Michael steered Francis in the opposite direction.

"Do yer fancy a bite to eat before we go shopping?"

"Do you?" Francis replied.

"No, I'm fine for now. Just don't want yer going hungry." He smiled. "Come on, this way."

He held Francis' hand and headed off up the main road until they came to the jewellers. Unusually, the shop front wasn't painted in a bright colour, as all the others were; it was painted black, which made it look very old-fashioned and quaint. There was one bow fronted window and one door to the side. Looking in the window, Francis could see so many rings on trays in lines from one side of the window to the other.

One ring stood out to her from all the rest.

"Michael, there are so many."

Francis' face was a picture, he thought.

"It's nice to have a choice. Der yer see anything that catches yer eye?"

"I do, Michael, but I'm not sure."

Francis was a little overcome. This was all so emotional. She could never have imagined herself, in her wildest dreams, choosing an engagement ring. She had been truly swept off her feet. She turned to look at Michael, wanting to remember this moment for the rest of her life.

"I can't believe what we're doing, Michael. It feels like a dream."

He looked back at her. "Yer do want to marry me, Francis?"

"I do."

He kissed her before she could say another word. They heard a man's voice say as they became deeply engrossed in each other's arms, "Good morning, Michael."

Francis and Michael stopped their embrace and smiled. It was Father Graham.

He had recognised Michael as he saw the couple arrive at the jeweller's shop. There were not many young men of his stature in the parish. He knew Michael and his family well. Francis flushed as the priest looked at her.

"Who do we have here?" he enquired of Michael.

"This is Francis Doyle, soon to be Mrs Connor, Father," he added with pride.

"We are just choosing a ring."

"So I see." the friendly priest smiled. His face was showing signs of amusement. "I look forward to seeing yer both soon."

He raised a questioning eyebrow.

"The finer points are yet to be decided," Michael was quick to reply.

"Congratulations to you both."

Father Graham carried on up the road, leaving them looking at his back. They didn't see the broad smile on his face.

"That was so embarrassing, Michael."

He laughed. "Not to worry. Which ring do yer want?"

Francis had her eye on a gold ring with a single oval emerald surrounded by small diamonds. It was not exactly an engagement ring but more of a dress ring. The band was open and plaited.

She pointed to it. "Can you see it?"

"Let's go in then and try it on."

He ushered her in the door. An elderly gentleman came to the counter.

"Morning to yer," Michael said. "There's a ring in the window."

The man went to the back of the window and opened it up.

"Can yer point which tray?"

Francis obliged. The elderly man placed the tray before them on the counter. Francis and Michael were huddled together as the jeweller picked out the ring she pointed to.

"Let me."

Michael took the ring and put it on Francis' wedding finger.

"It fits, Michael." Francis smiled up at him triumphantly. "It fits just right. That's amazing."

"Are yer sure, Francis? Take yer time."

"I'm sure," she said softly.

"A very nice ring," the jeweller said. "Good choice." The man smiled at Francis. "It's a good emerald yer have there. Congratulations."

"Perfect!" Francis said, turning her hand this way and that, loving the way it sparkled.

Michael didn't ask how much it cost. He just handed the jeweller his card.

While the jeweller sorted out the purchase, Michael turned to Francis and leaned towards her. His lips brushed softly on hers as he spoke. "Never take it off."

"I won't." Then she kissed him tenderly. "Thank you," she said and sighed.

CHAPTER 33

In London, an incident room had been set up at the police station. There were pictures of the recent criminals displayed on a large noticeboard. These were the faces of the criminals brought over from Ireland, awaiting trial. They were being held in the notorious prison known as Wormwood Scrubs in the borough of Hammersmith.

The officer in charge of the case was Inspector Frank Bennett. He stood now in front of the boards, looking at the faces of the men, a cup of coffee in one hand and a ham sandwich in the other.

He read the names under the photographs. Marius Radu, Daniel Andre, Leon Balan, Bacau Albu, Dalca Funar, Kostie Balan, Dario Dinu.

He threw half the sandwich in the bin and drank the rest of the coffee. Rereading the names, he went to his desk and wrote the names on his notepad. Inspector Frank Bennett was nearing retirement and would have liked to close this case before that event.

Things that the police force had to deal with these days were getting much worse in his mind. As he recalled, he had known most of the criminal fraternity in the past. He had joined the Met as a young man. Thinking how the crimes had changed for the worst, he thought about his patch, remembering how the crimes were mostly robbery. Thieves had been rife in London; murder was far less. Shootings were something that happened in America, not London.

Now it was drugs, people trafficking, and murders, more stabbings on the streets. Frank Bennett had had his fill. Still, he muttered, "If I can just wrap this one up, that's me done. Leave it to the youngsters. It's their world now."

Looking over the names again, he noticed the two surnames of Balan. Leon Balan had been shot dead. His brother Kostie Balan, on the other hand, had survived and was in the Scrubs, along with the others that had been caught in Ireland, except for Dario Dinu, the other man shot dead. He went back to the boards, where their faces stared back at him. He wanted that report from

Ireland. One of these, he thought, must have knowledge of Laura Popa.

Bennett had had a tip-off that a couple of these men knew of her. Which one of these would give him what he was getting desperate to know? They had all been questioned. None as yet had given up any details of any use. He picked up the phone again to Ireland. Aggravated now and in need of some action, he went to the phone on his desk.

"O'Rourke. Bennett here."

"Hello again," Jim O'Rourke said, his eyes rolling up to heaven.

Bennett asked in a very abrupt manner when was he going to get the reports. Would it be in this lifetime?

"I'm on it," O'Rourke barked back. "One of my officers has been stabbed, yer know. As soon as I have an update, I'll send it. We are doing all we can over here."

"I'm sure you are," Bennett retaliated. "Just not bloody quick enough."

"When the reports are done, you'll get 'em." Jim O'Rourke slammed the phone down.

Bennett slammed down his phone in response, though O'Rourke had hung up first.

Smiling to himself, Bennett said to himself, "Doesn't hurt to rattle the cage a bit."

He yelled out to one of his men, "Jackson," who was sitting at his desk on the far side of the room. "Get me an interview at the Scrubs. I want to interview the Romanians again."

"Yes sir, I'm on it."

"Jackson," he yelled again.

"Yes, sir," the younger man said through gritted teeth.

"Get me an interpreter, too, to join me there."

"Will do, sir."

Jackson was straight away on the phone.

Bennett went back to the photographs, wondering where Laura Popa was. He looked at each man as if willing them to tell him something, desperate now for anything to go on. He wanted to get things moving.

***

Patrick Logan was in O'Rourke's office in Bandon.

"I don't know what else there is to write, sir," he said. "It was all pretty well straight forward in Kinsale."

"Go on," O'Rourke said. "Try me. Tell me again."

"We were waiting." He paused, looking at O'Rourke and thinking he was in a bad mood. "Mick and me, that is, we were waiting in the car, watching. Dinu was on the side pavement by the harbour, waiting and looking like he was expecting someone. The boat engine turned over alongside where he was standing. He had a man standing by waiting, looking up the road in our direction. Then this redhead comes along and starts talking to Dinu."

Patrick paused again for a moment to collect his thoughts.

"I knew it was the woman he had been watching. So it was my guess she was his next victim. That's when Mick leaps out of the car, with his gun at the ready, as he recognised the redhead and called out that it was Francis."

O'Rourke kept quiet as Patrick carried on.

"I wasn't sure what was happening, sir. I got out of the car, gun at the ready, hearing Michael saying, 'Run, Francis, run,' which she did as the other big fella looked as though he was going to grab her. Mick shot the big guy, who went down, and then Mick went down. I shot the other guy, Dinu. Two dead bodies and Mick stabbed, end of. The other fella took off in the boat, and the water unit picked him up at the top of the harbour. The other men on the yacht, down in Union, were rounded up. What more is there?"

Patrick shrugged his shoulders.

"What more indeed," O'Rourke said.

Patrick thought and added more. "Dinu's car was loaded with drugs from the yacht, and the house they used had all the evidence of women and drugs. All that, sir, is in the other men's reports too."

Patrick looked at the superintendent. "I have put as much detail in my report, as much as I recall, sir."

"Sure yer have," O'Rourke said, rubbing at his chin. "I would have liked Mick's report too. Have you had word from him?"

231

"No, sir."

Patrick looked at his superior, hoping that was an end to it.

O' Rourke threw his hands up, then putting them on the desk, he stood up.

"I'll wait for Mick to turn up before sending off your reports. He just might add something. I'm not clear in my mind about the girl, and about her connection with Mick. Is this the new girl in his life?"

Patrick looked blankly back at him.

"I have no idea, sir."

O'Rourke came around his desk to stand at the window again, his hands deep in his trouser pockets. He left Patrick looking at his back while he looked out at the scudding clouds.

Almost to himself, he said, "London can wait a bloody bit longer." Turning back to Patrick, he smiled. "Did Mick tell you he wants out of the unit?"

"No, he did not."

Patrick was surprised and shocked. So, he thought, that's what's bugging him.

"As I say, sir. I've not heard from him."

***

Michael was the happiest man alive. His beautiful Francis was wearing his ring. All thoughts of work had disappeared from his mind. The couple strolled along the road without a care in the world.

Francis held onto Michael's arm. Every so often, she would look up at him. Almost as if to check that this was real, he was real. She had never felt so happy. This was a day she would always remember. Looking at his handsome face, she was trying to etch the whole episode of buying the ring into her brain, not wanting to ever forget the love she was feeling for him right now.

"Never take it off," he had whispered as he slipped the ring onto her finger.

That thought alone made her squeeze his arm. He looked down at her.

"Yer all right, Francis?"

"More than all right," she said, smiling up at him.

He was going to take her for something to eat and drink. They could spend the rest of the day thinking about each other and enjoying each other's company.

They would spend as much time together the next few days as possible. Michael was confident that O'Rourke would not hurry in finding him a new position in the Gardai. That was, in his opinion, in the hope that he might change his mind about leaving the unit.

At least they had until Sunday, when Francis would stay at her aunt's house.

***

Chief Inspector Bennett thought Wormwood Scrubs was a depressing place. He walked alone through its corridors. There was no sign of the interpreter as yet. Bennett's mind thought about the last time the Irish were there when the IRA inmates had staged a rooftop protest over their visiting rights. What a commotion that had caused. Sixty inmates were injured, and several prison officers too.

The governor, who he knew, had quit before things got rough. He had called the prison a 'penal dustbin' in his report. A very depressing place indeed.

Getting this case sorted was his priority. He wanted out himself, feeling his age and the new wave of crime that he thought was beyond what he could comprehend, or what he even wanted to deal with. His mind longed for decent images, away from the dregs of humanity.

He was just about to enter the interview room when he heard a click clack of heels hurrying along the corridor towards him. A woman in heels, he noted, as he threw open the door and went in.

The interview room was dark and gloomy. Pulling out a chair, he sat at the table, placing his notes before him. Then the woman responsible for the click clack shoes came in.

"Good morning," she said. "Campbell, your interpreter." She pulled out a chair at the table alongside the inspector.

Inspector Bennett gave half a smile and briskly replied, "Bennett, morning." He opened up his file. "There are five of them this morning," he said. "Some can understand English, but I don't want to leave any doubt that they haven't understood every single word I say."

"I understand," Campbell replied.

The door opened, and the first of the prisoners entered. He

233

was handcuffed, and a prison officer was with him.

With the recorder set, the officer stood beside the prisoner. He was Marius Radu.

"Sit," the officer said.

Radu sat. He was looking at the inspector with dark brown eyes; his face was unshaven, craggy, drawn, and without emotion.

The inspector looked back at him with disgust, flicked on the recorder and began. He stated the time, date, the prisoner's name, and his own and Miss Campbell's names.

"Do you understand English?" Inspector Bennett asked.

"Yes," he said.

"Do you know Dario Dinu?"

"Yes."

"Do you know Dario Dinu is dead?"

"No," he said.

His eyes flicked to the face of the interpreter. She sat silently, looking at him.

"Do you know Dario Dinu had a sister?"

"Yes," he replied.

"Do you know her name?"

"No. Dario Dinu was bringing some woman."

"Do you know what woman?"

"No."

"What was your job on the yacht?"

"Just to sail the boat. I don't know about anything else."

The inspector sat looking at him for a few moments.

"Do you know Daniel Adrei?"

"Yes. He was working on the yacht."

"Just to sail it?" the inspector asked.

"Yes, I think so."

"What about Baciu Albu?"

"Yes," Radu answered straight away. "He is a sailor."

"Now, tell me about Dalca Funar."

Radu shifted his position in the chair, wiping at the beads of sweat that just appeared along his top lip.

The inspector felt Funar was the man who would know more. He knew through his experience that the man in front of him was telling the truth.

"He is the captain," Radu said. "We were hired by him for this trip."

"Have you sailed with him before?"

"Yes."

"When was that, a couple of months back? Was that to Ireland?"

"Yes. He paid me well, so I took the job again. It was easy for me to make these short trips."

"Did you know he was dealing drugs?"

Radu hung his head.

It was the first bit of remorse the inspector had seen from him. He asked him again. Randu looked up at him.

"Yes," he replied.

"What about people?"

"People? No, I never seen any people." He looked long and defiantly at the inspector. "I do remember the last time there was a girl."

"What girl? Do you know her name?"

"No, she was in a cabin. She went on another boat while we were at sea. No other people. I don't know about people, only the drugs."

Inspector Bennett sat back in his chair. "Take him out," he said to the officer. "Bring me Kostie Balan."

He switched off the recorder. The inspector was deep in thought. He had almost forgotten the woman sitting next to him. He took a sideways look at her. She looked at him.

"Looks like you may not need me, inspector," she said evenly.

"I appreciate you being here nevertheless," he said.

He was writing something down as Kostie Balan came into the room. He was twice the size of the previous man.

"Sit," the inspector said.

Kostie kept standing. The prison officer pointed out the chair. Kostie kicked out at the chair to move it back and slumped into it. He was an ugly man. The sheer size of him was intimidating. His hands were enormous and robust. The inspector took in the measure of him. A right masher, he thought.

Once again, Bennett flicked the switch to the recorder and was ready to start with the questioning. Many of the same questions were asked and answered, as with the previous prisoner.

Inspector Bennett touched on a raw nerve when he asked Balan about his brother. The prisoner was visibly in a state of distress as soon as Bennett mentioned the death of his brother, Leon Balan. He banged his fist on the table. A thump resounded with each blow of his meaty fist as he spat out words.

"Why did they have to kill him? My brother Leon."

The interpreter sat up in her chair and was visibly flinching.

The inspector kept his cool and talked steadily and evenly. "Who is responsible for asking you to deal with drugs and traffic people?"

The inspector waited.

He was looking at the top of Kostie Balan's head.

"Dinu and his sister," Balan said without hesitation.

Balan's head still bowed down as tears rolled down his cheeks. His shoulders jerked as he tried to hold in the sobs. He had been, and still was, grief stricken about his brother. Balan didn't care what became of him now. His brother was the only person in the world he took notice of. His brother had looked after him and understood him. They had always been together. Kosti Balan was a simple man. His brain was limited. He relied on his brother to get by in life. He was alone now and totally bereft.

Kostie's size made him look hostile and could be very dangerous under his brother's guidance. It was now very apparent to the inspector, looking at the giant with a brain the size of a pea, who was now sobbing like a child.

Perhaps Kostie Balan could tell him a lot more.

"What do you know about Dinu's sister?"

Campbell took a tissue out of her handbag, showing it to the inspector, who nodded. She handed it to Balan, and he took it from her like a child. He wiped his face and blew his nose.

"Will you tell me what you know about Dinu's sister, Laura Popa, Kostie?"

Bennett waited.

CHAPTER 34

Francis and Michael ate their fill at the pub and washed it down with wine. From time to time, Francis held out her hand, gazing at the beautiful ring adorning the third finger of her left hand.

"Yer happy with that then, Francis?" Michael asked.

"You could say that, Michael," she teased him.

He smiled. "I think yer made the right choice. The green is almost as beautiful as yer eyes."

Michael put an arm around her shoulder. "When shall we get wed then?" he asked softly into her ear.

Sheer pleasure ran through her. Michael's voice was so seductive, accompanied by the warmth of his breath on her neck.

"Ask me again," she said, pushing her ear to his face.

Michael went along with it. He knew she was up to something.

"When shall we get—"

Francis had turned her face to him and enveloped his mouth with her own. He responded, and she felt him push his tongue until her lips opened wider.

She pulled away first, laughing at him. Michael pulled her to him, his eyes searching her face.

"I've told yer before, yer really are the most wanton woman."

She giggled. "Only with you, Michael. Only with you."

His eyes had turned into deep pools of expectation. "Yer can show me how much yer are tonight, Francis Doyle."

Francis' face flushed at the thought. It was his turn to laugh.

"What do yer think about the date?" he asked, all humour gone.

Francis looked at him.

"I suppose as soon as possible, judging by your appetite," she said with a saucy look that he loved.

She really turned him on.

Francis was giggling again.

"Don't start again, Francis. Yer won't win. Let's take a walk, shall we?"

Michael stood up and offered out his arm in a playful way.

"Why thank you, kind sir. I would be delighted." Her voice was sweet and playful, like a southern belle. "Why, I do believe we can chat along the way."

It was his turn to laugh again.

Back out onto the street, they both looked up at the sky. The clouds had moved off, leaving tempting bits of blue sky, reminding them the sun would shine again soon. Arm in arm, the happy couple strolled further along the road, laughing and chatting, with eyes for only each other. They would spend the rest of the day and evening together, and Michael hoped through that night, too.

He would not be disappointed.

CHAPTER 35

That evening, Nuala was sorting through a hoard of papers. She was looking now for something that would prove who she was, never having bothered about such things before. It had been David who kept all that sort of thing. He had been far more methodical than she had ever known how to be. But where to look, she had not a clue. David's room was full to capacity.

Nuala was fishing about in the tallboy in David's room again. Her mind went to when she had found the bundle of letters, with Robert's picture and letter. With that in mind, Nuala guessed she had been lucky to find it. Still, she couldn't be doing anything about that now.

Rummaging in the next drawer down, she began muttering.

"All this is too much for me. Why did yer keep all this stuff, David?"

Look in the desk, popped into her mind, as sure as someone had said it in her ear.

Nuala stopped and looked about the room.

After a pause, she spoke out loud again. "I will. I'll look in the desk."

Anyone watching Nuala alone in her home would think she might be a slice short of a full loaf.

The truth was, she was as sharp as a tack. It was just her brain worked on a different level than most. It was a clever brain. Nuala had a dislike for formality. Although she believed there was a place and time for everything. There was order in the universe and a plan for all.

She lived her life according to her own talents. True also to say, they had not tested her in the greater world. Nuala had no mind to go wandering away from the place she was born in. She loved her home, counting the blessings she had known there, with the love of one fine man that had sustained her, she could feel his spirit. He sustained her still, whilst she remained there, so did he. She had enough money to live a modest life, enjoying a quiet existence. People knew her, and she knew a few others, primarily from church. They were her kind of people. Nuala liked to keep within the church family, and her faith in the Almighty was deeply rooted in her psyche. She liked the priest, Father Graham, when he came to take Mass at Rosscarbery. Life there on the outskirts of the small village suited her fine. Her plants, the birds and her garden were more than enough. She felt well-balanced in her life. It would suit her till her time was done. Then she knew most confidently that she would go happily to the other side, to rest and perhaps start over and even meet her David again, there or in a new life.

Her soul was an old soul. She felt in touch with the natural world and lived in a rhythm that was harmonious to her life, to her very being and then into death.

Opening up the bottom drawer first, her eyes fell on several folders as she sat in David's chair. Lifting them out, she placed them on the desk before her.

"What have we here?"

Opening up the first folder, she soon realised there was nothing remotely of interest to her. She placed it aside. The second one had her name on the front.

"This looks promising. Would yer look at that? Putting me name on the front and all?"

Nuala, Onagh Doyle, Mrs Nuala O'Leary.

Nuala stroked her hand over the writing, remembering David. He must have sat in this very spot to write it. She opened it up. The first thing lying on the top of the contents was a picture. It was just her on their wedding day. Nuala took a long look at herself in the picture. It surprised her just how much she looked like Francis, or Francis looked a lot like her. Either way, the similarity was striking. No mistake; they were of the same family.

Next, she picked up her baptism record. Pinned to a bit of material like lace, the colour had changed from white to a snuff-coloured brown.

"My shawl," she said. "Or maybe a small bit of my gown."

Her dear David had kept all these things safe for her, and she hadn't even thought about them.

There was her marriage certificate and another piece of card that had turned brown. Pressed to it were forget-me-not flowers.

"Would yer look at that?" Nuala said to the empty room.

As she sat at the desk, her mind travelled far back, as she recalled David handing her a bunch of sweet little flowers. It had been a glorious spring morning. The sun shone. Unexpectedly outside their little home, she heard his bicycle bell ringing. Robert was at work, but she knew it was David. Flinging the door open wide, she stood within its frame.

"And what would yer be doing here at this time of day?" she had asked.

Propping the bike beside the old wall, he came to her, the flowers held out in front and a smile from ear to ear on his handsome face. Nuala had put out her hand to take the flowers.

Before he handed them to her, he had said, "They'll cost yer."

"Cost me what?" she had replied.

"Come with me for a walk."

David handed her the flowers, and she took them in and found a cup to put them in. He waited outside until she appeared with a shawl around her shoulders. David was now astride his bike, and Nuala perched herself on the cross bar. She remembered so clearly the day that he had decided to take her to the woods and make her his. Forever.

A tear had trickled down her cheek as the memory came flooding back, filling her with the overpowering feelings of him.

"Forget yer not, ever, David," she whispered.

Nuala placed all the items back in the folder. Got herself up from the desk. The light was fading now. Drawing the curtains and switching on the lights, she went to the kitchen. Nuala was in a thoughtful mood as she made herself some tea. Finding the folder with the pressed forget-me-nots had surprised her. David had saved a sprig of sweet little flowers. Now her mind was full of that first time she had lain with him.

Francis would be feeling like that, she mused. The chemistry between Francis and Michael was just the same as that between her and David. Some things are just meant to be. They made a lovely couple.

Nuala told herself there were things to get on with, now that Francis would be coming to stay.

"I think I'll take the bus tomorrow. I shall pop into Clona, sure I need one or two things for the trip to London."

London, she thought again, to see Robert's house. Who would

have thought it?

Nuala was excited and nervous about the journey. Still, she told herself she had a few days until the event. A few days to get used to the idea and a few days to get her courage up. A few days to get things in order.

The following morning Nuala was out of bed with a purpose, as she was going to catch the bus as it passed through Rosscarbery for Clonakilty at nine-thirty. Luckily the day was decent. Just a jacket would do, and her strong walking shoes for the walk down the lane.

Nuala put her purse in her basket and checked around the kitchen before leaving by the back door. She walked purposefully down the drive and off down the lane. After ten minutes, Mary Murphy was driving along the same lane and came alongside her, slowed her car, and stopped.

"Morning, Nuala," she called through the open window as she stretched across to the passenger side. "If yer off to Clona, hop in."

"I was going to catch the bus." Nuala smiled.

"No need. I'm going."

Nuala gratefully opened the door to the little car.

"Oh, that's grand," Nuala said as she swiftly got in.

Mary Murphy was a happy soul. Nuala quite liked the woman. She had a jolly way about her. Even in school, she was a jolly child; rosy-faced and rotund in stature then as she was now.

"Yer wouldn't believe if I told yer," Nuala started off.

"Go on," Mary said. "What's happened?"

"It turns out I have a niece."

"A niece?" Mary's head nearly spun off her shoulders. "How did that happen?" Mary's voice was a little higher pitched than was normal for her.

"Do yer remember my brother Robert?"

"I do. He went to England, as I recall, am I right?"

"That he did," Nuala replied. "Well, it's his daughter, Francis."

"Francis. Well, I never. That was a shock for yer?"

"It most certainly was. She's a lovely girl. She will be coming to stay with me for a while."

"That nice fer yer, Nuala. A bit of company about the place."

Nuala decided not to tell her about Francis getting married. That was Francis' news, after all. It was now Mary's turn for a bit of news, and she relished telling Nuala about it.

"Did yer hear about Mrs Brown's consequences after the op?"

Nuala was smiling inwardly. Mary Murphy had a way with words that amused her no end.

"I'm all ears," Nuala said.

"It was just a week ago now, so it was. There's her other half, telling her didn't she think she'd had enough time to recover." Mary turned her face from the quiet lane to face Nuala for emphasis, saying, "And when did she think she going to get back to the cooking?"

Nuala's eyebrows shot up at that. "He never did?"

Mary went on with both hands high on the steering wheel, negotiating the bends in the lane with skill.

"He said it was enough time to go without his pleasures, but he was fed up with going without dinner too."

"Poor Biddy Brown," Nuala replied.

"'Tis true."

Mary risked taking a peek at Nuala, and then both the women laughed.

Mary Murphy added, "I've always said two of the most important things to yer man is food and sex."

The little car was virtually wobbling from side to side as the two women shook with laughter, making their way down the lane.

They had enjoyed each other's company on the way to town. Mary always had something interesting to say, whenever they met.

They parked up.

"Shall I pick you up later on the way back?" Mary asked.

"I'll be stopping for me lunch," Nuala replied.

"See yer at the hotel then, shall I? I am having a bite of something too."

"Fine." Nuala smiled. "About midday, then?"

Nuala got herself out of the car.

She thought it was good to catch Mary as she set off toward the solicitor's office. Before entering, Nuala muttered, "If Mr O'Shea is busy, I can always leave a message."

Nuala stepped in over the threshold.

"Good morning, how may I help yer?" a cheery young woman greeted her.

There was a young woman seated behind her desk. It left just enough space to get around, should anyone be lucky enough to see the solicitor, Mr James O'Shea.

Nuala had known of him since her school days. A local man who had taken over from his father. These days he was looking more than ever like his father, with spectacles perched on the end of his nose and wispy white hair curled about his ears. He was a gentle man with a kind manner and softly spoken.

Mr O'Shea came out from the back room where his office was situated.

"Good morning, Mrs O'Leary. It's a while since we had the pleasure of a visit from yer good self."

Nuala smiled at his greeting.

"It's a fine morning. I was just passing, and I thought I'd pop in on the off chance you might spare me a minute or two?"

"I'd be delighted, come on through. Yer lucky to catch me this morning. I have half an hour to spare. Would that suit yer?"

"More than enough time," a grateful Nuala replied.

He ushered her into his small back office. There was a tiny window that looked out onto a yard, a desk and three chairs, with a filing cabinet in the corner.

"Have a seat there," he said, holding out his hand.

Nuala sat down, pulling at her jacket so it sat neatly at the front, her basket on the floor.

"Mrs O'Leary, what can I do for yer?"

James O'Shea placed his hands together on the desk and leaned a little towards her, waiting for Nuala to start.

"It's like this, Mr O'Shea. I have a niece I didn't know I had."

"I see," Mr O'Shea said.

"She's a lovely girl, my brother's only daughter. Do you remember my brother Robert?"

Mr O'Shea looked thoughtful for a moment.

"Now you come to mention it, I do. Didn't he take off for England?"

"He did that. We lost contact, you see," Nuala said.

"I see," he said again, this time with a gentle nod of his head.

"Is he well?"

"He passed away some time ago now. Francis, that's my niece, is now moving over here. She will be staying with me for a while. Until she gets her own place." Hoping that he was making sense of it all, Nuala carried on. "Now I was thinking, Mr O'Shea, that since we are all each other has, I would like to leave her my house when I die and everything in it."

"I see," he said for the third time.

"Will that be all right then?" Nuala asked naively. "My bit of money too."

"Of course, it will be fine. You need to make a will."

"I want to do that if that's the right thing to do."

"It is the right thing to do. It's a simple matter," Mr O'Shea said. "Let's take down a few details. There are no complications, as I see it."

Mr O'Shea couldn't have been more helpful. He asked her to sign, and he called in the receptionist to witness. Half an hour later, Nuala was shaking his hand as he saw her out to the front office and through the front door.

"Good day to you, Nuala. A copy will be in the post. There's nothing for you to worry about at all."

They shook hands, and Nuala made her way along the pavement.

She was grateful it was sorted before going to London. Looking at the shop windows as she walked, she spotted a nice jacket, thinking that it would do nicely for the trip. Perhaps some slacks, she thought. All the ladies seem to be wearing them these days. They're practical, and she thought she might go the whole way with a couple of tops. Why not, she thought. She hadn't been shopping for clothes in a while.

She didn't think she wanted to hold much more, so she headed off to Conolly's Hotel, situated conveniently amidst all the shops. Conolly's was a firm favourite for the locals who came in for a bit of shopping. Most of the ladies would stop for a bite at lunchtime. There was always a choice of something hot and tasty. They served food all day long and evenings too.

When Nuala arrived, it was almost twelve and Mary Murphy had already found a table and was chatting away with another lady at the next table. Nuala made her way to where Mary was.

"There yer are." Mary looked at her bags. "You've been busy."

Nuala was smiling. "I didn't mean to buy so much. I'm going off to London for a few days."

"London?"

Mary's voice was loud and high-pitched for the second time today. The woman on the other table pricked up her ears as she looked at Nuala with interest as Nuala sat down.

"Don't go telling the world," Nuala said.

Mary apologised. "Yer took me by surprise, is all."

"It's all right," Nuala said. "I'm surprised meself. Didn't ever think I would be going to London of all places."

She slipped off her jacket and hung it on the back of her chair.

"When are yer going then?"

"Monday," Nuala said.

"That soon?" Mary was on to the next thing before Nuala had a chance to answer. "What shall we get to eat then?"

"My treat," Nuala said. "I was thinking fish and chips."

"Lovely," Mary replied.

Nuala took out her purse from her basket and got up to go to the counter, where she stood behind two women who were getting their choice plated up. It was an hour later that Mary and Nuala set off for home.

CHAPTER 36

Martha and Joseph had been up quite a while before Michael showed his face in the kitchen.

"Late night, was it?" Martha teased, looking at her son.

"Morning Ma, is there any tea going?"

At least he was showered and dressed, thought Martha. "Francis all right?" she asked with a raised eyebrow.

Joseph came into the kitchen. "Morning, son."

"Morning, Da."

"Did yer have a nice day then, meeting the auntie?"

"We did." Michael nodded to Joseph.

"That's good. She's a grand lady. Did yer tell him, Ma, about the call?"

"Call? What call?" Michael asked, looking at Martha.

"I've not had a chance yet, Joe. He's just come down."

She looked back at her son and handed him a mug of tea. "O'Rourke called yesterday. I told him you were out visiting. He asked if yer would give him a call."

Michael sighed. Just then, Francis came in.

"Morning all," she said, bright and chirpy.

"Tea?" Martha asked.

"Yes, please. I'd love a cup. Did Michael tell you he bought me a ring?"

"No," Martha exclaimed. "He did not. He's just come down."

Francis approached Martha with her hand held out.

Martha looked. "That's just beautiful, suits you a treat. Green is your colour, that's for sure."

Joseph came over to take a look. "That's a cracker." He kissed Francis' cheek.

"Do yer want any breakfast?" Martha asked.

Michael, clutching his tea, went over and stood next to Francis. "I'll have some toast if there's any going," Francis asked. "With some of your lovely marmalade, please."

"What about you, Michael? Surely you want more than just a bit of toast now?"

Michael gave his Ma a half smile. "Whatever you got going,

Ma."

Michael looked at Francis and told her, "I'm just going to make a call." He gave her a quick kiss on her cheek and left the room.

Francis sat down at the table. She felt more comfortable in Ash House with a ring on her finger.

Joseph took himself off outside to see to the dogs. Martha set about cooking up for her son a plate full of eggs and bacon.

"How was it at yer auntie's then?"

"We had a lovely time. My aunt and Michael got on really well. I have asked her to come back to London with me." Martha's head spun around to look at Francis. The look on Martha's face caused Francis to quickly add, "It's just for a few days. I thought it might be nice for her to see where her brother lived, seeing as I'm going to sell it."

Martha took the pan off the heat. She had nearly caught the bacon.

"Is that so? When will this be?"

"Monday," Francis said with a smile.

"I'll say this for yer, Francis. You don't let the grass grow, that's for sure."

"Like I said to Auntie Nuala, there's not much point in waiting, is there?"

"No love, I guess not. Not once yer mind's made up."

"It is, Martha. I just want to be here with Michael."

Martha put a plate of toast on the table. "Of course yer do. Help yerself to everything else."

"If it's all right with you, I would like to stay here until Sunday. When we come back from London, I plan to stay with Auntie until I find my own place."

"I see," Martha said. "That's just grand. It will be nice for yer auntie and yerself to get to know one another."

"That's what we thought. We are very much alike, you know. I'm sure we will enjoy one another's company."

Michael came back and sat down at the table opposite Francis.

"Everything all right?" Francis asked, taking a mouthful of toast.

Michael rubbed his hand through his hair. "O'Rourke wants me to go in."

"Work?" Francis asked. Her brow furrowed at the thought.

"Surely not yet, Michael," Martha chimed in.

"No, not work as such. Just to get the report finished. London's on his back. They need our report as soon as possible. I'll go in. It shouldn't take me long. Paddy's done most of it already."

Martha put his breakfast down in front of him. "Not before you get that inside yer," she said.

He raised an eyebrow at his ma. "Don't mind if I do." He smiled as he tried to be light about it all.

He looked at Francis. "Do yer want to come with me? Not to the station, but yer could look around Bandon for the morning. Shouldn't take me long."

"Yes, that would be great," Francis said.

"Any more tea, Ma?" he asked. "This is lovely."

Martha smiled. She loved having this opportunity to feed her son, happy that he was staying there to recuperate. That dreadful stabbing. Just the thought of it made her make the sign of the cross over her ample bosom.

Seeing Michael so happy with his girl now was all she had been dreaming of for her son. *They are so in love with each other*, she thought as she looked at them.

She made the couple a fresh pot of tea and left the kitchen.

CHAPTER 37

Inspector Bennett was addressing his team in the incident room of the police station. He was pacing up and down as he spoke, informing them of the facts so far. He wanted answers, and he wanted them fast. The operation had already gone on for far too long.

His voice boomed out across the room.

"A composite artist will be going to the Scrubs this morning with Jones to speak to the two men, who may have seen the elusive Laura Popa. Perhaps that would give us some idea of what she looks like. I am beginning to think she is a myth."

Cooper called out. "Sir, I think we might have something."

"Speak up, man, don't keep it to yourself."

"The names of Dinu and Rominov, there is a match in the records for a marriage. It's quite some time ago, sir. Over ten years ago or so," he added a little sheepishly.

"Get on it. Find out all you can. We need to follow all leads."

"Yes, sir."

Cooper was pleased to have found this connection, but it might prove to be nothing at all.

"Right, men… and ladies," he added as an afterthought, taking into account the two women who were now on his team. "Let's have some action."

Bennett went back into his office and sat behind his desk.

***

Michael had finished his breakfast and went outside to speak to Joseph. He found him out in the stable, mucking it out. The dogs escorted Michael in the hope he was going to give them a run over the hill.

"Not this morning," he said to Murphy as the hound tapped away at Michael's hand with his wet, cold nose.

Joseph looked up when his son approached.

"Yer all right, Da? Can I ask yer if you'll drive me and Francis to Andrew's? I need to get me car."

"What's a do then?" Joseph had stopped his sweeping and was now resting on the broom.

"I'm going to the station to finish off the report."

"Francis is going with you?" he questioned, looking a little surprised.

"I thought she might like to look around Bandon for an hour or so."

"Not much to look at there," Joseph laughed. He thought better of it; his son was looking serious. He quickly said, "Of course I'll take yer. Give me ten minutes to finish up. Need to get this done. I'll be picking up the donkey later and bringing her friend too. Seems you're not the only ones to have hit it off lately. They have hit it off too."

He laughed again.

Michael looked at his da and smiled, returning to the house. He turned. "Yer might end up in there yourself when Ma finds out."

When he came back in, Francis was alone in the kitchen doing the washing up. He took advantage of her hands in the sink and grabbed her from behind. He started kissing her down her long neck.

"Da's driving us to Kinsale." Francis was hardly listening. She was getting lost in the feelings he was creating. His warm lips were gently caressing her neck, interspersed by his softly spoken words. "So, I can pick up me car." His lips glided down her swan-like neck. His hands found their way to her breasts. Francis withdrew her hands from the soap suds of the washing-up bowl and turned. Their faces were just an inch apart.

"Then we're off to Bandon," he said.

Francis sought those tempting lips of his again. She felt her passion rising, and then remembering where they were, she stopped kissing him and said, "We could have taken my car."

Reluctantly he stopped and looked at her when all he really wanted was to devour her there and then.

"I know, but I need my car, anyway."

Then he quickly covered her mouth with his. That kiss was interrupted. Martha had returned to the kitchen, coughing politely.

**

All went according to plan. It would have been easier for Joseph to have driven Michael straight to Bandon, but he understood Michael wanted to be with Francis as much as he could during this time.

They were certainly smitten. They could hardly keep their hands off each other. It was not lost on Martha or Joseph. Joseph smiled inwardly as he remembered well what he had felt like at Michael's age. So, it was with a happy heart Joseph took them both to Kinsale and the parochial house where his eldest son lived.

When they arrived, Andrew's car was not there. Michael's was where he had parked it before he was stabbed.

"Yer brother must be out in the parish somewhere. That's a shame, we could have had a cuppa. Never mind," Joseph said. "You get off now. See yer both later."

Michael thanked his father as he fished in his trouser pocket for the keys to his car.

"Mind how you go," Joseph called as Francis and Michael got out of his car.

Pleased that his car had started straight off, Michael looked at Francis. "Ready?" he asked.

"Ready," she replied, buckling up her seatbelt.

They were now heading off to Bandon. Francis was quiet and looking out the window at the passing countryside. The sun that had been hidden from time to time was now peeping out from behind the fair-weather clouds as they drifted and started to disperse, leaving a bright blue sky.

"At least yer seeing the lay of the land," Michael told her as they drove along the quiet lanes to Bandon.

"It's all so lovely, Michael."

In no time at all, they had arrived in the small town.

"Will I leave yer here in the town to look at the shops for a while? I'll come and find yer."

Francis smiled at him and reminded him about the last time he had said that to her.

"Sure, I remember, and I did, didn't I? Come and find yer."

He leaned over to give her a quick kiss. "I'm thinking a couple of hours at the most."

"I'll be fine," Francis said. "Off you go and write that report."

He was reluctant to leave her. "Just don't go talking to any men," Michael jested.

"I won't. I don't want to."

They looked each other in the eyes, smiling, and then got out of the car. Michael handed her the keys. "You keep hold of these now, in case you want to wait in the car for me. I'll find yer wherever yer are."

Francis just smiled at her man. She loved his way. She knew he was true to his word.

CHAPTER 38

Laura Popa was drifting around her palatial office within her house, located in the upmarket area of Bayswater. She had just seen Coral and Vinnie for the second time since their return from Ireland. Laura had listened intently to what her darlings had to say. Their recent trip had proved to be fruitful. Coral, Laura thought, had potential. She was showing an initiative now that Laura hadn't previously seen in her.

"If I can be of any further help, Laura," she had said before leaving.

"You, my dear, have been the biggest help. How vould you like a trip abroad again?"

"Where?" she had asked keenly.

"Romania, my dear."

"Yes, I'd love that, Laura."

Coral had looked excited. Vinnie looked down in the mouth.

"What about me?" he'd asked.

"Vell yes, if you von't to," Laura had purred.

She had no intentions of sending him anywhere. His work was done now. Laura had had enough of him, though he never knew it. Coral, on the other hand, was a different story.

"Run along now, the pair of you. I have things to do," she had told them both.

Laura's plan was beginning to hatch. When they had left, she went to sit behind her desk. Picking up the phone, she dialled a number, and after a few rings, a male voice answered.

"I have a job for you," she said. "I von't you to keep vatch at a house and let me know as soon as a young woman with red hair arrives." She paused. "Yes, that's right, you'll know, I assure you. Francis Doyle. It might be day or night. It could be any day." She paused, listening. "Then you vill tell me. It's a simple job. I know you von't let me down." She paused again and listened, stroking her long black hair. It had been pulled back tight at the scalp and fell down over her shoulder to her waist. She pulled at the fastening and let it fall about her. "The same rate. From today. No matter how long it takes." She paused again. After she had listened, she replied, "It's in a row of terraced houses. 657 Vands Road. It's in Vandsvorth. Good. You know it. I look forward to hearing from you."

She put the phone down. Her red lips curled.

It won't be long now, Dario, she thought as she flicked her hair back from her shoulder.

Slinking from the room, she closed the door quietly behind her.

Within a few hours, an unknown car arrived on Wands Road. It slowly made its way while the driver was checking the numbers of the properties. Finally, it had come to a halt as it found a parking space just two doors from number 657.

There were two men in the car. They spoke to each other in a foreign language. Anyone who had had the time to watch them would have realised that their behaviour was unusual.

After an hour had passed, one of the men got out of the car and walked off up the road. He reappeared a couple of hours later, getting back into the car, as the other man left.

There hadn't been anyone to take notice as the two men proceeded with their strange activity.

Laura was back in her office. She had summoned Vinnie. There was one other in the room, one of her henchmen. He was sitting almost behind the door on an upright chair.

After Laura spoke at length to Coral, she knew Vinnie's time was spent. He had become very obsessed with Coral. Not surprisingly, she mused, seeing how well the two had performed together.

Theirs was a strange relationship. They had known one another intimately for quite some time. Vinnie was a bit of a loose cannon these days. Coral felt that she couldn't trust him. Laura had listened when Coral had pointed out some of his disloyalties. Coral also found his sexual appetite was changing. There had been times, she told Laura, that she had feared what he might want to do to her next. Laura had had first-hand knowledge of Vinnie and his sexual appetite, though now Coral was telling her things she had previously not known.

"I understand," Laura said. "Vell, you can do the Romanian job on your own if you're happy to go. If you're happy to say goodbye to Vinnie."

She was now longing for a change. Coral was now very happy

indeed. "You can count on me, Laura. I'll do anything for you."

"I know." Laura brushed her hand gently around Coral's face and down her neck. "Ve vill chat later. Go now, come back later."

Coral smiled and left. Half an hour later, the scene was set for Vinnie. Laura knew it had to be the end for him. When he came into the room, it was dimly lit. He hadn't noticed the other man sitting behind the door as he entered.

"Hello, Vinnie," she purred as she sat astride the corner of her desk, her bare legs dangling.

Laura had his attention as he took in the sight of her. She showed him that she wasn't wearing anything apart from a flimsy top that softly floated below her breast.

"Come to me." She beckoned him with her fingers.

Her long red nails danced at the tip of her hand as she twisted her hand around and around, her back arched as she pushed her chest out to him.

He slowly walked towards her, already feeling aroused. He knew how she liked to play the game. They had played many times before.

As soon as he reached her, he slowly wrapped his arms around her waist as she yielded her scantily covered body towards him. Putting her head slowly to one side, she offered her neck to him.

With her free hand, she reached down behind her, and deftly without notice, she picked up the thin stiletto knife.

Vinnie was totally lost in himself as he thought about what he was going to do to her.

While his head was tilted, his lips sucking hard on her neck, his mind was lost. She slowly, firmly and surely slipped the knife into the side of his neck. Once it had pierced his flesh, she simply plunged it deeper to its hilt. For a moment, she felt his arms grip tighter about her. It had given her a thrill, and she let out a whimper of delight.

The man, silently watching, got up from his chair, moving swiftly now to catch him before he fell to the floor.

"Take him out," Laura purred, sliding off the desk, adding an unemotional remark. "Dispose of him and ask the cleaner to come."

CHAPTER 39

Michael had taken the stairs two at a time to reach O'Rourke's office. En route, he had encountered several of his colleagues. Everyone was pleased to see him back on his feet. As he had expected, there was plenty of banter from the men who worked in his unit of the Garda.

Finally, there was Jim O'Rourke. Michael entered the room. Patrick Logan, looking miserable, was seated opposite O'Rourke. He got up and looked at Michael.

"So, yer leaving then?"

Before Michael could answer, the superintendent asked Michael to sit down, and without hesitation, he did so. Paddy could wait to speak to Mick about leaving. He was not in the mood.

"Let's get down to business, shall we?" He eyed the two men with a stern look. "I've the Met breathing down me neck. We need this report finished today." He looked at Michael. "I want yer, Mick, to go through it with Paddy right now. Every last detail. I don't want any more comebacks from London, is that understood?"

His voice was soft, but it was meaningful. He looked from one to the other. Michael and Paddy got to their feet and left O'Rourke's office. Once outside, Michael looked at Paddy, "Coffee?" he asked, almost like a peace offering.

"Yeah," Paddy replied and went and sat at his desk.

Michael got him a coffee and sat down, his arms resting on his legs. He leaned towards Paddy. "I was gonna tell yer, but I haven't had the chance. There's been a lot going on. It's just time for me now to move on, yer understand. I want to settle down a bit, that's all."

Patrick looked at him. "It was a shock for me when yer got stabbed, but I didn't expect... well, yer know." Paddy hesitated. "I'm going to miss yer. Who do yer think they'll team me up with?" He didn't wait for any reply but blurted out, "Who's this Francis then? Is that it, turned yer head, has she?"

Michael laughed. "Yer could say that. I'm gonna marry the

girl."

"Yer kept that under yer hat. I'm pleased for yer." He held his hand out, and Michael shook it.

"Truth is, Paddy, she's blown me mind." Michael winked at him.

Both men took a swig of their coffee.

Michael wanted to get the report done. Standing up, he put his hand out to Paddy. Paddy, in turn, stood up and gave him a manly hug.

"I hope it turns out well for yer, Mick," he said, patting Michael's back. "But I'm still going to miss yer."

They set about the report and, a couple of hours later, presented it to O'Rourke.

Jim O'Rourke smiled at the two. "Well done. I'll get this off." Michael and Patrick turned to leave. "One more thing," O'Rourke said. Both men turned to face him. "You've got yer new position, Mick."

Michael hadn't expected that this morning. "That was quick."

"Report to Clonakilty Monday morning. It's all yours. Dooley's off to Dublin." Jim O'Rourke didn't look up but kept his head bent, looking at the report. "Good luck," he offered. "I'll look in if yer need me at all."

It was Michael's turn to be shocked. He looked at the top of Jim O'Rourke's bent head and walked back to his desk. "Thanks, sir." Michael put out his hand. Jim O'Rourke then stood up, looking Michael in the eye, as the two men shook hands across O'Rourke's desk, he added,

"Mind how yer go Mick" His voice was soft, but his handshake was firm.

Outside the office, Paddy wished Michael well and then shot off, thinking, *Who is going to be my partner now?*

After Michael had sorted out a few more things at his desk and had said some more goodbyes, his mood was mixed. He left the Gardai station, feeling almost light-headed, walking along, trying to make sense of what had just happened. It was all so quick, it had felt strange, and the unexpected nature of it had unsettled him. Clona, he thought on, not too far from home. What home? Michael's mind was jumping all over the place. He took a deep breath. Slow down, he told himself. There's no rush.

Monday morning, Clona. Monday morning! Hell, he thought, that meant he couldn't take Francis to the airport.

He picked up his pace along the pavement and up to the shops. He needed to find Francis.

It was Francis who saw Michael first. He was striding out towards her. His height gave him away as he was taller than the average Irishman. His hair, as it bounced over his head, made her smile.

She raised her hand and waved as they were on course to meet. Francis had been shopping and was holding several bags.

"Here, let me have those." Michael took hold of all the bags and kissed her cheek. "Are yer hungry?" he asked.

"Yes, I'm starving." Francis beamed her smile at him. "Shopping makes me hungry. I've had such a lovely time."

"I can see that," he said. "What have yer been buying?"

"All sorts."

She almost skipped alongside him as he led the way, his long legs striding out.

They reached a café he had in mind and went in. The place was lively, a lot of chatter was going on, and Francis looked about. She caught sight of a waitress carrying two plates full of food, admiring it as it wafted by.

"There's a table over there." Michael nodded in the general direction, and they made their way.

Francis sat herself down. "I think I've overdone the shopping."

"That'll teach yer." Michael handed her the menu card.

"How did it go?" she asked as she looked at what she might choose.

"We finished the report, glad to say. It was not much fun reliving those events. I've been offered the Clona station."

Francis looked up from the menu card she was holding. Michael was looking at her, waiting for her reaction.

"It'll be far less activity. A lot less than I'm used to."

"Will that be better for you?"

Francis was sincere in her reply. Michael took hold of her hand.

"It will be better for us, Francis."

She smiled, but she was not sure. She didn't want to be

responsible for him giving up a job that he was happy in.

"The thing is," he went on, "I'm to start Monday, this Monday," he added.

"I see," Francis said.

She couldn't help but look crestfallen.

"There's no problem. I've already thought I could ask Da to drive you and your auntie to the airport. He'll jump at the chance."

"That's a big ask, though." Francis was looking at him. "I'm not so sure, Michael."

She looked worried.

"Go on, Francis. Let me at least ask him?"

Michael was looking at her. Eager for her to agree, he went on. "I'd feel happier knowing he was taking yer. He knows the way like the back of his hand. Go on, please. He'll be pleased. I know he will."

"If you're sure he won't be put out."

Michael let go of her hand and put his to her cheek in a gentle caress. "It'll all be fine. Now that's settled, what yer going to eat?"

Francis and Michael spent the next couple of days enjoying each other's company as much as possible. They took long walks with the dogs, made their plans, ate out and went to bed early. They seemed to be avoiding Martha and Joseph. The truth was, they just didn't want their time together interrupted in any way. It was only a couple of days now before they would say goodbye. Neither was looking forward to that. Francis had made her mind up to return as soon as she could. Michael was confident that Auntie Nuala would not want to be in London for long.

***

Martha and Joseph had left them alone. Martha was in mixed moods. She loved having them staying, but now she was sad that Francis would be off to her auntie's the following evening.

"How long do yer think they will be over in London, Joe?"

Joseph came up from his newspaper. They were both in the kitchen at the table.

"What's that, Ma?"

"I was just wondering, how long do yer think Francis will be, before she gets back?"

"How do yer think I know the answer to that? We will find out soon, no doubt."

Joseph looked at his wife. He could see the puzzled look on her face. He put his paper down on the table.

"All things considered." He was looking at Martha now, with authority to give her the reassurance she was after. "Knowing how the pair of them are, between themselves, like, Francis will be back before yer know it."

Martha smiled at him. "That's just what I was thinking."

That evening Francis and Michael stayed home. Martha made a nice meal for the four of them. Joseph picked out some wines for the table. After they had all enjoyed Martha's dinner, they left the big kitchen for the comfort of the sitting room. Michael wanted to take this opportunity to tell his parents about his new position.

"I have some news," he said when they were all seated. Joseph and Martha were all ears. "I've been given a new post." He looked from one expectant face to the other. "Yer looking at the new inspector of Clonakilty."

Martha's hands flew to her face, and Joseph was on his feet. He took hold of his son's hand and shook it, just the same way he had when his son told them Francis and he were to be married.

Michael laughed. "Steady on, Da."

"I'm that pleased for yer, son. Can't say how much that means to me."

Joseph had been the inspector at Clona Gardai for many years. He had always hoped that Michael would follow in his footsteps.

"This is cause for a drink."

Michael nodded to his da.

"When are you starting?" Martha asked.

Joseph went to the cabinet for the whiskey.

"Monday," Michael responded. "This leads me to ask a favour. We were wondering, Da, if yer wouldn't mind driving Francis and Nuala to the airport?"

"Dublin?" Joseph asked, knowing full well it would be. He handed Michael his glass.

Francis felt a little uneasy and spoke up. "I understand if you'd rather not. Perhaps it was a bit much to ask."

Joseph's response squashed that thought right out of her mind.

"Not a problem. Ma can come too. Can't yer Ma?"

"Try stopping me, Joseph Connor. Now, where's me drink?"

Joseph chuckled and set about a glass for Martha and Francis.

"Slainte," Michael and Joseph said in unison.

The rest of the evening was spent in a jolly atmosphere. Martha and Joseph couldn't have been happier. They all downed a few more drinks while Francis told them what she hoped to achieve in a week.

"I want to be back by next weekend."

Michael looked at his da. "She had better be, or I'll go and get her."

Francis smiled at him, then told them she had booked her flights and felt confident that her employers would take on a lot of the responsibility of selling her house, along with the agent.

She told Martha and Joseph that all this sort of thing had been in her line of work for many years. Plus, she had a good friend in her office. He was the solicitor who had been her boss.

Martha praised her. "I know yer not the one for letting the grass grow, Francis. I wouldn't know where to begin."

Francis thanked Michael's parents and told them she would have been lost without their kindness.

"I can't believe just how lucky I am."

A tear trickled down her cheek. Michael put his arm around her shoulders and wiped it away. Joseph yawned and gave a nod to Martha.

"I think I've had me fill. I'm off to me bed." Easing himself from his armchair, he stood up, and nodding to Francis, he added, "Don't forget I'm picking up yer auntie after Mass tomorrow, Francis, and we're all going for our dinner at the Carbery Arms."

"I won't. Goodnight."

Francis stood and gave Joseph a quick kiss on his cheek.

"Night, Da." Michael got to his feet. Going over to Martha, he gave her a peck on the cheek. "Night, Ma."

"Night, son."

Michael left the room. Francis gathered the glasses and took them to the kitchen.

"Leave those in the sink," Francis heard Martha call.

She carried on and washed them, anyway. Martha turned off the lights and made her way to the kitchen. Francis was giving the glasses a polish. Francis put the last glass down, smiling at Martha as she came into the kitchen. Francis went to Martha and gave her a hug.

"Thank you, Martha, for all your kindness. You have made me feel so welcome. I shall miss being here with you in your lovely home."

Martha felt a rush of emotion as Francis held her in her arms.

"Yer more than welcome, Francis. I loved having yer here. We have plenty of time now to spend together. I want yer to know I'm here for yer anytime. Night love."

Martha left the kitchen for her bedroom, touched by the girl's sincerity.

Francis sat at the kitchen table to gather herself. She knew Michael would come to her room, if he wasn't already there.

She sat in the quietness. Tomorrow she would be spending the night under a different roof. She thought as she looked about the kitchen that she would miss being in this lovely house with Martha and Joseph. She had never felt so comfortable since losing her own parents in London.

Yet here, her parents now seemed closer to her than ever. Francis felt she was trying to fathom the unfathomable, recalling her dream or vision or whatever it was of seeing her father in the room upstairs, telling her to follow her heart. Then her mother, right there in Nuala's garden! That was such an amazing thing to have happened to her. Yet, it did happen.

Michael, her lovely Michael, lying now waiting for her upstairs, waiting to love her.

Francis sighed and went to the sink for a glass of cool water.

"Thank God I came to Ireland," Francis whispered.

She climbed the stairs, her heart full of love and thanks. Francis now wanted to be in Michael's arms, where she belonged.

CHAPTER 40

A gentle rain fell the next day, creating a misty blanket across the fields and hills. The temperature was mild, and there was no wind to speak of, so it remained there throughout the morning, soaking all beneath it. Despite the weather, the little church had a large turnout. The holy father only came here once a fortnight these days.

The Mass ended, and folk gathered in conversation.

Outside, Father Graham stood at the door, chatting and shaking hands with his grateful flock. A few would be going into the square for their dinner, whilst others beat a hasty retreat to the comfort of their own homes.

As the Connors came out through the porchway, Father Graham stretched out his hands in greeting to Joseph.

He had known Joseph for many years and respected him. Joseph had maintained his respectability through his long service to the Gardai. He and his family were well-liked by all. Now the kindly Father had a broad grin, stretching almost from ear to ear, as the two men came face to face.

"I hear congratulations are in order." He nodded in Michael's direction. Michael was right behind his da with Francis.

Joseph looked down at the priest, a little taken off-guard.

"Congratulations?" he inquired, still holding the priest's hand.

"Yes," said the kind priest.

"I understand young Michael is going to be married." Father Graham was searching Joseph's face.

"News travels fast," he said.

Michael grinned while Francis recalled the last time she had seen Father Graham, and her cheeks blushed again.

"We saw Father Graham in Clona when we bought the ring, Da."

"Quite so," Father Graham said and smiled. "Have you set the date yet?"

"No," Michael replied. "Not yet."

Martha and Nuala were waiting behind Michael. He now stood aside and gestured.

"Nuala here is Francis' auntie."

"You must be very pleased, Nuala." Father Graham reached towards Nuala and offered his hand, adding, "They make a handsome couple."

Francis' cheeks were hot. She hadn't had many dealings with a priest since her parents' passing.

Nuala was delighted that the priest knew Francis was indeed her niece. She stood straight and told Father Graham, "I couldn't be more delighted. I'm looking forward to Francis staying with me before the wedding."

"Is that right, Francis?" His twinkling blue eyes rested on her.

"Yes, I'm going to stay with my aunt for now. We haven't set the date yet as I need to sell my home in England, and as you can imagine, there is a lot to sort out."

"That all sounds grand. You'll be letting me know when and if you need me."

Francis gave a polite reply. "I will, Father, thank you."

He stood aside and let the family pass. There were more waiting behind who were eager for a chat with the kind Father Graham.

The Carbery Arms was buzzing. Joseph was stopped a couple of times as he tried to lead his family through to the back. As they passed the long bar, a couple of the men called out to Michael. Father and son stood shoulder to shoulder at the bar, surrounded by men.

The three women finally made it to a table. The smell of the roast meats for dinner was tempting.

"It's very busy in here," Nuala said. "I hope they have something left. I'm feeling hungry."

"Me too," Francis said. "It smells so good."

Martha looked between auntie and niece. With a nod of the head and a little wriggle into her chair, she told them, "It's always good, that's why it's so busy. I'm for the roast."

Nuala and Francis both agreed at the same time. Just then, a roar of laughter from the men went up at the bar. Francis looked over to see Michael laughing and his da's shoulders shaking.

"Must have been a good joke," Francis said.

Martha and Nuala raised an eyebrow.

"Think they have forgotten all about us."

Martha spoke in jest. There was no irritation in her voice as she looked over with pride at her husband and youngest son.

"Like two peas in a pod, your husband and son," Nuala told Martha.

The two were getting on well together. Francis kept her eyes on Michael while they were chatting about all sorts. Francis became lost in her own world. She enjoyed watching Michael, seeing how easily he fitted in with the other men. He was well-liked as she watched him throwing his head back, laughing. She didn't want to take her eyes off him. Martha nudged Nuala at the look of her looking at her man.

"Love is a truly wonderful thing," Nuala remarked.

"Thanks be to God," Martha replied.

Everyone seemed in high spirits. Francis had never encountered this kind of atmosphere before in a public house. The pubs in London were lively enough. The difference here was all the people seemed to know each other. It was a happy gathering. Francis realised that most of the faces she was seeing there had all been in the congregation at the church.

There were other women in the pub, and children. They all seemed content to be chattering amongst themselves. They left their men, who appeared to be enjoying each other's company at the bar. There was the exception of those families who were seated and eating already. Francis looked around and saw a group of children sitting around a big table in the corner. Well behaved, she thought, with their drinks of pop while they waited. Perhaps someone would bring them some food. She looked back to where Michael was, and at that moment, he happened to look over at her. He motioned with his hand in asking if she would like something to drink. She smiled and nodded back.

He was soon back at their table with a small tray. He had brought over two glasses of whiskey, one for Nuala and one for his ma, with a glass of red wine for Francis.

"Are you all for the roast then?"

The three women said yes, and with a wink and a smile, he was back off to the bar.

As soon as the food was ready, Michael and his father were back at the table.

Michael sat next to Francis and squeezed her hand. Francis

was getting educated as to what the protocol was here for a Sunday lunch out. She was really enjoying it all. She was the happiest she had been since losing her parents. There was her father's sister alongside the man she was going to marry and his lovely parents. She felt truly blessed.

After lunch, it would be tea at Ash House and then off to Nuala's home.

The time had flown by. Joseph and Martha had been their usual endearing selves throughout. Nuala had been full of life and laughter.

Now back at Nuala's home, the time had come for Michael to say goodbye to Francis.

It was dark outside, and Michael said he had better get off. Nuala, Francis and Michael had enjoyed the evening together. They chatted about the fun day it had been. Nuala assured Michael that they would return as soon as possible. She congratulated him on his new position and wished him every success. Michael gave Nuala a peck on the cheek and said goodbye.

Francis walked outside with Michael.

He held Francis in his arms while they stood outside under the clear starry night sky. He told her that the next day was a big day for all of them and they should get a good night's sleep. Francis had tears welling in her eyes. She walked with him to his car.

"I'm gonna miss yer so much," he said, looking at her with love in his eyes.

He took her in his arms one last time. They kissed and wished each other good luck for the week ahead. Michael got into his car and drove off swiftly down the drive. Francis, with tears on her cheeks, waved him goodbye.

That night Nuala lay in her bed. Her little case was packed and ready for the trip to London. She had thought very carefully about what to take.

Not too much, she had told herself. She had never stepped foot outside of Ireland. While she was excited, she was also apprehensive. Listening to her inner voice, she had a very strong feeling that she needed to go with Francis, that there was a reason.

All her life, she had listened to her own thoughts and feelings, acting upon them with conviction. She could be overcome by an emotion or feeling from time to time, then a knowledge of what would happen. Usually, she had been proved right, when and if certain events had unfolded. Other times she would feel compelled to advise people. Though these days that was less, as she kept herself to herself.

Francis coming into her life at this time was extraordinary, but Nuala knew there was a reason for it. It was part of the "big plan", a turn of phrase Nuala liked to use when referring to the turning points in life.

Lying there in her comfortable bed, she became calm in her mind. All was going to be well. Nuala's thoughts turned to her brother. She felt his love around her, almost like a hug. She felt it right there in her heart. Her last thoughts were of David. She relived the times they had enjoyed together. They'd been so much like Francis and Michael. Nuala turned on her side, snuggled down into her pillows, and drifted into a deep sleep.

Further along the landing, Francis lay comfortable in her bed. Her aunt had given her the large bedroom at the front of the house. No one had used this room in years.

Nuala had spent the past couple of days preparing the room for Francis. It was old-fashioned but had a grandeur that Francis thought homely. Her aunt had made up the double bed with the finest Irish linen. A thick, soft quilt topped off the bedding. Over on the dressing table was a posy of spring flowers from the garden. There were some lovely paintings on the walls. Francis was snuggled down, thinking of Michael. *I'm going to miss him for sure*, she thought as she turned the beautiful ring around and around on her finger.

Never mind, she told herself, it's just one week. There was much to do in that week. It was going to be fun to take her auntie with her.

Francis thought she would leave the furnishings behind in her house. There was nothing that she was prepared to bring over to Ireland. In fact, there was nothing she wanted to keep. Michael had said they could buy everything they needed. That included a home of their choice.

First things first, she thought. She would call an estate agent, cancel electricity etc, and contact Gerald Bagster to give him the details. She thought on. She'd give anything to her neighbours, including her plants. She needed to sort out her clothes. Things she didn't want could go to the charity shop.

As she tried to think of anything else, she put her fingers to the cross around her neck. Nuala had given her a very precious gift. She thought she'd never take it off, the same as Michael's ring. Finally, she drifted off to sleep.

The house creaked a little before it settled, and then all was quiet. The planets and stars silently and slowly moved through the heavens, while they all slept peacefully in their beds until the dawn of a new day.

CHAPTER 41

Joseph had arrived bright and early as promised. Martha had a basket stuffed to the brim with food for the journey. Joseph loved a drive and looked forward to taking Francis and her aunt to the airport. His car was his pride and joy, and it was immaculately kept by him.

He had filled up with petrol, checked the oil and even the tyres. All was ready for the journey; he was eager to get going. The main new road that had been recently finished would be a delight to drive on for him. He relished the thought.

In no time at all, the ladies were ensconced, Martha up front and Francis with Nuala in the back.

They had chatted most of the way, stopping only once. Joseph had been a knight of the road and was duly kissed and thanked as they left him and Martha at the airport.

Before they knew it, Francis and Nuala had boarded the plane. Nuala had crossed herself before the take-off, which had made Francis laugh. Francis and Nuala chatted their way across the Irish Sea.

It was just over an hour later when they had landed. Nuala dutifully crossed herself again. She offered up a prayer of thanks. Having left the airport, they caught a taxi, arriving outside 657 Wands Road late that afternoon. Nuala had been a true tourist, enjoying looking out of the taxi's window at the passing sights. Excited yet weary, Francis and Nuala arrived at their destination.

They hadn't noticed the two men parked up in their car two doors down the road. The men watched eagerly as the pretty young woman with flowing red curly hair paid the taxi driver. He then jumped out of his cab, taking the two small cases to the door for the women.

"Here we are, Auntie. Let's get in."

Francis fished in her bag for the keys.

The men in the car looked at each other. They had seen all they needed to see. Their job was done. All that was needed was a quick call to Laura Popa. The redhead had arrived. They could put their bill in. The driver started the engine, and they drove away.

"Isn't this cosy?" Nuala said as they made their way down the hallway.

"You mean small," Francis said with a giggle.

"I'll give yer that, but all the same, it's all yer need."

"All that I did need," Francis corrected her aunt.

They were in the kitchen-come-dining room. Francis had had it knocked through a few years back. It made an informal place to sit, and Nuala liked the atmosphere. It was colourful and cheerful. Francis' taste was certainly akin to her own.

Long, thin French doors led out onto the small patio to the back garden. Nuala stood there looking out at the variety of tubs and flowerpots. She could see how her niece loved her little patch. A small table with a couple of chairs was tucked into the corner. The boundaries were hidden by the lush planting. It was a secret place that was full of surprises.

"Do you like it, Auntie?"

"I do. I do, for sure."

"I know it's nothing to what you have achieved in your garden."

"That's taken me years of gardening. I didn't have a job for one thing, like yourself. I think you've done a grand job. It looks like a very nice place to sit. You've a lot of variety in a small area. Do yer get any birds here?"

"I do, but again, not so many as you. There are some huge trees further down. They seem to attract quite a few."

"That's understandable, given the difference of London to the countryside in Ireland."

Francis had made them some tea, apologising for the long-life milk she had found in the cupboard, placing it down on the table. Nuala came away from the window and sat herself down.

"Just what I need, the milk's fine fer now." She smiled.

The two women were comfortable in each other's company. They chatted about one thing to another without effort. When they had finished their tea, Francis showed her auntie where she could sleep. The spare bedroom upstairs faced over the back garden. Beyond the garden were the backs of another row of houses in the same design.

"This will be lovely, Francis. Think I shall be very

comfortable here."

Nuala was looking around the room.

"This used to be my room, but I took Mum and Dad's at the front. It's a little bit bigger. Come and have a look."

Sure enough, it was bigger, but not by much. Suddenly Nuala thought about her brother and his wife. This was their room. She could feel them there. There was happiness and laughter within it. The room still held on to the love and joy they had shared.

Francis spoke just at that moment.

"I'm not sure why, but as soon as I came into this room to sleep, I felt happier and found that I could sleep better."

Nuala smiled. "That's because you felt closer to your parents. It makes perfect sense to me."

"You, dear auntie, have taught me they are always with me, wherever I am."

Francis put her arm around Nuala's shoulders and gave her a squeeze.

"Yes, dear girl, 'tis true. They are always with us."

The evening was soon upon them. Francis had run down to the corner shop and bought some food. There was also food in the freezer that they could use up. By the time they had cooked and eaten, there was not much time left before both women looked forward to their beds.

Francis had her list of things to do ready for the morning.

The next day was damp and was drizzling with rain. It didn't dampen Francis' enthusiasm for getting on with her things to do list. By lunchtime, she had spoken to an agent. They were eager to call around and do a valuation on the property. They had said they were confident of a quick sale. An appointment was set for the day after next.

Gerald Bagster, her friend and boss, whom she had so tirelessly worked for at the solicitors, was now in the driving seat regarding her finances after the telephone call she had made this morning. He would take charge of all the legalities and anything to do with the swift sale of the house.

They had chatted for some time, and he was delighted her life was heading in a new direction. Though once again, he reminded her he was sad to lose her and if she ever needed to return, she would be more than welcome. He assured her he would do all in his power to facilitate an easy move. Francis put the phone down, took a deep breath and got on to the next call.

This call would be less personal.

Francis was now onto the utilities, cancelling her accounts. Now, one last call had to be made to her bank. She needed to change her address with them. It felt wonderful telling them it was her aunt's address in Ireland. They wanted a confirmation letter and told her there was also a branch in Clonakilty. Finally, with all that completed, she entered the little front room next to the front door. There was her auntie looking through the photograph albums.

Nuala had been clearing out the sideboard, as Francis had asked.

The doors to the sideboard were open, and the contents were placed on a table, ready for boxing up.

"Would yer look at yourself here," she said, looking up as Francis entered the room.

Nuala held out the photograph. There was Francis in her school uniform, with a shy smile on her face.

"That was taken at school. Mum and Dad kept one for each year. I think I was twelve in that one." Francis smiled at her aunt. Nuala was sitting surrounded by the albums.

"I've finished with the phone calls. I need to get some boxes, labels and some strong tape. Will you be all right if I just pop to the shops now?"

Nuala turned another page without looking up "Sure, you pop out then."

Francis could see she was happy just sitting there looking through the albums.

"We can pack them ready for shipping to Ireland when I get back."

"Good idea," Nuala replied happily, looking at her brother and speaking without taking her eyes off the photograph. "I'll be fine. You get to the shops."

Francis smiled at her aunt again, though she never noticed. Nuala was engrossed in the photographs.

When Francis returned, she found her auntie in the kitchen. She had made them some lunch.

"I've put together a bite to eat."

She turned to see Francis struggling with a flat cardboard pack, with another bag swinging from her arm.

"Here, let me."

Nuala rushed to help.

"Thanks." Francis was flushed with the effort. "Think this will do. I'm not going to pack much."

"Think yer right there."

She relieved Francis of the carrier bag swinging from her arm.

Released from her cardboard flat pack and the bag, Francis drew breath. "It's just things like the photographs and Mum's dressing table bits that I really want to keep, and my clothes too, of course. I've suitcases for those. We have a busy afternoon coming up, Auntie."

"Not before we have eaten. Sit yerself down. I'll dish up."

Grateful for her auntie's thoughtfulness, Francis sat at the table to eat.

The afternoon was busy after they had eaten lunch and cleared away. Nuala was packing up the albums in the little front room, but not before she had first looked at each photograph.

She was reliving her brother's life. All the years they had missed. She sighed and smiled, seeing his wife smiling back at her, knowing now they had had a good life together. She was pretty, Nuala thought, and she could see some of the looks of Francis in her, but more of her brother's and even her own mother's.

Nuala looked at every picture of Francis as a baby, then at school. Some with her father, some with her mother. Shame she didn't have a brother or sister. All these thoughts and photographs were helping Nuala to see the life of her lovely brother Robert.

It was while she was engrossed, reliving the life of her brother, there was a knock on the front door.

Nuala got up from the armchair and put the album down. She took a peep out of the window. She could see a tall thin woman with her back towards the window. Her long black hair was tied tight into a ponytail. It reached her waist.

Nuala took an instant dislike to the look of her.

Who is that? she thought. Perhaps the agent? She withdrew from the window and listened. Nuala could hear Francis coming down the stairs to answer the door.

"Hello." Francis looked at the woman with an inquiring look. "Yes?"

"Hello. You don't know me, but we have a mutual friend."

"We do?" Francis questioned.

"Yes. Coral. You met her in Ireland. I am sorry to arrive uninvited."

Nuala had the door to the lounge open enough to hear what was being said, and she became curious when she heard the woman mention Ireland. An uneasy feeling was wrapping itself around Nuala. She could see Francis' back as she spoke to the stranger. There was just enough space to see through the gap in the door, where it hung from its hinges. The foreigner carried on.

"Coral mentioned your house vas going up for sale. I live down the other end of the road, and I am interested."

Francis then remembered Coral. She recalled she had had a friend there.

"Yes, I remember Coral. How is she?"

Nuala was seeing the darkness around the women as she watched and listened.

"She's in Romania working," she replied.

Her foreign accent was strong. Francis listened and then told her, "Coral is right. I have just put it on the market today."

"Do you mind if I could come in and look around? I von't take long."

She made to take a step in.

Nuala had become extremely tense. She felt troubled. Then, as if someone had told her to, she went to the fireplace and picked up the iron poker. Creeping silently, she stood ready behind the door, holding the poker tightly.

Francis looked at the woman and quickly recalled what Coral had said to her that day as they sat in the little cafe in Clonakilty. She was thinking now, this woman was out for a quick deal and that's why she had taken it upon herself to call in, knowing Coral had told her she wanted to return to Ireland as soon as possible.

"Well, I do want a quick sale. I suppose it won't do any harm, but you will have to go through the agent. You will have to excuse the mess. I'm packing up."

The woman held out her hand. "I'm very pleased to meet you.

Francis, isn't it? I'm Laura Popa."

Francis smiled and took her hand. "Pleased to meet you," Francis answered sweetly.

The woman was now in the hall waiting for Francis to close the front door behind her.

Nuala was holding her breath. She saw the woman reach into her bag and take out a knife. Francis passed the woman and the lounge door saying, "Please come through to the kitchen this way."

As soon as the woman with a knife in hand walked by the door, Nuala came out behind her. All three women were in a line along the small passageway. Nuala didn't wait as she saw the knife glint, raised in the stranger's hand, ready to stab Francis. With all her might, Nuala lifted the poker and brought it down, hoping it would land on Laura Popa's head.

She missed. It had slammed down onto her shoulder.

Within a second, Laura Popa staggered and turned to see what had hit her. She fell forward straight onto Nuala, the knife held high, then plunging it into Nuala's chest. Nuala pushed away with all her might, the knife still held in Laura Popa's hand, covered in Nuala's blood. Within a second, an already unsteady Laura Popa fell sideways, smashing her temple on the iron radiator that ran along the wall.

Francis screamed in horror as both women lay on the hall floor. Blood was pouring from Laura Popa's head. Blood was also seeping from her auntie's chest, spreading as the material of her top absorbed her life's blood with the last pumping of her heart. Carefully stepping between the women, Francis reached her auntie.

Nuala was on her back. Francis knelt beside her and lifted her head carefully.

"Auntie, please don't die," she whispered, pressing her hand on her auntie's chest.

Nuala opened her eyes and looked at her, smiling. She spoke softly as her life was ebbing away.

"I've done what I was meant to do. Go home now, Francis, to Michael. He's waiting for you."

She looked away from Francis and beyond. Tears flowed down Francis' face as she knew there wasn't anything she could do but hold her in what she knew were her last moments.

Nuala's face changed suddenly, her eyes opened wide, and she spoke again. "David, my David, you have come for me." Francis watched as both her arms reached out in greeting, and she smiled, closed her eyes and was gone.

Francis lay her auntie's head carefully down and stood up. She needed to move, she told herself. Get to the phone. The hallway was like something from a horror film. Blood was seeping from both women, and Francis was covered. She couldn't think straight. Why had this happened?

Why was there a knife in the woman's hand? Trance-like, Francis managed somehow to get to the phone in the kitchen. Blood and tear-stained, she dialled 999. When she knew they were coming, she phoned Michael.

***

As the weeks passed into months, the case of Laura Popa had unravelled bit by bit. Slowly but surely, fresh evidence had been gathered almost daily. The police in London had been amazed at just how big her empire of crime had been.

It had come to light that she had murdered three so-called husbands, though there was a lack of evidence to prove the fact that she had married any of these particular men.

During the period she had spent with each of them, Laura Popa, after she had disposed of them, had taken over their illegal operations, which included drug running, people trafficking, and prostitution. Latterly she had ventured into brothel keeping in two properties in London.

All the men and women in her employ slowly completed the picture for the police. Criminals pleaded for lesser sentences for the parts they had each played, now feeling safe that she was dead, for most had lived in fear of her. They gave their individual evidence freely. It had become a case of monumental proportions.

Finally, they could close the case of Laura Popa. The woman who, after many years of crime and living a life of debauchery and lawlessness, had finally been brought down by a little Irish lady who was simply looking out for her niece.

Frank Bennett of the Met had enjoyed his retirement party

down at the local pub. His fellow officers had congratulated him on the wrapping up of the case.

He could not believe his luck when a phone call had come through alerting him to the crime scene of Laura Popa.

He would remember the little Irish lady in his prayers ever after. He would also remember Michael Connor and the pretty girl, Francis Doyle.

Michael had flown to London that day to be with his would-be bride Francis. He could give a full one-to-one account of the case.

He was more than happy to deal with the Met in London and in Kinsale, armed with his first-hand knowledge.

His meeting with Frank Bennett would speed the case through, so he could get back to Ireland, taking Francis home as soon as possible. He was instrumental in arranging for Nuala's return to Ireland.

With the gravity of the situation Francis had found herself in, Michael's assistance in all police matters had helped enormously.

Inspector Frank Bennett assisted the couple through the ordeal of the tragic outcome that Francis had so bravely endured. Not only was it in his interest to do so, but he had taken to the couple who had been through so much in their apparently short time together.

Michael had told Francis they would get through it, just like they had in Kinsale. He also told her he would never leave her side again. Michael had been impressed by how calm and in control Francis was.

Later when he asked her how she was feeling, she had told him softly that her dear Auntie Nuala had been pleased to go. Francis recalled to Michael those last moments, telling him she was sure she was now with her husband David in a land they both knew so well.

Whatever Francis believed was fine by him, as her belief, as he saw it, was truly a comfort to her.

Nuala had opened Francis' eyes to the land beyond the veil. Francis did feel comfort, drawing her strength from it day by day. She knew for sure her family would always be there watching over her. Her heart was full of love and gratitude. Francis knew beyond any doubt that she and Michael were indeed meant for each other.

She could not wait to be his wife.

EPILOGUE

September 28th 1980 was the chosen date for the wedding of Francis and Michael. It was the night before the big day.

Bridget giggled in her bed, recalling to Francis her own wedding night.

She had travelled up with Con, her husband, and their two adorable children. They were back at Ash House, being spoilt by their grandparents. How Martha cooed over the new baby. Martha Bridget was a blessing. Her namesake couldn't get enough of her. A doting grandmother indeed.

"We should get some sleep now," Francis suggested, though she thought it would be a miracle.

She took one final look at her gown hanging in the wardrobe and ran her hand across the silken fabric. Climbing into bed, she lay down and sighed a long final sigh of contentment, stretching as her tired body relaxed.

"Yer right," Bridget said. "It's getting late."

Lying there now in the dark, Bridget sent up a silent prayer for Michael and Francis. She knew that she and Francis would get along from the first time they had met. It was so nice to have another female in the family, one that shared the same sense of humour. This meant there would always be much laughter and frivolity whenever they got together.

The morning was bright and the sun would shine on the bride. Francis stood looking at herself in the long mirror while Bridget, now dressed in her long dress of pale tangerine, attached Francis' veil. Francis had chosen to wear her hair up, like she had on her first date with Michael. Some of her titian, long curls had been gently coerced to fall around her shoulders. She was watching now as Bridget adroitly arranged the small tangerine rose buds and gypsophila into her hair, forming a crown. Bridget was not holding back as she ventured into a wealth of genuine compliments.

Francis was a vision in ivory silk and lace.

"Michael will fall to his knees when he sees yer. One last thing. He gave me this to give yer."

Bridget went to her bag and fished out a small box.

"I have no idea what it is."

Francis opened the little black box and there, lying beneath some tissue paper, were a pair of the most fabulous earrings.

She gasped. "Oh, look! Look what he's bought me."

Bridget's eyes opened wide as she said, "Put them on, then."

They were the same bright green emeralds as her engagement ring. Francis went back to the mirror.

"How do they look? What do you think?"

"Bloody fantastic is all. I love them."

Francis put her fingers to the cross about her neck that her Aunt Nuala had given her. The feeling of it between her fingers was calming to her.

"I love them too," she said.

Francis had been true to her word and had not taken off the necklace that had been her grandmother's, nor Michael's ring that flashed on her finger. She knew she never would be parted from them.

Just then, there was a gentle tapping at the door. Bridget opened the door to greet her da.

Joseph Connor beamed at the sight of the two girls.

"My, look at the pair of yer." He puffed out his chest, saying, "I'm the luckiest man in Clona this morning, two beautiful daughters for sure."

The girls smiled at each other and then at Joseph.

"Will we do then?" Bridget asked cheekily.

"I should think yer will, and you, Francis, are stunning."

Frances smiled at her kind soon-to-be father-in-law.

"Are we all ready now?"

He offered his arm to Francis.

"Wait a minute, Da," Bridget said, hurrying into the bathroom, where the bouquet of flowers for Francis was standing in a jug of water.

"Yer can't go without yer flowers."

She smiled.

Francis was a picture as Joseph, with Bridget in attendance, walked out and down the street. Bystanders wished her good luck as they stood aside to let her pass. All eyes were on Francis as a proud Joseph escorted her along with his head held high. He cut a handsome figure in his wedding suit, with a tangerine rose in his buttonhole. In complete unison, Bridget was close behind Francis, holding the hem of Francis' gown to prevent it from soiling on the pavement. She kept in step perfectly.

Inside the church, the organ played hauntingly serene music. Francis cast her eyes to the front of the church. There was Michael, standing facing the altar, waiting for her. His brother Andrew was standing next to him. At first, Andrew was thought to have been the celebrant of the marriage. Instead, Michael had asked Andrew to be his best man rather than officiate the ceremony. Andrew readily agreed, accepting it might be better to take a much-needed break from his parish in Kinsale and spend some time with his family.

Gerald Bagster, her ex-employer, had accepted Francis' invitation to the wedding. He had arrived from London with his wife for a few days. Francis could see him now sitting with his wife. She was pleased he had made it. Her eyes fell upon Martha and Con, seated together with the children. The baby was fast asleep in Con's arms. There were a few of Michael's work colleagues. Patrick Logan was pleased to be there, showing off his newfound girlfriend. The rest were the general congregation that had attended Mass earlier and lingered on to watch the wedding.

"Are yer ready, Francis?" A kindly Joseph patted her hand.

"Yes, I'm ready."

She smiled. Bridget rushed around to stand in front of her and carefully lifted the veil, that part of the veil that would hang over Francis' face.

"You're ready now!" she said to Francis with an encouraging smile.

The two girls exchanged a knowing look of understanding between them.

"Thanks, Bridget."

Bridget winked a response.

Francis saw Father Graham raise his hands to bid the congregation to stand as he caught sight of her.

The organ music had changed, and right on cue, Joseph led a smiling Francis down the aisle. The congregation turned in unison and all eyes were on the beautiful bride.

Michael had turned, watching her with a pounding heart, as

Francis made her way to stand at his side. It was an hour or so later, after much singing, blessings and prayers, the married couple exited the church to a hail of confetti. Michael finally lifted the veil from Francis' radiant face to kiss her for the first time as his wife.

Only Francis had seen the three golden spheres of light as they came to rest nearby the altar. She had watched in wonder as she saw her parents and Aunt Nuala come into clear sight. As silently as they came, so they faded away.

The three had watched from beyond with the knowledge that Francis' life was on the right path at last.

Francis and Michael, united once more, were to continue a union that was theirs for all eternity.